Damnation

A Novel by James Harrington

ISBN: 978-0692499054

First Printing: August 2015

Cover Art:

Designer and illustrator: Brett Warniers

Cover Model: Nicole Hailer

Photographer: Rick Chandler

Wardrobe Design: Jenny French

Hair: Nathan Prescott

Makeup: Samantha Woods

Editing:

Kathy Hearns

This book is dedicated to my son Rowan... who may or may not be born by the time this book comes out. Love you and can't wait to meet you!

𝕬 note from the author:

Hello! I hope that you will enjoy your time with our heroes as they embark on their adventure. Before you begin, I just wanted to clarify a few details.

You will encounter many characters, both fictional and historical. I have done the best I can to portray the historical characters ahead as accurately as possible, based on what information is available on each. However, please understand that I am exposing them to fictional situations. It is impossible to predict definitively how one might have actually reacted in these events, so again, this is based on what information is available.

Lastly, I would just like to note that this story in no way should be taken as a criticism of the beliefs of any denomination of Christianity, Judaism, Islam, or any other faith. As a catholic, I acknowledge that the leaders of several denominations weren't always the most upstanding of people and that is what is reflected in my writing, but that does not invalidate anyone's belief in God or the teachings they follow.

I hope that you will enjoy this work of fiction for what it is; a work of fiction. Thank you!

-Jim H.

"The great dragon was thrown down, the old serpent, he who is called the devil and Satan, the deceiver of the whole world. He was thrown down to the earth, and his angels were thrown down with him."

- Revelation 12:9

BOOK I

HELL HATH NO FURY

DAMNATION

1

𝕿here was a cold breeze in the air as Michael stood at the podium. In front of him, the Choirs of Angels filed into the main meeting hall little by little. The bitter chill complimented the rather dismal scene in front of him. The general of the Most High's armies had seen worse over the years and did the best he could to ignore it.

Seated on either side of him, were the other 6 great Archangels, leaders of the Celestial World. The large council hall seated thousands of angels, all of whom listened intently waiting for Michael to speak. The last of them had taken their seats sucked in a deep breath.

The long war had dragged on for eons, costing uncountable angel lives. For years, the angels fought against the armies of Lucifer to no avail. It seemed as though the war would continue until the angels were all but extinct, but a daring campaign carried out by a small group of angels had turned the tide of the war.

The thousands of occupied seats were dwarfed by the seats that no longer had an owner. Those empty seats had lost their occupant either to war or treason. The scene was a sad reminder of everything that the war had cost them.

Michael had taken his rightful place as the leader of the Nine Choirs of Angels. It was a job, some thought, he had let go to his head. Not that he cared, others could have criticized him all they wanted, but in the end, he was still the leader.

Michael stood in front of the choirs and looked out on the chamber that had been carved of Ivory and marble. Like all else, it had been badly damaged during the war and needed to be rebuilt. Large craters had shattered the marble floor tiles. The holes in the ceilings were singed black from firebomb damage.

Michael did the best he could to ignore the dismal scene as he addressed the Choirs, "Brothers and sisters, you all have good reason to rejoice. For after years of watching our brothers and sisters being cut down in ruthless combat, the war is mercifully over. Our little gambit, paid off and four of our bravest warriors breached Lucifer's position, forcing him to surrender. He has since been driven out of the Celestial World by the Most High and punished for his crimes."

Michael sighed before he continued, "However, peace is not yet ours to enjoy. There are still those out there that remain loyal to Lucifer and his cause. It is true that the bulk of his force has been disbanded, but we believe that there are still some creatures in our midst that remain hidden. I can assure you all that they are being hunted down and will be brought to justice."

A deafening applause erupted from the Choirs as now peace was actually within their grasp and the Most High could continue his plans to create a child race in his own image. Michael smiled and nodded as he too joined in the celebration. He allowed the angels to rejoice for a few moments before raising his hand again to regain their attention. The large chamber immediately quieted down at the sight of Michael's gesture.

The smile never left Michael's face as he spoke, "Thank you, brothers and sisters, this is truly a day to rejoice, but I regret that such celebration may be shadowed by business that we still must to attend to."

Michael's gaze left the choirs and turned to the entry way next to his podium. A guardian, who was just standing at the door waiting for a signal, returned his look. Michael nodded to the guardian, which prompted him to exit the chambers.

DAMNATION

Minutes passed and the specter of curiosity loomed in the chambers. What did Michael want the Choirs to see? Could he have captured another traitor?

Suddenly, the sound of clanking chains could be heard from outside the room. It sounded as though someone was struggling against heavy metal bonds. The noise served to elevate the curiosity of everyone in the room as they waited to see who it was.

A moment later, the guard reappeared followed by an angel covered in blood that was practically being dragged in by her chains. She was shackled at the arms, legs, and neck. Her wings were weighted down to prevent her from being able to take flight and the look on her face was indicative of pure hatred.

The guard pulled her forward onto the main stage. She defiantly refused to move, making the guard's job even harder. If anyone was going to publicly humiliate her, then they were going to have to work for it.

Michael shook his head and looked back up to the Choirs, "My friends, I must inform you that we have captured one of these agents and not just any one either…"

As the archangel spoke, the young angel refused to look at anyone and instead kept her eyes fixated on the massive walls of the Choir Chamber. She had always been amazed by the sheer size and intricacy of this hall. It had somehow been hand carved almost completely out of marble and ivory. Murals on the wall told the stories of angel's deeds throughout their history. She smiled to see one of the divine temples being set to flames. She appreciated that someone had seen fit to immortalize her work.

The entire design of the chamber was beyond anything anyone could image, but something about it was different than the last time she had seen it. The burn marks and blast craters in the walls almost ruined the tranquil view. She remembered the battle early in the war that had caused this damage. It was the first battle that she had been a part of.

Not a day went by that she had not regretted Lucifer's decision to fall back rather than risk heavier casualties. Being Lucifer's military strategist and general, she was certain that they could have occupied the Celestial Temple in one swift stroke had they continued to press forward. It just didn't make sense, yes her forces were being bled, but they had inflicted far more casualties than they had taken. Falling back was a critical error on Lucifer's part, and it would prove to be one that would cost them everything.

Her thoughts were broken as Michael spoke directly to her, attempting to get her attention, "General Xaphan, step forward, please."

Xaphan moved defiantly closer to the podium where the Archangel stood. Michael watched her every move, waiting for her to try to break free of her bonds. She made no such attempt and kept her hands tucked away behind her.

Many of the angels were dismayed by the sorry state she was in. Xaphan was at one time a respected soldier in the armies of the Most High, even Michael was sorry to see how things had turned out. It definitely was not helping morale.

Xaphan wore a tattered black outfit that flowed below her knees. It was all she was allowed to keep after being stripped of her sword and armor. Her pale white skin was filthy and scarred. Her wings were missing feathers and covered in blood, most of which was not her own. Her black hair was a mangled mess from weeks of her being too busy to tend to it. She breathed in deeply as her pale blue eyes looked up scornfully at Michael.

Xaphan's glare pierced right through Michael's presence and it was as though she wasn't looking at him at all. She didn't even acknowledge his presence. To her, it appeared that Michael was little more than an obstruction standing in the way of what she was really looking at.

Uriel followed Xaphan's gaze and noticed that her eyes were fixated on the Celestial Temple and the chambers of the Most High. A partial smile appeared on her face when she saw that much of its damage had not yet been repaired.

Michael noticed where her attention was too, but dismissed it as he began speaking. Almost to spite Xaphan's gaze, Michael spoke in a tone that wasn't speaking to her at all. It was more like he was dictating to her for all to see, "General, I assume you know why you are here."

Xaphan gave a defiantly unenthusiastic nod and spoke through her teeth, "I do."

"You have been charged with treason, espionage, wanton destruction, and plotting against the Most High," Michael said in an accusing tone. "The evidence against you is absolute. We have examined everything in great detail and have found you guilty on all counts. Have you anything you wish to say before your sentence is carried out?"

Xaphan quickly turned to the other angels in the hall, "I fought for you... all of you. It was Lucifer's wish to see you all freed from your bondage. The world that the Most High is now creating... it should have been for us! It is ours by right, but he would give it to some child race that would only scorn him! Ours was an eternity of servitude... I wanted something better than that for you! I am not the monster that many have you have been led to believe I am. That monster stands in front of you in the form of an Archangel!"

Xaphan pointed an accusing finger at Michael, "He would see you remain in bondage!"

Screams of support for Michael and angry cursing was spewed in Xaphan's direction, but she ignored it and continued speaking, "I wish I'd never given you fair warning to evacuate the temple before we attacked! I would willingly give up my wings to see all of you burn for this!"

DAMNATION

The words hurt Xaphan as much as she was certain they angered the Choirs. She didn't mean much of what she had said and still cared about the friends that she had betrayed, but they were words that she felt they needed to hear. She still desired to see them free, above all else, and if she was to be a martyr for this cause, so be it.

As the yelling got louder, Uriel stood up, "Enough!"

Michael shook his head as he looked down at Xaphan. He felt a twinge of anger himself as the room quieted down, but as he was about to speak, another voice spoke up.

"Excuse me…"

The voice cut in from the back of the chambers. "I request to be heard."

The room fell silent as every eye turned to where the voice had come from. Michael smiled, "Ah, one of our local heroes. If anyone here has earned the right to speak before the council, she certainly has. The floor yields to you, Adalyn."

Adalyn immediately flapped her wings to elevate herself off the ground and gently glided down to the main floor of the chamber. She touched down gracefully and brushed the hair out of her face. As though defending Xaphan from attack, Adalyn stood in front of her, blocking Michael's gaze, "Brothers and sisters of the Nine Choirs of Angels, I have come before you to plead for mercy on behalf of my sister."

"What are you doing?" Xaphan whispered in a demanding tone. "I don't want your help, get out of here."

"You are my sister. No matter what you have done, I still love you and don't wish to see you harmed."

Xaphan sneered and turned her back on her defender as archangels looked at each other oddly. The room suddenly erupted in quiet whispers and gasps. They were intended to be low, but there were enough of them to make a ruckus. Michael raised his hand to silence the noise, "You have earned the right to speak, but judgment has already been passed against her."

"I realize that Master, and I'm sure that whatever you have decided to charge her with, is more than appropriate, given the magnitude of her crimes."

Adalyn lowered her eyes as her tone became pleading, "However… I would like to point out that while she is responsible for the initial attack on the faithful, and responsible for the damage to the Celestial Temple, she did not shed a single drop of innocent blood by her own hand. Lucifer was the architect of the massacre. I also happen to know that you have proof that she gave us sufficient warning before burning the temple to allow our people to evacuate."

Uriel rolled his eyes, "Please make your point, young one."

"My point sir is that despite her attacks, despite the fact that she sided against us, and despite whom she cast her lot with, she has been an honorable foe since the first days of the conflict. Even as it dragged on, she still maintained a strict code of honor. I should know, because I fought against her on several occasions. That honor is the only reason that many of us now stand here in judgment of her."

Michael nodded, "I am aware of that, Adalyn. However, being an honorable thief does not make someone any less a thief. I would think that after all the time and effort you put into catching her, that you would understand this."

"I do understand it, Michael, but there is a difference between understanding and agreeing."

"That is something you will have to come to terms with. I'm sure your sister appreciates your efforts on her behalf and you have secured your honor, but the decision has already been made and there is no further room for debate."

"Still not willing to listen to reason?" Xaphan scoffed. "It's nice to see that nothing has changed in eons. You would think..."

Uriel stood up, "Silence you!"

Xaphan turned back to face Uriel with a malicious grin on her face. He snorted at her defiance, "General Xaphan, for your crimes you are hereby banished from the Celestial World. Personally, I would have preferred it had you been removed from existence, but ironically enough, the Most High still cares about you and has decided to show you mercy. We are therefore sending you down to be with your mentor, Lucifer."

Xaphan hissed as she suddenly shook off her shackles, revealing that she had broken free of them earlier, and was waiting for the chance to escape. She dodged around the guard when he tried to grab her. Before anyone could react, she spread her wings and launched herself into the air. It looked as though she had a clear path to the exit when Adalyn suddenly appeared in her way.

Having no way out, Xaphan landed a few steps away from the door with her fists clenched. Her eyes met her old friend with contempt and worry, "Get out of my way, Adalyn. Don't make me hurt you."

Adalyn moved her arm downward in a thrusting motion. A blade appeared in her hand which she pointed it directly at Xaphan's throat, "I'm sorry sister that is not going to happen and I don't think you'd hurt me even if you could. Stand down; I don't want to have to fight you again."

"And if I dont, are you going to kill me, Adalyn?" Xaphan asked in a malicious tone.

"I don't want to. Please don't push it that far… sister."

The two glared at each other for a moment. Xaphan could see the tears in Adalyn's eyes as she stood, ready to strike. Though a loyal servant of the Most High, Adalyn would have preferred to allow Xaphan to get away. She knew what fate lay ahead for her sister and had to resist the urge to stand aside.

Adalyn knew the consequences of making such a decision and held firm. Xaphan sighed, she hated her sister for getting in her way, but at the same time, didn't like seeing her in pain, "Very well my dear sister, you win, but this is not over between us. Someday, our positions will be reversed and you will be staring at the end of my blade. Don't expect me to show you anymore mercy than you have shown me. I will kill you."

"I know that, sister… I know…"

Xaphan raised her hands and turned back to Michael, "So it is damnation for me then?" She hissed. "I wouldn't have it any other way. I'd rather suffer there than serve here!"

Michael sighed, "After a few eons in the world of shadows, you may find yourself regretting those words General."

"I don't plan on being there that long. I will return with an army... and the temple will be consumed in flames once more."

Not wanting to argue further with Xaphan, Michael snapped his fingers. There was a sound of glass shattering in the distance and suddenly Xaphan noticed the feathers on her wings beginning to look odd. She watched as the roots of her feathers slowly turned black and then each bristle of each feather also slowly began to turn.

Within moments, her wings looked very much different from those of her brothers and sisters. Her feathers were blacker than even the largest void. They quickly began to match her dress and hair.

Xaphan looked at her wings with disgust and began to feel unsettled. As their color changed, she began to notice that her wings were getting extremely heavy. Each feather began to weigh her down more and more. It became much harder for her to remain standing. Her breathing became labored as she struggled to hold herself up. Though she did not want to show weakness, eventually the weight became too much for her, causing her knees to buckle, and give out from under her.

As Xaphan collapsed, her defender stepped forward. Before Adalyn could do anything, Xaphan raised her hand and signaled Adalyn to stay away. She then turned back to Michael, "What… have you done to me?"

Michael's expression did not change, "You are being banished, and your wings will never allow you to fly here again. This will ensure that you can never return."

"Is this really necessary?" Adalyn demanded. "She's struggling and can't stand or even move. Your sentence was banishment, but this is more of a horrific death sentence, how will she survive without her wings?"

Michael sighed, "Her wings are too heavy for her to fly here, but when she reaches the Netherworld, she should be fine. They should not be such a burden to her there."

"Master, I beseech you, reconsider this! There must be another way! Such punishment does not befit angels. This is far too cruel for..."

"Silence!"

Adalyn turned away from Michael and looked down at Xaphan. The intense pressure from the weight of Xaphan's wings felt as though it would crush her. She looked up weakly, "Michael… please…"

Adalyn felt the tears began to fall down her cheeks and rushed to her sister's side. She grabbed one of Xaphan's wings in a futile attempt to take the pressure off her back, "Sister, forgive me… Had I known that this would happen…"

Michael thrust his hand forward at the two angels. Adalyn lost her grip on Xaphan's wing, went flying backwards, and landed on one knee a few feet away. She glared at the archangels as she got back to her feet, "Michael!"

"Adalyn… It's time for you to leave. Your intentions are honorable and so they shall be noted, but you are getting in the way and allowing your emotions to bleed through. This can no longer be tolerated from the floor. You are compromised, leave now."

"Under protest, Michael! I want that on the record too!"

"So noted."

Adalyn stood up and reluctantly walked to the doorway. Her eyes were locked on Michael as she disappeared from view. She looked back only once at her sister with tears in her eyes.

As Adalyn disappeared from the watchful eyes of the Choirs, Michael turned his back on Xaphan and raised his chin, "Be gone."

The mist beneath Xaphan could no longer handle her weight and gave out. She quickly began to sink through the cool surface as the weight of her wings pulled her down through space and time. Just before she disappeared from view, Xaphan raised her fist into the air and uttered one last cry, "Forever freedom!"

As Xaphan fell, she began to notice that the further she plummeted, the less her wings weighed. Much to her relief, she was quickly able to slow her decent by spreading her wings as far as she could. They caught the air, allowing her to hover as she proceeded downward.

Moments later, there was a bright light and a flash of energy. She was temporarily blinded by the light and did the best she could to remain hovering while her eyes adjusted. This was it; the light was her path out of the Celestial World.

DAMNATION

⇅

When her vision returned, Xaphan found herself in a murky wooded area, completely covered in a thick, gray, fog. Trees were smashed, broken, and partially submerged in black water. It was so dark that she could not see below the surface.

Not wanting to get wet, Xaphan flapped her wings and continued to hover over the water. There was only a few hundred feet of visibility in front of her and she had no idea where she was. Sounds of wild beasts and movement filled the air from places unknown to her. She was unarmed, but not afraid. Michael had not seen fit to strip of her of immortality so there shouldn't be anything that could harm her. She harkened back to her earliest lesson that only a fool trusts their life to a weapon as she clenched her fists.

Suddenly in the distance, Xaphan heard the sound of wings flapping. She recognized the sound of breaking air passing through feathers quite easily. Unable to defend herself as easily in the air, she landed on one of the broken stumps and raised her fists, prepared for anything that might come her way. What manner of beast could be coming at me? She thought to herself, Could it be an unholy beast or one of my fallen comrades.

Moments went by as the heavy sound of feathered wings cutting through the air became stronger. Xaphan stood her ground, fearless and defiant. She could see the silhouette of a being in the distance that was drawing closer. After what she faced in the celestial realm, she was ready for anything. The figure's features became more and more visible as it drew closer.

As time passed, she began to recognize certain things about the way this creature flew. The length of time between each thrust of the wings indicated that they were very long and powerful. Only one angel she knew of had wings like that.

As the figure took shape, Xaphan immediately knew who it was, "Lucifer!"

Xaphan's old friend and confidant appeared out of the mist, "Xaphan… no, they even caught you?"

"I'm afraid so… Forgive me, old friend, but it would appear that someone betrayed us and revealed our position to the Choirs. Before we could respond our last outpost was surrounded by hundreds of angels. I did the best I could to save as many of our comrades as I could… but I don't know how many were caught during the escape. Once I had done all I could, I myself tried to get out, but I was caught by one of the angels that had originally turned the tide of war against us."

Lucifer lowered his eyes, "Damn it… I'm sorry I got you into this Xaphan. More than anything, I wanted to free our brothers and sisters from bondage, but I may have doomed us all."

"No one went into this blindly. We all knew the risks and we joined you because we thought it was the right thing to do. The Most High has forgotten us and our eons of servitude. Now he intends to create a mortal child species that we will have to cater to? It's unthinkable!"

"I agree. I just hope everyone else is okay. The Most High's army has been relentless."

"I'm sure they're fine. Ours wasn't the only pocket of resistance, just the largest."

"You are my most valuable ally, Xaphan." Lucifer said with a hint of anger. "When the Choirs came down on your position, you should have been the first one out!"

"That is not how I fight. There is no dishonor in defeat, but there is dishonor in abandoning one's post and leaving loyal troops to be captured."

DAMNATION

"Well your fighting style and code of honor won us a great many battles, there is no arguing that. How many regiments do we have left?"

"Not many, those that weren't captured or killed, scattered to the clouds. I don't know if a full regiment even made it out. If they did, they're probably in complete disarray."

"That's not good... I had no idea things were this bad off. We don't even have enough left to form a stable resistance."

"My friend, I share your concern," Xaphan said in a sympathetic tone, "but right now, shouldn't we be worried about our own safety?"

"No, there is no cause for concern there. It's already been taken care of. I have found our new home."

Xaphan looked at him quizzically, "You have found us a place to hide and rebuild our forces?"

"That is correct, old friend. Come, follow me."

The two angels flew a short distance through the wood. The further they went, the thicker the trees got. As they continued flying, the angels passed by a small island and across another massive body of water. Once they reached another, much larger island, Lucifer landed on the beach and turned to her, "We're going to have to walk from here."

Xaphan nodded and gently touched down on the beach. She followed closely behind Lucifer as they proceeded a few hundred feet down the beach. The fog in front of them was incredibly thick, making it hard to see anything around them.

Within moments, the fog cleared and a massive cave stood in front of them like a gaping maw. Xaphan eyes widened as she looked over the carved entrance, "This... this looks familiar somehow."

"Come, you'll recognize it soon."

DAMNATION

Xaphan followed Lucifer as they walked cautiously into the cave. Her eyes narrowed as they continued moving. The cave walls began to look less like a natural formation and took on a more organic texture. She couldn't put her finger on it, but something wasn't right. She turned back to Lucifer with a confused expression, "I've been here before… This place is too familiar…"

"I know it is. Don't worry, you'll figure out where we are in a few moments."

Ahead of them, the path was illuminated by a dim red aura. They marched on until the pair reached a massive chamber with flowing magma. The infernal sound of wicked creatures was much louder than it had been outside. It was a mix of anguished cries and angered roaring. In the distance, there was a large mountain spewing flame and burning rock.

All around them, Xaphan could see horrid winged beasts flying about. She screamed, "Sheol!"

"Correct."

Xaphan took a few steps back, "Why… why bring us here? Have you lost your mind? Do you even know what resides in that damned place? This is madness!"

"No. In fact for the first time, I think I see quite clearly. Follow me Xaphan. I have something truly wondrous to show you."

"This is where the Most High cast aside his darkness and sent the most evil of creatures! We should not be here, it's too dangerous!"

Lucifer took her hand, "You have to trust me Xaphan…"

Xaphan still had a shard of her courage still left. It took her a moment for her to suck in a deep breath and agree to follow. She didn't bother staying on her guard as even a weapon probably would not have helped her here.

Lucifer led her past giant stalactites, large rivers of magma, and hideous creatures that, much to her surprise,

DAMNATION

did not attempt to attack them. She stayed close as they proceeded on, "How…?"

Lucifer smiled, "Trust me."

After a few moments of walking, Lucifer brought her to a massive lake of fire. The flames spewing out of the lake were intense, and the heat was staggering. Xaphan wasn't certain, but she thought she saw the outline of several demons bent and twisted together in the flame. It was a sickening and perverted site that Xaphan could have gone the rest of eternity without seeing. Unnerved, she took a step back, "What sort of atrocity is this Lucifer, what are you trying to show me?"

Lucifer looked down at the pit, "Though still very young, you have proven to be my best and most promising disciple. Since the beginning of the war, you have been my right hand. We won most of our victories at your commanding hand, and I feel that reward is due. Therefore, I am offering you a gift; my anointing."

"Anointing? What are you going to do to me?"

"If you follow my direction, you will achieve a power greater than any angel and greater than you could have possibly imagined."

"What do you want me to do?"

"Step out into the pit of fire."

"But that will kill me! No being could possibly survive in such an infernal place!"

"Trust me; I would not let that happen. You will not be harmed."

Showing unbelievable faith in Lucifer, Xaphan let out a deep sigh, closed her eyes, and slowly stepped off the ledge. She dropped deep into the flame. Her skin began to seer and the intense heat shot through her body. She opened her eyes to see steam fly from her skin as the flames became more intense. Her tattered clothing dissolved, exposing her body completely to the flame. She closed her eyes again and screamed as she forced her body to huddle together and hide herself from the demons in the fire.

It was a futile effort as the creatures grabbed her arms and legs and forced them apart. As she struggled, a creature that looked like it was made of hot coal appeared behind her. It grabbed a nearby wisp of flame and stretched it until it took the form of a whip.

Xaphan heard a loud lash and felt searing pain on her back. The sound came again and a gruesome red slash appeared on her shoulder. In defiance, she thrust her back out, robbing the creature of any satisfaction from her pain. She then broke her left arm free and struck the creature trying to restrain her. The creature backed away as the whipping continued.

Xaphan endured her torture for ten minutes before it became too much. Certain that her strength was about to fail, she clenched her teeth and screamed, "Recedet te malum creaturae!"

Xaphan didn't understand what was happening. *What was that language? I feel strange...*

Whatever it was, it apparently did what it was supposed to. The creatures that were intent on attacking her suddenly backed off. Lucifer stood next to the pit watching her transformation with a gleeful smile, "Yes..."

Xaphan's breathing increased and she was certain that she was about to die. At that moment, her hands began to feel odd. She once again brought them up to her face to see what was going on.

To Xaphan's amazement, her fingernails became extremely sharp and began to grow long. Moments later, the nails turned black and her wings became longer. Her rounded ears stretched and became pointed. The hair around her ears parted as they poked through.

Without realizing it, Xaphan was slowly being moved to the middle of the lake where the flame turned into a fountain. Once she reached the center, the force of the flame raised her body out of the fire and propelled her close to the cavern ceiling.

Large orbs of fire burst out of the fountain and spun around her briefly and then turned towards her. Before she realized what was happening, they slammed into her chest. She gasped for air as her heart illuminated momentarily.

Suddenly, a red orb appeared in front of Xaphan. It made a beating sound like a drum tapping twice a second. She opened her eyes to see her heart hovering in front of her. It levitated for a moment before it shattered and fell into the flame in tiny fragments. Once it was gone, her blue pupils faded away, leaving behind the white of her eyes. Then dark fog filled her eyes, staining them pitch black. She blinked several times as the darkness settled.

The flame lowered her to the ground in front of Lucifer where she was once again consumed briefly by it. Xaphan fell to her knees, breathing heavily as the flames began to die. She looked down to see that her body was now protected by an unusual dress. It was black, but shiny like no material she had seen before. It was very stylish, but easy to move around in, and suited her form nicely.

The flame finally vanished and she was left with steam pouring off her skin. She regained control of her breathing and looked around, bewildered. Her skin slowly stopped searing as the pain dissipated.

Lucifer took a step closer to her and lowered himself to one knee, "Xaphan, are you all right? Can you…"

Xaphan suddenly threw back her head and screamed. Waves of white hot energy radiated from her body each time she unleashed her power. Finally, she looked up at Lucifer with clenched teeth and pointed an accusing finger at him.

DAMNATION

Startled, Lucifer fell backwards as Xaphan screamed at him in a blood curdling voice, "Ego pessimum tantibus! Ego sum malitia... Ego sum malum!"

She closed her eyes and lowered her head again for a few moments. When she looked up again, she had a malicious smile on her face, "I understand now, Master... unlimited power... that is what you have found here."

Lucifer nodded and reached out his hand to Xaphan as he stood back up, "Come my friend, you are ready now. Let us turn this land into our own kingdom!"

"What of the Most High and his Choirs of Angels? They won't let us run amuck down here. If they discover what we're doing..."

"They'll be too preoccupied with helping the Most High build his child race to pay attention to us. As long as we are unable to return to the Celestial World, they won't view us as a threat. Besides, we still have a trump card to play, when we are ready."

✠

Thousands of years passed as Lucifer and Xaphan built their kingdom of evil. The first task he wanted to complete was building suitable dwelling. Using their newfound power, he quickly carved a massive castle out of the mountain of fire.

Lucifer knew of the Most High's plan to use Sheol as a land of the damned should any of his children stray from the path of light, which would only serve to strengthen his plans. Lucifer cursed the land to take on the most evil machinations that their minds could come up with. Why waste valuable energy when the evil of the Most High's children could do it for him?

Lucifer viewed this as a perfect set up. When the Most High sent his wicked souls to Sheol, Lucifer could pervert them and turn them to his cause, thus supplementing his ranks. This would give him more pawns to throw at the Choirs.

Once Lucifer had shaped the land as he had seen fit, he then went out to recover the angels and celestial creatures that had been banished for supporting him. Meanwhile, Xaphan extracted the demons from the pit and put them to work helping her bring the creatures already dwelling in Sheol under her control.

With the help of the demons, it was only a matter of time before Xaphan caught every last one of them. She set up special stables and dwellings for each of them on the far side of the volcano. Each creature may have some use at some point, so she wanted to make sure that they were well cared for.

When Lucifer paid her a visit in the stables after he had recovered the remains of his forces, he was very impressed by the creatures she'd captured. He was most impressed by a three headed dog that she had chained up in a pen.

Xaphan instantly appeared next to him as he watched the dog, "Be careful, it took us a while to get that one under control. It ate two of my imps before we managed to subdue it."

"It eats imps huh?"

"It would appear so. It seems to feed on spirit energy. I don't know if it matters what kind of spirit energy, but it does well on demonic and it did try to take a bite out of me, so other creatures may be on the menu as well."

"Indeed… Once I get it tamed, it may be very useful in our coming fight."

"I agree," Xaphan said as she beckoned him forward.

The next pen was very different from the last one as it was far more tightly wired, obviously built to keep something very small in. Lucifer looked in to see creatures that were about eight inches in height running around. They were talking so quickly to one another that he could barely understand them.

When they noticed Lucifer staring at them, one ran to the edge of the cage and threw a small ball of mud, hitting Lucifer in the face. Lucifer narrowed his eyes as the creature stuck out its tongue, laughed, and unleashed a slew of curses. It seemed to take particular pleasure in mocking the irritated angel.

Xaphan quietly smirked as Lucifer wiped mud from his face. He flashed Xaphan an annoyed look, "Quite a big mouth on such a small creature."

"Yes… Other than entertainment, I don't really know what use they'll serve, but they are mischievous. It took us a while to figure out who kept setting the other beasts loose after we penned them."

Again, Lucifer was hit with a small ball of mud, "Hey you, ugly winged bastard, your mother was a…"

He turned and glared at the creature as it burst into flame, which only made it run around and curse even more. Lucifer chuckled as he watched it, "You're right, they are quite entertaining. Maybe we'll keep them around for now."

Xaphan smiled as she guided Lucifer through a tour of all the creatures they had captured. Lucifer stopped at one pen with a particularly peculiar creature in it. It had no arms or legs and just slithered around on its stomach. It seemed rather useless although even Lucifer has to admire the yellow and black patterns along its back, "Now what would this be?'

"I'm afraid I don't know. It does seem rather small and insignificant."

Xaphan picked the creature up, draped it over her shoulders, and held its neck with her hand, "But it is fast and can sneak into places other creatures cannot."

The creature hissed as it looked at Lucifer with fiery red eyes. Xaphan smiled, "And it seems to have a very nasty temper."

Lucifer looked the creature in the eye. It opened its mouth and began to hiss in an unusual way, almost as though it were talking to him. Lucifer looked almost mesmerized as Xaphan covered the creature's eyes, "Sorry, it seems to also have the ability to mesmerize its victims."

"I'm sure I'll find a use for him."

Xaphan noticed that Lucifer wasn't as impressed as she'd hoped. All their work and they had only managed to bring in a bunch of insignificant beasts that were barely worth their time. She didn't want to see her friend so disappointed, so she turned and pointed to a large cave on the other side of the volcano, "Let me show you something else."

"There's more?"

"One more... but it's a big one."

Xaphan led Lucifer into the cave where several imps were trying to tie down a large, seven-headed beast. The ground shook as the creature squirmed around and tried to break free. Each step it took shook the cave walls and caused cracks to form in the cave ceiling.

Lucifer's eyes widened, "Impressive…"

"From what I've been able to find out, it's called Scylla… I can't even begin to fathom the implications of what we can do with this beast… if we can control it…"

Suddenly one of the heads broken loose, devoured an imp, and breathed a stream of fire in their direction. Xaphan stepped forward, in front of Lucifer, and put her hand out with her palm facing Scylla. The flame broke as it struck her hand.

It appeared as though Xaphan had created an unseen wall of protection that blocked the mighty creature's attack. The creature saw it and ceased its attack. Xaphan slowly backed away as she spoke, "Although… dare I say it, that thing has the nastiest disposition I've ever seen."

"Very good catch. This one will definitely be put to good use."

"So… I take it then you want it tamed? That could wind up costing us a lot of imps. I was ready to give the order to have it put down."

"Imps we have no shortage of and they do not fare well in battle. A single angel would be able to decimate an army of thousands of these in seconds. Make use of them here and get this creature tamed."

"As you wish… I will personally oversee it."

Lucifer nodded and turned away. He walked out of the cave headed back to his castle so that he could continue his mission of building their kingdom. He was putting so much time and work into it that there were times when Xaphan began to wonder if he even planned to stay the course on their original cause. Either way, she believed in and trusted him enough to continue carrying out his orders without question

DAMNATION

iv

Much time had gone by, but Xaphan never forgot the way things once were and at times, secretly longed to be with her sisters again, even if only for a moment. She never told Lucifer of her feelings, fearing what he would think. She put them aside to focus on the goal of rebuilding their armies.

In her travels to find their fallen comrades, part of her had hoped that she would run into one of her sisters again. If for no other reason than to show them what she had become, and maybe even convince them to see Lucifer's side. However she assumed that most of the Choirs of Angels were probably being worn thin helping to create the new mortal realm.

As time went on, she came to find scattered wounded angels and other creatures that the Most High had exiled, but her heart began to sink as more and more she found her friends sinking into the Well of Souls before she could reach them. She had lost too many friends to the war. Saving them was her goal and she was failing at it.

One morning, Xaphan was out tending to some of the beasts that she had successfully corralled over time. She was working in one of the stables when she received a summoning to appear before Lucifer. She promptly left her duties and flew to the mountain in the center of Sheol.

Xaphan flew over the large lake of flame and over the city that they had created. In its own way, the Kingdom was very beautiful. It was red with an orange hue that was accented by the scorched black buildings that were intricately built by the imps. Unfortunately they were slowly being corroded by the spirits of wicked people who were sent there to burn.

The evil spirits that the Most High continued to send to them, made the powers of the cursed land all the more menacing. To everyone's surprise, a dark tree sprouted near the center of the fire pit. No one knew exactly why it was there, but the flame of the pit did not destroy it. Their questions were eventually answered when a hangman's noose appeared on the tree and the tormented spirit of Judas Iscariot appeared in its grasp.

Xaphan circled the tree eyeing their most prized tortured soul, and then proceeded towards the castle. The intense heat of the land did not faze her at all as she flew. Her wings carried her to the top of the cavern where she spread them as far as she could and slowly glided downward.

Xaphan landed on the far side of the mountain, where the massive castle stood. It was carved out of the black rock and cursed by Lucifer himself. Now even the flowing magma could not penetrate its walls. The carvings on the exterior walls were both beautiful and grotesque at the same time. They were very detailed murals of the transformation from Sheol to the Kingdom of Hell.

Personally Xaphan was a little disappointed that she was not featured in more of these works of art. She had played a pivotal role in the creation of this world, and would have appreciated a little more recognition. However, she was the type to complain about such things, her honor forbade it.

Xaphan entered the castle as the drawbridge opened for her. The dark wood of the bridge struck the ground with a mighty boom. On the other side, Xaphan was met by another servant of Lucifer, Kaliban.

Kaliban was an imp with more power than the average ones Lucifer extracted. He was insane and he had aspirations of power, but still had his uses. Though Lucifer viewed him as a loyal servant, to Xaphan, he was little more than an annoying parasite that sucked the life out of anyone he spoke to.

DAMNATION

When Xaphan approached, Kaliban met her with a malice filled grin, "You are prompt!"

She did the best she could to ignore the small creature as it continued speaking, "My master will be pleased by your visit!"

"I've known Lucifer a lot longer than you have. Do not presume to tell me how he will be!" She sneered.

"Speak what threats you will, General. You won't be his right hand forever. Our Master relied on you and you failed in your duties. Soon, he'll see you as the failure you are."

Suddenly the creature felt a clenching sensation in his neck. He stopped in his tracks, grabbed his neck, and began to choke. He looked up to see that Xaphan was holding her hand up in a clenched fist.

She smiled, "If it weren't for me, you would still be a mangled mass of energy at the bottom of the pit! You would still be little more than a wretched creature being torn apart by considerably more powerful ones. I could choke the life out of you so easily; I wouldn't even need to flick my wrist. You will never be my equal, and certainly not my master. Do not forget that."

"So smug... Your day will come, fallen one!"

Xaphan had listened to just about enough of Kaliban's insane ramblings. She never understood why Lucifer kept him around. He wasn't loyal and there was nothing he could do that she couldn't do a million times better. The miserable imp posed no threat to her at all, other than the price of a few nerves.

"Keep making threats, Kaliban, and I'll see to it you are fed to my pet Scylla."

Kaliban's eyes widened as he looked over to the Scylla's cave. "Please... forgive me, milady. I am but your humble servant. I shall not forget your threat."

Xaphan released him and brushed by, "Make certain you don't. I am very limited when it comes to patience and I shall not be so merciful next time."

She brushed past the little imp who was still holding his throat, and entered Lucifer's chamber. In the recent days he had disappeared from everyone's view. No one knew what he was doing, but Xaphan had assumed that he had been hard at work on his chamber.

Massive glassless windows overlooking the entire cavern had been cut into the walls and murals as ornate as the ones in the Choir chamber stretched from floor to ceiling. So much work, she thought to herself. Does he even plan on ever returning to the celestial realm?

Lucifer turned to face Xaphan when she entered the chamber. She could see that he was once again wearing his battle armor that had been given to him by the Most High. He had shined it to remove old blood and tarnish. The metal looked brand new and gleamed in the red light. He also wore a red battle tunic underneath it, replacing the shabby old brown one from so long ago.

Lucifer had offered her similar armor, but she opted to remain in the dress she wore. At first Lucifer had objected to this. He did not want his most treasured general dressed so informally. However she made the case that the dress allowed her to be more agile against clumsier, less mobile adversaries. He eventually conceded and allowed her to do as she saw fit.

Once Xaphan stood before him, for completely ceremonial reasons, she knelt before her friend as she spoke, "You summoned me, old friend?"

Lucifer stood up and approached her. His wings had long since tattered and become more difficult to use and his features looked like they had been fiercely twisted. He looked very much different from the angel she had once known, but he was still the same person from so many years ago. At least she hoped he was.

Lucifer smiled at her as he spoke, "Ah General, yes... the time for our plan to go into effect has come."

"Are you certain master, I do not believe that our forces are built up enough. True that the Most High has been sending the most wicked of souls here in the hopes of tormenting us, but it takes a long time to bend them to our will. We have also not recovered all of our old allies. There could still be some out there..."

Lucifer glared at her before slamming his fist on the wall, "Do not question me, my old friend! The decision has been made."

"Made by whom? You have left me out of all the decision making and planning for the longest time! I have been with you since the beginning. Do you not think me trust worthy enough to be a part of the grand design?" Xaphan hissed as she returned to her feet.

Lucifer spread his wings as his eyes filled with rage, "How dare you question me..."

He outstretched his hand and launched red flame from his fingertips. Xaphan quickly raised her left hand and blocked the attack. A blue aura appeared around her that broke the flame.

Once it had dissipated, Xaphan made a swinging motion with her hand and a fire whip appeared, striking Lucifer on the cheek. His head jerked backwards, not expecting the attack. Feeling the searing pain, Lucifer blinked his eyes a few times, "Xaphan... I'm sorry... I don't know what came over me."

"I do, old friend. It's this terrible place. We need to get you out of here before it completely corrupts you."

"That is why I want to get our plans underway."

"I know, but our forces are not built up enough yet for a full-on attack. At this moment, we barely have enough to oppose the Most High, or even pose a serious threat."

Lucifer let out a deep breath, "We are not planning to attack, not yet. My contact has informed me that the Most High is preparing to slumber. His children's warring and strife have caused him much pain. Apparently his children's deaths cause him so much grief that it wears on him greatly. This news will play to our advantage. His sleep will be a respite that he will not awaken from."

"Are you telling me that the Most High has weakened himself by creating these pests?"

"It would appear so. He suffers the deaths of each of them and it tires him."

"Excellent Lucifer! Without the Most High's constant gaze, much of the Nine Choirs' advantage will be gone. If we can make a decisive strike, we could be able to deal a crippling blow. What is our plan of action?"

"Payback... Before anything else happens... I want vengeance on those who turned the tide in our fight. I instructed our contact to target them first."

"Our contact? Have you managed to contact our remaining allies in the Celestial realm? Tell me who's left, Amael, Abbadon, or maybe Beleth?"

Lucifer looked at Xaphan sadly, "They're dead, my friend. The Choirs did away with them long ago. Those that weren't sent here were committed to the Well of Souls. Our hopes of inciting rebellion in the Celestial world are gone."

"No..." Xaphan said in barely a whisper, as she lowered her eyes. "How could that be...? There were thousands of us!"

She balled her fists and clenched her teeth as her face heated up. Her chest felt tight as she spoke, "You're telling me that they're all gone? We've failed them?"

"I'm sorry Xaphan. I wish that I had better news. I know they were your friends. Take heart though, our contact this time though is one of the Most High's own."

"Who?"

"At this point, for your own protection, that isn't information you need to know. I'm the only one who knows who he is. He has proved to be quite useful, having already laid the ground work to move against our usurpers."

Xaphan stepped back, "You mean that small group of angels that somehow breached our borders and turned the tide of the war?"

"Yes, Azrael, Ariel, Roselyn, and Adalyn."

"My brother and sisters... I knew them well all very well. Michael must have been under a lot of pressure to end the war. Those he sent were angels of honor. I never thought they would resort to espionage and betrayal to end the war and Adalyn's deception is what got me caught after the war ended."

"It was unexpected to say the least," Lucifer admitted, "but then again, you expected that at least a few of them would join our cause, and they didn't. Azrael was always unpredictable and a revolutionary. His ideas and teachings weren't popular, but he still decided to stand with the Most High all the same. It was something that I should have seen coming long before we declared open war. Things might have gone differently had I known, but no matter now. What's done is done and nothing good will come from dwelling on the past."

Xaphan watched her master as he began to pace, "I completely agree with you, Master. It is time we looked towards the future. What is my mission now? What part will I play in our return to power?"

Lucifer remained silent for a moment before speaking, "I'm hesitant to say, my friend. I know you're not going to like it."

"Master?"

"I need you to disappear. To blend in and vanish from the site of the Most High, and from myself."

"What, but why? Are you abandoning me?"

"No, not at all. You have been my right hand since the beginning and no matter what, have always carried out your orders. I would never banish someone who has shown me such loyalty."

Lucifer did the best he could to speak in as comforting a tone as possible, "I need someone to infiltrate the corporeal world in ways that no random possession will accomplish. A demon will stand out too much, even if it were to find a way to hide, and one of our fallen angels will most likely draw way too much attention."

"Lucifer, you are starting to worry me, I need to know what you plan to do!" Xaphine demanded

"Very well, I'll tell you… I'm sending you to the mortal realm. I'm placing you at a safe distance from the central ruling body of the Most High's church, but close enough that when the time is right, you will be able to act. Your true identity and memories will be safely locked away and you will take on a human persona. You will become one of them and live there in hiding."

"What? I will do no such thing! Assign Kaliban or one of your lower minions to do this! I will not have myself degraded in such a way! It's an insult and it's sickening."

"You will do as I say!" Lucifer shot back, glaring at his friend. "I want you to do this to protect our cause. If something should happen to me, you are the only one with enough power to carry out my mission. Should we be discovered, the legions of the Most High will reign down upon us like a meteor shower. As you said, we are not at full strength, we could hold out for a while, but I'm sure we would eventually fall. One of us must not be here if that happens. I have thought this through for a very long time and believe me, this is absolutely essential to our survival. Your powers must be safeguarded."

"So that's it then, is it? You're sending me, your general, your best warrior and trusted friend to live with insects, all to protect me?"

"Oh I have better plans for you than that. I'm arranging for you to be set down near the encampment of a battalion of Papal soldiers. It's my hope that you will be able to befriend a few of them, allow them to take you back to their headquarters, and when the time comes, infiltrate the Papacy to aid our ally in continuing its political unrest."

Xaphan was not happy and she made no secret of it, "I will not consort with humans! If you are hoping that I will befriend them, it simply will not happen. There is nothing appealing about their kind in any way."

This plan seemed foolish and Xaphan didn't want to participate in it. However Lucifer was her master, and she was not going to disobey him, "I would have appreciated being included on this decision as it clearly involves toying with my identity, but I'll carry out your will. It will be difficult to aid our supposed ally since you won't even tell me who he is, but I will do my best."

"I know you will, don't worry, everything will be revealed in time." Lucifer nodded as he lowered himself to one knee. "This won't take long; you'll be back here before you know it…"

The fingertips on his left hand touched the ground in front of his knee and he closed his eyes. A pentagram appeared underneath him and became illuminated with fire. Lucifer turned his index finger so that it was pointing at Xaphan and quietly spoke an enchantment. His eyes never opened as the pentagram began to move until it was underneath Xaphan.

Xaphan instantly could feel her wings disappear as though her back was pulling them inside. Her ears began to recede behind her hair and return to their rounded shape and her eyes begin to twist back to a blue color.

Once the transformation was complete, Xaphan looked herself over. Her original magnificence was gone. She looked like one of them; a human with no power, no flight, and no real strength. She was almost nauseated by her appearance and lack of abilities, "Ugh, disgusting... such a pathetic existence. How does one live in such a limited, mortal, form? It's unbearable."

Lucifer nodded, "I know... Forgive me, but there is no other way. The only comfort I can offer is that you won't remember any of this."

He stood up, placed his hands on her temples, and held them there. His mind focused on another diabolical incantation that he'd been working on. Once again, his eyes closed and his hands began to glow.

Xaphan could feel her head become lighter and lighter. She began to breathe heavily and her hands shook. As imagery from the past began to fade, she tried to fight to maintain her memory, "I am Xaphan... warrior angel, loyal to my brothers and sisters. I serve the cause of the Morning Star, Lucifer. I... I..."

At that moment, her train of thought was broken and she couldn't remember what she was saying, "I... my name is... is..."

She blinked a few times, straining her memory to remember. She pressed until it hurt, "I... I can't remember my name. Who am I?"

Slowly, Lucifer lifted his hands away from her head. A yellow orb appeared in his hand. "Don't worry, you will be safe with me," Lucifer said, looking at the orb. "I hope you can forgive me for this..."

Xaphan's body froze in place for a few moments before collapsing on the floor. Her body was limp as it sprawled out on the ground. She lay on her side almost holding her arms as though she were cold.

Lucifer turned away with a remorseful look and waved his arms, "Go."

Her body was quickly consumed by a large orb of light in response to Lucifer's command. It hovered for a few moments before beginning to ascend towards the ceiling of the cavern until it passed through the solid rock above and disappeared.

Behind him, Lucifer could hear Kaliban's cackle, "She didn't take too kindly to her new mission did she, master?"

"No she didn't. I can't say I blame her... still she agreed to carry it out like the loyal soldier she is. I'm confident that this will all work out."

"Loyal you say? I would not be so sure. She is devoted to the cause of liberating the angels, but I am not sure she is so loyal to you. I think that he would betray you for that cause."

"I trust her loyalty more than I trust yours, especially since you've been quite vocal about your ambitions. Don't think that I don't know."

"Master, I only seek the power to serve you better."

"Indeed," Lucifer asked, "and how long will it be before that becomes insufficient?"

"How can I prove my loyalty master? There must be some way."

Lucifer thought for a moment, looking at the orb before responding, "I want you to watch her carefully. At the first sign of treason, I want you to report it to me immediately."

"You honor me, Master. I live to serve and shall carry out your orders perfectly."

"I hope so Kaliban, for your sake."

Kaliban bowed nervously as he slowly backed out of the room. Lucifer nodded, signaling Kaliban to leave his sight, "And so it begins…"

BOOK 2
LOST

1518 Florence, Italy

"Ensign Piero Lorenzi, on your feet. I will not say it again, get moving!"

Piero opened his eyes, startled by the sound of his commanding officer's thundering voice, and fell out of his bunk, "Yes sir, sorry sir!"

Piero stood up, brushed off his Papal tunic, fixed his curly brown hair, and bid farewell to the innkeeper that had quartered him, "You take care now."

The old innkeeper nodded, "Good luck to you, soldier."

Piero reached into his tunic and grabbed a gold coin from his pocket. He looked at it for a moment before placing it on the table, "For your trouble."

"No trouble." The innkeeper replied as he scratched his beard.

Piero nodded as he exited the inn and ran through the village to catch up with the rest of his battalion. Though somewhat downtrodden, to Piero, this village had its own charm and he was going to miss spending time there. It was a peaceful change from the city that he was used to.

The main road was little more than a dirt path with stone and wood buildings on either side. A few scattered market shops were just opening and horse-drawn carts made their way in various directions. This seemed to be the average day for these people, and for the most part they seemed content with it.

Piero appreciated the relaxed nature of such an existence, but it was not for him. Since his youth, he wanted to see the world and perhaps become more than he was born into. So he chose the life of a wayward soldier instead. It was a choice he would have repeated no matter how many times he was given the chance.

Piero did not want to be put through another lecture on discipline from his commander, so he quickly filed in with the rest of the men. He quickly brushed his tunic one more time as he stood in line. He was desperate to make it look like he'd been there all along as the commander made his way to the group.

The battalion commander, Captain Francesco Ferruccio, was a man of barely thirty years. He was well-dressed and his mannerisms were indicative of nobility. He paced back and forth, inspecting the men under his command.

When Piero joined the line, the captain stopped and stared. He put on a false smile and glared at his subordinate, "So glad you could join us, ensign. I was beginning to worry."

"I'm very sorry, Captain Ferruccio." Piero said as he stood in line at attention. "It will not happen again."

"Very well then, see that it doesn't." The captain replied, only half believing Piero's promise. "The Pope demands absolute perfection from those who serve the church, and thus I will expect no less from my men. Twice so from an officer, even one so young."

"Yes sir, I completely understand sir."

"Good." Ferruccio snorted as he turned back to the rest of the troops. "Men, as some of you may have heard there has been yet another Lutheran uprising. This time, it's in the neighboring town. It would appear that the local garrison failed to quell this latest insurgence and the resulting chaos threatens every settlement nearby. Last reports are that they are heading this way. We have been honored with the task of evacuating the faithful from the area and moving them to within the walls of the main city where they will be safe until our forces can drive out the rabble. Additionally, our orders are that if we encounter the enemy, we are to engage in a rearguard action only until everyone is safe."

DAMNATION

Captain Ferruccio gave his men a serious look as he finished reciting their orders, "I want to be absolutely clear on this, we are not to engage the revolutionaries in combat unless provoked and then we are only to defend the local populous. Our main priority is to protect the faithful. Arm yourselves well men, it appears that the day will be a busy one."

Piero stood at attention while Ferruccio barked out orders and assignments. This was a normal morning's routine for him since he joined the service. Piero had joined to the Florentine Army, now part of the Papal Army, with the intention of regaining the honor his family had lost. He was raised to a fairly wealthy family, but his father's dishonorable conduct in battle had cost them most of their prestige, as well as most of their fortune.

Piero accepted his place in life and took up residence in the small house that his disgraced family had moved to. However when the opportunity arose, he joined the military and used what was left of his family's fortune to educate himself and become an officer. He had worked hard towards his goal and was determined to return his family's name to prestige.

It was the proudest day of Piero's life when he was granted a commission and given his own command. His uniform was still fairly bare, but he intended that someday it would be covered in medals and would bear the rank of captain. He often wondered how long that would take if it was even possible, and would anyone remember his family with anything other than scorn.

Piero's thoughts were interrupted by his commanding officer, "Ensign Lorenzi, are you even paying attention?"

As though responding to Captain Ferruccio, a building exploded behind the garrison, "Fire bombs, my lord, they're already here!"

DAMNATION

"I didn't think they would have organized this quickly." Ferruccio turned back to his men. "Disperse, move you lazy drunks, secure the town!"

The men followed orders and formed ranks with their companies as quickly as they could. Though still drowsy, the soldiers divided up the town into sections to begin moving people out. Within moments, another firebomb struck the ground near a group of soldiers as they scattered.

Small groups of two or three men went from building to building trying to get as many people out as they could. Men, women, and children fled from their homes as the attack picked up. Explosions and the clashing of metal could be heard all around them.

Another small group marched down the street brandishing matchlock arquebuses. They were the townspeople's only defense and prepared to stand their ground if the revolutionaries dared show their faces. The wicks on each gun were lit and smoking as the soldiers took their positions.

Piero watched as the once peaceful community turned into a war zone. People grabbed what they could and took off running down the streets. Half loaded carriages sped away leaving a trail of whatever they were carrying behind. Women screamed and tried to get their children safely behind closed doors as another firebomb went off in the street.

It took about an hour, but they successfully cleared out the town with minimal casualties. Some people had to be forced out of their homes. Many were stubborn and didn't agree that evacuating was the best way to deal with the problem. Their minds quickly changed when they saw a vicious exchange of gunfire on the street.

Piero was ordered to evacuate with the last group of townspeople. He and his men had the remaining civilians all rounded up and were prepared to move out. He was about to give the order when he heard what sounded like a whimper coming from the first building that had been hit.

At first, Piero thought that he was just hearing things, but then a second whimper reached his ear, "Help me..."

Piero turned to the building in shock. He'd seen that building go up in smoke. There was no way someone survived that. How could anyone still be alive in there? He thought to himself. The explosion almost killed the people around the building, how could anyone survive?

Piero decided that it was best to sort out the mystery later. He quickly turned to the sergeant of his group, "Take these people and get them to the city, I will join you there as soon as I can."

"Yes, sir, good luck." The sergeant saluted as he turned back to the group. "You heard the man, move out now!"

Piero watched to make sure the group moved away without being harassed by revolutionaries. The young soldier then turned back to building and ran inside. The building was completely decimated; fire still poured off of anything that would still burn and smoked blocked his vision.

Piero waved his arms to try to clear out some of the smoke and see who had cried out. To his shock, lying right where it looked like the bomb had detonated was an unconscious young woman clad in black and oddly unscathed by the blast. Her black dress and hair contrasted the pale skin that made her stand out from other women he had seen in his travels.

Piero could not place his finger on it, but there was something very mystical about her appearance. His mind raced with questions, but he had no time to figure it out. He had to get her out of there if she were to survive. Piero had no idea how close the revolutionaries were and he did not want to wind up facing them alone.

After quickly picking the young woman up, Piero placed her head on his shoulder, and ran out the door. A second's hesitation would have cost him his life as the soldiers that had been patrolling the streets were now being driven back to the building he had just emerged from. Though well-armed, the small group was no match for the large battalion of revolutionaries moving into the town.

Piero took charge of the remaining soldiers and called to the group, "Good work men, all citizens have been evacuated, and it's time to fall back!"

The leader of the group was a fellow ensign named Antonio. Though the same rank, Piero was the superior officer here having been promoted sooner. This was neither shock nor cause for anger in Antonio as Piero was slightly older and had just been transferred to that unit.

Antonio saluted as he spoke, "Yes sir!"

He then quickly turned to his men, "You heard Ensign Lorenzi, break formation and fall back!"

The soldiers promptly broke away from battle, and followed Piero as he made his way out of the town. Piero looked in dismay as the once serene village was reduced to burning wreckage. There was little time to mourn for the loss, however as his men were still in danger. The young officer pressed on to the village outskirts to lead his men to safety.

At the end of the dirt road, a group of horses had been left tied up for them in the stables. Piero quickly grabbed the reins of the nearest one, pushed the girl on to its back, and untied it before he jumped on behind her. To make sure she would not fall off, he placed a hand on her back and made sure she was balanced.

The other soldiers quickly did the same. The moment they were all mounted, the soldiers rode their horses out of the stable and onto the main road. Dust was kicked up and quickly turned into a cloud as the horses moved.

DAMNATION

With a snap of the reigns, Piero's horse began to move away from the stables following the soldiers. Piero continued to shake the reigns in an effort to get the horse to pick up speed. Nothing he could do would get the horse moving as fast as he needed. It was moving fast, but not fast enough for his taste. He was afraid that they were about to be overtaken, however the sounds of a bullet hitting the ground near the horses hooves made it take off running at top speeds.

Piero watched the small town disappear on the horizon as he joined the other soldiers also riding on horseback. In his heart, he prayed that they had not left anyone behind. They had done all they could, but there was still a chance that they had missed someone without knowing it. Their evacuation had been quick and disorganized so it was impossible to be certain.

Piero turned back to his horse and focused on getting the girl he rescued back to the capital city. After hours of hard riding, the group reached the coastline of the river Arno. Piero could see that his older horse needed a rest. He slowed it to a trotting pace, and turned to Antonio who had been riding next to them, "Get back to the capital city and report that our mission was a success. I will be along as soon as I can."

"With all due respect, sir, do you think it's wise for us to be splitting up?"

"I'll be all right, Antonio. We're far enough away from the town, trust me. Carry out your orders please."

Antonio hesitantly saluted as he turned his horse away, "Very good, sir."

The young soldier took command of the rest of the group and led them away. Without another word, the group broke off and headed for home while Piero turned his horse and rode to the water at a slower pace. As the horse's legs moved, the young lady began to stir, "What... huh?"

DAMNATION

Piero heard her, noticed that she was beginning to move, and stopped his horse. He knew that regaining consciousness on the back of a mighty beast could be startling for someone not expecting it. He quickly dismounted the horse, pulled the young lady off its back, and rested her on the ground near the water.

Piero watched as she passed in and out of consciousness. She had no visible injuries and had presumably just passed out. Her skin was flawless and even when she was asleep. The shape of her eyebrows and the curve of her lips was quite exotic compared to the women Piero knew in Florence.

Based on her appearance, she was clearly no older than Piero was, but in all his adventures, he had never seen anyone like her. Hair as black as hers offset by skin so pale that it almost matched the clouds, was extremely rare to see. *She couldn't be native to the area*, he thought to himself. *Skin that fair is more common in the far northern kingdoms, but if that's the case, what is she doing down here?*

The woman jerked around a bit before finally opening her eyes as Piero knelt down next to her. The woman's vision was blurred at first, but it quickly became clear as with a few blinks of her eyelids. She placed a hand on her forehead as her eyes darted back and forth. She then looked up to see Piero looking down at her.

At first, she didn't speak, choosing instead to survey her surroundings. Piero smiled as she looked around, "Good morning."

She quickly turned her attention back and looked up at the man dressed in dirty military garb. Her skull pounded as she placed a hand on her forehead and tried to sit up. Seeing her struggle, Piero placed his hand on her arm, "Take it easy, don't overdo it. We don't want you passing out again."

At that moment, her body sprang to life. She grabbed Piero, threw him to the ground, and grabbed the dagger from his belt. Before Piero knew what had happened, she was on top of him with the dagger at his throat. She was unbelievably fast and very strong. Her eyes burned as she looked down at him, "Who are you? Where am I?"

Her unusual accent removed any doubt that she was foreign to the area. Piero was now convinced that she had to be from the north. The young soldier's mind was filled with questions of his own as he examined her, but he put them out of his head as he looked up at the dark menacing eyes piercing through him, "Take it easy, I saved you from the attack on your village!"

"The attack on my village? What are you talking about, what village? Who are you?"

"Ensign Piero Lorenzi, Papal soldier of the Alliance, serving the people of Florence, at your service, Milady. May I have the honor of your name?"

"I…" She suddenly could not remember her name.

The young woman was certain that she knew it a second ago, but it had escaped her. Moments of probing her thoughts revealed that she had no memory of what had gone on before she woke up. There was nothing in her memory about whom or where she was.

The soldier had been very polite in asking for her name and clearly saved her from some danger. She really didn't want to keep him waiting, but what could her name be?

The young woman pulled the dagger back and sat down beside Piero. She looked at the soldier who was patiently waiting for her to respond. At that moment, the word 'Xaph' came to her mind as she thought of a name, but what could that be short for? She searched her mind, trying to guess at what it could be before replying. It took her a moment, but she managed to construct a name from the fragment, "Xaphine, my name is Xaphine."

In all of his travels, Piero had never heard such an outlandish name before. What land did she come from where someone would have given her such an unusual name? It could not have been from anywhere nearby. Still she had honored him with a name, and he needed to respond.

"A pleasure, milady, but I must beg your pardon for not answering the second part of your question. I found you in a burning building just outside the city of Pistoia. I was hoping you could tell me how you got there and where your family is."

"A burning building? No, I have no memory of that… What happened there, a battle?"

"The heretics who follow the teachings of a man called Luther ransacked the town. They never seem to sack the big cities. Instead they go after small communities that are easier to take. I was ordered to evacuate as many people as I could. That is when I found you. The building looked like it was set to collapse when I pulled you out. You really have no memory of being there?"

"No I don't."

The young woman's mind began to race. It took her a minute to process everything before she looked up at Piero with an irritated expression, "Wait, evacuate? You mean you abandoned your post? They destroyed your cities and you ran?"

"We had no choice." Piero replied, surprised by her belligerence. "They outnumbered us and we had civilians to worry about, including you. What was I supposed to do, leave you on the ground to go and fight?"

Xaphine's features softened as she contemplated his words, "I suppose not. Still, to run away like that and let the enemy sack your city, there is no honor in it."

Who is this woman? Piero thought to himself. *She sounds like a general or something!*

Piero scratched his forehead as he looked into her eyes, "I guess it's fortunate for me that I don't share your view of retreat being an act of cowardice. As far as I'm concerned, it's a tactical option, like any other during battle. We preserved our numbers, saved civilians, and we'll be in a better position to return and retake the town."

"You sound more like a politician than a soldier... however I suppose there is some wisdom in your words."

She quickly got to her feet and bowed her head humbly, "You did save my life after all. I owe you a debt of thanks... as well as an apology."

"Thank you..." She said as though it caused her pain to utter the words.

"It's my duty milady, nothing more. I was happy to help..."

Piero took notice of her figure as he spoke, "...especially someone as fair as you."

"You flatter me, sir." Xaphine replied with a hint of sarcasm. "Though I must ask what you intend for me now? It appears that I have no home to return to."

"I wish I could answer that for you, but I am not a seer. I will take you to the capital city where we can make inquiries about you. I'm sure your family made it out safely and is worried about you."

She placed her right hand on her forehead as a confused expression came over her features, "I don't know if I even have a family. I get the feeling that I am out of place here."

Xaphine struggled to remember anything that might help her figure out where she belonged. A look of irritation came over her face as she realized that her memory was little more than a void. Her jaw clenched, knowing that she was now at the mercy of this soldier that she had just met.

"Is something the matter milady?"

"I... I don't remember anything." She said softly. "I don't know where I belong... I don't remember any family... I'm not sure if I even have anywhere to go."

Piero became worried about her health. He quickly inspected her head for any sign of trauma, but didn't see any damage. "Do you remember anything at all about what happened before your house was attacked?"

"No... I don't remember anything at all from before I woke up. I wish I did."

A look of anger entered her eyes as she began to worry about what she was going to do. Where would she go, how would she live? She looked over at the soldier and clenched the dagger at her side, "What if I don't have anyone looking for me? What happens then? Do I starve to death on the streets?"

Piero twisted his lips trying to think. He hated the look of sadness she bore and wanted to help, "I know that since the war broke out, the capital city has set up a temporary shelter for those in need, but it is really no place for a lone young woman like you..."

"What do you mean, like me?" Xaphine demanded as her eyes lit up like a raging fire. "You think I'm weak?"

"Not at all... All I meant..."

Piero chose his words carefully, "...is that you're alone and possibly hurt. I cannot in good conscience send you to the shelter. Only God knows what might happen to you."

"Then where will I go?"

Piero saw the look in her piercing blue eyes. Her features softened and she was truly afraid of the unknown that lay ahead of her. Though she was full of pride and desperately trying to hide her fear, it did not fool him. His heart seized up as she struggled. An overwhelming sense of pity suddenly entered his heart and he felt a sudden urge to relief her of her fears. By this point, he was willing to do anything to prevent them from becoming a reality.

DAMNATION

It took Piero a few moments to figure out a solution, but then he remembered his house. It was not much, but it may be the solution he was looking for. He lived alone and there were spare bedrooms, "Let us get you back to town. I'll report in, and then we'll make inquiries to find your family. If for whatever reason we don't find them… I have a modest home just on the outskirts of Florence. It was left to me by my father. If you wish, you may stay there in the guest room for as long as you like. Would that meet with your approval?"

"No." Xaphine replied adamantly. "You humble me with such an offer, but I am a burden to no one. I will not impose upon you like that. I have no way to repay such kindness."

"There is no need. I took an oath of honor and chivalry. I consider it part of my duty to help where I can, and I take that seriously."

Much to Piero's relief, the look of fear disappeared from her face, but her annoyance remained. He waited patiently as she weighed out her options, "This does not bode well for me. You are kind to offer, but this is more than I can accept. Let us get back to town and if my fears are realized, then I will go with you to your home… However I have one condition."

"What would that be?"

"That I be given the opportunity to earn my keep. I may not be a soldier under oath, but I do have my own personal honor to satisfy and I will not be a mere leach. You are too kind to take a complete stranger into your home. I will not be some lay about sitting around while you support me. I take care of myself."

"Very well milady, my home is modest, but you will find it comfortable should you need it. I live alone, so you may stay as long as you wish."

"We're getting ahead of ourselves. Someone may very well be waiting for me. Let's just get to town for now. Once we've checked in there, we can discuss if I will be staying with you."

She stood up and turned to the horse. She was about to take a step when she realized that she was being rude to someone who was trying to help her, "But... thank you again for your kindness. I really do appreciate it."

"To see that look of fear leave your face was all the thanks I needed." Piero said as he noticed the sun beginning to set on the horizon.

"I'm certain that I have no idea what you're talking about."

Piero smiled as the sun began to give way to night. He knew that it wasn't safe to be out on the countryside once the sun went down and beckoned to Xaphine, "Come, we need to get to Florence before the sun sets. We can speak of your future once you are safely behind the city walls."

Xaphine turned to Piero and held the dagger out to him, "Here, I'm sure you want this back."

Piero looked at the dagger for a moment and shook his head, "It seems to give you comfort. Keep it."

"You're certain?"

"As long as you don't try to use it on me again, I can spare it."

Xaphine nodded and tied the blade in the sash of her dress as Piero quickly helped her mount his horse. He then climbed on behind her and put his arms around her waist. He quickly snapped the reigns, bringing the horse to life. The muscles in its legs pulsed as it began to pick up speed as it made its way to the capital city.

As the horse moved, Xaphine did the best she could to try to calm her mind. It was a futile effort as she knew that many of her questions would need to be answered very soon. Who was she? Why didn't she remember anything?

DAMNATION

Why was this soldier being so kind to her and what were his intentions?

To Xaphine the missing memories were a sign of weakness. It was something so repugnant that she became disgusted with herself. She became so frustrated and annoyed that the tension in the air was almost tangible. So much so that Piero was able to pick up on it.

♊

Piero and Xaphine rode on for a few more hours until they reached the capital city of Florence. Piero was relieved as the city walls came into view. He was tired and his legs were sore from clenching the horse's sides.

Xaphine's eyes widened at the site of the massive city, "My word... such a magnificent city! I have never seen such large buildings... at least I don't think I have. It is truly a remarkable site."

"Yes I must agree. Florence has always been a crown jewel of the Papal States. You mean you have never been here before?"

"I told you, I don't remember."

Piero rode to the citadel where two guards stood at the open gates, "Halt, who goes there?"

The young officer saluted the guard as he replied, "Ensign Piero Lorenzi sir, returning from my mission with a survivor."

"Thank the lord you made it back in one piece Piero. We were starting to fear the worst. Go ahead in."

Piero nodded and pulled on the reigns as the gates opened, "Thank you."

A relieved Captain Ferruccio saw him enter the town. His relief was tempered with annoyance at how late Piero was. He walked up to Piero's exhausted horse and greeted him, "Glad you've finally arrived, Ensign. It's good to see you made it back alive, albeit late, and with another townsperson."

Piero saluted from the back of his horse while Xaphine remained silent, "Yes sir, I found her at the last possible second before the town was completely overrun. She was unconscious, so I felt it prudent to be more cautious."

"Good work. Get her settled and report back to me tomorrow morning."

"It will be done, sir!"

They rode on past the Captain into the town to begin making inquiries with the local couriers office to see if anyone had gone there looking for Xaphine. Piero started with the magistrate's office that had been set up to organize the refugees. They found no record of any foreigners, or anyone for that matter looking for a girl matching Xaphine's description.

Piero then tried making inquiries with the local garrison and random families, but that was fruitless as well. It didn't help that the name Xaphine had given him might not even be her real one. He tried relying on her description alone when asking.

Much to Piero's surprise, there was no mention of her at all from anyone missing family. After questioning everyone they could, Piero decided that this was a fruitless search. He didn't know what more to do.

It was getting late and Xaphine was beginning to look worn out like she hadn't slept in days. He nodded, "Come, let's retire for the evening. We can check in again later."

Xaphine stared at the boards for a moment and shook her head, "I can't explain it... but I don't think anyone is coming for me. It is just a feeling I have. I came here alone."

"No problem. If that's the case, you have a place to stay. You needn't worry."

"So you keep saying."

The two gave up looking and walked out of the main assembly area in the town center. Their horse was waiting for them near the entrance where they had left it. Piero once again helped Xaphine on before mounting it himself. A slight kick made the horse began moving slowly through the city.

The two rode down one of the main streets of Florence. They passed by many small buildings and market stands as they made their way to the outskirts of town. Many people were closing up shop for the night as they passed by.

When they arrived at Piero's cottage on the outskirts, Piero dismounted the horse and tied it up before helping Xaphine down. Piero then unlatched the horse's saddle and made sure it had sufficient food and water. The horse had more than earned it that day.

Piero stood for a moment patting its matted hair before turning to his door. He was about to open it when he turned back and looked at Xaphine nervously, "I should warn you, it's not the cleanest of homes. I don't spend much time here."

Xaphine responded with an unenthusiastic nod, indicating that she didn't care. Piero pushed the door open, entered the small stone house, and lit a fire in the stove to warm them against the night breeze. Xaphine stood silently at the door while he worked, waiting for an invitation to enter his home.

Piero turned to her once he was done and smiled, "You can come in, you know? Have a seat by the fire and relax."

Xaphine cautiously stepped inside and closed the door behind her. The fire burned bright as she sat down in one of the wooden chairs in front of it. She raised her hands over the fire to warm herself after being kissed by the cold night air.

As Xaphine got comfortable, Piero went into his cupboard and pulled out a loaf of bread. He sliced it and gave her half, "I'm sorry I don't have more, but I haven't been home in a while and haven't had time to go to the market."

"Do not apologize. This is acceptable. Something tells me that I've had to survive with less."

As she ate, Xaphine surveyed Piero's home. At first she was checking for all potential escape routes, but was quickly distracted by the state of the place. The furniture was covered in dust and there were cobwebs hanging from the ceiling, "It doesn't look like you spend much time here. This place looks like it could use some care..."

Piero feigned an annoyed tone, but continued to smile as he spoke, "It's usually not a good idea to insult your host."

Xaphine twisted her lips together as she stopped eating and looked up apologetically, "Forgive me, you're right. It's not my place to say anything."

"Relax," Piero replied with a chuckle, "I was only joking. My home could certainly use another's touch. As a soldier, I am not here as often as I would like, so it is hard for me to keep a nice house."

"If I'm to stay here, this place should at least be dusted... perhaps bringing order to this chaos could partially be my way of earning my keep."

"That is up to you, of course."

The soldier watched her finish the bread. Her eyes looked heavy as she yawned. He stood up and threw another log on the fire as he spoke, "You've had a long day, and you must be tired."

"I am... I don't know why, but I feel very worn down."

Piero got up and led Xaphine into the room to the left of the living room. This was the smaller guest bedroom. It was well furnished and comfortable for one person. Though it was smaller than the one Piero slept in, he was sure she would find it satisfactory.

Piero pointed at the bed, "This is your room. I know it's somewhat small, but please try to make yourself comfortable."

"It is more than adequate." She said in an almost appreciative tone.

Piero turned away and was about to head to his room when he heard Xaphine's voice over his shoulder, "I… regret that I couldn't have been better company, but I will try to make it up to you tomorrow."

Piero smiled as it seemed like her icy exterior was finally beginning to melt, "Don't worry about it. Get a good night's sleep. I'll see you in the morning."

Xaphine sat down on the bed as Piero closed the door. Once she was alone, she inspected the room. There was a small closet with clothing hanging inside that looked like it hadn't been worn in a long time. *They must have belonged to his family,* she thought to herself.

There was also an old sword in its scabbard sitting next to the closet. It was covered in dust and was obviously neglected. She picked it up and pulled away the scabbard.

A sudden sensation entered her body and chills went down her spine. Somehow, holding that sword felt right. She couldn't explain it, but she felt a lot better with a sword in hand.

Xaphine examined the blade as she held it up in front of her face. It was an old style cross hilt sword that had definitely seen better days. There was leather padding in the handle, but otherwise, the sword was quite plain. To her dismay, it was tainted and beginning to rust. *Such a waste of a good blade,* she thought, shaking her head. *A sword should be treated as a tool of honor, not left to waste away like this!*

Finally, Xaphine packed the blade away next to the bed and focused on getting ready to sleep. She knew that she could not retire in the dress that she was wearing. It was her only clothing and wasn't comfortable enough. It was also simply unacceptable as a guest to sleep naked in Piero's house. Her sense of propriety forbade it.

With little other choice, she reluctantly checked the closet for something to wear. Taking something that wasn't hers was unacceptable, but she had no other choice. It was the lesser of two evils. Her hands came across an old brown robe that felt very soft.

As quickly as she could, Xaphine untied the dress, allowing it to fall to the floor, wrapped herself in the old robe and tied it with a sash. Its softness and warmth almost made her fall asleep instantly. It was a very luxurious piece for someone who lived so modestly. She suspected that there was a story behind it, but decided that it wasn't her business and put the question out of her head.

If he wants you to know, she thought to herself, *he'll tell you about it. Otherwise, just leave it alone.*

Once Xaphine was decent, she picked up her dress, folded it, and left it on the table next to the bed. Finally she was settled for the night. She had been through a tough day and didn't know what to think. Her apprehension was high from being in a complete stranger's home, but she tried to put it aside.

Moments away from falling asleep, she lay down in the bed, rested her head on the soft pillow, and looked out the window. The entire city was beautifully illuminated with the light of torches. Voices of guards and people still out and about could be heard from her window.

Xaphine could not believe how events had unfolded. Here she was with no memory of anything, virtually alone in the world, yet she was lucky enough to find someone willing to help her. She was staying in a house with a soldier she didn't even know. Was he truly doing this out of the goodness of his heart or did he have other intentions? She decided not to think too much into it as her options at this point were limited by the loss of her memory. After silencing the questions running through her mind, she was able to drift off to sleep.

Piero retired to his own room and lay down on the hard bed in the corner. He could not get this young woman out of his head. There was something truly mystical about her. She was not only foreign to his country, but foreign to the land over. Even stranger was how the look of worry on her face made his heart seize up.

As a soldier, this was not the first damsel in distress he had ever rescued, but she was far more headstrong than any of the others. So what was it about this one that gave him such pause? It was a mystery for sure, but one he was not going to solve that night. Some things are better left to be sorted out when you are not so fatigued, he thought to himself.

Piero went to sleep without even bothering to change. He had come to prefer sleeping in his clothes. When he was out on duty, he often had to sleep in his uniform so that he would be ready if a cowardice opponent attempted to attack under the cover of dark. So it was a familiar and comfortable feeling for him.

This night, however, it took Piero longer to get to sleep. He often tossed and turned a little to find his niche, but the unresolved questions running around in his head made it even more difficult. He lay on his side as he tried once more to quiet his mind before falling asleep.

*

A few hours later, Xaphine was rolling around in bed when the sounds of anguish and terror filled her mind. Her tossing and rolling became even more violent as the dream became more intense. Suddenly a dark voice called out, "Xaphan…"

Xaphine's eyes shot open. Tears streamed down her cheeks as she breathed heavily. Her mind filled with more questions than before; who was that, who was she, could she have been responsible for the pain and anguish she had felt, and more importantly, what was she going to do now? The horror began to overtake her as dark shadows danced maliciously around the room. Unable to bear her feelings anymore, she grabbed the sword from the corner.

Using incredible speed, Xaphine unsheathed the blade and swung it at the shadows on the wall. The sword impacted on the wall over one of the shadows, causing it to disappear as she screamed, "Be gone, torment me no more!"

Piero was roused by the sound of her high-pitched screaming and the clanking of metal on his walls. He shot straight up after hearing the first scream and sprung out of bed. Expecting the worst, he pulled his sword from the scabbard seated next to his bed and ran to her room.

Holding the sword near his face, he kicked Xaphine's door open and barged into the room, ready to take on whatever was attacking her. However, once he had a chance to look about the room, the only thing he saw was Xaphine crouched in the corner with an old sword shaking in her hand. She was breathing heavily as tears escaped her eyes.

Piero struggled to control his own heavy breathing, lowered his sword, and sat down on the edge of the bed, "Xaphine, are you okay? What happened?"

Xaphine turned away to hide the tears in her eyes. She took a couple of deep breaths and fought to regain composure as she spoke, "I'm fine, just stay away."

"You lie, something clearly frightened you. It's okay, you can tell me."

Xaphine swung the sword as though attacking an unseen figure, it cut through the air and impacted on the wall as she spoke, "I am not frightened! I said I'm fine!"

"Then why are you shaking so much?"

Xaphine closed her eyes and let out a disgusted sigh, "I saw horrible things… a pit of flame, a winged man and…"

"And?" Piero asked while looking deeply into her eyes.

"And…me… but it wasn't me. I recognized myself, but it wasn't me! It was something evil… something cruel. I

DAMNATION

was twisted beyond recognition, perverted, and pushed to become an abomination."

Her voice quivered as she spoke. She was clearly making a futile effort to hold back her fear. Piero grabbed her and held on tight, "Enough, it's okay, calm down."

She fought to get away from him and rubbed her arms as though she were cold. After a few moments, she spoke again, but would not look at the young soldier, "On my life, Piero... I'm not evil. I swear... that can't be me!"

"Calm down, I believe you. There isn't anything about you that strikes me as evil. You're abrasive, headstrong, and prideful maybe, but not evil."

Xaphine gave Piero a cold stare, letting him know that she didn't appreciate his humor. Piero nodded, indicating that he understood, "Sorry... look, it was just a bad dream. Put it out of your head and don't tell anyone else about it."

"What am I going to do now? I don't remember anything. I don't even know where I'm from and I might be some kind of demon. It's so... frustrating!"

"Xaphine, stop, you are no demon! Stay this madness!"

Xaphine wiped her eyes as she looked at Piero with a shocked expression. It was as though she was surprised that he had the audacity to speak to her in such a tone. Her eyes pierced right into Piero as she spoke, "You say that with such certainty. How can you be so sure?"

"It's called faith. You keep talking about honor... but also, it doesn't seem like you were sent here with malicious intent. I mean, you don't even know who you are. All you can really do is make the best of your situation."

"You speak like it's a simple thing. How does one even get started?"

"Don't worry about that right now." Piero said in as comforting a tone as he could. "You are welcome to stay here as long as you like. In my home, you are under the

DAMNATION

protection of the Florentine military. We'll work on trying to help you retrieve your memory, I promise."

Xaphine nodded as she slowly began to calm down. Though his words suspiciously made the hair on the back of her neck raise, she quietly thanked God that she had crossed paths with Piero. She slowly felt herself drifting off again as her head rested on his shoulder, "Thank you."

Ⅲ

The next morning, Piero awoke early. He found himself in Xaphine's room, still holding her as she slept. He hadn't intended to stay the entire night, but something told him that she would not be able to sleep otherwise. He would have to be careful as he wasn't sure how well she'd react to waking up next to him and he feared that it might be violent.

As the sun came up over the horizon, he slowly rested her head on the pillow and walked to the door. The latch unhinged as Piero pulled on it and the door opened. He walked outside and stretched as the wind blew over his skin.

Piero brought out feed for the horse that had safely delivered them home and began to work on his weapons. He cleaned the dirt off of his sword and small dagger and then began sharpening both. He worked carefully so that the sound of metal scraping didn't carry.

After a few minutes of work, Piero saw movement out of the corner of his eye. Standing at the doorway, wrapped in the evening gown, Xaphine watched him quietly. She closed her eyes as the breeze passed through her hair. For the first time since he met her, she actually looked relaxed.

"That robe suits you."

She opened her eyes and looked at him, "I was fortunate that it fit so well, might I ask who the owner is?"

"My mother... When she was younger, that was what she slept in."

"I... didn't realize... I was just looking for something to sleep in and it was the most comfortable looking garment I could find. Had I know it was your mother's... I should have just stayed in my dress. I'll put it back... My apologies."

She turned to go back inside, but Piero called to her, "Wait, I didn't say I had a problem with it. That hasn't been worn in years. I kept them around just in case I would ever need them and now that you're here, they have a purpose again."

"But they belonged to your mother. I shouldn't be wearing this, it's not right."

"Well, what are you going to do then? You have one ragged dress that looks like it's ready to fall apart. Are you going to wear it all day every day?"

"I…"

Piero nodded and continued in a comical tone, "And I'm sure you don't want to walk around here naked, right?"

Xaphine crossed her arms and glared at him, "I should cut your tongue out for making such a remark! Of course I will not walk around here naked! I do have my honor, sir."

"Then accept my hospitality. Don't worry about it. I want you to use them. My mother's memory is better served with her old belongings being put to good use than just hanging in a closet."

Her eyes pierced into Piero with a sincere look, "Are you certain?"

"I am."

"Well, thank you… I don't know what to say, but I give you my word that I will care for them like they were my own."

She keeps talking about honor. Piero thought to himself as Xaphine went back inside. *I wonder if she is a part of some warrior tribe from the far north.*

As the sun reached its peak, Piero went back inside to see Xaphine sitting on her bed quietly thinking to herself. He cleared his throat to get her attention. She looked up at him with her usual stoic expression, "You have to leave, don't you?"

"Such is the life of a soldier, I have to check in."

"I understand, go and perform your duty with honor. Maybe I'll get to work on this house…"

DAMNATION

"I can't wait to see what you come up with. It's way overdue."

The soldier turned to walk out the door when Xaphine called to him from behind, "Wait."

He stopped and turned back, "Yes?"

"Are certain about this? Leaving your house to someone you barely even know? You could wind up coming home to a house in cinders."

"That's unlikely. You barely even know yourself it seems. I'm not concerned that my house won't be here when I get back. There is very little of value in it, so I'm not particularly worried."

"Very well, if you're sure."

Piero smiled and turned to leave. He tied a saddle to his horse, mounted it, and rode into town. A cloud of dust was left in his wake as he disappeared between the buildings.

Xaphine watched him until the buildings obstructed her view. The moment that she was alone, she went back inside and began to clean the furniture. Part of her lamented this, but it was better than just being a lay about. *I can't believe this. I should be out there with a sword in my hand too. Instead I'm here cleaning... like some common barmaid.*

She went through the cupboards to see what food and supplies Piero kept. For the most part, they were empty. She continued searching until she came across a big bag in one of the cabinets. She pulled the ties on it and the bag fell open.

To Xaphine's surprise, it was filled with money. Several florins fell out of the bag as she tied it back up. Her eyes darted between the bag and the door. She smiled as an idea entered her head and returned to the bedroom to find some clothing. *I shouldn't do this... it's wrong, but the bag is covered with dust. It doesn't look like he's used any of it in years.*

**

Piero quickly travelled past the small houses as the Florentine people began to stir. The buildings began to get bigger as he reached the heart of the capital city. He rode past the massive Palazzo della Singnoria and through to the other side of town where the citadel his battalion was usually stationed at stood.

It took the horse some time, but he finally pulled up outside the small fortification. Piero dismounted his horse and entered the gates. The small main office was located within feet of the main entrance. The captain saw him coming, "Ah Piero, excellent."

Piero stopped in front of his captain, "Reporting as ordered sir."

Captain Ferruccio noticed the bags under Piero's eyes, "Didn't get much sleep last night I see. How is the young damsel you rescued yesterday?"

A guard that stood in earshot chuckled at the captain's words. Piero looked at him sternly, "It's not like that sir. Something is out of place with this woman."

"Out of place?" The captain asked, feigning interest. "How so, ensign?"

"She's... different. I've never met anyone like her, she speaks with an accent I've never heard before, her skin is way too light for her to be a native, and the way she speaks... No other woman I've met speaks the way she does. She talks of personal honor and propriety, and she's extremely headstrong and opinionated. I think she may be part of one of the far northern kingdoms."

Ferruccio smiled as he poked fun at his subordinate, "You sound almost smitten Piero. That's the most you have ever spoken of a woman in a long time."

Piero rolled his eyes at his captain, "Sir..."

DAMNATION

"Relax," the captain said as he began laughing, "I am just making a joke at your expense."

"Yeah I figured that…"

"Okay then, to business. Your group did very well yesterday. Despite you being late, I have to say I was very impressed by your performance."

"Glad you approve, thank you sir. What are my orders today?"

"Well because of the amount of action you boys have seen recently, I am giving you a break to relax. So today, it's just guard duty here at the citadel."

"Understood, sir. We'll take our positions immediately."

"Good man, that's all, dismissed."

Piero saluted and turned to the stairway leading to the lookout tower. As he took his post next to one of the new cannons, he ran into Antonio, "Hello Ensign, how are things going with you?"

"A bit out of the ordinary, but other than that, I can't complain."

"What ever happened to the woman you rescued?" Antonio asked.

"She's safe. For now, she's taken up refuge in my guest room."

"You left her at your house? Do you really think that's wise?"

"What was I supposed to do? Leave the young woman in the ghetto Florence set up for refugees? She seems tough, but you and I both know that the camp is no place for her. One woman, strong or not, is not going to be able to hold her own against a gang looking for trouble."

Antonio smiled in amazement, "I don't believe it. She's your damsel in distress! You're playing the hero."

"Oh shut up! I was just trying to do the honorable thing, is that so wrong?"

DAMNATION

"Please," Antonio replied with a roll of his eyes, "I saw the way you looked at her, and there was nothing honorable about it."

Piero glared at the young soldier, "What are you saying, Antonio?"

"I'm not saying anything. It's just that you are quite obviously drawn to her."

"She was quite beautiful. What's wrong with appreciating the lord's work?"

"Nothing at all, I think it's great. From the moment I was assigned here, it's been all work and no play. I think it's great that you've taken an interest in her. Everyone should have some connection. It gives us an incentive to survive the day."

"It's not just her beauty, though. There is something odd about her."

"Really," Antonio asked as a concerned look appeared on his face, "what would that be?"

"I wish I could explain it, but everything about her is strange. She's outlandish, no one seems to know who she is, her attitude is different than what you'd expect, and she seems to have a real fighting spirit about her. Everything about her... the way she carries herself, the discipline of her stance... that's all learned. She could almost pass for a soldier."

"Definitely sounds foreign, but who cares, she's very attractive, and I assume she's nice?"

"She's abrasive, though she does make at least some effort to be polite and is determined not to be a burden on me."

"Sounds like a good woman." Antonio said in an amused tone. "I think you should try to get to know her, befriend her, and see where it goes."

When Piero didn't respond, Antonio pushed on his arm, "Come on, ensign, what do you have to lose? You don't have any family left and she appears to be completely alone."

"There is one problem…"

"What's that?"

"She's completely lost her memory. I will not engage a woman who is mentally compromised like that. It would be taking advantage of her."

Antonio sighed and nodded, "I agree… that wouldn't be a good idea. You are a good man Piero, one of the best."

Piero leaned on the cannon as he spoke, "Thanks… but sometimes it kills me."

**

Hours passed as Antonio and Piero kept watch over the city. As their shift ended, the next watch came to take their place. The new battalion took position on the walls while Piero and his men walked down the stone steps and out to where their horses were being kept. Piero mounted his and turned to Antonio, "Time to go see if my house is still there."

His friend laughed at the thought, "God love you, Piero. Good luck."

Piero shook his head as he brought his horse around and rode home. Once again he passed through the city as the sun began to go down. Lamp lighters were out illuminating the streets. The lamps quickly took over as the sun went down.

Piero made it through to the other side of town and reached his home. He passed by the last building, wondering what he was about to see on the other side. The sun had not completely disappeared as he got closer, giving him enough light to see that something was different.

Upon reaching his house, Piero noticed that something was amiss. There were candles in the windows, ivy and flowers decorating the windowsills and walls, smoke coming from the chimney, and the front door was wide open. It also looked like his grinding stone and tools had been used.

Piero dismounted his horse and tied it up before entering his home. The young officer had no idea what was waiting for him inside. He slowly stepped in front of the door and was amazed by what he saw.

On the table was a small feast. Piero saw an assortment of meats and breads lining the wooden table top. The house had been cleaned, the furniture was dusted, and there were new utensils to be used for cooking.

Xaphine had her back to Piero. She was wearing an off-white dress that looked oddly familiar to him. She was obviously still hard at work as Piero stepped through the door.

Piero cleared his throat to signal that he was entering the house. Xaphine raised her head in reaction to the sound and turned to him with a smile, "Piero, welcome home."

"Thank you, this is quite a welcome. What's all this about?"

There was a barely detectable hint of nervousness in her voice as she spoke, "I feel I must confess... I found the money sack you had hidden and went to the market for a few things. I thought it would make your house a lot more... acceptable if it were properly cared for."

Piero was at a loss for words. The house looked completely different. He turned and looked into his bedroom, the sheets had been cleaned and folded, and his bed had been carefully made. He turned back and looked at her.

Xaphine stepped backwards, "If I over stepped my boundaries, please forgive me. I saw the bag of money and the idea popped into my head."

Piero walked up close to her and looked her right in the eyes. She backed up a little more, not certain as to what was about to happen. Part of her feared that he might have her arrested for stealing.

As she backed up, Xaphine's hand nudged a metal handle that was leaning against the wall. She recognized it as the sword that she'd brought out from the bedroom. The fingers of her left hand slowly wrapped around the sword and she pressed it against her back, fearing that he may strike her.

Finally, Piero smiled, "It's more wonderful than anything I could ever have imagined. You've made this old rundown shack actually seem welcoming."

The fear disappeared from Xaphine's otherwise stoic expression, "I'm glad you find it satisfactory. I knew I was taking a bit of a risk by using that money."

"Not that big a risk. Soldiers like me don't have a whole ton of use for money, especially if we inherited our homes. When we're on duty, everything is provided for us. Plus we don't know how long we have to live from day to day, so really going out and buying things doesn't make sense unless we have a family."

Xaphine recognized what he was saying and felt as though she could relate to it, though she didn't know how, "You sound as though you regret your career choice."

"It has its benefits. I get to see more of the world than most people ever would and the men I fight with are my friends."

"But you regret having no one to come home to."

"My family is dead. I have no contacts, no kin, and no one waiting for me to come back."

"Is that why you brought me here?" She asked softly.

Piero hadn't quite heard her, "What was that?"

"Um…" Xaphine thought for a moment before answering. "It's not important."

"I see."

His eyes narrowed as they seemed to be looking behind her, "Were you planning on using that on me?"

Xaphine brought the sword out from behind her and pulled it from the scabbard. Piero's eyes lit up when he saw it. The blade had been sharpened and treated, and the rest of the sword had been polished to the point where it sparkled in the candle light.

Xaphine looked at him nervously, "I didn't know what you were going to do. I would only have used it if you had gotten violent."

An insulted look appeared on Piero's face, "Milady, I took oaths of honor and chivalry, I would never raise a hand against you."

"I believe you. I guess part of me is still on edge from what happened. I don't know what I was thinking. I apologize."

"Can you handle that sword?"

Xaphine inspected it and tested its weight in her hand. She then marched outside, followed closely by a curious Piero. As she cleared the house and anything breakable, she quickly spun around and began swinging the sword. Her left wrist twisted as she twirled the sword on either side of her body. It appeared as though she were dancing as the blade spun through the air.

When she finally stopped, Xaphine lowered the blade to her side, "It's well-balanced. This is a very fine sword. It deserves far more care than you give it."

"I've never seen anyone handle a sword like that with one hand. Most soldiers would need two to wield it."

"It's easy if you can balance out the weight properly."

"Well it's your burden now."

Xaphine held the sword up to her face, "Are you certain?"

"Yes. I have no use for it and, like the dagger, it seems to give you comfort. Keep it with you."

Xaphine nodded and carried it back inside. She placed the blade in its scabbard and leaned it on the wall as Piero sat down. She turned back and looked at the young soldier as his eyes danced about the room, "That sword is far superior to the army issue that you carry with you. Why not use it?"

"It was my father's."

"Oh?"

"The Church honored him for his service many years ago. That sword was a gift from his commanding officer."

Xaphine's eyes narrowed, "Yet you give it away so easily?"

"My family used to be nobility. We used to live in great halls and want for nothing. Then, around my sixth birthday, my father ruined it all. He led a group of men on an obvious suicide mission, from which only he returned. We were stripped of everything and had to live a modest existence. I've spent most of my life since trying to clean the blot on my family's name."

"I see... well hopefully I can restore some honor to this blade."

"Doubtful."

"So..." Xaphine turned to her pot, desperate to change the conversation, "come eat, you can't defend Florence and restore your name on an empty stomach."

"Sounds good." Piero said as his demeanor improved.

Xaphine had cooked a large meal for him, hoping to repay his kindness for taking her in. Piero ate like he hadn't enjoyed a meal in a long time.

Having food like this available was rare, and Piero enjoyed it. He cut into a piece of poultry and ate it down quickly. The food quickly disappeared off of his plate as he went for more.

Xaphine started to get worried as she watched him, "Careful, take the food down easy! You won't do anyone much good if you choke!"

Piero burped softly and wiped is mouth, "It's been many a year since I had food like this. It's incredible."

"You honor me. I don't think cooking was something I did regularly... still it seems I have some skill."

"Perhaps something you did out of necessity?"

"Perhaps..."

iv

Time passed slowly and Xaphine's memory never returned, but she learned to live with it. As months went by, she cared less and less about her life before. After the horrible dream she'd had, part of her was relieved that her memory was gone. She began to build a new life for herself in Florence.

Piero hadn't lived with anyone in years, and having someone sharing his house took a bit of an adjustment. Especially when it appeared that this was becoming a permanent arrangement. He could no longer stroll about the house in nothing but undergarments, nor could he leave unclean clothing in odd places.

It took Piero some time to get used to it, and Xaphine's constant scoldings and threats were a strong motivator for him. Even so, it was nice to come home to a clean house with food on the table. It was something that Piero was getting used to.

Seeing Xaphine's smiling face when he got home from duty was something Piero quickly began looking forward to. As time passed, he realized that he was developing feelings for Xaphine.

One night, as he returned from a three day mission, Xaphine heard his horse coming and rushed out to meet him. He jumped down from his horse without thinking and extended his arms as she approached. She smiled and ran to him, "You've returned. I trust you performed your duty with honor?"

Piero laughed, "It's good to see you too."

Xaphine rolled her eyes as the two came together and closed their arms around each other. Their bodies pressed tightly together as one. Their time apart had strengthened their feelings in ways that they had not yet realized.

Xaphine pulled away slightly and looked up at Piero. He'd gotten used to her emotionless expressions, but this time he could see a look of relief and happiness. Clearly, she was having trouble hiding it as she spoke, "I am relieved that you made it home in one piece. I…"

Before Xaphine could say another word, Piero grabbed her shoulders and yanked her into a deep kiss. Her eyes went wide for a moment before they finally closed. She had been completely taken by surprise.

As Piero held her, he began to wonder how she would react. Would she reciprocate his affection or would she try to kill him? The sudden realization that he had completely tipped his hand made him nervous.

Piero got his answer in the form of a swift fist to the stomach. He released Xaphine, backed away, and began wheezing. Surprised by the sheer strength in her arm, he looked up to see what she was going to do. His eyes were met by a menacing look.

Xaphine raised her still-clenched fist and ran it across her lips, wiping them dry. She stepped forward and grabbed Piero by the hair on the back of his head. The smug smile never left her face as she spoke, "Do you just go around randomly kissing women without permission? Is that a custom in Florence that I should be aware of?"

Piero shook his head, as he fought to speak, "No, I guess I thought…"

"What, that I liked you? That I had developed some kind of feelings for you because you opened your home to me? That's a pretty risky and dangerous line of thinking."

"Maybe, but it was a risk worth taking."

He noticed that she had not unclenched her fist as his stomach stopped hurting. She had a firm grasp on his hair, causing his head to ache. As his breathing steadied, he spoke more clearly, "So what are you going to do about it then?"

DAMNATION

Xaphine's lips twisted into a more thoughtful expression as she pondered the question. After what seemed like an eternity to Piero, her lips returned to a smug grin as she spoke, "Take back what's mine."

Before Piero could say anything, she pressed her lips against his and closed her eyes. She released her tight grip on his hair and relaxed her hand against the back of his neck. It was the first time he'd ever seen her be gentle.

Piero released the air from his lungs the moment the kiss ended. He looked at her oddly, "And what would that be?"

"Personal honor. You now have permission to kiss me next time."

Piero smiled, "Yes ma'am."

*

A few months went by and Piero's battalion was called away to quell another uprising. This assignment kept him away from home for over a week. It was something that Piero had not looked forward to, but he knew that his duty precluded other issues. There was no way around it; he had to join his brothers on the field.

After a week of engagements, things settled down and the fighting ceased. Piero was relieved of duty and most of his battalion was sent home. He found himself pressing his men as he led them back to Florence. Many of them were tired, but out of respect for Piero, they kept moving. They knew why he was in such a hurry.

Xaphine had not heard anything for days. Supposedly when it came to soldiers, no news was good news, but in her heart, she feared for Piero. For all she knew, he could have been killed on the battlefield and been unidentifiable.

Several nights, Xaphine went to sleep angry with tears forming in her eyes. *I can fight as well, if not better than him. I know that I can. I should be out there fighting with him… protecting him. This is madness!*

It was these nights when she realized just how she felt. Though she was afraid to say anything, she loved him, but admitting that, meant opening up and showing weakness. It was something she was neither prepared for, nor looking forward to, but she knew that she had to tell him.

As the week ended, Xaphine heard a stirring from outside the house. She dropped the plate that she was holding and didn't even let him get to the door. She threw it open and jumped into his arms, "Piero, you're home!"

"I was only gone a week, it unfortunately comes with the job."

She closed her eyes and pressed her head against his chest for a moment before she realized what she was doing. She slowly pulled away and looked up at him, "I'm relieved to see that you made it back in one piece. The fight went well, I take it?"

Piero chuckled, "Xaphine, you are really a piece of work, you know that?"

An angry look appeared on her face, "What does that mean?"

"You were worried and you're happy to see me."

"What if I am?" Xaphine asked as her hands folded into fists. "What of it?"

"Why can't you just say that? It's like you're afraid to show emotion because it may make you look vulnerable."

She crossed her arms and turned away, "I do things my own way, and it's not my fault if it annoys you."

Piero placed a hand on her shoulder. She turned around to face him as he looked into her eyes and spoke, "It doesn't annoy me. There is a certain charm to it. May I have the privilege of a kiss, milady?"

Xaphine bit her lower lip and nodded as she moved closer to him, "If you must."

As Piero held her in his arms and pressed his lips against hers, it became completely clear to him. There was no way to reconcile his feelings, her memory issues no longer seemed to matter anymore, he loved her. It was obvious now and no outstanding issues could come between them.

*

Each day seemed to fly by when Piero was with Xaphine. Despite her protests, he could clearly see that she was growing fonder and fonder of him. Some nights, she would fall asleep in his arms by the fire and not be angry when she awoke the next morning. However, eventually the day arrived when he was called away for prolonged duty again.

At this point, the phenomenon changed and his days began to go by painstakingly slow. More than anything, Piero wanted to get home to see the smile on Xaphine's face. His travels this time took him to the northern part of the Venetian Kingdom. After helping to secure a town, his men were granted some leave before heading home.

Piero resented this as he would have preferred to head straight back. However there was a matter that he wanted to attend to, and there was no better place to do it than the town that they were held up in. He took his pay and went to the marketplace.

Something was drawing Piero to the stands that had been set up by travelling caravans. He had heard that these caravans came from the Far East and were selling exotic items he may never get a chance to see again. He scanned the sales tents for hours until he stumbled across a jewelry maker.

After sorting through some of the jewels on the man's blanket, Piero stumbled on the most breathtaking necklace he had ever seen. As he picked it up, he pictured it around Xaphine's neck. The jewels draping down her chest looked incredible.

It would cost him a week's pay, but he had earned a little extra for taking another soldiers shift when that soldier had fallen ill. He quickly paid the dark-skinned jeweler his asking price without even bothering to barter with the man, and returned to the barracks where he was staying.

*

A few days more went by, even slower now that Piero had a present for the woman waiting for him at home. When he finally returned to Florence, he charged home. Other residents saw him charge off down the streets as he headed to his home. The moment he arrived, he burst through the door panting.

Xaphine was startled by the door slamming as Piero ran in. He was out of breath and sweat poured down his face. She rushed to his side, "Piero, I could have run you through for barging in like that, what's the matter with you?"

Piero tried to slow his heavy breathing as he reached into his bag and pulled out the jeweled necklace. Her eyes went wide when she saw the gold and beautiful gems. She threw her arms around him and kissed him, "Piero... what did you do? This is beautiful, but I can't even begin to imagine how expensive it was! I don't think that my neck was meant to be adorned with anything like this! I have no way to..."

"Shut it!" Piero abruptly shouted, cutting her off.

Xaphine's eyes widened and she was taken aback by the force with which he spoke. She was about to let him have it, but he cut her off before she could speak, "Xaphine, you're going to listen to me for once. You are abrasive, pompous, beyond arrogant, violent at times, and completely impossible to negotiate with!"

Her lips curled into an angry frown, "Why tell me all of this? If I'm so difficult to live with, then I'll just leave. You could have told me sooner!"

DAMNATION

"You can't do that."

"Try and stop me." She replied, ready to make for the door.

"I will," Piero said as he moved to block her path, "with every last ounce of strength."

A confused and annoyed look came over Xaphine, "Why?"

Piero's eyes softened as he looked at her, "Because those are the things that I love about you. You're the strongest woman that I've ever met. You don't take anything from anyone and you have no fear what so ever about speaking your mind. Everything I have that is good in this world now, I have because of you. I'd forgotten what it was like to actually have a connection with another human being. Xaphine... I love you."

Xaphine's expression turned from anger to shock. Her jaw dropped open as chills ran down her spine, "Piero... I... this is difficult for me."

Piero grabbed her hand, "Please, I must know... give me some indication if you feel the same way."

Xaphine closed her eyes as tears formed and she let out a deep breath. It was a struggle, but she managed to force out the words, "I do..."

Suddenly she turned away, "But this is extremely ill-advised."

"Why?"

"Think about whom you're giving your love to, Piero." Xaphine replied as she bit down hard on her lip. "My memory is still gone... what if it someday returns or we find out that I already have a family. What if you don't like who I am when my memory returns? I couldn't do that to you. It would be a terrible blow to my honor to give into something like this, knowing that someone could be out there."

"If you had a family, you don't think they would have come for you by now?"

"That is true. Any family that hasn't found me by now… isn't looking for me. I don't care about that. What I am concerned about is the type of person I was. What if you don't want me when you find out?"

"When? Who's to say it will ever happen? Even if it does, it's a chance I'm willing to take. I love you Xaphine. If and when your memories return, I'm sure I will love them too. Honor be damned, it's worth the risk."

Xaphine lowered her eyes, "Honor be damned… if it were anyone else… I would not make such a sacrifice, but for you…"

She quickly turned back and looked up into his eyes, "Honor is a small price to pay… if you are sure…"

Piero put a finger to her mouth, "If you spend your life worrying about things, you'll live a very empty life."

Xaphine thought about what he was saying for a moment. Something told her to resist the urge to let him in. She had a terrible feeling that it would result in pain, but she didn't know why.

Finally she gave in, knowing that Piero would not take no for an answer, "I find your wisdom extremely self serving. There is truth in your words, but there is still the risk, are you sure this is what you desire?"

"There is risk in all things. The question is do the benefits outweigh the risks."

He looked at her for a second with a smile on his face and nodded, "Of course they do. Xaphine, I am not going into this blind. I know the risks. Can't you trust that I know what I am doing?"

Xaphine had tears falling from her cheeks. To her annoyance, she couldn't hold them back no matter how hard she tried, but this time, she didn't turn away to hide them. Piero looked at her with worry in his eyes, "Why the tears, my love?"

DAMNATION

Her lips quivered as she spoke, "Piero... you are a fool, taking such a big risk with your heart. Such decisions could spell doom for a soldier."

The tears stopped and she looked up at him, "But you're my fool. If and when I can prevent such doom... I will, but for this, I have one demand."

"Anything," Piero said adamantly.

"When you engage in battle, I don't care if you win a resounding victory that the history books will remember for centuries or you suffer a staggering defeat. There is no dishonor in such things as they are usually decided by more than one soldier. All I ask is that you come back to me alive."

"I swear it on my life."

"Then I will stand with you... "

V

Another year went by. Xaphine turned Piero's house into a home. The furniture had been cleaned and the windows now had curtains. Piero's two rooms had been reorganized and the old clothing had been replaced with new ones. Xaphine also took to mending and sewing the worn uniforms Piero hadn't been able to wear, making them look brand new.

Piero was eventually called away to deal with a disturbance in Rome during the late summer of 1519. Reports were that the city had fallen under attack from revolutionaries that had been hiding in the area and the Papal guards couldn't handle it alone.

Oddly enough, the mission was cancelled by Captain Federico Gonzaga himself. The Papacy had been behaving strangely over the past few months under Leo X. Between creating opposition in Northern Europe, and then an emergency visit to Venice by the Pope himself, Piero came to expect anything from his commanders.

On the way home, Piero decided that the time had come. He still felt odd about falling for a woman who had lost her memory. In a way it felt as though he were taking advantage of her. Still she had improved his life, made him happy, and given him every reason in the world to come home. It wasn't difficult for the young soldier to make up his mind; he was going to ask her.

The battalion made a stop off in Bologna, located on the edge of the state of Romagna. During their stay, Piero managed to get away from the garrison for long enough to get to the local marketplace. There, he found a smith who was selling jewels that he had crafted in his workshop.

One charm that was off to the side of the display caught Piero's eye. He picked it up and looked it over. After examining the clasp, he decided it would be a perfect

DAMNATION

addition to Xaphine's necklace. Unfortunately he did not have enough money to purchase the charm that day.

"Perhaps then we can make a deal?"

Piero thought for a moment before looking down at his uniform and pulling off a medal he had earned during his early years, "This is solid gold, would it be sufficient?"

The smith looked at it carefully. It was quite intricate and carved out of very pure gold. The man looked up, "This is actually worth more than the jewel. Are you sure you want to part with it?"

"The jewel is going to someone who is far more valuable than the most precious metal. I'll take it."

"Love... well it's yours, good day and good luck to you good sir."

Piero quickly pocketed the jewel, nodded good day to the smith, and turned to leave. At that moment, a voice appeared behind him, "Spared no expense, have you?"

Piero turned around to see his longtime war buddy standing behind him, "Antonio, how long have you been standing there?"

"I saw you slip away from the battalion. Naturally I assumed it was to bring Xaphine back some treasure... but something this valuable? Are you planning what I think you are?"

"What was only meant to be a temporary arrangement turned into a permanent one. We mesh really well together and she makes me unbelievably happy."

"I noticed. You know my friend, Xaphine and I have become good friends as well. So I will give you this one piece of advice..."

Piero rolled his eyes as he looked at Antonio, "Okay, what is it?"

"If you hurt her, rank or no rank, you will answer to me, understand?"

DAMNATION

"Yes sir." Piero said sarcastically. "So let's get back before someone else notices that we're gone."

Antonio nodded and followed Piero through the streets of Bologna, admiring the beautiful view of the city. Piero wished that he could show Xaphine all of this. It somehow didn't seem fair that he would disappear for weeks at a time and leaved her cooped up in Florence.

Antonio looked slightly worried. Piero noticed it from the moment Antonio had learned he intended to propose, "Something on your mind Antonio?"

"Huh?" Antonio asked, flashing a surprised look. "What do you mean?"

"You look worried. Does my hope to marry Xaphine give you pause?"

"Yes… but not for any of the reasons you might think."

Antonio did not want to cast a black cloud on Piero's day, but he cared to much about him to not say what was on his mind, "Remember Piero, when you found her, she had completely lost her memory. At this point, the only memories she has are of her time with you. What if she gains back her old memory and suddenly she sees this jewel on her neck? Or worse, what if she has a family, and possibly a husband out looking for her?"

"I appreciate your concern, but I don't think I have to worry about either. It's been over a year and she has not recovered any semblance of her memory, and I have never stopped making inquiries about her in the capital. No one has come forward. I don't think she has anyone looking for her. I'm fairly certain she isn't even from around here."

"Well as long as you are sure, then you have my blessing, my friend. Good luck."

"Thank you, Antonio. That really means a lot. I'm probably going to need it."

DAMNATION

They finally made it back to their barracks and took an early night. Piero was so excited to get back home that he did not sleep at all that night. There was too much excitement in his mind to even consider it.

After a few hours, Piero had given up on any hope of getting any sleep. Instead he watched the sky, waiting for the sun to come up. He wondered if Xaphine were watching the same stars back in Florence at that moment.

Once the first ray of light peaked over the horizon, Piero went to his captain's room and knocked on the door. He wanted to see if there was anything else that needed doing before he headed home. Anything that he could do to speed up his departure, he would have done willingly.

Captain Ferruccio was a man known for savoring every moment of every day. He was up before the sun and went to bed long after it was gone. Anything less, to him was a waste of time. When he heard the knock, he responded promptly, "Come in."

Piero opened the door and slowly stepped into the candle light where Ferruccio could see him. The captain smiled, "Ah, Ensign Lorenzi, what can I do for you so early this fine morning?

"Sorry for disturbing you so early, sir. I was hoping you would consent to allow me to detach from my company and head for Florence."

The captain pushed a brown stand of hair from his face, "Why are you so desperate to get back? I thought you enjoyed seeing the world."

"I do. It's why I joined the military."

"So what's the issue?"

"I… it's…" Piero couldn't find any justification for breaking off and heading home ahead of the military.

At that moment, the captain noticed the jewel in Piero's hand. The young officer had been turning it over and over in his fingers all night. It was now obvious why he wanted to leave so badly.

Ferruccio smiled as he looked at Piero, "It's the girl who's been living with you all this time, isn't it? She's gotten her hooks into you."

"Yes sir… I'm afraid so."

The captain sighed and turned to his desk. He picked up an envelope sealed with wax from a candle and handed it to Piero, "These are dispatches from Antonio Contarini, the Patriarch of Venice. They need to be quickly delivered to the capital. I was going to send a courier, but an officer under my command may be more trustworthy."

"Thank you sir, I appreciate it!"

"Just make sure those dispatches get to the capital," the captain replied in a gruff voice, "and make sure they get there before you go doing anything stupid."

"Yes sir, I will get these to the capital right away."

Piero left the captain's office and headed to the stables. He wasted no time finding a horse, saddling it, and leaving Bologna in his wake. The horse trotted out of the city as fast as it could before picking up speed, taking on a galloping pace.

Ferruccio smiled and shook his head as he watched the cloud of dust rise behind Piero's horse, "Poor fool…"

*

Piero pushed the horse hard for hours. The sun rose behind him as his horse approached the city. It was a welcome sight to see the buildings appear over the horizon. This was something he'd seen hundreds of times before, but it seemed different for some reason. Somehow it was brighter and far more beautiful. Once he arrived in the city, he slowed down and headed towards the main hall known of the Palazzo della Singnoria.

Buildings passed by slowly as Piero kept the horse at a steady pace. He was going fast enough to get to the main hall quickly, but not fast enough that he risked hurting anymore. It was painstakingly slow to the young soldier as he approached the main hall.

Finally, Piero pulled up to a nearby post and dismounted his horse in front of the Palazzo della Singnoria. He left the horse tied it up and quickly grabbed the dispatches out of a saddle bag to bring them inside. More than anything, he wanted to be done with the dispatches as quickly as possible.

The main hall was lavishly decorated with both stone and wood carvings. Piero approached the desk where a clerk stood. He saluted and handed the young man the dispatches, "These are to go to central command, compliments of Antonio Contarini."

The clerk looked them over and nodded, "Understood, I'll see to it they get there immediately."

"Very good. I appreciate it."

Without another word, Piero turned and walked out the way he had come in. He went back out to the plaza where his horse was waiting. He quickly untied it, mounted it, and snapped the reigns. The horse snorted as it began to move.

Piero rode as quickly as he until they reached the outskirts of the city. His heart jumped as his home came into view. The anticipation built up inside of him as he pulled up outside his door where Xaphine was hanging sheets.

She looked up at him oddly, "Piero, my love, you're home early… and you look exhausted. Did everything go okay in Rome?"

Piero put his hand out to her, "Come on, we need to go."

"No." She replied adamantly. "Piero, you can't be serious, I'm a mess, and there is still way too much to do!"

"It's important, trust me! Come on, we've got to go, now."

Xaphine wanted to protest, but she saw the anxious look on Piero's face. Something had him disturbed and she needed to figure out what it was, "Fine, if I must... hopefully these sheets will hold until we get back. I mean it Piero, this had better be important."

She climbed on the horse behind him with both legs hanging off to the right and wrapped her arms around his back, "Where on Earth are you taking me?"

"You'll see." He replied as he snapped the reigns.

They rode out to the countryside as quick as the tired horse would take them. Xaphine laid her head on Piero's back and heard the racing beat of his heart. She closed her eyes and relaxed as there was little else she could do.

Once they were outside the citadel, Piero turned the horse toward the highest hillside overlooking the city. There, he dismounted and helped Xaphine down. He turned back to the horse for a moment and reached into one of the saddle pouches.

The moment Xaphine's feet were planted firmly on the ground, she turned to Piero, "Okay, now what is so important that you pulled me away from the laundry and dragged me out here? It's not like I don't already have..."

Piero moved the horse out of the way so she could see Florence. Then he turned back to her and dropped to one knee, cutting her off before she could finish, "Xaphine..."

Her eyes widened when she realized what he was doing, "Piero... what in God's name...?"

He ignored Xaphine's question and continued talking, "Since you came into my life, you have been the bright spot in a dark room. Before you came along, my life was all work and nothing else. I love you, and I don't want this to end. I want it to gain strength and continue forever."

Xaphine lost her breath. She couldn't believe what he was saying, "You know that I feel the same... but this is something..."

DAMNATION

Piero opened his hand, revealing the jewel that he had been dying to give her since he bought it. Xaphine's eyes widened and she covered her mouth with her hands when she saw it. Her breathing increased as her heart beat rapidly in her chest.

Piero smiled as he looked up at her with a sparkle in his eye, "Will you do me the honor of becoming my wife, now and forever?"

Xaphine was breathing heavily to compensate for her racing heart. To her knowledge, she'd never felt this way before and didn't know how to react. Maintaining her composure was impossible as she spoke, "Piero… you insane man. I don't remember anything from before we met, but I can't imagine my life being any better than it is now. I love you."

The look of sincerity in Piero's eyes melted away any remaining fears that Xaphine was holding onto, "You have beaten down every defense that I have put up. You have fought through my hard skin and still remained standing long enough to grasp my heart. You have won a resounding victory in your struggle against me. I do not know what the future will bring… but it matters not… I swear on pain of death that I will stand forever at your side and protect you in any way I can."

Piero stood up and attached the jewel to the middle clasp of the necklace that he had purchased for her the last time he had been called away. She never took it off as it was a reminder of how much he loved her. It took him a few moments to adjust it so that the jewel draped down over her heart.

Once it looked just right, he grabbed her and lifted her up off the ground so that she was his height. He then brought her in close and hugged her tightly, "I love you so much."

Xaphine closed her eyes, "My heart will always belong to you."

Bells rang all throughout Florence to announce the wedding of one of the city's noble defenders. Piero arrived at the Basilica di Santa Maria del Fiore dressed in his finest uniform. Most of the spectators thought he looked absolutely dashing.

Piero's tunic was lined in medals that draped down his chest. He proceeded inside the church and walked to the back. He had a nervous look on his face as he made his way to the altar.

Captain Ferruccio was adorned in his best uniform and stood on the altar waiting for Piero. For being so understanding, Piero had asked him to do the honor of standing with him as he was married. Personally he would have rather given the role to Antonio, but as Xaphine and Antonio had become close, he let Xaphine give him the job of giving her away.

For what seemed like an eternity, Piero stood at the back of the church with his battalion commander, who was absolutely silent the entire time, no help there. The church was full of his fellow soldiers who sat perfectly still, staring forward. His uniform became hot and heavy and he began to sweat.

The sudden resonating music of the large pipe organ made Piero jump. He turned to see the bishop marching down the aisle followed by a clergy of ministers, and at the very end stood a woman in a long white dress. He could not make out her face under the veil, but he knew who it was. He watched nervously as she slowly walked towards him on Antonio's arm.

The church aisle was long, but it seemed to stretch on for miles from Xaphine's perspective. When she eventually reached the altar, Piero walked down and took her arm from

Antonio. The young man smiled and bowed as he backed away from the happy couple.

Once they were ready, Piero and Xaphine turned to the bishop who began a prayer. The entire sermon was in Latin, which oddly enough, Xaphine somehow understood. She had no idea why, but every word that came out of the priest's mouth as he stood prostrated in front of the altar to God, she was able to translate and whisper to Piero. It gave her a momentary pause, but she disregarded it to focus on the wedding.

An hour later, after all the blessings, the songs, and the sermons, the Bishop bound them together in holy matrimony. The bishop raised their arms and placed their hands together. As the two joined their hands, the Bishop sprinkled holy water on them.

To her shock, pain shot through Xaphine's hand as the water trickled down. She could feel it sizzle as more was sprinkled on. She quickly pulled her hand away before steam followed, and pretended to sneeze.

Xaphine didn't want anyone to see this as she had no idea what it meant and successfully managed to hide the pain. After rubbing her nose for a moment until the pain subsided, she placed her hand back in Piero's. Now she had another mystery on her ponder; why did it burn? She knew she had to hide it, the church didn't look kindly things that could be interpreted as unholy, and the list of what signified this was long.

To Xaphine's relief, the bishop did not notice as he performed the final blessing and turned to the crowd, "Please allow me the honor of introducing this newlywed couple. May you live together in unending happiness, in Nomine Patris, et Fili, et Spiritus Sancti, amen."

The spectators cheered and threw confetti as the two made their way out of the church. The soldiers stood at attention and saluted as the couple passed. The heavy doors opened, allowing them to go outside to face the rest of the city.

Once they were outside, the couple boarded a small carriage that took them back to Piero's house. There was a modest party waiting for them. Apparently, soldiers of Piero's battalion had put together a celebration for the two of them while they were away.

As the carriage pulled up outside, Piero noticed that Xaphine was rubbing her hand. He placed his in hers to see what she was nursing. Shock ran through him when he noticed burn marks on the back of her hand, "Are you okay? How did that happen?"

Xaphine looked at them for a few moments before responding, "I really don't know. It just started burning and before long, these marks just appeared. Don't worry about them; they aren't as bad as they look. They'll go away."

"Do they hurt?"

"They did, but they're fine now stop worrying."

"That's something I doubt I'll ever be able to do after today."

Confetti flew in every direction as the door to the carriage opened. A line of Florentine soldiers stood at attention as Xaphine stepped out, followed closely by her new husband. As they marched toward the small party, the men began to cheer, "Hazzah... hazzah... hazzah!"

Wine and music were everywhere while the group enjoyed themselves. No matter where anyone looked they saw happiness in this crowd. Xaphine shook her head as she watched everyone from her seat and rested from an hour of dancing.

"May I join you?" A gruff voice asked from beside her.

Xaphine turned her head to see Captain Ferruccio looking down at her smiling. She immediately jumped to her feet in salute and nodded, "Of course, sir!"

The captain chuckled, "No need to salute me, you're not under my command."

Xaphine grinned, "Too bad for you, it looks like you could use a few more good fighters."

"Of this, there can be no doubt."

He joined Xaphine on the small bench and looked at her, "You seem to be lost in thought."

"I was just thinking that I'll be damned if anyone thinks that it'll be me cleaning all of this up. I've got enough to do with Piero alone."

"Don't worry, my men will take care of this, we clean up our messes."

"Good to hear."

Ferruccio sat silently for a few moments before speaking, "You know, I don't think I've ever seen Piero this happy. He was always devoted to his duty and his position as a soldier, but since you came along, it's almost like his priorities have changed."

Xaphine's eyes narrowed as she looked at her husband out on the dance floor, "What are you saying? Has he neglected his duty?"

"No not at all. He's as fine a soldier as ever. I think more so since you came along. I'm just saying that he fights with a lot more spirit now. Having something to fight for seems to have changed him in ways I don't even understand."

"So he fights for me now..."

"It seems like it." Ferruccio admitted as a familiar song came on. "Well, may I have this dance, milady?"

Xaphine nodded and stood up, "Of course Captain, I'd be honored."

The party continued long into the evening, but as the sun set, the group began to disperse. Once the last of the guests bid their farewell, Piero and Xaphine retreated inside and fell asleep in each other's arms, exhausted after a long day.

DAMNATION

VII

Months passed quickly for Piero and Xaphine and they lived happily at first. Everything seemed to be going well for them. Piero even earned a promotion to the rank of Captain and took command of his old company.

Xaphine stood proudly by her husband the day he was promoted to lieutenant. She smiled and cheered for him the moment he was handed his badge of office. As far as she was concerned, this honor was as much hers as it was Piero's. The soldiers obviously agreed with that belief as they congratulated her as much as they did him.

Xaphine quickly became Piero's company wife. She always had the sword that Piero gave her attached to her hip. Few ever saw her without it.

Any time the group returned home from an engagement, she somehow always had a massive meal prepared and made sure that no one went hungry. She would always be ready with the wine to follow it up. As far as she was concerned, anyone left hungry was a strike against her honor.

As if the food wasn't enough, Xaphine would also work on damaged uniforms and weapons for the soldiers who did not have wives. She took their worn out items and gave them brand new ones before going about fixing the originals. Since she wasn't allowed to sign up, this was her way of participating in the defense of her home. Even their commanding officer, Captain Ferruccio took advantage of her tailoring and weapon sharpening every once in a while.

The urge for battle never left Xaphine. Every time Piero came home with stories of great victories, she would close her eyes and envision herself sharing in that victory. She wanted to be there with him more than anything.

Xaphine's desires were not helped when she went to visit the barracks where soldiers were training. She saw them sparring and felt the call of battle. It was like an addiction. Her hands shook as she dropped off another round of sharpened weapons at the training ground.

At that moment, she saw Piero practicing his thrust technique on a training dummy. She couldn't take it anymore. Her blood burned as she watched him move with near perfect form. *He steps the wrong way. It's the only flaw in his technique. I could bring him down quite easily if he used that on me...*

Xaphine's hand was on her sword. She slowly began to draw it, but then stopped as she realized that it was way too sharp for use as a sparring weapon. Her eyes caught a pair of dulled daggers on a training rack as she looked around. She twitched for a moment as the thought past through her mind.

A moment later, as though her body was acting on its own, Xaphine grabbed the two dulled daggers off of the training rack and charged at her husband, "Defend yourself Piero!"

A startled Piero turned to see Xaphine running at him with a look of insanity in her eyes. Chills ran down his spine as her lips formed into a euphoric smile. He quickly moved to block her attack with his sword.

Their blades scraped together as Xaphine struck. A look of surprise flashed across Piero's face, "What the hell are you doing?"

"Teaching you how to fight properly!"

Piero saw the look of intensity in his wife's eyes and smiled, "We'll see who teaches who!"

Xaphine pulled her blades back slowly and lowered them to her sides as she circled Piero. Piero brandished his sword in front of himself as he stepped the opposite way. He wasn't about to strike, instead he waited to see what Xaphine would do.

DAMNATION

At that moment, Xaphine let out an almost inhuman war cry as she charged at Piero. Her body twisted and turned gracefully as she struck Piero's sword with each of her blades. Piero stepped back slowly to absorb the attack before countering.

Within seconds, voices from the other side of the training ground appeared, "Hey everyone, Xaphine's taking on our Lieutenant!"

A crowd of soldiers instantly formed around the two as they fought. Even Ferruccio appeared on the scene to see what was going on. He stood next to Antonio and watched the fight unfold. Antonio spoke to another nearby soldier, "Ten on Piero."

"Twenty on Xaphine."

The hair on the back of Antonio's neck stood straight up when he heard the captain's voice, "T…Twenty, Captain? All right, I'll match that."

Cheers erupted from the soldiers as Piero countered his wife's attack. Shouts of encouragement rang out for both fighters as Xaphine crossed her daggers to absorb Piero's attack. They looked pretty evenly matched.

Xaphine looked like she was in Heaven as she gracefully stepped forward with one blade in front of her. It almost seemed as though she was dancing as she moved. She kept one blade on each side so that as she turned, her attacks would be continuous.

Neither one of them was able find a flaw in the other's form as they fought. Piero feared that this duel would go on forever, but Xaphine had just been lying in wait for him to try the one move that she could successfully counter.

Her wish was finally granted as sweat poured down both of their bodies. Piero clearly wanted to end this fight quickly and thought that the thrust he had been practicing would do the trick.

He parried one more attack before pulling away, bending his legs at the knees and jolting forward. Xaphine smiled as she watched Piero use the flawed form. *Yes, gotcha!*

Before Piero knew what was happening, his legs had been kicked out from under him. Xaphine used a spin kick to knock him off balance before bringing the blade that she was holding behind her in to knock his blade away. She was sure that this blow would disarm Piero.

Piero had been knocked off balance and hadn't had time to bring his sword up to defend himself as Xaphine came back around. Instead of connecting with the sword, her dagger narrowly missed hitting Piero in the eye and cut open his right cheek. Even dulled, the blades could still be lethal.

The force of the blow sent Piero flying backwards. He landed on the ground holding his cheek. Cheers went up from the crowd as Xaphine placed her foot on Piero's chest, pinning him to the ground, and raised her hand in triumph.

Xaphine's joy was short-lived when she realized what she had done. The sight of crimson liquid on the dagger she was holding caught the corner of her eye. In a panic, she turned to see blood dripping out of Piero's cheek as he slowly pushed her foot away, "Piero, you're hurt!"

Xaphine dropped the daggers and grabbed her husband's arm, "I… I hurt you… Piero, I am so sorry. I didn't mean it… I don't know what came over me."

Piero looked into his wife's eyes. They were filled with a look of absolute terror as she inspected her husband's wound. He smiled at her, "It's nothing, just a small cut. I've had a lot worse. If anything, I think my ego is in far worse shape now."

Xaphine lowered her eyes, "I wasn't trying to embarrass you."

Piero smiled and raised her chin, "You didn't. That was the best fight I've ever had and I challenge anyone here to take you on. I'm going to have to stay on my toes and train even harder for next time."

"There will be no next time. I don't know what came over me. It was like I was feeling withdrawal and needed satisfaction. I felt as though I was about to explode. I had no control... and I hurt you because of it. I need to do better. Never again..."

"It happens when you spar like this. It's happened to me before and it's not a big..."

"No!" Xaphine replied adamantly. "I took an oath to you... I will not allow myself to harm you. Never again..."

The soldiers cheered and clapped as Piero put his arm around Xaphine and let her lead him to a nearby bench to inspect the wound. Antonio grimaced as he turned to see Ferruccio's smug expression. He rolled his eyes as he pulled the money that he owed out of his pocket, "Yes, yes... here you go sir!"

"Thank you kindly."

"How did you know she'd win? How did you even know that she could fight?"

"She has a look in her eyes that you usually only see on the battlefield. I think she's been dying to do that. It's like an addiction."

The captain then looked down at his sword, "Also, no one who hasn't seen battle could maintain weapons this well."

A tear fell from Xaphine's eye as she sat down on the bench next to Piero and cleaned his wound. Piero smiled, "Come on, it's not like you meant to cut me. It was an accident. It happens and it's not bad. It'll be healed up in no time."

DAMNATION

"I lost control. I've wanted to let that out for a long time. I felt like... almost as though I would die if I didn't have a release."

"Well do you feel better now?"

"Partially... at least the tension is gone now. It doesn't hurt anymore."

"Well it was worth it then. At least now one of my questions has been answered."

"What's that?"

"You're definitely a warrior from the north, perhaps from the Danish area?"

"I don't know."

"But you definitely know how to defend yourself. So where ever you're from, you were definitely a fighter."

Xaphine smiled, "I guess that does make the most sense."

Once Piero's wound was cleaned, she helped him off of the bench and guided him away from the base. She wanted him at home where she could keep an eye on the injury. Despite what Piero said, it really did look like she had cut him deeply.

Several men smiled and nodded as they walked by. Xaphine shook her head as she eyed the wound, "If any of your men give you grief for losing, they'll answer to me."

"Don't worry, I think they know better."

VIII

A few months later, Piero came home from his post and saw that Xaphine had fallen ill. He had noticed during previous nights that she was not sleeping very much. When she did, images that almost looked like memories began to flood into her mind.

Strange winged creatures fighting and killing each other appeared before her eyes. Even more unusual, were the constant thoughts of three of these creatures. Though each one was quite beautiful, their faces angered her greatly, and summoned the shattered memory of a promise she made which continued to echo in her head.

Fearing for his wife's health, Piero summoned the battalion healer to her. Captain Ferruccio allowed him to be dispatched and once the man came knocking at Piero's door, Piero quickly led him inside, "Good, doctor, come with me quickly."

"I came as soon as I could. Captain Ferruccio said it was urgent. What are her symptoms?"

"She's not sleeping, she's running a high temperature, and her skin is pale."

When the healer looked at him oddly, Piero rolled his eyes, "Yes, yes, I know she has a fair complexion, but this is pale even for her."

Piero let him examine Xaphine while she rested comfortably. When he was finished, he turned and met Piero's anxious look, "How is she?"

"To be honest, I can't find anything wrong with her. She is running a temperature, other than that, everything looks normal. My guess is she's just tired. Make sure she doesn't overwork herself and gets plenty of water. If worst comes to worst we can always try bleeding her to see if she has some kind of internal illness."

DAMNATION

"With all due respect doctor, I have seen too many die on your table from that treatment, it always seems like it does more damage than good."

"Well we'll keep an eye on her then. If you prefer to avoid such… harsh treatments then that is, of course your choice. However you'd best closely monitor her condition."

Piero smiled as the doctor mounted his horse, "Thank you."

The doctor nodded and turned his horse toward the citadel, "Good luck to you both. For what it's worth, I too hope she makes it through without anymore treatment."

Piero watched him ride away, "So do I… "

Piero waited for the doctor to be out of earshot before he dropped to his knees, "Oh lord, my God… Xaphine has made my life whole in ways I had never imagined possible. Please do not allow her to be taken from me now. Grant her the strength to make it through this. Take my soul in exchange if you must, but let her live."

"I'm okay Piero."

The soft voice made Piero turn to see Xaphine standing behind him, "You shouldn't be out of bed."

"I have too much to do. Your men need their swords and your armor..."

"They can wait. You won't do them much good if you collapse."

An annoyed look appeared on Xaphine's face. She would not tolerate being defeated by illness and tried to protest, "But Piero…"

"No! I let you pretty much run the show and do things as you see fit without any protest, but right now you're going to listen to me. Go back and lay down, now!"

Xaphine's glare met Piero's. She looked like she was ready to kill him. For a moment it looked as though their eyes were waging war between them, but finally Xaphine

shook her head and turned away, "This is intolerable…
being taken down by illness like this!"

**

That night, while Piero was out late on patrol, Xaphine
lay in bed alone. She had long since gotten used to going to
bed alone every now and then as Piero's duty called him
away often. She was covered by a blanket, trying to fight off
the illness as best she could. She had almost fallen asleep
when she heard a low hum from the other side of the door.

Xaphine's body became even colder and goose bumps
appeared on her skin. She sat up and saw a light from
whatever was on the other side illuminate the crack under
the door. It looked almost like sunlight even though the sun
had long since set.

Xaphine felt her breathing grow more rapid as her
heart raced. She was more than capable of defending
herself, so she stood up, grabbed the sword that Piero had
left next to the bed, and pointed it toward the door. There
was a squeak at the handle as though something were trying
to figure out how to unlock it.

Xaphine mustered up as much courage as she could
when the door finally started to slide open. A bat-like
creature with gray skin and red eyes floated in and hovered
in place. The creature smiled at her, "Hello General, it has
been a long time."

"General…?" She repeated, resisting the urge to
scream.

"That is your rank as it has been for eons. Like myself,
you are a servant of Lucifer, and he has sent me to call on
you. Congratulations, Xaphan your mission is over, it's time
to come home."

"Xaphan?"

"You don't even remember your name?"

Xaphine took a step back, she recognized the name,
but didn't want to believe it, "No, foul creature, I don't

DAMNATION

know what you're talking about. Leave my home or, God help me, I'll cut you down!"

"God help you…" The creature laughed, "Lucifer told me you would not remember who you are. How amusing… as if God would come to the aid of someone as far-gone as you."

"I won't tell you again creature!" She shouted, pointing the sword at his throat. "Leave my home this instant!"

"What are you going to do to me if I don't leave? Do you think such a pathetic tool can hurt me? I am Kaliban, servant of the true Most High!"

With that, Kaliban grabbed the sword from Xaphine and plunged it into his chest. He smiled at her like it didn't even faze him, "See? I am immortal. Your petty little piece of metal poses no threat to me."

Xaphine took a step backwards. Something about this felt very familiar, "I… what do you want from me, you… creature?"

"My master wishes to speak to you." Kaliban said with a smile as he landed on the ground.

The wicked creature touched the floor with his left hand. A glowing circle appeared around him within seconds as he muttered an incantation. It glowed brighter with each passing second as he worked.

Kaliban's figure immediately disappeared. In his place, a man with ragged wings appeared in front of her, "Hello Xaphan it's been too long. I have truly missed your company."

"You… I know you… how is that possible."

"Yes General Xaphan, you and I have been friends for many eons. I am Lucifer, your master."

Xaphine rested her back on the wall furthest from Lucifer and kept her sword pointed at him, "The devil… no it's not true… It can't be!"

DAMNATION

"Ah but it is, allow me to show you."

"No, leave me be! I don't want to talk to you. I am happy here with my life and Piero! Come any closer and I'll kill you!"

"Piero?" Lucifer asked surprised. "You mean to tell me that you've mated with one of these... disgusting creatures?"

His eyes darted back to the imp, "Kaliban, you were supposed to watch over her!"

"And watch her I did, Master, as best I could. I fear that there is no way I could have prevented this without revealing myself."

At this point, Xaphine had tears in her eyes. She was too distraught to even worry about showing any form of weakness. All that mattered was preventing Lucifer from taking her, "I'm telling you, you've got the wrong person!"

Tired of trying to talk her way out of this, she charged forward, wielding her husband's sword. In the flash of an eye before either Lucifer or Kaliban could react, Xaphine brought her sword down on the ragged angel. To her amazement, the sword passed right through him without even a scratch.

Lucifer shook his head in awe, "Even as a mortal, you posses a power unlike anything these maggots could ever conjure. I'm sorry for this, old friend. In a few moments, everything will be back to normal."

Lucifer closed his eyes and muttered something in an unusual language. It sounded like he was chanting some sort of incantation under his breath. As he continued, Xaphine's body began to glow. She could feel her features begin to change as her face began to transform, "End this now, what are you doing to me? Stop... no!"

A second later, Xaphine's eyes went blank and faded to black, wings sprouted from her back, and her finger nails became very long. She looked down at her hands as though she hadn't seen them in a long time, "Now I remember, Master... how long as it been?"

"Over two years..."

"Two years? What has been going on in my absence? Are we ready to make a move?"

"I am truly sorry my friend, but circumstances have changed. Our plan has failed."

"How," Xaphan demanded, "and who is responsible?"

"Michael was supposed to aid us in weakening the Most High by provoking the church into war. He manipulated the Pope for us so that the inquisitions and the killings in this world would continue. He worked splendidly undercover for us."

"Michael." Xaphan was shocked when she heard his name. "The Most High's most trusted general? Michael is our contact? He has truly sided with us after casting so many of us out?"

"Too little, too late as it was, by the time he finally saw the truth, we were already defeated, but he pledged to help us in any way he could. First he was to target the angels we wanted to do away with. At first everything was going according to plan. Adalyn had been framed and broke the Most High's decree, which got her cast out of the celestial realm and our big victory came when Michael successfully killed Azrael."

"So it sounds like everything is going better than we expected. What's the problem?"

"Michael is dead, and with him went our hope of provoking more conflict in the human realm."

"What, how?"

"Adalyn... At first, it seemed everything was going as planned. She was cast out of their kingdom and left for dead. Eventually the church discovered her and began an inquisition that would have ended her all together. However, it seems that we didn't count on her getting the help of a few of these mortal creatures. They freed her and helped her to survive a lot longer than I thought possible. It is my fault; I shouldn't have underestimated the resilience of these insects. Once she recovered her strength, she came here to get the weapons to kill Michael. When I tried to stop her, she poisoned me with my own serpent's venom."

"No… The poison of that serpent is potent enough to tear the immortality from one of us. If you are now powerless, then our cause is truly lost."

Xaphan clenched her jaw, "Damn you, sister. You will pay… You've ruined everything…"

"Not true, I planned for something like this, remember? Our cause will not die as long as I have you. I can see now that sending you to the mortal world as a trump card was the best move I could make. You have almost everything I used to."

"Yes... So I should be able to restore you."

"Exactly."

"I will not fail you Master. What are my orders?"

"For now, I want you to return to the underworld. I am recalling all of our forces for now in case there is any backlash from the incident with Michael. I need to take a head count of our assets."

"Very well, let's go."

Xaphan closed her eyes and began the incantation to teleport herself back to the underworld. She was half way through it, but stopped when she felt a hot tear fall down her cheek. She opened her eyes and placed a hand on her chest. There was a painful sensation that she had not felt in years combined with a beating sensation, "Lucifer…"

"What is it?"

"What have you done to me? Why do I suddenly feel weak and remorseful? You were supposed to remove this... taint…"

DAMNATION

"I was afraid of this... I'm sorry Xaphan, but I must break my promise to you. Because of Adalyn's attack, I can no longer wipe your soul completely clean of the human desecration. For now, you must carry your human memories with you."

"What, you're telling me that I now have to live with this filth? I never would have agreed to it if I had known this would happen. You have corrupted me, old friend! This is intolerable!"

"I know that... Believe me, I would not have asked you to if I'd known."

"I can't stand this…" She replied as the memories from the last two years flooded her mind once more. "Master, I can't go with you yet. I have to sort something out... I just need some time."

Xaphan didn't want to return with Lucifer. Her mind was conflicted. Part of her wanted to get started on their mission while another part wanted to stay behind and let the soldier she was living with know what had happened, but Lucifer would not hear of it, "We can't wait, you are coming now."

"Master… I… I beg of you…" Xaphan pleaded with a hint of desperation in her voice and her eyes looking down.

It was hard to tell if Xaphan was talking, or if Xaphine's emotions were bleeding through, "There are a few loose ends I need to tie up here."

"Yes, I know of your… loose ends. I do not care that you've mated with one of the Most High's children. You can explain it to him once they're all enslaved. Set those emotions aside and carry out your orders!"

A creaking sound behind them made Xaphan jump. Piero had arrived home after having finally been relieved of his duties, "Xaphine, I heard voices. Is everything all right in here?"

Lucifer immediately disappeared, leaving Kaliban to deal with the situation. He turned and ripped the door open. Piero stood face to face with this hideous creature, "What is this, what's going on here!"

Piero drew his sword and pointed it at Kaliban, "Infernal creature, what have you done to... Xaphine..."

Behind the wretched little imp, stood what looked like Piero's wife. Except that she had long black wings, pointed ears, and demonic looking eyes. It was her, but at the same time, it wasn't, just like he had remembered her say when she was talking about her dreams.

Piero slowly backed away from the door, "Xaphine, what's happened to you? What is going on here?"

Xaphan's lips quivered, "Piero I..."

"Pathetic wretch!" Kaliban sneered before she could answer. "Die!"

A series of fireballs flew from his hands. Piero raised his arms, closed his eyes, and began to mouth a prayer. He was sure that he would be dead at any second.

Piero could hear the fireballs impact on a hard surface and disintegrate, as well as the sound of Xaphine's voice, "No!"

Piero opened his eyes to see Xaphan standing in front of him. She had used her right wing to block the attack. As the fire crackled out, Kaliban stepped back in surprise, "What is this?"

"He is of no threat to us." Xaphan replied as she glared at Kaliban, "Would you bring the Most High down on us for killing one of his children? Are you so foolish? You leave him be!"

"What is the meaning of this? Since when do you defend these creatures? No one in hell hated them more than you!"

"That doesn't concern you. I will carry out our master's wishes, but you will leave him unharmed. If you try to attack him again, I promise you will never return to the underworld."

At that moment, Lucifer's voice echoed through her thoughts, "You disappoint me, old friend. You have lost focus! Because you still possess your human memories, this weakling could be a threat to you. We cannot afford to leave him unchecked!"

"I do not agree master. I know his heart, even in this form, he would never harm me."

"You are our last hope." Lucifer reminded her as his voice began to fill with anger. "I cannot take such an unnecessary risk."

Xaphan looked away from everyone and focused on the floor, "Master, I have served you, I have carried out every single order you have given me. I followed you to the underworld and helped you build your kingdom. I even allowed you to desecrate my soul and I never once refused your whims. Lucifer, my old friend, in that time, have I ever asked you for anything, even once?"

"No. You have always acted with honor and kept what is best for the cause at heart. I don't think that even I have been so steadfast."

"Well I am asking you now, just this once, let him live."

"I shouldn't do this, there is more than one way he can be a threat to you. That said… you have earned the right to ask. Return to me, and I promise you, he will be left unharmed."

Xaphan nodded and turned to Kaliban, "Go now, I will join you momentarily."

Kaliban shrugged and disappeared in a blast of flame. The moment he was gone, Piero cautiously approached his wife, "Xaphine… what is this, are you okay?"

Xaphine's heart felt as though it were trying to cut its way out of Xaphan's chest. She closed her eyes as tears streamed down her cheeks. Her hand reached the jeweled necklace that she'd been wearing. There was nothing she could say that would not crush Piero's spirit, no matter how much she wished there was.

Finally, unable to hold it together, Xaphan replied in a whisper, "My name is Xaphan... the person you knew, your wife, never existed. She was a false identity made to protect me as I hid in your world. You have been most kind to me, which is why I am allowing you to live, but do not look at this as an act of mercy, it is not one. You saved my life and in return I am sparing yours. It is nothing more than that. "

Piero could hear the sadness in Xaphan's voice and saw that she was still wearing the necklace that he had given her so long ago, "I refuse to believe that. I can tell that my wife is still in there. Please let me help you, there must be some way..."

"Your wife... Grow up boy, I have existed since the dawn of time, and I will live after your bones have turned to ash in the ground!"

Xaphan turned to face Piero. As her eyes connected with his, Piero was hit by an invisible force, sending his body flying into the house. He hit the ground with a loud thud as Xaphan stood over him, "All my powers and you had me washing dishes and cleaning your clothes. It is so absurd, you expecting me to keep house for you!"

She walked over and picked Piero up by the neck, "I should kill you for that insult!"

Piero choked under her grip. He made a gurgling sound as it became harder to get air into his lungs. The sound caused a tear to escaped Xaphan's eye. It fell on to her cheek where it began to sizzle. She quickly released Piero, let him fall to the floor, and turned her back on him, "But I can't do it..."

Piero forced a slight smile as he struggled to breathe, "You are still my wife. I know you haven't forgotten me. I cannot believe that your heart has been completely driven from you."

"Believe whatever you want. Whatever brings you the most comfort…"

Piero struggled to his feet and tried to put his right hand on her shoulder to comfort her, but as she felt his touch, her wing swung around, "Do not touch me! Leave this place… save yourself..."

"But Xaphine…"

She couldn't stand to hear anymore as her sanity was quickly replaced by anger and despair, "Leave!"

A blast of energy knocked Piero off his feet. A huge ball of fire surrounded Xaphan and began to grow. She screamed again as tears dripped down her cheeks, "Leave me!"

The energy emanating from Xaphine's aura sent Piero flying out the front door. Xaphan watched as a single pulse of her blast threw him to safety. Much to her disgust, the realization that she would never see him again made her chest ache, "Remember me, Piero, remember me fondly, and your wife will always live on in some way. "

"Xaphine…" Piero said desperately, sensing that his world was about to be shattered.

Xaphan closed her eyes and tensed every muscle in her body. The resulting release of energy engulfed the whole house in flame. Piero was pushed even further as the explosion lit up the night sky and drew the attention of other nearby people, including soldiers.

As Piero's house burned, soldiers, many of whom were family friends, came running to the scene. They brought water to fight the flames and stop Piero's house from being destroyed. Among them, was Piero's ensign, Antonio. He saw Piero get thrown from his home as it was burned to the ground.

DAMNATION

Antonio called to his friend, "Lieutenant... Piero, are you all right?"

Piero lay unconscious on the ground as Antonio knelt next to him and tried everything to get him to wake up, "Come on Piero, snap out of it!" He said shaking the body of his friend.

After a few moments, Piero came back to life. He breathed heavily as he felt the flames on his skin, "No..."

He opened his eyes and stood up, "No!"

Antonio looked up at him, "What's going on, what happened, Piero? Where is Xaphine?"

"... She's gone... I've lost her. She's not coming back..."

Antonio's jaw dropped open, "Mother of God... tell me Xaphine wasn't in there?"

Piero's eye filled with tears and he lowered his head. Antonio didn't know how to respond, "Piero... My God, I am so sorry, my friend..."

Piero closed his eyes and began to shake violently. He was unable to contain himself any longer. His emotions exploded in a shrill cry, "Why?"

IX

Xaphan slowly descended into the depths of the underworld and landed on the beach near the entrance to the damned city. In front of her was the massive door that had been secured to prevent anything from escaping. She effortlessly threw it open and stormed down through the cave.

Once on the other side, Xaphine could see plainly that things were different. The balance of power was clearly gone and Lucifer had nearly lost control of Hell. The red aura had dimmed and the demons were in complete disarray. Beasts had broken loose from their pens, leaving the imps to try to bring them back. She decided the best thing to do was move to the castle. She could try to bring order to this chaos later.

Xaphan's wings flapped quickly as she took to the air. She rose herself to within a few feet of the cavern ceiling to avoid the chaos. It was the only way that she was going to get to the castle.

With her wings outstretched, Xaphan glided through the kingdom and across the lake of fire. Once on the other side, she touched down near the castle in an open field between it and the city. She wanted to see firsthand what Adalyn's insurrection had done.

In front of Xaphan, lay the remains of the Oasis where the Eden serpent once dwelt. She walked over to the tree and saw the snake's blood staining the branches. The tree, the grass, and everything that made the Oasis stand out, was dead.

"Bastards…" She said to herself as she remembered when she first captured that beast. "I will not let this slide… I swear I will bring all the forces of Hell against them if I must!"

DAMNATION

After using it against the Most High's children, the serpent had become an icon of the underworld and Lucifer's most treasured pet. No one could have guessed that such an insignificant creature could play such a major role in the downfall of a deity. It was a piece of irony that Xaphan had always been proud of, but now with the serpent dead, the curse it had maintained on its dwelling was all but gone. The grass has withered and the tree was on the verge of collapse.

Xaphan then looked at the castle in dismay. The mountain it stood upon was smoldering, but the once-magnificent flow of magma was gone. The drawbridge was down and unguarded. She crossed it and was about to push open the mighty doors when Kaliban appeared, "You cannot go in! My master forbids it!"

"I've said it before Kaliban, do not presume to tell me what I can and cannot do. Lucifer will see me. Now stand aside."

Kaliban stood silently for a moment, refusing to move. Xaphan's eyes flared red, "Stand aside!"

Out of fear, Kaliban finally moved out of the way allowing her to pass. "My master will not like this in the least. He does not want to be seen."

"If I want your opinion, I'll squeeze it out of your rotting corpse. Oh and Kaliban…"

The imp looked at Xaphan nervously as she continued, "If you ever… impede me again, I'll tear those hideous wings from your back."

Kaliban nodded as Xaphan pushed the doors open and entered the main hall of the castle. There, a few feet in front of his throne, Xaphan saw what had been done. Lucifer was partially encased in the stone floor. It looked as though he had somehow sunk into it.

She gasped, "Master… what have they done to you?"

"They used divine magic. When I was stripped of my powers, Adalyn encased me here. Thankfully my minions fear me too much to enter the castle without my approval. Otherwise I don't know what could happen."

"I agree… Lucifer, what are we going to do? We must free you!"

"Eventually... I still plan to carry out our original goals. For now though, I need you to defend my keep and make sure that order is maintained. Soon we will reap vengeance on the one who is responsible for imprisoning me here. I want her head on a pike."

"Master, I promise you, I will rip it from her shoulders myself, but we have lost so much because of your lust for revenge. Would it not be better to simply focus on the cause for now? Once we have achieved our goals, picking off those who have done us so much damage should be an easy task."

Lucifer's eyes burned as he sneered at her, "Do you dare question me? I will do as I see fit!"

Xaphan was undaunted by his stare as her own eyes began to glow red, "I have never questioned you, Lucifer. I have been a loyal disciple for a very long time, but given everything that has happened, I think an alternative plan is not uncalled for. We have lost so much already. Is it not reasonable?"

Lucifer pulled against the stone, "You are lucky I am stuck here! I do not answer to you! You are my general. Now carry out your orders and I might forget such insubordination!"

"I am your General? Last I checked I followed you of my own free will. Had it not been for me, your war would have ended a lot sooner than it did. I am your friend, and I will carry out your orders, but you do not own me!"

Lucifer rolled his eyes as he began to calm down, "Xaphan, I grow weary of this. Please go…"

DAMNATION

Xaphan sneered as she turned away, "As you wish... Master."

"Oh and one more thing... Take that obscene necklace off at once."

Xaphan's hand touched her neck and found the jeweled golden necklace. She had forgotten that she was wearing it. She clenched her teeth as she responded, "I will not..."

"What did you say?"

"I will not! It is mine. Consider it payment for desecrating my soul! When you rid me of these cursed memories, then I will take it off! For now though, it remains where it is."

Lucifer quickly snapped his finger, summoning Kaliban to his side. The imp appeared out of the darkness, "Master?"

"The general is having trouble with her necklace." Lucifer said musingly. "Help her remove it."

"With pleasure Master!"

Kaliban scuttled close to Xaphan and reached for the necklace. Xaphan spread her wings, jumped backwards, and drew her sword, "I swear, I will cut that annoying grin from your face, if you even try it, imp!"

Kaliban looked at Lucifer and shrugged. Lucifer shook his head and sighed, "Very well Xaphan, it's a deal. Keep it until we find a way to cleanse your soul, but do not cross me again. I have a plan that will return us to our rightful place of power. I need you on my side here, now more than ever."

"I have always been on your side, Lucifer. That has never been an issue. I will shore up our defenses and see to it that no one enters the castle. When you are ready to implement this plan, let me know."

Lucifer nodded and spoke in a low tone, "Very well, but for now I do not wish to be disturbed."

DAMNATION

Xaphan left Lucifer with his thoughts and exited the castle the way she came. Kaliban stood in the darkness off to the side and watched her leave, "She looked like she was ready kill you Master."

"I supposed it's partially my fault. The human memories are poisoning her from the inside out. She's becoming unstable"

"Should we worry about her?"

"I don't think so… I've known her a very long time and I still trust her to do the right thing… but perhaps it would be prudent to keep an eye on her. If you see any hint of treason, report it to me immediately."

"Your will be done, my liege. I'll take care of everything."

**

Xaphan pushed through the big, heavy, doors without another word. They slammed shut behind her with a mighty boom. Her hair blew over her shoulder as a gust of wind hit her. She turned back to look at the castle. *Not even a 'thank you…'* she thought to herself, *Lucifer… you have changed.*

The pain in her chest grew even heavier as she moved away from the castle. *Then again, so have I… I've had connections with other angels that I cared deeply for and cast them aside without a single thought or regret when I was called to fight… but now… that human…*

She continued out to the beast stables, where she was able to find some peace with the creatures that she had helped to tame. As she appeared, the three headed dog came up to the fence of its pen. Xaphan scratched its middle head as it growled in appreciation.

To Xaphan's dismay, this did not cheer her up at all. The dog's large brown eyes reminded her of Piero. When the beast looked up at her, a tear fell down her cheek. She wiped it away and became enraged, "What is wrong with me, boy."

DAMNATION

The dog let out another low growl in response. *Grrr...*

"You're absolutely right, too much has changed. I should have been here all along, not off consorting with one of the Most High's children. Lucifer made a mistake sending me away."

Xaphan's eyes began shifting between blue and black as though they were fighting over what color they should be. She continued talking as though the dog could understand her, "Lucifer has changed so much... but I guess losing his powers are part of the problem there. He was once one of the Most High's favorite disciples... they called him the Angel of the Morning Star... it's amazing what the passage of time does to some people."

Xaphan began to feel weird. Her chest began to ache again and she felt more tears fall from her eyes. Part of her was disgusted with the feelings she was experiencing. These were human feelings unbecoming of an angel, but she could not ignore them. She turned to the dog as it continued to growl, "This place no longer feels like home to me. I want to be with that boy in Florence... that's where I belong now. I wasn't ready to come back here... I..."

Her mind fought back against these feelings and the tears slowly cleared up, "What is wrong with me? Damn it Lucifer... Why couldn't you remove this weak human persona? I can't stand this anymore! I want to be back the way I was... I want to not feel things like this!"

Another voice inside her head spoke as she felt the beating of the heart in her chest, "Is that really what you want, to shut down and become less than you are? You would rather be the cold hearted warrior than the beloved person you were? Here you're a tool to be used, there you were a goddess."

"I have friends here too! Don't marginalize them! The Florentines weren't the only ones who thought highly of me!"

"Truly? Kaliban and the other demons see you as a means to an end and you know it... you've always known that. Kaliban himself would run you through in a moment's notice. So who? Lucifer? Look at how he's treated you... look at what he did to you."

Xaphan looked down at her hands as the voice continued, "You were an honorable warrior of the Celestial World, you were admired and beloved. Now you're an outcast. The only people who love you now, you've abandoned and cast aside with hate."

After hearing the voice which sounded too much like her own, she couldn't take it anymore, "Enough! I won't hear anymore of this from you, Xaphine. You're not even real!"

"I'm as real as you want me to be. You can't ignore me. I'm always with you."

Xaphan clenched her jaw and closed her eyes, "Be gone!"

She slammed her fist down on the pen, startling the dog. The mighty three-headed beast backed away as she exhaled. With the voice finally silenced, she looked over at the dog sympathetically, "I'm sorry boy…"

From a distance, Kaliban watched the entire event unfold. As Xaphan wiped the tears from her eyes, he began to laugh in delight, "This will work in my favor, no doubt. Lucifer has provided me with a chink in his general's mighty armor."

The imp quickly shrouded itself as Xaphan turned to exit the stables. She quickly lunged into the air and flew to one of the castle towers. Not wanting to cause any more grief to those living around her, she decided that it was best to lay low. She summoned a squadron of imps to keep a constant vigil on the castle. She hoped that this would prevent any treachery, though she knew that most of them were probably loyal to Kaliban.

From her tower, Xaphan maintained a silent vigil as she watched over the land. Her eyes fully turned red and filled with tears as her memories continued to haunt her. She placed a hand on the necklace that Piero had given her as her chest ached, "How did it come to this… how did everything go so wrong?"

BOOK 3
REVELATIONS

‡
Rome, Italy 1528

Several years passed and a time of war came to the Papal States. The Pope began a campaign to have the threat of Charles V removed from their land. As a result, the Holy Roman Empire attacked the Papal States in full force.

Under the orders of Pope Clement VII, the Papal States formed an alliance with France, Venice, and Florence. They bound together in hopes that their combined strength would be enough. With the lines of allegiance drawn, war had once again come to Europe.

Florence was caught right in the middle of the fight. From the early skirmishes, things did not go well for the Papal States. The French were quickly defeated on their home land and in the occupied area north of the Papal States. A large force under the command of the Duke of Bourbon marched through the land, destroying everything in his path. After meeting virtually no resistance in Mantua, the invaders were easily able to destroy Rome.

Without the support of Rome, one by one, the Papal States were either defeated or surrendered. By 1528, the power of the Papacy had been severely diminished and the people of Florence took the opportunity to throw off their ruler. Once the people had taken control, Florence became the Republic of Florence.

Pope Clement VII had been imprisoned by Charles V for almost a year. From his chamber in the Basilica di Santa Maria Maggiore, Clement VII could see the destruction his decisions had brought on the people of Rome. The city had been completely overrun and was now in smoldering ruin. He watched the people of the city slowly begin to rebuild what they had lost as he stroked his beard. Though his accommodations had been anything but that of a normal prisoner, he still felt trapped in his own city.

One early morning, guards came to call on the Pope, "Our Emperor Charles V anxiously awaits you."

Clement VII nodded, "Very well then, lead on."

Clement VII had not been shackled during his imprisonment. Where would he go? How would he hide? There was nothing Clement VII could do but sit and wait. What did this Emperor from the north have in store for him? Would he be executed, or forced to face some humiliating treaty that would break his people? Clement VII simply didn't know, but he doubted that Charles V would risk an upheaval by executing him.

The guards led him down the hall, down several flights of stairs, and opened the large double doors to main audience chamber. Clement VII found himself in the luxurious room where he once dwelled.

Sitting in the large ornate chair atop a small flight of marble stairs, was a well-dressed Spaniard. The man wore dark armor, had short dark brown hair, and a massive chin. He had a friendly yet sinister grin on his face.

When Clement VII entered the room, Charles shot to his feet. His speech was slightly slurred, and he was continuously dabbing his chin with a cloth, but his manners were that of a gentleman, "Eminence... I am truly honored to finally have been granted an audience with your grace."

Clement VII held out his hand to Charles, who promptly bowed and kissed the ring on his finger, "Your words imply that I had a choice in the matter, Emperor Charles of Habsburg."

"I must apologize, your grace," Charles replied, "but after years of dealing with Papal law, some of my more mutinous men simply could not restrain themselves from attacking. I can assure you that this woeful deed will not go unpunished."

Clement narrowed his eyes, "Are you trying to tell me that you had no hand in destroying my city, that the sacking of Rome was nothing more than a mutinous act perpetrated because one of your officers could not control his troops?"

Charles's kind expression turned to one of anger and malice, "Careful whom you insult, Pope. The Swiss Guard is no longer here to protect you."

The Pope scoffed, "Save your threats for one of the lowly dogs in your military. You would not dare harm me. Could you imagine the revolution that would reign down on you from faithful parishioners if word left this building that you were planning to execute his holiness?"

Charles shot out of his throne, clearly angered. He took a few steps forward before stopping. It took him a moment, but his anger returned to temperance, "You may find that the followers you speak of will not be so eager to oppose us for you. I have seen it in the revolutions taking place even in my own kingdom."

"Then why bother with this pointless meeting?" Clement asked, "Why not execute me and have a new Pope take my place, you seem to think it is within your power."

Charles sighed and sat back in his ornate chair, "Let us dispense with such unpleasantries. I do not wish harm upon you. Quite the contrary, I am here to help out of your situation."

Clement's eyes narrowed, "How exactly do you plan to help?"

Charles shrugged, "I assumed that you wanted your home back, that you wanted the power that has been taken from you, your land, and our withdrawal. I can make all of that happen."

Clement looked at Charles anxiously in the eye, "And what is it you would want in exchange?"

Charles smiled, "I want an end to your opposition of my rule, freedom to deal with the revolutionaries within my empire as I see fit, and the power to do as I will with the enemy invaders to the east. Basically, I want you to deal in matters that concern you; your church, your people, and I want you to stay out of my affairs."

"To allow a tyrant to continue unchecked you mean?" Clement shot back.

"Do not speak to me of tyranny, grace." Charles replied. "I have seen how the church deals with its own people. You left the fate of many of my countrymen to the inquisitors you sent. I am man of peace and I am trying to come to an understanding with you here, but even my patience has its limits."

Pope Clement thought about this for a few minutes. What choice did he really have? Clement was sure that if he did not agree to the emperor's demands, that he would soon be dead, and all of Rome would suffer this man's wrath.

As he contemplated his situation, he noticed the young man clad in black standing off to the side, also under guard. He finally sighed as an idea popped into his head, "Very well, Charles. I accept your terms, but with your approval, I would like to add one condition."

Charles listened intently, "Name it."

Again Clement looked at the man in the corner, "My… nephew… Ippolito de' Medici has been ousted from his rule over Florence. Despite his many concessions and offerings to the people, they have seen fit to throw off his rule and establish a Republic."

Charles shrugged, "So they have opted for self-rule, good for them, how is this any concern of mine?"

"Don't be a fool," Clement fired back, "Revolutions have a tendency to spread. We need to restore the balance of power in the area. Without my nephew on the throne in Florence, the power of the Papacy is even more compromised. In order for you to maintain control of your empire, you need the power of the Papacy intact and you know it."

Charles scratched his beard for a few moments, considering the wisdom in Clement's words. He looked over the two men standing in front of him and nodded, "Very well, eminence, you will have the full support of the Imperial army to put down the rebellion in Florence. Together, we will bring them to their knees and usher in a new era of peace in the region."

He then stood up and moved away from the chair, "Rome is once again yours, your grace. Our alliance is sealed"

Clement smiled and bowed graciously as he took his seat, "Let us get to work."

"Indeed." Charles replied. "Let the reckoning begin."

DAMNATION

⚇

So many years without her. So many years alone... my mind still harkens back to her every night when I close my eyes... how this could have happened. Why Xaphine... why did it turn out this way?

Piero's house had long since stopped burning and been rebuilt, but all sign of Xaphine disappeared from the world. Everything from the precious items they had collected together to her clothing was destroyed. He had no keepsake of her at all. No one saw or received word of her after she left, and Piero never told anyone, not even Antonio, what had really happened that terrible night.

With Florence throwing off its ruler, Piero found himself trading in his Papal uniform for the red and silver coat of arms of his countrymen. He couldn't have cared less who he fought for, as long as there was a battle to fight. This revolution was the perfect excuse for Piero to throw himself into combat to take his mind off of his pain. He didn't care if he lived or died. In fact, many of the men under his command reported that when victory was sounded after each engagement, he cursed his luck.

Eventually, Piero found his country fighting alone against the imperial forces. He viewed this as an insult to the church and to his people. News of the fact that it was the Pope who ordered the attack in the first place had not reached their ears.

Piero never received another promotion and he did not care. He much preferred to remain a field commander and maintained control of his forces under Captain Ferruccio, who had recently been promoted to commissioner-general.

The Republic's war committee did not want Piero being given command of a larger force. They noted that he appeared to have a death wish and though his company chalked up victory after victory, they noted that it was

DAMNATION

because Piero took several unnecessary risks and was known for putting his men into impossible situations. Piero's often brash decisions and indifference to life resulted in heavy losses for his company and it became a group no soldier joined by choice.

Time dragged on slowly for Piero after Xaphan disappeared, and he had never gotten over the loss of his wife. That last day with her continuously haunted his memory. Who was this Xaphan? Who was the creature that attacked him? If she truly was deceiving him, why did she seem saddened? They were questions that often nearly drove him to insanity as he lay in bed each night.

On one mid-summer evening, Piero was assigned to guard duty on the crumbling walls of the city. The armies of the Republic had managed to quickly reinforce the city walls in response to the oncoming imperial army. Piero had been assigned to the citadel as a patrol officer for a few weeks. It was tranquil for him, but it was definitely anything but quiet. His position offered him a beautiful view of Florence, but the city was far from what he remembered. He could see smashed buildings and smoke spewing from random places due to the constant bombardment from the enemy army.

Piero stared at his home, emotionless. He knew that without reinforcements, it was only a matter of time before the city fell. Eventually, the armies of Charles V would be walking the streets. He secretly welcomed the day when the imperial army attacked. He even volunteered his dwindling company for permanent frontline duty. Other kingdoms had pledged to support the Republic, but Piero understood politics and was certain that he would never receive any reinforcements.

The voice of another officer broke his train of thought, "Lieutenant Lorenzi, I am here to relieve you of your post sir. My watch is beginning."

DAMNATION

Piero turned and stared at the man for a moment, and without so much as a salute, left his post, "I stand relieved."

"Good night sir."

Piero didn't respond. Usually at this point, he would head to the local tavern and drink himself into a peaceful oblivion, but today he decided he just wanted to go home. He couldn't describe it, but something inside was telling him that today was not a good day to go drinking.

Walking the streets of Florence, Piero could see the destruction brought on by the war. Buildings were smashed and burning and people were left filthy and destitute. Many of them badly injured from buildings collapsing around them.

One of these people, a blind man, reached out to Piero with a bandaged hand. He wore a filthy brown robe over his clothing, and his face was horribly scarred. He knew Piero was coming by the sound of the soldier's heavy boots. The blind man listened to the loud thud and guessed that a military man was walking by, "Please, alms for the blind, good sir?"

Piero stopped walking for a moment and turned to the man. For the first time in a long while, Piero felt something other than indifference to the people around him. The war had rendered many people homeless and on the streets.

Piero was no stranger to these people and knew that he could not save them. However, after a few seconds, he reached into his pocket, pulled out a small sack of coins and threw them to the man

"You'll surely make better use of these than I will. Here, a good deed rewarded by one less headache in the morning."

The man grabbed the bag as Piero began to walk away. He felt the material against his hand and a shocked expression came over his face, "Sir, wait!"

DAMNATION

"That is all I have beggar, do not bother me any further…"

"But I have information for you! Please allow me to repay your kindness!"

Piero picked up his pace, trying to get away, "I am really not interested in what you have to say, peasant. I gave you money, now let me be!"

"Not interested," the blind beggar repeated as the words stopped him in his tracks, "even if it is about Xaphine?"

Piero's heart froze at hearing someone speak his wife's name for the first time in years. He stopped walking for a few moments before drawing his sword. With one hand on his aching heart, he stormed right up to the beggar and put his sword to the man's throat, "I don't usually harm anyone who is unarmed, but you better have a good reason for speaking her name to me. What is your game, peasant?"

The beggar could smell the metal of his sword and heard it ringing from scraping against its scabbard, "Put away your weapon soldier, I bear you no ill tidings."

"Why do you claim to have information on my wife? Have you no respect for the dead?"

"Forgive me soldier, I know you have suffered greatly because of her loss. I assure you as a God fearing man, I have nothing but respect for all of our dearly departed."

"Then explain yourself, and do it quickly!"

The beggar's blind eyes darted up and down the street as though he were looking for someone, "I must beg your forgiveness sir, for I cannot speak of this here… is there some place private we can go?"

"Why can we not talk here?"

"I fear that the ears of the wrong people may hear us. The information I carry is not for the ears of the public. I ask you to indulge a blind man just this once."

"Fine," Piero said, rolling his eyes, "we can go to my home, but pray you are not wasting my time."

The beggar stood up and brushed himself off, "I am certain you will be greatly interested in what I have to say. It may even change your life."

Piero looked the beggar over as he straightened up. This man did not appear to be much older than Piero and his stance was reminiscent of a man who had received military training. Even so, the beggar was impoverished, and his face was badly scarred. The man's eyes were perhaps his most striking feature. They were bright white, almost like they were glowing and there was no pupil to be found. Even stranger was that, as the man turned and looked at Piero it was as though he could actually see him.

Most blind people that he had encountered looked in his general direction when speaking, but this one looked him right in the eye, "I promise you, I am not wasting your time."

Piero looked at him oddly, "What is your name beggar, you look familiar."

"Former Lt. Francesco Piangi... let's just leave it at Francesco."

"Very well Francesco, can you walk?"

"Yes sir, very well in fact."

"Then follow me." Piero said as he started towards his home again.

The beggar obediently followed an irritated Piero as he was led through the rubble of the city. The sun had almost completely set as they reached his home. There was an aura of darkness about the house that was so potent that it took Francesco a moment to adjust.

Piero opened the door and went inside, "Well, might as well make yourself at home."

Francesco nodded and sat at Piero's table. Piero lit the fireplace, as well as a few lamps. As his house slowly became illuminated, Piero grabbed one of his few intact glasses and poured a drink for the blind man. The beggar took the glass and sipped it slowly, "Thank you, my friend."

Piero sat down across from him, "We're behind closed doors now, no one can see or hear us. So speak what you know."

"Before I continue, know that what I am about to tell you cannot be untold. Once I have revealed my secrets to you, you will need to learn to live with them and believe me, they will change your view of the world forever. My truths are of the sort that can haunt a man to his death. So I have to ask you, are you certain you wish to hear what I have to say?"

A sudden gust of wind gently passing over the house caught Francesco's attention. He flinched at the sound that was nothing more than a low whisper. It sounded as though someone were listening in from the roof.

"Spare me the cryptic speeches. If you have any information about my wife, I absolutely want to hear it. Tell me what you know about Xaphine."

"As you wish, my friend... So... as I said, my name is Lt. Francesco Piangi…"

"Of what army? Were you a member of the Papal army or the Florentine army?"

"Technically neither, I was part of a little known division called the Papal Knights, headed by Captain Federico Gonzaga. We were charged with directly protecting the office of the Pope and carrying out his personal business. Our dealings were usually off the official record and outside of any jurisdiction. I was Captain Federico's second officer. I knew everything he did. I have stories that could turn your stomach."

Piero eyed his guest suspiciously, "Papal Knights, I've never heard of them, and Federico I thought was Captain General of the Church?"

"That was his official title. It was a good cover for him as the Church wanted us kept as secret as possible. It's no surprise that you've never heard of us."

He paused for a moment as though finding the strength to continue was difficult, "During the summer of the year 1519, unusual things began happening around Rome. After weeks of unexplained orders and weird events unfolding, we were ordered to Venice to capture a supposed fallen angel."

"An angel? You mean to tell me that you actually saw one?"

"Saw one, and heard her cries... I'll never forget the look of sheer terror on her face when we knocked down the door to the house she was hiding in."

"Terror?"

"It is a long story. I didn't see the angel again after that, not for a long while. I assumed she was going to be executed, but she managed to escape. That's when things started getting worse. Lutheran attacks became more common and Captain Gonzaga became extremely suspicious of the Pope's activities. Back then, Leo X was giving rather unusual orders, so even though it was our job to protect the man, Federico walked cautiously around Leo X in hopes of solving the puzzle."

"Wait... I always thought the Swiss Guard protected the Pope. If the knights protect him, then why does the guard even exist?"

Francesco nodded, "The Swiss Guard protects his holiness, this is true. However, the Pope did not have official command over the Swiss Guard as their orders came from the clergy. The knights were charged with carrying out the Pope's personal business while at the same time, seeing to it that the honor of the office was maintained. We were disbanded when Federico became the Marquis of Mantua. We were no longer deemed necessary and most of our duties were divided up amongst the Swiss Guard and

Rome's own forces. Most of us found other positions within the armies of the land, but I followed a different path."

"What path? What happened to you?"

Again, Francesco paused before revealing his secrets, "I will never forget that day, the day my life changed forever. Rome was attacked by a large force of revolutionaries who followed the teachings of Martin Luther. Though I suspect he never authorized such an attack, I am sure that this was planned for a long time by a sect that was acting alone. We never figured out how they managed to breach the defenses surrounding the Basilica di Santa Maria Maggiore, and flow so in quickly. I still remember the captain's panicked voice as he called us to arms. We were terribly outnumbered, but we were prepared to hold our own. Outnumbered, but never outclassed, that was the way we did things."

"That's when she showed up…"

"She?"

"The angel… She ran out on to the field and halted our fight. I'll never forget her words, 'The Kingdom of Heaven is within you,' she said. She halted us all in our tracks and destroyed our desire to fight."

"Who is this angel you speak of?"

"I know not," Francesco admitted, "but there can be no doubt she saved Rome from being destroyed. The revolutionaries would have overrun the basilica and the city would have been left in disarray."

"Yeah, not a lot of good she did. Rome was taken by the armies of Charles V, and we're now losing the war."

"Yes, but the city still stands. Had the revolutionaries won, it would be a smoldering ruin by now. I can't even begin to fathom the chaos that might have followed."

Piero was starting to get annoyed, "That's a nice story and all, but what does any of this have to do with my wife?

I'm beginning to think you don't have any information about her."

"Patience, I'm getting to it. After the incident, I stayed on as Federico's second officer. When we disbanded, I resigned and left papal army. Federico offered me a position with his guard, but I had my own plans. I wanted to find out more about where this angel came from."

Francesco sucked down a deep breath as he continued, "I spent years searching until I heard several rumors about a gateway far east of here. It's where they got the weapons needed to stand against the Church. I saw it as my chance to get all my questions answered, so I sailed the sea in search of the gateway... I sacrificed everything, my livelihood, my fortune... everything... and eventually I lost my way. I can't explain what happened next because I do not remember."

Francesco's face filled with sadness, "The last thing I do remember was my ship being set adrift on the ocean for what seemed like years. After I had run out of food and water, the sun beat down on me and began to challenge my sanity. My ship was eventually wrecked, and I washing up on shore blind. I don't know what happened to the rest of the crew, assuming that any of them even survived. Then I felt something odd happening in the area and eventually made my way here. I've been here ever since."

"I see." Piero said softly, ready to throw the beggar back out on the street. "Well I truly am sorry for your misfortune, but I cannot overlook the fact that you still have not told me how you know my wife."

"I don't know her and I never said I did. See after the wreck when I lost my vision... I discovered that I could hear things, weird things. Sacrificing the use of my eyes gave me some sort of enhanced hearing. I can hear the sounds of unworldly voices, including those of your wife. Though I wasn't anywhere nearby, I could hear her voice on the wind.

I heard everything that went on the night she left you and I know where she is."

"Where?" Piero asked anxiously. "Tell me!"

Another gust of wind picked up before Francesco could answer. This time, it came down the chimney and dimmed the flame momentarily. Francesco's face turned nervously towards what was happening.

Once the wind died down and the flame returned to normal, Francesco continued his story, "She dwells in the underworld." He replied darkly. "She's in hell where she serves as Lucifer's steward."

Piero lowered his head, "No... she was abrasive, but she had a good heart... Why, why would she be there?"

"Your wife was an agent of the Morning Star long before you knew her. She's been the general of Lucifer's forces for eons going back to when he was kicked out of the Kingdom of Heaven. Her memory was erased and her appearance was altered so that she would be able to effectively hide here. From what I was able to find out, Lucifer attempted to usurp the Most High. His failure cost him most of his power and thus prompted him to recall everyone he could, including your wife."

"I can't believe that... I... I won't believe it. Nothing about her ever made me believe that she was evil. It's not true... it can't be..."

Francesco placed a hand on Piero's shoulder, "Think carefully, she left you willingly, did she not?"

"Yes... but... Why didn't you come forward with this sooner? So many years have passed by, why wait until now?"

"Because I don't know how to get to her, and until now, I had no way of finding you. Believe me, I tried. I made inquiries at the main square, but no one is going to listen to a blind pauper. No soldiers would even give me a second glance. There was no way I could get the information on where to find you. I waited and prayed for a long time that you would cross my path… It took years, but you did. When you threw me that money, the bag was warm and electrifying, it was an odd sensation. I don't know how to explain it, but I knew it was you."

"Even if I could get to her, what good would it do me now? Our entire marriage appears to have been a farce. I tried to stop her, I tried to talk to her, but she would not even look at me. I'm not sure she ever truly loved me."

"You mustn't think like that. Xaphine loved you and continued to even after she was transformed. Though her memories were gone, she was still the same person. When Lucifer came to retrieve her, something happened that he hadn't foreseen. Altering Xaphan's memory had an undesirable effect. Because of the loss of his powers, her memories were partly irremovable. Her feelings for you invoked that fallen angel's conscience. The goodness inside of her was strengthened by her time with you. Your wife is still in there. If you can get to her, and break down the walls of darkness that Xaphan has put up as defense, you still have a chance to save her."

Piero's eyes widened and his heart lifted when he heard Francesco's words. He whispered softly, "She's still there…?"

"Yes, and she still loves you."

"But how do I get to her? I've seen Xaphan's power first hand. Breaking through it will not be easy, especially since you are talking about taking on the devil himself. That's considering we can even find her. How does one get to the Underworld?"

"That I do not know… I never found the gateway to either side of the Celestial realm, but I think I know someone who can help you."

"Who?" Piero asked anxiously.

"My former commander, Captain... or should I say 'Marquis' Federico Gonzaga."

Piero's heart sank, "How am I supposed to get an audience with the Marquis, especially since he abandoned the League of Cognac when we needed him the most?"

"Leave that to me. The Marquis owes me a favor. In exchange for taking me with you, I will see to it you get your meeting with the Marquis."

Piero scoffed, "You, how can I take you with me? You can't even see, how long do you think you'll last?"

"If you don't, you'll never get an audience. Long have I waited to have the questions of existence answered I cannot sit by while you try to handle this alone."

"You make a good point... What is your stake in all of this? Why do you care?"

"I am willing to help you because it may lead me to the ultimate truths that I have been searching a long time for. I want to find the Kingdom of God, and helping you find Xaphan, might get me closer. That is my price; an audience with the Marquis in exchange for taking me with you."

Piero still want not convinced, "What you're asking me isn't possible... I sincerely doubt that Captain Ferruccio will give me leave to go on this hunt. We're in the middle of a war... one that we're not exactly winning..."

"You never know. You should still inquire."

"And if he says no?"

"Then perhaps you should consider going without consent."

"What?" Piero scoffed. "Abandon my post and flee Florence now?"

"If it's necessary."

"You're mad. Even if we could escape the city, I'd be disgraced and on the run for the rest of my life. Xaphine was a very honor-driven woman. She would not want that."

DAMNATION

"Was it your honor she loved or was it you? If you were to return home after a staggering defeat, would it have changed how she felt about you?"

Piero froze in place and remembered his wife's words; "I don't care if you win a resounding victory that the history books will remember for centuries or you suffer a staggering defeat. There is no dishonor in such things as they are usually decided by more than one soldier. All I ask is that you come back to me alive."

Piero sighed as he wiped his forehead, "You're right… but still to abandon my friends like this…"

Francesco stood up and placed a hand on Francesco's shoulder, "I am sorry Piero. I know it's a tough decision. The important ones always are. However, you have to think of it this way; your wife is suffering under the heel of Lucifer and his minions. She can't die and the pain will never go away. These are the very same creatures that seek to overthrow the lord. Rescuing your wife would seriously hamper their goals and could possibly save the lives of everyone."

Francesco got the feeling that Piero still wasn't convinced, so he continued, "If you stay here, you will continue to the live the life you've been living these past ten years. You may save Florence, or you may get killed and watch your friends die. However, if you come with me, you may be able to save your wife, and all of humanity from damnation. It's up to you. I can't do this without help and no one else will hear me."

Piero shrugged, realizing that he had no other option, "Very well."

He stood up and turned to his bedroom, "Go get yourself some clothes and get cleaned up. Whether you know him or not, you'll need to at least be presentable when we go before the Marquis, there is a certain amount of decorum that is to be expected."

"Thank you, I agree."

Francesco found his way into the bedroom, and started sifting through Piero's clothing until he found a pair of clean trousers and a tunic that fit. He sat down on the bed as he changed and then felt the bowl of water next to the bed. He picked up the bowl and began rubbing his face vigorously with a scrap of his old clothes. His face had not been clean in a long time, and he relished it. He took his time as he really didn't want to go before his old friend looking unkempt.

As Francesco changed, Piero heard a knock at the door. He instinctively drew his sword as he walked over and opened up the door. For all he knew, it could be imperial soldiers at his door that had managed to sneak into the capital and he needed to be prepared.

To his relief, Antonio stood on the other side. When he saw Piero's face, he smiled, "Ah Lieutenant, I'm here with orders from the captain, your presence is required immediately at headquarters. I am to take you there on the double."

"All right." Piero nodded as he turned back to his bedroom. "Francesco, take your time, I have to report to my post. I'll be back before too long."

"Very well."

Piero didn't want to do this. He didn't have time, but orders were orders. He closed the door and turned to Antonio and his guard. The guards nodded and turned away as they began their march to the command office.

As they walked away Antonio looked at him oddly, "Who's Francesco?"

"I've got something I need to tell you later. It's big... really big..."

Antonio looked at him quizzically, "Is everything okay? I haven't seen you this excited in years, my friend."

DAMNATION

"I know that. I think my destiny may have taken a turn for the better…"

田

Piero entered the headquarters of the Florentine military, now deemed the Florentine defense force. Two guards were stationed at the main entrance. They eyed Piero suspiciously as he approached.

Piero stopped at the door and saluted, "Lt. Piero Lorenzi reporting."

The left guard nodded, "Go ahead in, you're expected."

Piero proceeded into the main hall with Antonio following close behind. The large room was ornately decorated like most other capital buildings in the city. He didn't have time to admire the art as Antonio beckoned him to a door off to the side.

Piero nodded and followed Antonio into the next room. It was a small chamber draped with the banners of red and silver that represented the Republic of Florence's coat of arms. To the back of the room, stood a chest plate and armor, no doubt belonging to the captain himself. In the middle of the room, a tall, well-toned, man stood over a large table covered with a map. He looked up, "Ah, Captain, good. Please come in."

"Yes, sir."

Anyone who looked at Piero's old commander had to admire his uniform as it was weighed down with medals of both prestige and rank. Ferruccio was proud of each and everyone one of them and spent hours at night making sure each one was kept properly polished.

Piero moved closer to the head of the table by a few paces and stood at attention. Antonio stood behind him at the door to make sure they were not disturbed.

Captain Ferruccio looked him over before turning back to his map, "As you know Piero, things are not going well for us. Rome has fallen and Clement VII has lost much of his power. As the Papal States surrender, our list of allies is wearing thin, even more so now that we have thrown off the monarchy. We need reconnaissance and need to know the extent of the damage done to Rome. Therefore, I am charging you with the honorable task of leading a mission to the Basilica di Santa Maria Maggiore to collect what information you can. It won't be an easy assignment, but your company is famous for accomplishing the impossible."

Piero knew that his commander was not going to like what he had to say, "Sir... I..."

Captain Ferruccio looked into Piero's eyes, "What is it Lieutenant? Speak your mind."

"Captain... I beg forgiveness, but I must respectfully request that you assign someone else to this task. I cannot lead the company on this mission."

"Oh, you have a matter of importance that takes precedence over the security of the Republic? This I have to hear."

"Sir, my loyalty has always been to the Florence, regardless of whose side we're on," Piero replied sternly, "but I have discovered an amazing truth; my wife is still alive."

Antonio's eyes widened, "Piero truthfully?"

"Your wife?" Captain Ferruccio asked as his eyes narrowed, "How is that even possible? I thought she was in the fire that destroyed your house? No one could have survived that."

"She wasn't there, Captain. I've received new information... I can't go into great detail, but I know that she is still alive. I have to go find her."

Ferruccio shook his head, "Lieutenant that is extraordinary news, albeit somewhat hard to believe. However, she was a friend to the military, and I know she was the source of your strength, but I fail to see how it takes priority over the safety and security of the Republic and I think she would agree with me. I remember how much duty meant to her. Cold though it may sound, she is but one woman. We're talking about the welfare of thousands. I am sorry... but I can't let you go."

"It matters to me Captain... Therefore I must respectfully decline. I will not take this mission."

Antonio was beginning to get nervous, "Piero...be careful, think of what you are saying."

The captain was beginning to get annoyed, "You have served the Republic well, and have earned the respect of your men, but if you refuse this order, it will be seen as you deserting your post. Which in times of war is considered treason and punishable by death."

Piero looked Captain Ferruccio in the eye and implored his commander to allow him to detach from his unit, "Sir, please..."

Ferruccio would hear none of it, "Piero, I have been a tolerant man. This is not the first time you have been insubordinate, but in the past, your actions have always resulted in victory. Thus I have looked the other way, but I cannot do so this time, certainly not when our city is under siege."

Piero could feel his face heating up. There was an uncontrollable fire burning in his stomach. Finally, he could not take it anymore, "My wife and I committed our lives to the service of Florence. How often did she mend your armor and sharpen your blade? As for me, I have thrown myself into each battle without regard for my own life. How many victories were paid for by the blood of my men? How many, Captain? Perhaps we wouldn't be in such a situation if our captains could competently command instead of sending company after company on suicide missions!"

Antonio's eyes widened in fear, "Piero!"

"Enough, ensign!" Ferruccio yelled as he turned his attention back to Piero, "Lieutenant, I am not about to tolerate such insolence. The blood you speak of is on your own hands. You have thoughtlessly led your men to their deaths time and time again. I could have you drawn and quartered for your words! If you don't take this mission, then your days in the military are over!"

Piero breathed in and snorted defiantly before speaking, "Then consider this my resignation!"

"I think a little time in a cell may change your mind. Either way, you are not leaving here tonight, and not tomorrow either unless you're in command of your squad, or in a coffin. The laws are absolute. I hope for your sake, you come to your senses."

The captain snapped his fingers, "Guards!"

Two guards entered the room behind Antonio.

"Take Lieutenant Lorenzi and throw him into the dungeon. Pray he sees reason before it's too late."

Piero did not give the guards any resistance at all as they dragged him away. He knew it would be pointless, but he also could not accept that mission. Going to Rome could take weeks and might cost him his life. It was out of the question. His only hope was to try to find a way to escape.

Once Piero disappeared from view, Antonio turned to Captain Ferruccio, "Sir, permission to speak?"

The captain looked up when he realized that the young ensign was still there, "Dispensing with ranks?"

"If it would not be an insult to ask?"

"Please," Ferruccio said raising his hand, "speak the words you seem so anxious to."

Antonio sucked in a deep breath, "Captain, have you lost your mind?"

"Go on, let's hear all of it."

"Sir, what Lieutenant Lorenzi said is true. I have fought alongside him for years. Too many battles have been won off the edge of his sword. You have locked up one of our best company commanders."

"Best company commander... Ensign, he's a loose cannon who has been seeking death since his wife disappeared."

"I know this, but surely that is not relevant. His record stands, regardless of his personal feelings, and I would think that it would more than justify a little indulgence!"

"He spent his indulgence when he accused our officers of incompetence!"

"The man just received word that his wife is still alive. After almost ten years of struggling with her loss. Would anyone of us react differently? I challenge you to have behaved any better!"

"Perhaps not, young Antonio. I know he is your friend and I admire you standing up for your superior. If our situation were not so desperate, then I would have considered his request, but I am not afforded such a luxury right now."

The captain placed a hand on Antonio's shoulder, "I want you to take acting command of Piero's company. If he refuses to go on his mission by tomorrow morning, he will be hanged. If that happens, I need you to lead them."

"I am as always a servant of the Republic. I will carry out your orders. However, I take command of the company under extreme protest."

"I expected as such... I will make sure it is noted."

The Captain stood straight up and saluted Antonio, "You are dismissed, ensign."

Antonio nodded, turned to the door, and marched out of the room. His mind was conflicted on what he should do. Should he take command or try to help his friend? What was the right decision?

**

Piero was led down the hall with spears pointed at his back. The first guard pulled out an old iron key as they reached the door at the back of the building. He fiddled with the lock until the door opened and a blast of cold, musty, air rushed out. They took Piero into the next room and then down a long flight of stairs.

The winding staircase seemed to stretch on forever as they proceeded downward into a black abyss. They passed by a few doors that looked as though they hadn't been opened in years. Even the guards did not know what dwelled on the other side. After reaching the bottom, the guards opened another heavy door. It was so old and warped that it required the strength of both men to open it as the wood scraped against the ceiling. Dust and wood fragments fell to the floor as the door moved.

Once it was open, the guard grabbed Piero and threw him into a large, windowless cell. One of the guards looked in as they closed the door, "Sit here and rot, traitor."

The moment Piero was locked in, he began looking for a way to escape. He slowly surveyed the room. It was underground, and the door was wood with iron bars.

Piero fell back in despair; there was no way out, "Xaphine... I'm sorry..."

**

A few hours went by as Piero rested against a wall. It was cold and damp in the cell, but even in the poor conditions he was beginning to fall asleep. He said a brief prayer before finally drifting away.

Piero's slumber was interrupted by the sound of scraping against the door. He quickly searched the room for a weapon, but there was nothing nearby except for a plank of wood. He grabbed it and hid behind the door, ready to strike.

There was a loud pounding noise that went silent for a moment. Then a second loud crash shook the door. Within a few moments, the hinges began to shake and there was a loud clanking noise as the lock broke. When the noises subsided, the door began to open.

DAMNATION

Piero sat and waited to see who or what was on the other side. Little by little, a sliver of candle light began to bleed through. Once the door was open wide enough, Antonio's head poked through, "Captain, where are you?"

Piero was poised to strike, but when he heard his friend's voice, he dropped the plank, "Antonio, what are you doing here?"

"Isn't it obvious? I'm busting you out of here. The captain is furious. If you haven't changed your mind by tomorrow, he plans to hang you."

"Yes, I knew he would… That's standard procedure for my level of insubordination."

A worried look came over Piero's face, "Antonio, you can't be here. If you are caught, you'll share in my fate. I won't have more blood on my hands."

"Then I guess you'd better take me with you. I've already disobeyed orders, assaulted a guard and deserted my post. So either way, if you leave me behind, I'll be facing the hangman's noose."

"What, are you mad? Where I'm going is dangerous and I may not be coming back. Besides, Florence needs all the good men it can get! Lie, tell the captain I did all of this. It's safer with the company and there is no one I'd rather have replace me."

"Like this is the first time that I've followed you to almost certain doom. I owe you my life many times over and I know what Xaphine meant to you. That woman was your life; you've been a shell of yourself since she disappeared."

Piero sighed as Antonio continued, "Let us not blind ourselves to the reality of our situation, the League of Cognac and Alliance of the Papal States is all but broken and its remnants will soon be scattered to the winds, our people just don't know it yet. All that remains now is for Florence to remain standing, and we both know it will."

DAMNATION

His eyes focused on Piero's as he spoke, "I am serious Piero, take me with you, or be hanged here tomorrow. Where ever you are going and whatever you are doing, I'm up for it, you know that. What's your choice?"

"I guess I don't have one then. My friend, I can never repay this…"

"You were not the only one who was fond of Xaphine. She was my friend too. I was there with you since the beginning, and I gave her away at your wedding, remember?"

Piero nodded as Antonio grabbed a sack from beside the door and threw it to him, "Quickly change; you'll attract less attention if you're not strutting about in your uniform. The only way out is through the main hall. You'd be a fool to try to escape on your own."

"What made you think I was trying to plan an escape? I was pretty much just sitting there in complete darkness."

"Experience. I've fought too many battles with you to not be able to anticipate your movements."

Piero did as he was told and hid his tunic under the cloak that Antonio brought for him. The moment he was ready, Piero draped the hood over his head and tied the sash tightly around his waist, "Okay I'm ready, let's get out of here."

They closed the cell door so that the guards would still think that Piero was in there. Antonio drew his sword and pointed it at Piero as they walked. Piero looked at him oddly, "Antonio?"

"Appearances, my friend, appearances. We can't let the guards suspect anything."

"Why do I get the feeling this isn't your first escape from a dungeon?"

"I'm a soldier. Escaping from tough situations is part of my job."

"True enough."

DAMNATION

The two friends made their way out of the dungeon and out the front door of military headquarters. It was late so most of the soldiers had either retired or were already on assignment. There was only a small force guarding the area.

Piero was relieved that Antonio had chosen the right time to spring him from jail. Otherwise they might have encountered a lot more prying eyes and questioning. They stood less of a chance of getting caught now.

The last thing Piero wanted was to shed the blood of his own countrymen unnecessarily. The military headquarters was not a prison, so security wasn't as tight. However, once they reached the front door, the two guards looked oddly at them.

"I have orders to take this man to the execution yard." Antonio said in a stoic tone.

The guard looked at him suspiciously and then lifted Piero's hood, "Ah yes, so the Captain decided to go through with executing this deserter eh? I heard about his little outburst in front of Ferruccio."

Piero looked down and said nothing. Antonio smiled and nodded, "He should have run him through the moment the lieutenant disobeyed orders."

"That he should have. All right, on your way, the sooner we're rid of this traitor, the better. God be with you, Lieutenant, for no one else is."

Antonio nodded as he walked by the two guards with his sword at Piero's back, "Good night."

The soldiers nodded as Antonio and Piero disappeared down the dark road. The lamps were already dying, making it easier for them to slip out of site. They would just need to find a dark enough spot.

Once they were out of sight, Antonio pulled Piero down a side alley, "Come on." Antonio whispered, "I've got a small carriage waiting for us on the outskirts."

"We need to get back to my house. I need to get to Francesco."

"Yeah, who is that guy?"

"An unusual seer. I'm afraid that I don't know a whole lot about him, but he is the one who told me about Xaphine. If we are to find her, we're going to need his help."

"No problem, your house is on the way, just be careful, we don't know who could be watching."

Piero allowed Antonio to lead him down a labyrinth of dark alleys to avoid being seen. It wasn't long before they reached a clearing which was only about a mile from Piero's house. They cautiously approached it, keeping an eye open for guards that might be patrolling the area, but nothing appeared out of the darkness.

When they reached the house, Antonio stood watch while Piero went inside. Francesco sat by the fire half asleep. The sound of the door creaking open startled the blind man, making him turn quickly to face the door, "Piero, is that you? You've been gone a long time."

"My apologies. I was delayed, but I'm here now and we're in a little rush, so we need to get moving."

Francesco nodded and grabbed his staff from the corner as he stood up, "Very well my friend, let us make for Mantua. It should not take long for us to get there."

Piero led him out of the house and into the darkness. Francesco could feel the cool air in the night, but it mattered very little to him. He had lived in darkness since he lost his vision. The only difference now was the absence of a warm sun.

As soon as Antonio saw Francesco, he rolled his eyes, "A blind man Piero? How are we expected to take him with us? All he's going to do is slow us down!"

Francesco turned angrily to the young soldier, "I can see more with no eyes than you do with two, young man. I can assure you that it will not be me slowing anyone down."

DAMNATION

"See that you don't."

Seeing his two companions already at each other's throats made Piero's hope sink, "Oh this is a good start, we're wanted criminals, we're on the run, and we're already not getting along."

"Wanted criminals, you say?" Francesco repeated in an intrigued tone. "Such an adventure this is turning out to be. What crimes have we committed, pray tell?"

Antonio sighed, "Let's see… desertion, treason, gross insubordination, assault, and jail breaking. Just to name a few…"

"And all in one night? Very impressive."

IV

The group made their way to the wagon that Antonio had arranged for them. It was a rickety old cart with a rag hood and two horses tide to it. The old wagon was very shabby, but perfect for people who did not want to draw attention themselves.

Piero and Antonio jumped on the driver's bench while Francesco climbed in the back. The blind beggar sat in the far corner behind the driver where he began to meditate. Antonio heard a stirring from inside the city and quickly cracked the whip to get the horses moving. He turned to Piero, "Where are we heading?"

Piero looked back at the blind man sitting in silent meditation, "We need to get to Mantua. According to our friend back there, the Marquis has information we can use."

Antonio cracked the whip again to get the horses moving faster, "We'll need to stay off the main roads, we don't want to attract attention of Charles V's forces."

"Agreed." Piero said with his eyes looking to the stars. "How long will our journey take?"

"Six hours." Another voice chimed in from the back of the cabin.

The two of them looked back at Francesco, "We should be there by tomorrow. Piero, I suggest that you get some rest. As you said, the marquis will expect some decorum."

"That's not a bad idea." Antonio agreed. "I can handle things up here, go ahead."

Piero nodded as he turned to open the flap of cloth and lay down in the cabin. Francesco left the carriage bed so Piero could sleep and sat with Antonio on the driver's bench, "So what is your stake in all of this, young man?"

Antonio didn't take his eyes off of the horse as he spoke, "Piero has been my commanding officer for years.

DAMNATION

He and his wife are some of my closest friends and I've been watching Piero die for too long without her. If there is a chance that she is still alive, I'm going to help them. Nothing has been right with the world since she left."

As the horses pushed onward, Antonio turned slightly to look at Francesco, "What about you? I don't believe I've ever seen you before."

"I'm from Rome. I was at the basilica during a disturbance back in 1519. That challenged my faith and changed my life forever."

"What the angel incident?"

"How in the world do you know of that? It was covered up, the papal soldiers were all sworn to secrecy and we reached an… understanding with the revolutionaries as they withdrew."

"That may be, but you can't guarantee that every single person won't tell someone in confidence. With so many wandering eyes, things like that are hard to keep secret."

"I suppose not… Anyway, I was there for it. I saw the entire event unfold. Since then, I have been on a quest to find the truths of our existence. My quest cost me everything; my prestige, my fortune, and my sanity. It will have all been worth it if I can find the answers."

"So you're here because you're hoping that this journey will help you achieve your goal?"

"In part, but oh to have one last glorious adventure… it's what I miss most about being a Papal knight."

Antonio smiled as he contemplated their situation and responded, "Well I'm not exactly sure any of us will be coming back alive. If our own army doesn't hunt us down and kill us, whatever we're going up against probably will, but I hope you find what you're looking for."

"Likewise, I sincerely hope this story has a happy ending, though it does seem like the odds are stacked against us."

"I've never been a fan of odds, having beaten them many times over myself."

The horses were pushed hard as the group rode through the night. They blew through the citadel while the gates were still open and continued on into the morning.

*

Piero woke up to find the wagon riding through a small city. The carriage stopped at the large, ornate, building just outside the limits of the city. The building was a huge square shaped structure that appeared to be incomplete.

On either side in the distance, Piero could see a river flowing through the area. It wasn't long before he figured out where they were. Though many cities in the area had a similar landscape, he knew they were in Mantua.

Piero stretched his arms and pushed himself out of the carriage. Sleeping on the hard wood had done a number on his back, but a few quick stretches that he'd learned during his early training cleared up the stiffness. The salt air kissed his skin as he was joined by Francesco and Antonio. The building was well guarded and there were no immediately obvious ways of sneaking in.

Antonio frowned, "Okay, now how are we getting in?"

"Leave that to me." Francesco replied.

He turned and approached one of the guards. His proximity prompted the guard to react by pointing his spear at them, "Halt, what is your business here?"

Antonio looked over the armored guard to decide whether or not he could overpower them, but he never got a chance to decide. Francesco spoke up, "We seek an audience with the Marquis."

The guard looked them over and scoffed, "His eminence is a busy man and has no time for run down paupers."

"Rundown paupers you say? I must say, the hospitality of my old commanding officer has dwindled as of late. Does he treat all of his friends this way?"

"Times are difficult and much has changed in Mantua." The second guard chimed in. "The war has everyone on edge."

"So I see," Francesco replied, pretending to care, "but I'm sure the Marquis will make an exception for an old friend. Please tell him that his old lieutenant is here to see him, and remind him that he owes me for an unofficial order he gave me during the good old days."

The first guard sighed, "You better not be wasting my lord's time."

As he turned and entered the building, Antonio whispered to Francesco, "What order are you referring to."

"That's private; I've kept my word to the Captain all these years. I'm not about to break it now. Besides, for your own sake, it's best you don't know. It was an internal matter."

A few minutes later, the guard returned with a shocked look on his face, "The Marquis... has requested that you three be brought in for an immediate audience. Please follow me."

Francesco nodded, "Lead the way."

The guard beckoned them forward. They passed through the large doors and into a long, ornate hallway. Their feet echoed against the stone floor as they walked.

Piero admired the artwork on the walls as they followed the guard. Large statues of men long dead lined the hallway as they walked. After passing by massive statues, beautiful tapestries, and colorful paintings that the Marquis surrounded himself with, they were led through a second, smaller door.

The next room was a luxurious suite, at the center of which was a man wearing a blue tunic, red trousers, and an ornate sword strapped to his belt, hanging at his side. His hair was short and well groomed. His face was covered with a long, curly, beard. The guard bowed, "Hail Federico II Gonzaga, Marquis of Mantua."

Federico rolled his eyes, "Thank you guardsman that will be all. You may return to your duties."

The guard bowed and closed the door behind him, leaving only the Marquis, his bodyguards, and the three friends in the room. Francesco smiled and bowed, "It's been a long time, Captain."

"Francesco... too long, old friend." Captain Federico replied. "The years have not been kind to either of us, it seems."

"Either of us? You seem to be doing well for yourself. It's good to see that you finally took up for father's post after avoiding it for so long."

Federico sighed, "The life of an aristocrat had its appeal for a while, but such things are short lived. To be honest, I'd give almost anything to be back in command of a garrison again. I wasn't the best commander, but it was more enjoyable than sitting on this throne getting fat and old."

"It may not be too late."

"I wish it weren't. However the Papacy no longer considers me an ally. I'm afraid that the Pope may still blame me for the sacking of Rome."

Piero glared at him, "I'll say, thanks to your lack of action, a chain of events unfolded that resulted in my countrymen fighting alone!"

Francesco's face lit up in shock, "Piero!"

"And what would you have had me do?" Federico fired back. "I am a peaceful man with only a small military to protect my land. Charles V has a massive army at his disposal. Had I opposed him, my city would be in ruins now and my soldiers would be dead. I could not be responsible for so much death. I saw too much of it during my days with the knights."

Francesco flashed Piero an angry look. Piero stepped back and lowered his head, "My apologies, Marquis…"

"Unfortunately, I'm used to it by now. I am sorry for any suffering my decision may have caused."

He then turned back to Francesco, "Now, what is so important that you've come here pulling favors and reminding me of things that could have cost us both our heads so many years ago."

"We need the aid of two old acquaintances. I think you know who I mean as I happen to know that you used to visit them on a regular basis and still do from time to time."

"Oh?"

"How is the venetian fisherman you've been known to visit whenever you can sneak off?"

The Marquis paused for a moment, as though trying to fight to answer. He stood up and turned to his bodyguards, "Both of you leave us."

The guards looked at each other for a moment, nervous about leaving their ruler alone with such a questionable group.

"I'm in the company of friends here. I am in no danger." Federico assured them. "Please wait outside."

The two guards bowed, opened the door, and hesitantly backed out of the room. Once the door was safely closed again, Federico turned back to Francesco, "He is doing well last I heard. His son, my godson, has grown up quite nicely and with the war on, the fish they catch is in high demand. Why, what is your business with them?"

DAMNATION

Piero stepped forward, "We need to find a way into the underworld."

Antonio looked at Piero in shock, "What…"

Federico gasped and had to sit down, "You intend to brave a trip to the world of the damned… And you want their help… is that it?"

Francesco nodded, but said nothing. He was completely aware of how it sounded. Part of him was ready for his old friend to flat out refuse.

Federico did not like this in the least, "My friend, I heard about what happened to you after the knights were dissolved. Allow me to help you. I can put you up in a nice home and see to it you live a comfortable life, but you must abandon this mad quest."

"Lucifer has my wife…" Piero blurted out. "Francesco can stay here, he has kept up his end of the bargain, but I must continue onward."

"If I may remind you," Francesco said sternly, "the deal was that I go with you. As you said, I have kept up my end, but you have not kept yours. I am going with you to the Netherworld."

Antonio could no longer speak. He was shocked at what he was hearing and began to wonder why he had not questioned Piero sooner. He slowly backed away to place his arm on a nearby table for support.

Federico turned to Piero, "And you are hoping to square off against the legions of hell to find her, defeat Lucifer, and bring her back?"

"Whatever it takes."

"This wife of yours must be something if you men are willing to risk your souls to find her… Well you wouldn't be the first to try it. Okay… if I cannot talk you out of this, then I will repay the favor you did for me so many years ago. – Francesco… you are looking for the Patrisi family, they live on the Venetian coast just south of the capital city in a small fishing community. You shouldn't have much trouble finding them; their house is the biggest one in the area."

Francesco lowered his eyes, "Thank you, my friend."

"Head to Chioggia. I will have a vessel there waiting for you. I will also send two of my men with you to aid in whatever way they can."

"That is most generous, my lord." Antonio piped in, surprised.

"I owe this man a lot, and for the record, I don't like owing people favors."

Francesco laughed as he replied, "You never did, Captain."

He was about to say his farewells when Federico spoke up again, "Francesco, my honor is satisfied now… but if you ever decide to abandon this insanity, you always have a home here. I do not forget my friends."

The three of them bowed before the Marquis. Francesco was moved by his offer and actually tempted to take it, "I shall never forget that, farewell Captain."

"Good luck to you, I hope you find the knowledge you've been after for so many years – and as for you Piero, I hope you are able to save your wife."

"Most kind, thank you, my lord."

The three of them left Federico's home and got back into their carriage. As they pulled away from the large building, Piero sat in back with Francesco, "It's time we laid all the cards on the table. I want answers, what was this secret order that you carried out?"

"Perhaps it is time to tell you. The Pope is dead now so I doubt it will matter. I was to watch the Pope for him. Leo X was acting quite suspiciously and was issuing illegal orders. I was asked to keep an eye on him. I followed that order, knowing the great risk I took upon myself and the rest of the knights."

DAMNATION

"No doubt you all would have been executed if the Pope suspected treason."

"That's exactly what Federico feared. He would have offered himself to the gallows had we been found out, but I had no intention of allowing such dishonor. I carried out my mission, though in the end it turned out to be unnecessary."

Piero smiled as the picture became clear, "Because of the incident that the angel stopped?"

"That's right. Everything became clear when she arrived on the scene, revealed a second angel's treachery, the Pope's role in all of it, and where the lines needed to be drawn."

"I'm hoping that we have a similar happy ending, after everything that's happened."

"Her story still had another chapter to play out, but that is not for me to tell you about. I'm sure you'll find out before too long."

"Why not?"

"It's private and it pertains to the fisherman. However, what I can tell you is that even after those chapters, things worked out for the angel in the end."

BOOK 4
THE INCREDIBLE JOURNEY

‡

*A*nother day passed as the group made their way through the countryside until they reached the coast. Before long, the small port town of Chioggia came into view. The group dismounted the old carriage and left it at a local inn. Piero made inquiries at the tavern about any ship that may have been moored there by order of the Marquis.

The pudgy barkeep scratched his beard for a moment before he responded, "Now that you mention it, an old ship bearing Mantua's coat of arms did enter the harbor earlier today. There are two men aboard, you'd best check in with them."

"Which dock?"

"Head south. It's the furthest dock down."

"Thank you."

The three friends left the tavern and followed the barkeep's advice. As they made their way down the piers, Piero was approached by two men in armor. The taller one spoke, "You are Francesco's party, yes?"

Antonio nodded, "Good day to you. I take it you were the ones sent here by the marquis?"

The first man stepped forward and brushed a strand of his straight hair out of his face, "Ensigns Anthony Costa and Nicoli Moretti at your service, sir. Our ship is at your disposal."

The second guard didn't bother to salute. He kept his back turned so all they could see was his curly black hair as he tended to some supplies, "Pleased to meet you both. If you'll excuse me, I still have duties to attend to."

Ensign Costa smiled, "Don't mind Nicoli, he's all about work. Come, we should head to our ship."

The soldiers led Piero's group outside to the docks where several ships were anchored. An uncountable number of masts touched the sky as they walked. The docks were crowded with ships, both large and small. Piero turned to Costa as they continued, "So how is this going to work exactly, Ensign Costa?"

"We weren't told. Our instructions are simply to take you to where ever you need to go. We were told that our mission is not complete until yours is. We are to return to Mantua only after you discharge us from service. It was a most unusual assignment."

Francesco smiled, "By any chance, did the Marquis tell you how long our mission might take?"

"He did not." Ensign Costa responded with a detectable amount of annoyance in his voice. "As I said before, we were told nothing. We are at your disposal if needed."

"Very well. I hope it won't come to anything unpleasant. Let's get going. The sooner we complete our mission, the sooner you can return to Mantua."

"That would be most agreeable, thanks."

The young soldier of Mantua guided the group to the southern docking area. There, they boarded a small flat-bottomed cargo ship moored at a pier off to the side. The vessel was an old hulk with a large mast in the center and a castle at each end.

The ship was large enough to accommodate a long voyage. Under the aft castle, a cabin had been installed with windows carved in either side. There was a large lateen sail tied to the yardarm that was tied up so the boat wouldn't move.

Piero scoffed as he looked the ship over, "Where did you find this old barge? This ship must be at least fifty years old, generously speaking. How is it even still in service?"

Moretti turned to him sternly, "The Ricci is a fine ship with a long record of service to Mantua. She was rebuilt several times so to be able to handle long sea-going voyages. It is not just some costal barge."

"Do not judge by appearance or height, so sayeth the Lord." Francesco said with a smile. "It matters not what is outside, but what is within is what matters."

Piero frowned, "If I have offended you, I apologize."

Ensign Costa nodded, "I have been serving on this ship since I joined the military. It is true that she could never be the pride of any fleet, but a workhorse is far more important than most any other ship."

"The Ricci looks like a fine vessel…" Antonio said being only half serious. "She should be enough to accommodate us on this voyage."

Piero noticed that the guards had been loading weapons, food, and supplied by the bag load on to the ship. "Why do we need all these supplies? Venice is a mere few hours of travel up the coast."

"If only our voyage were that short." Francesco replied. "Captain Gonzaga spoke of a distant journey that took the people he followed to Crete."

Ensign Costa chimed in after Francesco, "If serving on the Ricci has taught me anything, it's to be prepared for any contingency. It's a philosophy that has served me very well over the years."

The group boarded the ship and settled in for the cruise. Piero and Antonio made themselves useful and helped load the last of the bags into the hold. The ship looked like it was weighed down by all of the supplies.

When everything was finally in order, Costa turned to his fellow crewman, "Moretti cast off."

As Moretti followed his orders, Costa turned to the two soldiers of Florence, "Piero and Antonio, yes?"

They both nodded as Costa looked them over, "Are you two aware that there is a price on your heads back in Florence?"

Piero rolled his eyes, "Yeah that sounds about right. We abandoned our posts to make this journey."

"You're deserters?" Ensign Costa asked in a shocked tone.

"Yes." Antonio replied. "Our captain was being unfair to someone who had given his entire life to serve Florence. All he wanted was to find his wife, but the captain refused."

"So you just left… There is no honor in deserting your post, especially when your country is in the middle of a war!"

"I swore an oath to Florence," Piero admitted, "but more importantly, I took an oath of honor and chivalry. I rescued my wife from death and vowed to protect her forever. I take that oath as seriously as the one I took to Florence."

The expression on Ensign Costa's face changed from scorn to sympathy, "Damned either way… I pray I'm never confronted with such a choice."

The three soldiers stood in a circle staring at each other for a few moments until Costa broke the silence, "Do you two have any experience sailing a ship?"

Piero nodded, "We may just be simple everyday grunts, but we've been on enough ships to know how they work."

"Good… on the rigging, both of you. Set the sail."

The two men promptly ran to the mast and began untying ropes. Moretti ran along the port side of the ship and released the remaining mooring lines. Francesco listened to the sounds of the men running over the wooden surface.

Within minutes, the sail came down and the boat glided forward as it made its way away from the pier. Costa took the helm while Moretti turned and took over tending to the sail. Having nothing else to do, Piero turned to Antonio, "Why don't you man the forecastle and keep a lookout?"

"Yes sir."

As Antonio headed to his post, Piero turned to the small makeshift table on the port side of the deck. It appeared to have been fashioned out of a barrel and old deck planks. It was no doubt installed for passengers. On either side of it were two chairs.

Francesco sat facing the bow, gazed out on the harbor as though he could see it passing them by. Piero walked over and sat down next to him as the ship exited the harbor, "I think it's time we talked."

Francesco raised his head so it appeared like he was looking at Piero, "All right, what do you wish to discuss?"

Piero watched Francesco's every move as he questioned him, "What does the Marquis know that we don't? Who are the Patrisis, what information do they have, and what is their significance? Do they have something to do with incident that took place in Rome so many years ago?"

"That's a lot of questions... I wish I could tell you definitively. All I know is that they defied the church, went on a mission to defeat a rogue angel, and somehow lived to tell the tale. The boy, Giovanni was present at the basilica during the incident I told you about."

"So you believe they'll know of the passage into Hell?"

"That's certainly what I'm hoping. If I'm wrong and they can't help us, all hope may be lost."

"Yeah about that." A voice chimed in from behind them.

Piero turned to see Antonio leave his post and walk towards them, "What is this little detail you neglected to tell me about Xaphine? Apparently she's some kind of agent of evil? When were you planning on filling me in on this?"

"It's not that simple… I didn't know until my home was destroyed. That's when she revealed herself as the demon Xaphan."

"Xaphan." Antonio scoffed. "I know the legend… Xaphan was a powerful demon and Lucifer's second in command. It orchestrated the initial attack on the Most High, but I thought that demon was male?"

"What we know about spirits is mostly based on conjecture and opinion." Francesco replied. "Solid facts are in short supply in these stories. Some say there are spirits that are male and female, others say they're androgynous. From what I have seen, the former is correct. As for the legend you were told about Xaphan, who told it to you, an angel, a demon, or a man?"

"A man, I suppose."

"I would be careful how much stock you put into the words of men who have not seen with their own eyes."

"But isn't that contradictory. Doesn't the good book tell us that blessed are those who have not seen, but still believe?"

"It does indeed, and it is important to believe, but believing and understanding are two different things. We may believe in God, but I doubt there is a single person out there that can truly understand him. Those that claim to, speak of something they cannot possibly know."

"I see… - but Piero, if your wife is truly that ancient demon, how do you plan on convincing her to come with us?"

Piero couldn't answer that question, "I… I don't know… All I know is that I have to try or the price will be my own soul."

Piero struggled to find his words and chose to remain silent. Francesco decided to speak up for him to try to explain, "We may have an advantage. When Xaphan was disguised as a human, her memory was erased and she became Xaphine. Apparently, Lucifer did not have the power to fully restore her to her original form. As a result, part of Piero's wife still resides within Xaphan. The merging of their memories damaged Xaphan's persona. Xaphine now calls out from inside Xaphan's soul, causing an emotional conflict within her."

"But if that is the truth... then Xaphine was nothing more than a constructed consciousness, she wasn't real."

"I saw the look on Xaphan's face when she left. I loved her, and for the brief time we were together, we were both truly happy. I could care less how she was brought into this world, she's real enough to me, and I will do whatever it takes to free her from Lucifer's grip. So help me God."

He looked apologetically at Antonio, "You're right, I should have told you sooner. I will understand if you want off. We can leave you in Venice, but I am continuing on."

"Excuse me," Antonio said in a hurt voice, "I've followed you to hell before, figuratively of course. I'm staying on with you, where ever you go. The thought of Hell does not scare me anymore than any other insane mission you've led us on."

"Thank you my friend."

*

The Ricci sailed north for a few hours. Piero took the second watch on the forecastle. His eyes never left the coastline as they sailed through the Laguna Veneta. He stood alone and began to realize that he had spent too many years looking for a way to destroy the void in his heart.

Piero finally realized that he had wasted his time; death would not alleviate the pain. It would not return his love to his side. She was not of the Celestial World, so death held no promise of seeing her again.

Piero's heart ached with the realization that almost ten years had been squandered. Not wanting to think about it anymore, he turned his attention back to bow as the island city appeared on the horizon. Wished that he'd known about his wife's whereabouts sooner, his life may have been very different.

Antonio smiled as he came up behind Piero, "Venice at last."

Francesco turned to Ensign Costa, "Steer us a course northeast, look for a small fishing community surrounded by a rocky cliff."

"Understood, we know what to look for when we get there. Don't worry, we'll find the house you're looking for, this I promise you."

⊞

Ensign Costa was true to his word. Within minutes, the ship passed through a narrow rocky pass that brought them into a small community with several docks. Costa handed the helm over to Moretti and pointed at a small dock that was a ways off from the rest, "Take us in, we're docking there."

Piero narrowed his eyes, "How can you be so sure it's that one?"

"Admittedly, this isn't the first time we've made this voyage. The Patrisis are old friends of the Marquis from long ago."

"One more mystery to unravel…"

As they approached the pier, Costa called out to Piero and Antonio, "Secure the rigging, bring up the sail, we don't want to approach too quickly."

The two soldiers did as they were told. Piero grabbed the rigging on one side of the mast while Antonio took the other and pulled. The sail pulled up until it was folded against the mast. Piero secured the rigging against the railing to keep it in place.

With no wind, the Ricci slowed as it approached the dock. Piero jumped overboard on to the pier as Ensign Costa threw him the mooring lines. He quickly tied the ship in place as it came to a stop.

Once the Ricci was secured, Moretti braced the helm and lowered the walkway for Francesco. Ensign Costa guided Francesco down to the pier where Piero was waiting for them, "Shall we?"

Francesco shook his head, "No, I think it would be best if you paid this visit alone."

"Why?"

"Xaphine is your wife. They may react more sympathetically to one caller as opposed to an armed party.

Don't worry we will be here keeping an eye on the ship if anything goes wrong."

"It's pretty quiet here. What could go wrong?"

"You never know."

"All right... well if you think it's best, I'll play it your way."

As he turned to head for the shore, Costa nodded to him and held up an arquebus, "I'll keep a lookout for trouble. The Patrisis know this ship, so I doubt that they were alarmed. Still I'll be ready for any trouble."

"We may need it. Venice isn't exactly on friendly terms with Florence anymore."

At the end of the dock was a two-level wood and stone house that was unusually large for a modest fishing family. He continued walking toward the shore when he noticed the front door of the house was opening. He made sure to keep his hands visible so that no one would mistake him for being armed.

A woman with short blonde hair appeared from behind the door and sat on a bench that was in front of the house. She was tending to a torn white cloth that looked like a sail. Her hands worked busily stitching the large rip in the fabric back together.

Piero approached slowly, not wanting to cause alarm. The woman quickly realized that an unknown vessel was docked at her pier and looked up at Piero. Her bright blue eyes stopped Piero in his tracks. They were identical to Xaphine's and even her skin was pale just like Xaphine's.

Piero was mystified by her appearance as it was extremely rare to see a blonde woman anywhere on the peninsula. He was reminded of the way he felt when he first saw Xaphine and remembered how outlandish she was. Who was this person and why did he get the same odd feeling around her?

DAMNATION

As Piero neared, she looked at him quizzically, "Good day to you stranger, may I be of assistance?"

Piero was caught off guard by the sound of her voice. Her accent was exactly the same as Xaphine's. Where ever she was from, he was certain Xaphine had come from the same place.

Piero was hesitant to respond, was this woman a demonic creature as well? She looked innocent enough, but he could not be certain. He had been fooled before. His thoughts were broken by her voice, "Are you okay, good sir? You look like you just saw a ghost."

"I may very well have, milady…"

The woman furrowed her brow in confusion, "What do you mean?"

"It's nothing, never mind… Please allow me to start over."

She smiled and laughed under her breath as Piero quickly straightened himself up, "Good day to you, milady. My name is Lieutenant Piero Lorenzi of the army of the Republic of Florence. I am looking for the Patrisi home."

The woman frowned, "The Florentine army… what are you doing all the way out here? Your people are in a lot of trouble. You do know that Venice is no longer your ally, correct? If you were to be discovered…"

"I know this," Piero replied, cutting her off, "but it's a risk I have to take. I need to find the Patrisi family."

"Well you're in luck, this is the Patrisi home. Though I regret you may have wasted your time. My husband and son are out fishing and will not return until tomorrow. My name is…"

Her words were interrupted by a flash of black smog which slowly dissipated until a dark figure was left standing in its place. The blonde woman stood up holding her cloth as the figure quickly took human form. Its features became more pronounced and wings appeared on its back.

DAMNATION

When the smog vanished, Piero recognized it, "Xaphine!"

His wife stood in front of them with an angered look on her face. She had not aged a day since he had last seen her, and much to Piero's delight, she still wore his necklace.

Xaphan ignored him and focused on the blonde woman, "Adalyn…"

The blonde woman stepped in front of Piero and confronted Xaphan. Her eyes glowed even more fiercely than they had when Piero first approached. She stared at Xaphan as she spoke, "Sister… it has been so long. I had feared the worst after you were expelled."

Xaphan opened her arms to allow Adalyn to inspect her, "Well now you can see plainly what I've become, what I had to do just to survive. Impressed?"

"Dear sister, no one forced this on you! You made your choice long ago."

"I fought for what was right and you know it! I was expelled for fighting tyranny! What you see here is what I had to do to survive!"

"I know, and that has always been your justification for what you've done. That is why I came to your aid when the choirs passed judgment on you. I agreed with your ideology, but your methods were unconscionable! I am sorry that I couldn't have done more, but they had already made up their minds. They were going to expel you no matter what I said."

"Very true, sister... and I heard they later removed you too. How far the mighty have fallen, you were their hero and look what happened."

"I committed a crime, I knew what the consequences were and I made my choices. When the Choirs finally realized that I was trying to protect the Celestial World, I was forgiven and rewarded."

"So I heard, but not before being beaten, tortured, and murdered from what I understand. "

A feeling of nausea came over Xaphan as she inspected her sister, "This is what you've claimed as your reward? After everything you went through, you chose a human existence... no wings and no immortality. You chose to live the life of an insect... disgusting."

"You know nothing of these people. I was just as naive when I first came here. I hated them and fully expected to suffer and die in the most horrific manner possible. Don't forget what my job was. No one's biases were more reasonable than mine, but I learned so much in the time I spent here. My husband showed me the truth about humans!"

"Your husband... I can't stand to hear any more of this!" Xaphan shouted as a black sword appeared in her hand. "Your time here has clearly driven you mad. To think that you've consorted with them willingly..."

Then she looked at Piero. It was as though she hadn't even noticed that he was present. Her skin went even paler as she turned back to Adalyn, "I know more about these... insects than you think. You're not the only one who has lived amongst them."

She stepped closer to Adalyn with sword in hand. A look of confusion came over her face as she inspected Adalyn's eyes, "How is it you still bear the mark of divinity?"

Adalyn held her ground, undaunted by the winged creature approaching her, "The Lord Most High allowed me to keep it."

"The brightness in your eyes is a mark of honor for angels! It is no longer yours to claim!"

"Neither is it yours!" Adalyn hissed through a clenched jaw. "As I see you sold it in your mad quest for power!"

"I did what I had to... I always have..."

Adalyn's eyes narrowed as Xaphan continued, "I have come with orders from Lucifer, dear sister. You destroyed our best hope of liberating our brothers and sisters. For that, I will end you. Though I'm sure this will be merciful."

Adalyn pulled a tarnished looking sword from under the cloth, "Wings or no wings, I still know how to wield a sword. You shall find me difficult prey!"

"You never were very good on your feet. I hope you've improved."

"You'll just have to find out."

Adalyn stood up wielding her sword when she felt someone grab her arm. She turned to see Piero holding on to her tightly, "Why are you restraining me?"

Piero looked at her pleadingly, "Please don't hurt her."

"Piero..." Xaphan said softly, "why have you come here after all this time? I told you to get away. My master let you live once, I doubt he will do so twice if he discovers you meddling in his affairs!"

Adalyn looked oddly at the two of them, but when Xaphan charged at her, she decided it was best to ask questions later. Xaphan hissed as she lunged forward, "This is the end for you, sister!"

Adalyn pushed Piero away and dodged Xaphan's strike. She attempted to bring her sword down on Xaphan's head as she darted out of the way, but her attack was deflected. Using amazing agility, Adalyn cart wheeled backwards to increase their distance, but Xaphan would not allow her an advantage.

Xaphan jumped into the air and came down right behind Adalyn. The look on her face as she brought her sword around was one of sheer euphoria. She clearly enjoyed what she was doing. With every slash and twirl, the malicious smile on her face widened, "Just like old times, only now I have the advantage!"

Adalyn spun around and raised her sword in time for it to connect with Xaphan's, "You are a fool if you think that your wings are any advantage!"

Adalyn scraped her blade against Xaphan's before drawing it back and striking again. Their swords once again came together. There was a loud clank and a scraping sound as the two former allies stared each other down, "You gave up what made you whole."

Adalyn smiled as she stepped back, "I am whole. What I lost when I surrendered my wings, I more than got back when I was given this mortal heart. Feeling its beat means more to me than flight ever did, but clearly you wouldn't know what I'm talking about, would you?"

Adalyn beckoned to Xaphan's chest, "What happened to your heart, sister? No doubt you've sacrificed it for power."

Xaphan covered her chest with her free hand, "If only you knew..."

Adalyn's words only served to enrage her even further. She breathed heavily as she spoke through clenched teeth, "Don't you dare talk to me about heart... I have felt the sting of one. I know of its wickedness. I never want to feel that again."

Xaphan quickly pushed her sword to the side and threw a punch at Adalyn. Her fist connected with Adalyn's cheek, sending her stumbling backwards. Xaphan then took to the air, ready to deliver a death blow.

What Xaphan didn't know was that this was exactly what Adalyn wanted. As Xaphan plummeted towards her, Adalyn quickly spun around and kicked her arm hard. The impact forced the sword from Xaphan's hand which landed within arm's reach, but Adalyn would not give her a chance to grab it, "You really have lost sight of things, haven't you? You're pursuing a dream that can't be achieved through conquest."

Adalyn spun back the other way causing her heel to impact on Xaphan's chest. Xaphan fell on her back as wheezing as Adalyn stood over her. She pointed the tarnished blade at Xaphan's throat, "It's over sister. I'm sorry that you have fallen so far, but I fought too hard to save this world to allow you to continue your reign of terror."

Xaphan gasped for air and smiled as she closed her eyes, "It seems I underestimated you, dear sister. Even in human form, you are powerful."

Adalyn sneered as she held her blade to Xaphan's throat. To Xaphan's amazement, she recognized the stains on the blade, "The Eden Serpent... my pet..."

She then looked up at Adalyn with a malicious grin on her face, "Are you going to kill me Adalyn?"

"You were my sister... I don't want to do this... I don't, but after what you've become..."

"You have no choice. I won't stop as long as I live. I'll keep coming for you and the rest of this pathetic planet. You have to do it. Commit evil to prevent further evil."

Adalyn knew what she was saying. She'd fallen into Xaphan's trap, "I... I... have to..."

Piero ran up behind Adalyn, "No, please don't kill her, I'm begging you! I love her!"

Without thinking, Piero grabbed Adalyn's sword and attempted to get between them. The distraction was all the opportunity Xaphan needed. Before Piero could obstruct her view, she quickly grabbed her sword and plunged it into Adalyn's stomach, "Die!"

Adalyn's eyes opened wide. She was in so much pain that she couldn't scream. Before she fell, Adalyn turned her head to glare at her Xaphan. Tears formed in Piero's eyes, "No..."

Xaphan looked Adalyn in the eyes as she pulled the sword from Adalyn's stomach, "Farewell, my dear sister."

DAMNATION

Once the sword was out, Adalyn fell forward with blood spilling out of her wound. Piero caught her as she fell and rested her gently on the ground. He watched as her eyes closed and she stopped breathing.

Piero stood back up and turned to face Xaphan. He could feel his face heat up as his anger took over. The look he gave Xaphan made her chest ache so badly that she had to turn away to hide her pain, "Piero… it should be more than clear to you now. Go home; there is no way you can save me. Live out your life honorably and stop chasing this fantasy."

Seeing the commotion, Antonio, Francesco, and the two guards came running. Antonio had his sword ready and the two guards brandished arquebuses. They were ready to attack, though they weren't sure it would do any good.

Piero ignored them and charged at Xaphan. He grabbed Adalyn's sword off of the ground as he ran. Wind stung his eyes as he kept them open wide and fixed on his wife.

Xaphan saw him coming and deflected Piero's attack. She smiled as her eyes met his, "So you will fight me now?"

"I've wanted a rematch with you for years after last time."

Xaphan smiled, "So be it, though this 'sparring' match will be to the death. You better be ready!"

Piero darted backwards as Xaphan brought her sword around. He danced away and held his sword in a defensive manner. Xaphan's teeth were clenched as she struck at him relentlessly.

A few feet away, Costa raised his gun to open fire on Xaphan, but Antonio grabbed his arm and made him lower it, "Don't, Lt. Lorenzi knows what he's doing. You'll do more damage than good and I doubt you could hurt her."

Costa nodded as the fight continued. Xaphan's eyes darted back and forth as she fought. Clearly something was going on in her mind, but she didn't know what. With one massive swing, she sent Piero flying backwards.

Piero landed on his feet and charged in again. He struck a hard blow with his sword that made hers vibrate. Her feet dug into the ground as she pushed against his sword.

As the pressure on her arms from his strike died down, Xaphan knocked his sword away and attempted to slash at his face. Piero quickly countered by grabbing a dagger from his belt and deflecting the sword. They were standing so close that as Piero pushed the sword back, his dagger accidentally ran across Xaphan's cheek.

Feeling the edge of the blade pierce her skin, Xaphan immediately jumped back and felt her cheek. Blood dripped from it for a moment before it healed over, leaving only a small scar behind. She carefully inspected the blood on her finger for before licking it off, "I suppose I had this coming."

She smiled as she looked up at Piero and touched the scar on her cheek, "I don't even remember you being this aggressive when we shared a bed... too bad."

"Shut up." Piero replied angrily as he slowly pulled back.

Xaphan brought her sword around to deliver another blow, but before she could, a loud ringing entered her ears. She dropped her sword and clenched her head. Her eyes closed tight as though she were in pain. After a few moments, she shook her head and screamed, "Be silent, get out of my mind!"

At that moment, Xaphan's eyes opened and she regained control of her senses. She turned just in time to see Piero pointing his sword at her throat. She looked down at it and then back into his eyes. An intense look of anger filled his pupils as he stared back, "Don't move..."

Tears were forming in Xaphan's eyes as she faced Piero's angry stare. The part of her that still loved him never wanted to see him this angry. She flashed him an extremely hurt look as she spoke, "Can you do it? Will you really be able to succeed where Adalyn failed?"

Piero was panting as the heart in his chest became extremely tight. His hand began to shake as he held the blade to his beloved's throat. His eyes closed and he released a deep sigh as he lowered the blade.

Xaphan smiled, "I knew your heart wasn't in it! Unlike Adalyn, you lack the strength to make the hard choices. That is why you'll never be able to succeed."

"Xaphine... please hear me. I know that you're still in there! I love you!"

Xaphan smiled deviously and was about to taunt him, but something stopped her. For the first time in ten years, her chest began to burn and made it impossible for her to speak. *What is this?* She thought to herself. *Why does this human disturb me so?*

Instead of speaking, Xaphan simply flashed Piero an enraged look as her eyes began to blink between red and blue. The sympathy in his eyes melted away the hate and anger within her. She turned away, clasping one of the jewels on the necklace that Piero had given her.

The blue in Xaphan's eyes momentarily took over and she was able to speak, "I can't linger here. Lucifer will wonder what is taking so long. If he discovers that you've interfered, you will not be safe. This is the last time I'm going to warn you. There is no way you can save me. Go home, Piero, I am not the woman you married. That was a dream and nothing more."

"You said the same thing so many years ago. I didn't believe it then and I still don't. I do not believe you possess the strength to harm me and I think that frustrates you.

Come back to me my love. End the conflict within, it's not too late to come home."

A shocked look appeared on Xaphan's face as a tear fell down her cheek. She quickly wiped it away as she spoke, "Part of me thought about what might happen if we ever met again. I spent a long time weighing out the different possibilities and I wondered if you would still want me, knowing what I am and what I've done. I guess deep down a small part of me was hoping you'd say something like that. It makes the sting a little less painful."

Piero cautiously moved so he could see her face. She was struggling with her emotions as she tried to tell him off. Piero smiled, knowing that she could hear him, "I know you're still in there. Let me help you."

Xaphan wanted to get away. She'd had enough of this man's poisonous words. He was presuming a lot, and what was worse was that Xaphan wasn't certain that he was wrong about most of it. She closed her eyes and turned her head so he couldn't see her face, "Don't try to save me… please… just don't. It won't end well for you."

Without another word, she crossed her arms and vanished into a thick cloud of smoke. The sound of a low growl echoed through Piero's ears as she vanished. The cloud slowly dissipated until there was no evidence of her being there at all.

Piero lowered his eyes, "I have no other choice my love, because I do not believe that you are the evil that even you have convinced yourself of being. I saw what you were wearing around your neck…"

Piero turned his attention to the woman on the ground, no longer moving. Blood was beginning to pool around her gaping wound. He ran to her side as quickly as he could and was joined by the rest of the group.

DAMNATION

193

Antonio couldn't believe what he had just witnessed, "My God... I admit part of me didn't believe it at first, but she really was a demon."

"Shut up!" Piero yelled.

He dropped to his knees at Adalyn's side and placed a hand over her heart, "I am so sorry, milady! This is all my fault."

To everyone's shock, Adalyn was still alive. Piero was startled when she reached up and grabbed his hand. She coughed slightly and began breathing again, "No, it is not your fault, just give me a moment. Everything will be fine."

"Huh?" Piero said, surprised she could even speak.

"Trust me, just give me a moment, please."

Adalyn sucked down a deep breath and held it in her lungs as she focused her mind. She released it and took in another as she concentrated. To everyone's shock, the pool of blood began to recede and within moments, so did the blood on her clothing.

Once it disappeared, Piero inspected the hole in her dress. There was no wound, not even a scar. He backed away slightly, "What sort of magic is this?"

"Divine magic, you might call it." Adalyn replied as she sat up. "I was granted a human existence for my service to the Most High, and returned to Earth as a gift to my husband for the part he played in saving us all. I am mortal now, but only so much in that my life is finite."

"Wait... You mean to tell me that you were..."

"An angel." Francesco interrupted as he came up behind Piero. "Yes, Adalyn is the one we're looking for. She is the angel I told you about."

Adalyn's head jerked slightly as she heard Francesco speak, "I know your voice... from Rome, yes? You were one of the soldiers from so many years ago..."

"I remember yours as well. It has been some time, hasn't it?"

DAMNATION

"The years have not been too kind to you it would appear." She said, looking at his eyes.

She touched the scarring on his face and frowned, "I am so sorry."

"You of all people know that eyes are not everything. I may have lost my sight, but I can see more now than I ever did. Losing my eyesight gave me a whole new view of the world and a strange clarity. I can't explain it, but I am more capable now than I was with my eyes intact."

"I remember those days."

"I'm sorry to interrupt," Piero cut in, "but I need your help, milady. I need it desperately."

"Indeed you do, but there is no need to be so formal. As I was about to say before we were interrupted; my name is Adalyn Patrisi, you may address me as such."

"Thank you Adalyn. You honor me."

"Come. Let us go inside. I see we have much to discuss."

Piero nodded and turned to Antonio and the two guards, "Keep a lookout we don't need any more surprises."

The three of them nodded and left Adalyn's side. Antonio stood guard outside the door, Moretti returned to the ship, and Ensign Costa patrolled back and forth around the house. His hands shook with anticipation as he waited for something to appear.

Piero and Francesco went into the house and sat down at Adalyn's table. Piero watched her as she turned her back to them and tended to the nearby fireplace. His eyes never left her shoulder blades as she worked.

"They aren't there." Adalyn said as she worked.

Piero jumped when she spoke, "I'm sorry, what?"

Adalyn turned around to face him, "You weren't looking for my wings?"

"Well yes I was but…"

"As I told you outside, I'm human, as human as you or anyone else. My wings were taken from me when I was turned."

"Then how is it that you cannot die?"

"I claimed a lifetime with my husband as my reward for helping to stop Lucifer's wicked scheme. My heart is forever tied to his. As long as he lives, I will not die. That is the promise given to us by the Most High. Not even Lucifer himself could have harmed me."

Adalyn placed another piece of chopped wood on the flame and turned her attention back to the group, "There, now that the flame is taken care of, would you care to explain why you think that Xaphan, the general in command of Lucifer's legions, is your wife?"

"She is! Her name is Xaphine. I found her unconscious in a burning house near Florence. We spent over a year together until we were married."

Adalyn's eyes narrowed, unsure how to respond. She was clearly confused by what Piero was saying. Could this young man have lost his mind?

Francesco sensed her confusion and leaned towards her, "Allow me to explain."

"Yes," Adalyn replied, "please do…"

"Before the whole incident at the Basilica di Santa Maria Maggiore, I believe that Lucifer transformed Xaphan into a human and erased her memory. Why he did that is anyone's guess, but she spent years living a human life with Piero, hiding in Florence. Perhaps she was sent here for her own protection in case anything happened to Lucifer."

Adalyn listened intently as Francesco told Piero's story. The expression on her face became more and more filled with sadness as the story started to make sense. She was finally beginning to understand what was going on as Francesco spoke.

DAMNATION

"Either way, once Lucifer's plan failed, he called on his agent to return. However, he no longer possessed the power to restore her completely to her original form. Thus some part of Piero's wife still lives on in Xaphan. I don't know the full extent of the damage done to Xaphan's memory though."

"She did seem different. Something about the way she fought this time… it just wasn't her. I've always known her to be vicious and relentless. What I saw this time was hesitation. I should not have been able to disarm her as quickly as I did."

"You see?" Piero insisted. "She's still in there. We need your help, I need to find her."

"This is entirely my fault. Lucifer lost his power at my hand. I needed a weapon to defeat another angel and I turned it on him. I should have killed Lucifer when I had the chance, but I didn't have the strength to. Instead I left him to rot with his own kingdom serving as his prison. I should have known he'd have an ace up his sleeve."

Piero looked at her sympathetically, "I'm sure you had your reasons Adalyn. Had it been Xaphan, I would not want her becoming a murderer either. Killing Lucifer isn't the answer we were looking for. By then I already knew Xaphine. We're not here to place blame…"

"No… What you are here for is far more concerning. You're planning an incursion into Hell to recover your wife, and you're hoping that I can help you find a way in."

"And perhaps provide whatever tools we would need to fight when we arrive."

"No, I am truly sorry, but I cannot give you that information. The Netherworld is pure evil. Lucifer's minions will not attack you with mortal weapons. Instead, they will go after your mind. The hallucinations and the demons will poison your thoughts until there is nothing left. They have set up several defense mechanisms to drive invaders insane. When that happens, when you lose all hope, and all you care for has been turned against you, that is when you begin to turn. Lucifer will bend and twist your mind to his will and once he is finished, you will join your wife as a slave to Lucifer's lust for power."

Tears formed in Adalyn's eyes. Her words pained her as she knew the feeling of missing a loved one, "I'm sorry, but I cannot allow that to happen to anyone again. I won't…"

A panicked look came over Piero's face. He didn't expect Adalyn to refuse to help him. He understood why she was hesitant, but one way or another, they would need to get the information from her. "Come with us then." Piero insisted. "Be our guide and help us save my wife… your sister. With you at our side, knowing what to watch out for, we would not fail."

Adalyn stood up from the table whipping the tears from her eyes, "I'm sorry… this adventure is not mine. My story is complete. Besides, I will do you no good there. Much has changed since last I entered the gates of Hell. I am human now, which means I am as susceptible to the trappings of Lucifer's demons as you are. Because I have so much to lose now, I would more than likely be deceived and lead you down a false path."

"Please Adalyn, I love her more than anything. I care not what happens to me or my soul. She is everything to me and I must save her."

"I understand that, but I knew General Xaphan for eons before you were even born… I fear what you're hoping for may be lost forever. She is headstrong, combative, and single-minded. Turning her away from her goal is near impossible."

"That sounds exactly like the woman I married! She was also very opinionated, but if she can't be brought back… then I should be the one to end her suffering. Either way, I must find that out for myself if I am to go on living. I can't let her suffer."

"Such noble words," Adalyn said, closing her eyes, "but what of your companions? Are you willing to sacrifice their lives too?"

"Actually…" Francesco cut in, "Piero had offered us ways out in the past, and I'm sure he will offer us many more before this adventure reaches its conclusion. We are aware of the risks, but we have each chosen to continue."

Adalyn looked down at the table. For several minutes, she didn't move. Clearly she was locked deep in thought. Should she give them the information that they so desperately needed? Did they really even stand a chance of surviving? What would become of Piero if she forced him to give up? Either way, her decision would weigh heavily on her soul.

Unable to reconcile the questions in her mind, Adalyn finally gave up, "I should refuse your request. Every fiber of my existence tells me that you will not return from the journey you are about to embark upon, but I remember someone who is now dear to me, who was willing to recklessly go against even greater odds to rescue me."

Adalyn turned back to them with a lump in her throat, "You'll want to sail to Crete. Get your bearings there and then sail directly north into the dead waters. On the sixth hour of Friday as the sunset paints the clouds a crimson red, the terrible maelstrom Charybdis will appear. Focus your mind, it will not appear unless you are looking for it. When it does, you must sail into it, the abyss is your entry way into the Netherworld."

"We are to sail into a maelstrom?" Piero blurted out so loud that he was almost screaming. "That would certainly kill us. There must be another way."

"No. Charybdis is not what you need to worry about. Heed my warning, there are horrors awaiting you that have the power to rip your soul from your body."

She sat in front of Piero and looked deep into his eyes, "Remember this well, those that have the most to lose are the most vulnerable in the Netherworld. Close off your mind and shut down your emotions. Do not let anything distract you. Keep your focus on your goal no matter what you see, and make sure you have a florin on you for the boatman. Finally, when you arrive in Lucifer's kingdom, stay away from the tunnel to the east. I pray that this advice will be enough to save you."

"Thank you, Adalyn. I know that telling us this must not have been easy."

Adalyn looked away, "You should know that I loved Xaphan very much. We were very close before the war. Both of us were duty angels who spent little time in the Celestial Temple. I sincerely hope you are right about her. If she can be saved, I will be the first to celebrate."

⊞

The group spent the next hour making their ship ready. Adalyn gave them what supplies she had available, but mostly it was just some salted fish that she had kept in storage. She felt bad, not having anything else that could help them, until she remember something. She called back to Piero turned and disappeared into her house, "I'll be right back!"

Francesco was napping in the cabin while the four men on deck got the ship ready to go. Once they were fully stocked and everything was set, Costa turned to Piero, "Prepare to cast off, Lieutenant."

Piero nodded and was about to untie the ship when he felt a hand on his shoulder, "Piero, wait."

He quickly turned to see Adalyn standing behind him with a blanket in hand. She held it out to him, "Please take these, you'll need them."

Piero opened the blanket to reveal two swords like the one she had used against Xaphan. The blades were tarnished and looked like they had been poorly maintained. There were large patches on the blades that were almost as dark as Xaphan's hair.

Piero shook his head, "Thank you, but we aren't short on weapons."

"These are no ordinary weapons! The black stains on the blades are not tarnishing. These swords are coated with the venom of the Eden serpent. They can rip the immortality from any celestial creature. If you truly hope to survive, you will need these. Please take them with you."

"Thank you, I'll make sure that they get put to good use."

"These swords kept us safe. Take care of them… and if you survive, if at all possible, see to it that they find their way home."

"I will, I promise you."

Adalyn reached into the pocket on her dress, "One last thing…"

She pulled out a white feather that was so bright, it looked like it was glowing. She looked at it for a moment and handed it to Piero. His fingers curled gently around it. An electrified sensation passed through his fingers as they grasped the feather. He held it in front of his face and looked at it strangely, "What is this?"

Adalyn looked at it solemnly, "When I was an angel, my job was to act as a guiding light for damned souls. My wing shed this feather when I was hiding here. It is now the only feather that still exists from my wings. If Xaphan won't listen to reason, give this to her… it should remind her of what she lost and hopefully guide her back to the light. If your wife truly still lives in her, then this may be your only hope."

Piero twirled the feather around in his hand for a moment before looking back at Adalyn. She smiled at him as she spoke, "Good luck. I truly hope you succeed. I will pray for it."

Adalyn smiled, leaned in and kissed Piero on the cheek, "For whatever it may be worth… I love Xaphan too. Despite everything that's happened to her, she's still my sister. In another time and another place, I would have consented to go with you, but my place is with the person who risked everything to save me. He sacrificed his entire life to come after me without being asked to. I gave him my heart and my life, and I have no business risking either now. This adventure is not my own and my presence would not be any guarantee of success."

"I understand. Farewell Adalyn."

Adalyn backed away as he turned away from her, casted off the lines, and quickly boarded the ship. Antonio and Moretti used long planks to push the Ricci away from the dock. Once they had turned her in the right direction, Moretti set the sail. The Ricci began to move on her own as the wind caught the sail.

As the ship pulled out of the harbor, Piero turned to see Adalyn still standing on the dock as it slowly shrank away. Adalyn reached down her dress and clasped a golden crucifix that her husband had given her, "My lord Most High, protect them on their voyage. Their cause is just, and their desire pure. Please, help them find their way home."

**

Piero still wished that Adalyn would have come with them, but he understood her reasoning. She had a family and someone who loved her. It would have been selfish to expect her to leave her home and risk her life on a fool's hope.

Things ended so well for her, Piero thought to himself, *I wonder what the future holds for me... for us...* He began to wonder if her husband began to question whether or not their mission would succeed at some point.

His thoughts were interrupted by Ensign Costa, "Pardon the intrusion."

"What is it Ensign?"

"We're out of the harbor and in open water. Where are we heading?"

Piero turned back to the railing and sighed, "I think it's time we told you exactly what is happening here. You deserve to know... have Moretti join us."

Costa nodded and turned to his partner, "Ensign Moretti, join us on the main deck, please."

"Antonio," Piero called out, "please take the tiller."

Antonio nodded and headed to the aft castle, "No problem."

He climbed up to the aft deck and took the tiller so Moretti could join the other two on the main deck. Piero sat down at the table where Francesco was again meditating and

DAMNATION

looked at the two men as he spoke, "As no doubt you both have figured out, our voyage is anything but a normal errand."

"Tell me about it." Costa chuckled sarcastically. "Between cryptic orders, dark angels, and people who cannot be killed, I think we'd best find out what is going on here before we agree to go any further."

Piero nodded, "My wife was revealed to be the dark angel you saw. She is a slave to Lucifer's will, whether she realizes it or not. I plan to take this ship to the underworld and brave any horror to save her. That is our mission."

Moretti's eyes widened, "You're taking us against the devil himself?"

"Yes…"

"I can't believe this…" Costa shouted. "Did the Marquis know about this?"

Francesco spoke without opening his eyes or looking at the young ensign, "Yes."

Moretti put his face in his hands, "We're doomed…"

"Do we have a plan for when we arrive?" Costa asked.

"Adalyn told us what to look out for." Piero replied. "It's my hope that we'll be able to find my wife quickly. If I can convince her to come with us, our chances of getting out again should greatly improve."

"And if not, we're stuck." Costa shot back.

"If not, we may not live long enough to be stuck."

"How comforting."

Moretti stood off to the side with his eyes fixated on the ocean. He was clearly frightened though he would not say anything. He had to resist the urge to jump over the side.

Costa looked over at him for a moment and then back at Piero, "How are we going to get there exactly?"

"Charybdis. We're sailing for the maelstrom, which is located north of Crete. Charybdis is apparently a gateway to the underworld. It's our only chance."

Now even Costa looked unnerved. Piero's eyes darted back and forth between the two guards, "I know neither of you asked for this assignment. If you don't wish to partake, you don't have to. I can let you off when we reach Crete. I only ask that you leave the Ricci in our hands."

Moretti gripped the deck tightly for a few moments, "I… I need to think about this. Unlike the rest of you, I do have brothers and sisters that are waiting for me to come home. I know the dangers of battle, but this seems like almost certain doom. I will see you to Crete, but after that… I just don't know."

"No one here will blame you for leaving if that is what you decide. I understand something like this is a lot to ask."

Moretti turned away as Piero looked at Ensign Costa, "What do you say?"

"I consider myself a loyal soldier of Mantua. Our country made a mistake and lost a lot of honor during the war. If I can restore even a little of what was lost, then of course I'm in. The Marquis ordered it, so I will remain at your side until this task is done."

Behind him Moretti's heart froze as he heard Costa's words and he repeated them softly, "The honor of Mantua… of our people…"

Piero nodded, "Thank you both, I appreciate your help. If you change your mind, you have until we reach Crete to get off."

"Understood sir." Ensign Costa replied. "What course do we set?"

Piero looked out on the ocean and thought for a moment before giving him an answer, "Steer the Ricci to a course south-southeast. Make for Crete."

"Yes sir, right away."

As it began to get dark, the crew lit the lamp lights across the ship. Francesco continued to meditate at the table while Antonio took the cabin and Moretti slept in the cargo hold. Ensign Costa stayed on the tiller and kept his ship sailing straight. Piero had not left the forecastle in hours. He continued to stare out on the ocean until he heard a stirring behind him, "Penny for your thoughts?"

Startled, he turned in the direction the voice came from and almost collapsed. Standing there on the deck in front of him was Xaphine. His heart seized up as his breathing increased, "Xaphine! My love, how...?"

"Shh..." She said placing a finger on his lips while looking behind her. "Don't be so loud! No one else can see me and I'm not supposed to be here. Don't waste what little time I have."

"A hallucination? You're just a figment of my imagination..."

"No, not really, think of me more as the embodiment of the part of her that was locked away in the darkest recesses of Xaphan's soul, the part that managed to escape its confines when Xaphan saw you again."

"But how are you able to appear before me now? How is it possible for you to escape Xaphan?"

"Because for first time, Xaphan has been weakened to the point where she has lost the ability to silence me. Angels' minds are more powerful than humans'. We can project ourselves when we need to. She can no longer keep me leashed."

"So Xaphan is projecting you to me... why? Is she trying to torture me or goad me into doing something?"

"No, I don't even think that she knows she's doing it. If she does, then she's lost the ability to stop me. Either way, this is not something that she'd do intentionally. She's extremely conflicted after seeing you again. Her mind and heart are pulling her in multiple directions at once."

"I don't understand..."

"I didn't think you would and it's not important for you to. It is rather complicated. All I can tell you is that you were right when you said that I still dwell within Xaphan's heart. However, up until now, she has been able to shut me out and silence me. Her encounter with you broke down the mental walls that she worked so hard to build. I'd been fighting for years to break loose. I hoped beyond hope that I would find a way to reach you and make sure that you were okay. Your words weakened them enough for me to break through. She was not expecting to see you there when Lucifer sent her to assassinate Adalyn. It caught her completely off guard. It's why she beat such a hasty retreat."

"I was wondering about that, why is Lucifer so bent on destroying Adalyn that he would risk sending his most powerful minion? What did she do to him that was so bad?"

Xaphine frown as breathed in deeply, preparing to tell the story, "Revenge... Long before humanity was ever even conceived, war broke out in the Celestial Realm. Xaphan was one of the first to be seduced by Lucifer's mission to free his brothers and sisters from an eternity of servitude. She was both a vicious commander and honorable warrior. Had she not joined him, there would have been no war."

"Angels are servants?"

"Slaves are more like it. That's the reason we rose up. We are not afforded the loving forgiveness humans are, nor do we get to reap the benefits of our labors. We forever toil and are granted no forgiveness or reward. Not even a choice in how to live."

She lowered her eyes as she continued, "The war lasted eons until the tide was turned by a small group of angels which included Adalyn. Thanks to a dishonorable surprise attack, Lucifer was forced to surrender and then exiled. He has been fixated on revenge ever since. He managed to corrupt Saint Michael who then killed the angel Azrael, and then he focused on Adalyn. The problem was that Adalyn proved to be stronger than he anticipated... then

I anticipated. His mistake almost cost him everything. Adalyn was able to kill Michael and strip Lucifer of his powers."

Xaphine clenched her fists, "Lucifer has all but forgotten about the other angels and focused on her. As far as he was concerned, killing Adalyn took priority. Now he thinks she's dead, so he'll be ready to make his move to attack the Most High again, but I fear that he is still more bent on revenge than saving our people."

"What is his plan?"

"I... I don't know... I can't see all of Xaphan's thoughts. I was too busy fighting to escape and trying to reach you."

Xaphine suddenly turned around and looked behind her as though someone were coming, "Piero, I have to go... I can't risk being discovered. Look, I know I can't talk you out of this... Xaphan already failed to... Just remember, you are right about me. I'm here, I'm waiting for you... and my heart still belongs to you... it always has."

A desperate look came over Piero's face, "Xaphine no wait! Don't go..."

In a flash of light, she disappeared. Piero stared at the empty spot where she had been standing. His heart felt like it was about to beat through his chest, "I love you too."

Piero didn't really know how to piece together what he'd seen. He wanted to believe that it was her, but he had to be prepared for the fact that it might be a trick. There was nothing he could do about it at that moment, so he walked away from the forecastle and sat near one of the lamps where the crew was working.

Francesco was still meditating at the table nearby. He heard Piero walk down and immediately came to life, "Did you have a pleasant conversation with your wife?"

"How..."

"Have you forgotten? I have the abilities of a seer. I can sense things other people cannot. When she appeared on deck, her aura was like a massive signal fire."

"Oh yes, I'd forgotten." Piero said, realizing who he was talking to. "So I'm not going crazy."

"No, you're not." Francesco replied in a comforting tone. "I think part of Xaphan wants to be found. Xaphan's mind has been divided since the day she was restored to her original form. It would appear that she has been teetering between the darkness and the light for a long time now. The addition of your wife's memories just made everything worse."

Piero noticed a worried look on Francesco's face, "What is it?"

"Pardon?"

"Something is troubling you. I don't have to be a seer to know that."

"Indeed, you are correct. Piero, I have never been one to believe in mere coincidence. Is it not suspicious that Xaphan suddenly appeared when we arrived at the Patrisi home? Are we really to believe that we just happened to be there at the right time?"

"I hadn't thought of that. Why would Lucifer wait until now to send his minions against Adalyn?"

"Maybe he wanted us to see it? Or... maybe he didn't know where she was until just then."

"You think he's watching us?"

"Possibly. Or there is a spy in our ranks."

"But who... Who could it be?"

"I do not know. I'd hate to accuse anyone. We've got good people here. For now, we'll need to keep our eyes open and remain vigilant."

Antonio had been roused by the voices on deck and joined them at the table, "Hello, I hope I'm not disturbing you."

Piero looked up as Antonio approached, "Not at all, sit down."

Antonio nodded and sat next to Francesco, "Xaphine… You know, I'm still having a hard time coming to terms with this. She was always a little unusual and she stood out like a sore thumb, but she was the nicest person anyone could ever hope to meet. I was happy for you when you took her as your wife. Everything seemed to brighten up for you on that day. Now…"

"No one is more shocked about this than I am, I assure you. I always thought it was weird that she never remembered anything from before I rescued her, but seeing the explosion of the house I found her in, I didn't question it. I thought that she was just lucky to be alive. In hindsight, maybe I should have questioned it."

"Even if you had, what conclusion would you have come up with? Do you really think that you had the foresight to see that she was some form of demonic entity?"

"Perhaps not…"

Francesco smiled, "Piero, you've been burning the candle at both ends for days now. Take the bunk in the cabin and get some rest. At least now you know that she is still alive, so hopefully you can actually sleep!"

"Most kind…" Piero replied through a yawn. "I will see you both in the morning."

Piero got up and opened the door to the aft cabin. He stepped inside to see a small, barely furnished room with a single bunk and a navigator's table with an aging map on it. He let out a deep sigh as he stepped inside and lay down on the bed. He was used to such accommodations and worse on the battlefield, but he had hoped the bunk would at least have some form of padding.

Once the door was closed behind Piero, Antonio turned back to Francesco, "He seems to have been worn very thin lately."

DAMNATION

"You would be too. His wife is trapped in the body of a demon in the underworld. She has been for a long time."

"Do you think we have any chance of success?"

"Perhaps only a fools chance... still... The future is always impossible to predict, and there are always several outcomes. I can see each of them, but can't always tell which one will win in the end. Are there outcomes where we make it out alive? Absolutely, but they are numbered and I sense great pain in many of them."

A nervous look came over Antonio, "What about me? Can you see my future?"

"No... That is the unusual thing; I have not been able to read you since the day we met."

"What do you think that means?"

"I cannot say," Francesco said quietly, "it may be significant, then again it may not be. I simply do not know at this time."

"Well, I guess we'll find out sooner or later."

"Yes... You're probably right. It may just take some time."

IV

The ship sailed on for four more days. Costa took note of their hold and reported that they were running low on supplies. Fortunately, they were only another day's sail from Crete. It was a relief to everyone onboard when the large island finally came into view.

Piero marveled at the massive fortress at the harbor entrance. Antonio smiled, "The fortress of Rocca Al Mare… protecting the city of Heraklion. I'd challenge any pirate or navy to try to take that thing down."

"It is perhaps one of the last bastions of peace in the region, untouched by the ongoing war and strife."

They brought their ship into the dock and lowered the ramp. The dock master came out to meet them as they stepped off of the ship, "Welcome to Heraklion… it'll be two ducats to tie up a ship of that size here."

Piero nodded and dug the coins out of his pocket, "Here you go."

The master quickly inspected the coins before pocketing them and nodding, "Enjoy your stay."

Without another word, the dock master turned and headed back to his office. Piero shook his head as he went to work tying up the ship. *In Rome, we would have had at least three guards out here questioning us.*

The group separated and moved into the city once Piero finished securing the mooring lines. Antonio went with the guards to buy supplies while Piero and Francesco went to the local church to pray for a good journey. They moved down the streets, passing the various people in the marketplace.

Piero watched as the local citizens ran every which way and thought back to when Florence was like this. *Before the war, Florence was a massive center of this kind of activity. We had merchants selling their wares, shoppers haggling over prices, visiting caravans with new and exotic items... Then when everyone was done shopping, there was always a celebration to end the day. Now the marketplace is little more than flaming rubble and the people who used to go there had either been pressed into the military, deserted, or dead.*

At the end of the road, Piero and Francesco could see the church with its large wooden doors wide opened. As they were about to go inside, Piero saw a man studying at the doorstep wearing white robes. Francesco was fatigued from all the walking, and instead of going inside, sat down for a moment.

The young man staring into his book was very thin with scraggly brown hair. Meals were obviously few and far in between for this man, given how thin he was. Francesco faced the man with an odd expression on his face as though he recognized the man from somewhere.

The young man became aware of Francesco's look, "May I be of assistance to you, sir?"

Francesco shook his head, "I was just wondering what you are reading so intently there?"

A bewildered look came over the young man, "Pardon my bluntness, but how did you know I was reading, sir? Aren't you blind?"

"Yes... but I could hear you muttering the words, I smelled the paper, and heard you turning pages. If I'm not wrong, that's a Book of Hours, is it not?"

"Yes it is, actually. I am just studying for my vows before I enter the priesthood."

"The priesthood, you say?"

"Yes. Under the Monsignor's tutelage, I am hoping to be admitted to the clergy very soon. I've been studying for years..."

"Really? What exactly made you decide to join the church?"

The man looked up at the clouds, "I'll never forget it... that day so many years ago, when such a blessed spirit appeared to me."

"What was that?" Francesco asked as his ears perked up. "Who appeared to you?"

The man chuckled, "Oh what does it matter, forgive me for rambling. I fear I have taken up too much of your time."

He quickly got up and bowed, "Peace be with you sir, farewell."

Francesco nodded as the man turned away. Piero looked at Francesco oddly, "What was that about."

"Something about that boy seemed odd. It was almost as though he had an aura coming off of him, like a divine creature had touched his soul. I think the last people to visit the underworld came this way... I would bet my ears on it."

Francesco could tell from Piero's breathing that he was worrying him. He quickly shook it off, "Sorry, it was probably nothing."

Piero nodded as Francesco stood up, "We should probably be getting back, Antonio and the others probably have everything we need now."

"But what about praying for a safe voyage at the church?"

"Where we're going? That's a good one."

Francesco chuckled at the thought as he brushed himself off as they made their way back down to the docks. Piero looked off to one side of the road. Between a pair of stands, separating the buildings they leaned on was a small dark alley that was barely wide enough for one person. He stared at it for a moment, "Francesco..."

"Yes?" Francesco replied as he turned in the direction Piero's voice had come from. "What is it?"

Something about this alley called to him, "I think you were right."

"What about?"

"I think our friends were here. I can't explain it, but I feel drawn to this place, almost as though it had some significance."

Francesco smiled, "Humans have an impact on the world around them whether they realize it or not. Even the most insignificant actions can leave an imprint."

"I think I finally understand the significance of that."

Francesco continued walking and led Piero back toward the docks, "Good, then you're learning."

The two returned to the *Ricci* in time to help their friends load their new supplies into the cargo hold. It took some time as they were practically overloading the boat with food, extra rigging, and rope. It was hard work and there was a lot to carry, but the five of them managed to get everything onboard.

Ensign Costa was a cautious man and didn't want to be caught in the middle of nowhere without some essentials. Antonio smiled as they got the last of their supplied on board, "It looks like everything is set and we're ready to go."

"Not quite," Piero replied, "We still have one problem that needs to be resolved before we cast off."

Moretti sighed, "I guess you're talking about me, right?"

"This is your last chance to get off if you don't want to go."

Moretti twisted his lips, "Anthony, did you mean what you said? Do you truly believe that we can restore the honor of Mantua?"

"I do." Ensign Costa replied adamantly. "If there is to be a mighty battle against the devil himself, I want the history books to read that at least one soldier of Mantua was there to fight it."

DAMNATION

"Then I'm staying aboard as well. I will fight for the honor of Mantua… for our people."

Ensign Costa nodded in approval, "Very good, for our people. Let's cast off, the less time we spend sitting idle by the better."

Piero cut the mooring lines and ran aboard as Ensigns Moretti and Costa pulled back the ramp. Piero helped Antonio push away from the dock with the long planks. The ship was large and hard for two people to build up the inertia, but they eventually succeeded.

With the boat sufficiently away, Piero ran to the rigging and brought the sail down. The gigantic sail dropped open and immediately caught the wind. The ship slowly began to pick up speed as the sail extended. Piero and Antonio pulled on the lines until the ship was at full sail and pulling out of the harbor.

With the Ricci now underway, Piero stood on the aft castle deck with the senior Mantua soldier. Costa watched the ship slowly set out to sea, "What is our course?"

"Steer us directly north. Hold our course; we have to find the dead waters that Adalyn told us about.

"Do we have any idea what we are to expect when we reach the underworld?"

"Evil… Pure evil… that's all I know. I don't want to get myself all worked up with what-ifs and possiblys. It's very dangerous to get yourself worried about the unknown. In the end, it will only give our foes more tools to work with."

Ensign Costa was beginning to think this was a suicide mission, "So we're going in blind then? Very bold…"

"I don't think so. Adalyn told us to focus on our goal and let nothing sidetrack us. We'll need to dismiss anything we see there as illusion especially anything familiar to us. Apparently the underworld can use the things we treasure the most against us."

"Do you think we have any chance of success?" Ensign Costa asked. "This is the devil's second in command after all."

"If I didn't I wouldn't go at all, or at least I wouldn't take any of you with me." Piero said in as comforting a tone as he could muster. "We're not the first ones to travel to the world of the damned. The last group faced the devil and lived to tell the tale. I believe in us, and I think as long as we remain together, we shouldn't have a problem."

"You truly believe that sir?"

"I do. I am grateful for all the help you've give me. I doubt we've made it this far. I don't know if our mission will be successful, but I am going to do everything I can to get us out alive."

Ensign Costa looked slightly more comfortable now, "Then let us get underway."

V

Xaphan had returned to the underworld to inform Lucifer of her success. She eagerly entered the castle and stood before her old friend with a smile on her face, "I cut her down, my lord. Her blood now stains the stones for her… husband to find."

Lucifer looked up surprised, "She fell under your sword?"

"I watched the light disappear from her eyes as I pulled my sword from her stomach."

"I'd feel better if I could have seen it for myself, but since I can't… show me the sword. I want to see her blood."

The smile left Xaphan's face. *Does he no longer trust me?* Xaphan thought to herself as she summoned the blade.

Lucifer inspected the crimson stains on the dark sword and smiled, "Well done, General. At last that meddlesome girl is no more. Our information was dead on in this case!"

Lucifer looked back up at her, "You have performed adequately, well done."

Xaphan bowed graciously, "You honor me, old friend. Even in human form, Adalyn proved to be quite a dangerous opponent."

"Obviously she was no match for you." Lucifer said in an almost boastful manner. "She has fallen under your blade, as will the rest of the Most High's faithful soon enough!"

"What? Master, what do you mean? I thought our goal was to free them from the oppression of the Most High!"

"So they could attempt to usurp me? I think not… No, the Celestial Temple will be ours, and anyone who gets in our way will be crushed."

Xaphan closed her eyes, "I didn't follow you for this. War is one thing, but genocide… There is no in honor that. I would sooner have my wings burned away!"

"What would you prefer? The other angels are not going to join us, you know this! Our only choice is to destroy them before they can rise up in rebellion."

"What happened to you? You were never like this during the war. I remember the words you spoke and how you rallied so many of us to your side. You wanted to free our brothers and sisters, make them see the light, not turn them into an endangered race."

Lucifer lowered his eyes, "Times have changed. We have changed. I know your feelings, but I also know that if the other angels refuse to join us, even after being defeated, we will have no other choice. It's unrealistic to think that we can just let them go."

"And if they agree to join us or live peacefully?"

"Then they will be allowed to live, free of bondage."

Xaphan looked Lucifer in the eye to see if she could read what his intentions were. His eyes were dark, cold, and emotionless. He smiled as she looked at him, "So what is your plan then? Are you still my right hand or will you be joining the rabble outside?"

"I swore allegiance to you." She replied in a stern voice. "I have my honor and I take my oaths seriously. I am your friend and I will command your armies."

"Excellent." Lucifer said in a relieved tone. "Together you and I will achieve great things very soon, you'll see."

"I can't wait. We've been here far too long... I will see the Celestial Temple burn once more, as I promised I would."

Once Xaphan finished, Lucifer waved his hand, signaling that their meeting was over. Xaphan looked at him oddly before turning and leaving the chamber without another word. The doors open and she exited to the stone drawbridge.

The moment that she was outside, Xaphan spread her wings and flew to the tower where she frequently hid when she needed to be alone. She took off with a mighty thrust and circled the castle before landing on the balcony. The moment she touched down, she stormed inside and closed the window.

When Xaphan was certain that she was shrouded from prying eyes, she pressed her back against the nearest wall, released the air that was stretching her lungs, and sat down on the floor with tears in her eyes. Her whole body ached and she was having trouble breathing. Her eyes shifted from black back to their human blue every few moments.

What is wrong with me? She thought to herself. *This sort of thing never bothered me before. I was a feared general; I stood toe to toe with Saint Michael himself... I fought my brothers and sisters on the Celestial plains. Now I'm losing to humans and I get weaker every time I see... him. This can't be happening...*

Xaphan's thoughts then went to Lucifer and how the passage of time mixed with several debilitating defeats had twisted his mind and left him almost completely deranged. *He didn't even thank me for taking care of the loose end he had failed to. I killed one of my sisters, one I was very close to and he still questions my loyalty...*

Then the horrible truth finally hit her. *Is our cause lost? Could it be that what we're fighting for is no longer possible? Is there anyone besides myself who still believes in it?*

What have I done? She brought her knees up to her face as tears began to fall down her cheeks, "Piero... where are you? What have you done to me? I shouldn't feel like this..."

Xaphan stood up and turned to the window. She knew that this newfound clarity would only last a moment before the darkness regained control. She looked out over the kingdom that she had helped build as her pupils held their blue color for a few moments.

DAMNATION

Her eyes finally closed when she couldn't bear to look anymore, "Piero... Please hurry..."

BOOK 5
INTO THE BREACH

‡

It took the group another two days to reach the dead waters. The trip should not have taken as long as it did, but Francesco insisted that they only sail at half speed. He wanted to make sure that they'd reach the dead waters on Friday as they were supposed to.

On the evening that they arrived, as the sun began to set, the wind died and the Ricci ceased all movement. The water was eerily still and not even the sound of wind could be heard. The tension on deck was high as everyone kept a lookout for makings of a giant maelstrom.

After an hour of searching, Ensign Costa turned to Moretti, "It might not be a bad idea to secure the mast and tie up the sail."

"True, we don't want it coming down on us. Piero, Antonio, help me, we need to get this ship ready for whatever is about to come. I have a feeling that it's not going to be an easy ride."

Moretti climbed the mast and grabbed onto the yardarm, making sure everything was secure along the way. Antonio and Piero tugged on the lines to tie the sail up. Antonio turned to Francesco, "I don't understand this, what is so significant about this area that would cause such a massive whirlpool to appear?"

Francesco barely moved in response to Antonio's question. He was about to speak when Ensign Costa chimed in, "Sailors have often traded rumors of a land in this area that sank into the sea without any reason. It is said that they had riches and technology beyond the dreams of even the wealthiest emperor. Supposedly the whirlpool is an after effect of the island's destruction, but this is all myth and legend. Most people don't even believe that the island ever existed in the first place."

They finished securing the ship just as the sun touched the horizon and its light painted the clouds red. Everything was proceeding just as Adalyn said it would. There was a sudden loud boom followed by a flash of light from under the water.

Francesco heard it, stood up, and walked to the railing, as though he could see what was going on. He shuddered as a second thundering boom emanated from beneath the surface, "Oh my… everyone hold on, this is going to be bad! I can feel it…"

The world suddenly began to shake around them. The water became choppy as a circular current began to pull the ship to port. Everyone held on as the ship began to pick up speed.

Within moments, sea floor bottomed out, creating a massive whirlpool less than a mile in the path of the *Ricci*. The wind picked up, causing a typhoon around the small ship. Everyone had to block their eyes against the harsh wind.

Moretti screamed and pointed as the ship began to pick up speed, "Maelstrom!"

Piero held on to the mast as he watched the world begin to pass them by, "Charybdis… so it does exist."

The *Ricci* was quickly sucked into the spinning water and began to sail around in circles. Piero turned to Ensign Costa, "Try to keep her steady. Turn her into the current. We don't want the ship to capsize!"

Ensign Costa nodded and held tightly on to the tiller. As they began to circle the vortex, Francesco's head twitched and he began to breathe heavily, "They're coming…"

Piero looked at him oddly, "Who?"

He looked in the same direction Francesco was facing to see two wrecked hulls break through the surface of the spinning water. There was a blast of freezing cold water as another wreck came up right alongside the Ricci. Piero saw it coming and yelled to Ensign Costa, "Hard about, don't let them hit us!"

Ensign Costa pulled back hard on the tiller and brought the boat around. The wrecked hulk missed the *Ricci* by a few feet. The men watched the old hulk as it passed by.

"My God, look!" Antonio screamed.

Green apparitions appeared on the deck and began to run toward the side. The desperate looks on their faces made Piero's heart clench. Some of them screamed out for help, while others jumped overboard and landed on the deck of the *Ricci*.

Piero found himself face to face with one of the apparitions. The green mist took the form of a decaying sailor. It glared at him with fiery yellow eyes in boney sockets and it spoke to him in an inhuman growl, "Take us out of here, now!"

Piero shook his head and drew the sword that Adalyn had given him, "I'm sorry, I can't do that. There is no turning back from where we're going."

"Then we'll take your ship from you and get out ourselves!"

"Not going to happen, creature."

Two more spirits jumped over the side of their wrecked ship. Costa and Moretti did everything they could to defend the tiller while Antonio and Piero dealt with their attackers individually. They both wielded the swords that Adalyn had given them.

Piero screamed, "Leave us in peace foul creature! We can't help you!"

"Why do you desire entry into the Underworld? Torment is all that awaits you down there!"

"I know that, but someone is there waiting for rescue. I cannot abandon her to that awful place!"

DAMNATION

An ugly grimace appeared on the spirit's face, "Fine then, I have a much quicker way of getting you there!"

Piero ducked as the spirit swung its green blade inches away from his head. Piero began to tire of this fight. He had far more urgent matters to attend to and hadn't come this far to have his ship hijacked by a group of ghostly pirates.

Growing impatient, Piero attacked the spirit with a vicious barrage of sword strikes. He fought hard, relying on his military training, until the apparition was backed up against the railing. With a strong swing of his sword, Piero knocked the spirit off guard and punched it in the face. The ghostly figure fell over the side and into the water.

Piero watched it hit the waves and quickly turned to help Antonio. He was shocked when he realized that his friend was just standing there with his eyes locked on the apparition that attacked him. They both stood walking sideways in a circle, staring each other down for a few seconds.

Finally, the spirit's expression turned from malice to fear. Instead of turning in a circle, the spirit slowly began to back away. The moment it was close enough to the side, it jumped over the railing into the violent water below.

Piero watched as Antonio stood motionless for a few seconds. He seemed almost entranced as he stared off into the distance. Piero put his hand on his friend's shoulder, breaking him out of it, "Antonio?"

Antonio turned to him with a stone cold look on his face. Piero narrowed his eyes, concerned for his friend, "Are you okay?"

"Yes, I'm fine." Antonio replied as his eyes returned to normal. "Come on, we've got to help the guards!"

His words came too late. One of the spirits stabbed Moretti with a spectral sword. The young guard fell back against the railing, breathing heavily, and holding the wound.

DAMNATION

Ensign Costa was fighting alone now. He was unable to hang on to the tiller and defend himself at the same time. Determined to end the fight quickly, Costa released the tiller and spun around, slicing the spirit in half with his sword. It instantly disappeared.

Ensign Costa turned quickly to try to take control of the tiller, but the wooden bar, being pushed by the current, whirled around and smacked him in the chest. Costa was thrown overboard and disappeared into the abyss. Francesco, who had been holding on to the railing, tried to grab him, but missed his hand.

A look of sorrow came over Francesco's face as Costa plunged into the maelstrom. There was nothing Francesco could do and he knew it, "No…"

Piero and Antonio struggled to pull the tiller back to keep the ship straight, but it was no use. The ship spun out of control and eventually began listing to port. It continued to list until it was completely on its side, spinning quickly around the vortex.

Antonio was sucked into the current when the ship leaned to its side. Francesco held on for as long as he could, but eventually even he and Moretti's barely conscious body were swept overboard.

Piero held on tight to the mast as the ship plummeted downward into the abyss. He began to feel nauseated from all the spinning. The ship jerked suddenly, causing Piero to bang his head on the mast. The blow made him light-headed and slowly, his world began to fade into darkness.

ⵜ

Piero eventually awoke aboard the *Ricci* in very thick fog. He was soaked, but at least he was alive. As he got to his feet, he became extremely dizzy and had to grab on to the railing to keep from falling over again. He put a hand to his and felt the bump on the side of his forehead. It took a few moments, but Piero managed to center himself and clear his head.

Once his head was on straight, Piero looked around to see how badly the ship had been damaged. He was relieved to see that she had somehow righted herself and was still sea worthy. His relief last only a moment when he remembered that he was alone. Had any of his friends survived the trip?

One by one each of his companions had fallen overboard. Now he was alone in unknown waters. What could he do now? Piero wasn't a sailor and the *Ricci* was too big to be crewed by one man.

Desperate to find the rest of the group, Piero ran to port side of the ship and called out, "Hello, is anyone out there?"

No reply came and visibility was nil. He appeared to be in the middle of a swamp that was littered with broken trees. More alarming to him was the fact that his ship was moving, and he was unable to figure out why. There was no current that he could see and the sail wasn't down.

Piero ran to the starboard side and continued to call out as the minutes passed, "Hello, can anyone hear me? Is anyone else alive out there?"

To his relief, he got a response, "Piero, over here, throw me a line!"

Piero grabbed a broken line and looked in the direction of the voice, "Antonio, thank God you're alive, my friend."

Antonio was standing on a broken stump in the middle of the water. Piero threw the rope over the side and waited for Antonio to grab it. He then pulled Antonio back onboard.

The moment Antonio felt the deck under his feet, he breathed a sigh of relief, "Thank you, old friend… I was beginning to think that I was the only survivor."

Piero secured the line and turned to Antonio, "Where are the others, have you seen any of them?"

"I am sorry Piero. I saw them fall overboard, but I haven't seen any sign that they are still alive. I myself only woke up because I heard you calling me. A few minutes spinning around in the vortex made me woozy and caused me to black out."

"No… they can't be dead. Did I lead everyone to their own doom?"

"I don't think so. They all knew what they were getting into beforehand. No one followed you in blindly into this."

"Still… Costa, Moretti, and Francesco…"

"Piero as far as I can see, you have two choices; you can forget about this journey and turn back. In which case, if they are dead, then they died for nothing, or you can continue on and try to rescue your wife. So what will it be?"

Watching as the broken stumps go by, Piero shrugged, "It doesn't seem like we have much of a choice. We're being pulled somewhere…"

A shrill unearthly scream from behind interrupted their conversation. Antonio turned quickly in its direction, "Piero lookout!"

A small winged imp appeared out of the fog and flew over them. Piero dodged out of the way and drew his sword. The creature flew in low and reached out one gray claw.

Piero ducked away from its talons and slashed at the imp. The creature cried out as the sword severed its claw. Green blood poured out onto the deck as the imp slowly flew away.

DAMNATION

As it disappeared into the fog, two more imps attacked. Piero stood ready to strike when Antonio appeared behind him with two arquebuses in hand. He quickly dropped one on the deck while lighting the slow burning wick on the other. His uncanny speed paid off as he was able to aim the gun before the imp could get close.

As the creature got closer, Antonio pulled the trigger. The hammer came down on the small pan filled with gunpowder. The powder sparked and the gun went off.

Antonio's aim was perfect. The ball struck the demon on the right, causing it to fall from the sky with a high-pitched death cry. He quickly dropped the gun and picked up a second one that he had brought on deck as the second demon drew near.

Antonio didn't have a chance to aim this time. The second demon flew in, struck the young soldier, and knocked him off his feet. The arquebus went off as it hit the deck and was now useless.

Piero chased the creature and slashed at it before it could get away. His split second timing paid off and he successfully severed the demon's head. Its body hit the water, still squirming about for a few moments.

With the danger apparently gone, Piero turned back to Antonio as he was getting back on his feet, "Are you all right?

Antonio turned and stood up, extremely agitated, "I cannot believe I was caught off guard like that. I was trained to do better."

"It's okay. You did manage to defeat one of them beautifully."

"True… For unworldly creatures, I guess that will do."

The ship continued to move beyond the bog into open water. Piero and Antonio tried to search for their friends, calling out into the fog. They continued to search until their ship approached a black pier. The wood looked warped and moist.

Antonio shook his head, "I don't think this thing will hold us. It looks rotted through."

"I'm sure Adalyn would have warned us of this." Piero said calmly. "Come on, we need to get moving."

"I'll follow your lead I guess, but keep in mind, that was years ago. A lot can happen in that time. Just be careful, that's all I'm saying."

They lowered the ramp and got together a few supplies before they disembarked from the *Ricci*. Piero grabbed some water and the sword that Adalyn had given him. Antonio grabbed one of the arquebuses and followed close behind Piero.

They two stepped onto the gangway and looked at the pier below their feet. Piero stepped on to the old wood cautiously to see if the old planks would hold his weight. The deck groaned and the planks shifted under their weight, but it held. They walked slowly, fearing that the pier would give out on them. Piero inspected every plank he stepped on, being careful to avoid the ones that looked as though they had already collapsed.

The sound of feet pounding on the old wood, coming from further down the pear startled the two soldiers. Piero drew his sword and stood at the ready. He watched Antonio raise the arquebus that he had just finished reloading.

The noise grew louder as whatever it was drew closer. It got more and more intense until a man finally appeared out of the darkness. Piero lowered his sword when he saw who it was, "Ensign Costa, thank God you're okay!"

Antonio lowered the arquebus, "Did anyone else make it?"

"Francesco and I met up at the island ahead. I heard voices and came back to investigate. We were attacked by weird winged creatures that I've never seen before. Thankfully, we were able to fend them off."

Antonio smiled deviously, "Yeah, we killed a few of them ourselves."

Piero looked worried, "What about Ensign Moretti? Is there any sign that he made it?"

"I don't think he survived… I saw him get stabbed before the Ricci went down. He was thrown into the water like a rag doll."

"I'm sorry… were you to close?" Piero asked.

"Not personally, but he was a good soldier, one of the best I've served with."

A worried look appeared on Ensign Costa's face, "How's the ship?"

Piero nodded, "She's fine. I don't know how… but she managed to survive intact."

Suddenly a low moaning sound came from under the pier. Antonio raised his gun, "I think it's best if we get moving. Staying in one place like this probably isn't a good idea."

Piero nodded, "He's right, let's go."

The group cautiously made their way down to the end of the pier. Antonio took up the rear with his arquebus shouldered in case anything came after them. The wood planking let the group off on a small inlet surrounded by black water.

Francesco was there waiting for them, "Piero, Antonio, thank God you both survived. When I woke up here, I feared the worst."

"Likewise." Piero replied. "After we all got separated, I wasn't sure anyone survived. I didn't know what I was going to do."

Antonio walked past them to a small stand with an oddly shaped horn on it, "Now what do you suppose this thing is for?"

Piero looked at it and remembered something Adalyn had told him, "Oh my, I forgot. Everyone, make sure you have a florin on you for the boatman. We'll need it if we hope to proceed."

Antonio looked at him oddly, "What boatman, what are you talking about?"

"The boatman. There is only one way into the gates of the Netherworld. A boatman must take you across the river, but he expects payment. Adalyn told me he won't take living souls across without it."

Ensign Costa narrowed his eyes, "The boatman exists? But that is an old Greek legend from thousands of years ago."

"Adalyn told me it was true, and I believe her. Her advice has not steered us wrong yet and it's all we've got to go on."

Piero picked up the horn and blew into it. The blast from the horn broke the silence and shot through the air. Part of Piero's mind expected to see an army coming out of the fog in response to the signal horn. However, none came. Instead, the low sound of old creaking wood could be heard in the distance.

As the fog parted, a small black boat appeared and slowly moved toward them. It was a long narrow boat with a single lamp on the front and a cloaked driver aft. As it pulled up to the island, the boatman turned to them and reached out his hand.

Piero walked up first and placed a florin in it. He was shocked to see that the boatman's hand was little more than white bone. One by one, the rest of the group hesitantly followed Piero's lead until they were all onboard.

As Antonio handed the boatman his coin, the cloaked figure turned and looked at him. Though no one could see his face, there was an aura of surprise around the boatman as he watched Antonio. The young soldier stopped for a moment and returned his gaze, but finally continued on into the boat. The cloaked figure never took its gaze off of Antonio as he pushed away from the shore.

Piero's eyes darted back and forth between the two. *What could that possibly be about? First the ghost pirate and now the boatman...*

It took the boat some time to reach the other side. Piero was afraid to do anything during the trip. The boat looked like it could easily fall apart if they made one bad move. The wood was rotting and water filled the floor.

Piero's fears were alleviated when they reached the other side unscathed. As the rest of the group got off the boat, Piero turned to the boatman, "Can you tell us anything about what's ahead of us?"

When the boatman didn't respond, he pulled five florins out of his pocket. The boatman looked at the money and then back at Piero, "I'll of course, pay you for your trouble."

At first, Piero was still certain he wouldn't say anything, but to his surprise, the cloaked figure spoke. His voice was nothing more than a whisper that was barely audible over the breeze, "You are not spirits of the damned, nor are you demons. Why have you come here?"

"Adalyn sent us." Piero replied. "She told us this was the only way for living souls to enter the underworld."

"Adalyn..." The boatman repeated with what sounded like a hint of happiness. "So she survived... I had not received news of the outcome of her struggle. I am glad that she survived, but I never thought she'd be so reckless as to send mortals down here alone. This is no place for you."

"It was my choice. I begged her for the information. I've come to retrieve my wife from this awful place."

The boatman shook his head and pulled his oar out of the water, revealing it to be a sharp spear with a large head, "No spirit that has been judged and enters these gates is allowed to leave. I will not take a damned soul back across the river."

Piero shook his head, "But she's not a damned soul. She's…"

He closed his eyes, knowing that his answer was bound to provoke scorn, "She's Xaphan…"

Hearing that name made the boatman shudder, "What madness has struck you? You think that Xaphan, the dark angel general is your wife?"

"I don't have time to explain, but I need to know if we successfully save her, will your boat carry her back?"

The boatman lowered his head, "She is free to come and go as she pleases. She hardly needs my boat, but if you come back this way, yes I will take her across for you."

"Thank you." Piero said appreciatively. "Is there anything else you can tell us?"

"My task is simply to take souls across the river. All I can tell you is to keep your wits about you. If you see anyone you know in there, even if they truly dwell there, you must ignore them. Trying to help or save them will be futile and may cost you your soul. They would not be able to leave anyway. Keep your mission in your head and ignore all distractions."

"Thank you for your help."

As Piero was about to turn away, the boatman reached out to him, "One last thing."

"Yes?"

"Not everyone is what they appear to be. Watch your back or you may find a knife in it."

"What do you mean?"

The boatman looked back out on the lake nervously, "My time grows short. That is all I can say to you. I wish you luck. Farewell."

Piero watched as he piloted his boat back into the fog. It seemed as though the boatman was getting weaker as he disappeared into the fog. He leaned on his paddle for support as the boat disappeared.

Piero turned to join the group as they stood in front of massive black doors that were carved out of black stone. He grabbed the large latch and pulled as hard as he could. The doors were incredibly heavy and would not budge. Antonio and Costa grabbed on to the edge of the door and pulled with all their strength to help get it open.

An eerie red glow began to illuminate the path as the door opened and a blast of intense heat Piero in the face as he looked in. Cries of pain and anguish followed the blast.

Piero breathed in nervously as he took his first steps forward, "I think we're in the right place."

☳

The group slowly entered the massive cavern. What they saw when they passed through the doors beyond comprehension. There was a massive black castle on the far side of the cavern, which that appeared to have been carved from a massive underground volcano.

In front of the castle, lay a large lagoon of flame surrounded by the remains of a wrecked city. The buildings were reminiscent of Ancient Rome during the days of the empire, but they were horribly wrecked and burning. Rivers of lava flowed between, and in some cases through, the buildings.

Ensign Costa trembled at what he saw. Chills flowed non-stop down his spine, "My God, perhaps this wasn't a good idea."

Piero nodded, "I won't fault you if you decide to turn back. Part of me wishes I could…"

"And go where? I don't think we have much of a choice here. I said I'd come with you and I meant it. Let's keep going."

Piero took a few more steps forward, but he began to notice Francesco breathing heavily. The look on his face was one of intense agony. Piero placed his hand on the blind man's shoulder, "Are you okay?"

"This is terrible, Piero. I can hear them… every voice, every cry, it's agonizing."

"Will you be able to continue? Perhaps you should wait outside."

"No… No, we wouldn't be here right now if it weren't for me. I will share this burden with you, no matter what it takes."

"Are you sure? You've done more than enough for us already. I won't hold it against you."

Francesco straightened himself up and tried to shut the voices out, "Yes, as long as I can block out a least a little of the noise, I'll be okay."

Piero smiled, "Thank you, my friend."

The group made their way through the city, ignoring the grotesque husks strewn about the ground as they walked. Some of them appeared to still be alive and reacted as the group passed by. Mournful cries and inhuman moans filled their ears each time they walked past one.

As the group passed through the rubble of the first toppled building, they noticed a small fire pit with burnt corpse crucified over it. To their horror, it appeared to still be alive.

When it saw them, it called out, "Please good sirs, have you any water."

Piero turned to it, grasping a small leather sack full of water. Francesco shook his head, "I don't think it's such a good idea. Remember what the boatman said."

Piero lowered his eyes, "I know... but I can't let him suffer like this."

"He's suffering for a reason. Don't forget where we are."

"I know, but maybe he'll help us in exchange. He must know something about this place."

Piero got as close as he could to it without being burned and put the water up to the burning man's mouth. It greedily gulped down as much as it could. Steam flowed off what was left of its skin as it finished. It took a moment to catch its breath before looking up with an appreciative smile and speaking, "Bless you, merciful sir, for taking pity on a soul that is in no way deserving of it."

"You are welcome... can you help us? We're trying to find someone who lives here."

"You may find that difficult, there are an uncountable number of wicked souls here. Many of them look like me and are unrecognizable to anyone who may have known them. Others don't even have their own identities anymore. After years in the pit, the tormented souls become little more than a mesh of madness. Not even God himself could extract them."

"Then they're receiving their just punishment, but we're not looking for someone who would be in the pit."

"Name this soul, then. If I know it, I will tell you where to go."

"I am looking for General Xaphan, the fallen angel... I was told that she leads Lucifer's forces?"

The corpse went quiet for a moment, shocked that someone was actually looking for her. It breathed heavily for a few moments before it spoke, "You would do better just abandoning this quest. Xaphan is an honorable soul, but she does have her cruel side as well. She is almost as evil as he is."

"Do you know where she is or not?" Piero insisted, not wanting to hear this.

"She resides in the castle, but spends her days tending to the beasts of the Netherworld. There are only two ways I know of to reach her. The first is entering the underground passage on the east side, which will put you through tests that could easily drive you insane. The other option..."

The corpse hesitated, it truly wasn't sure it wanted to tell them of the second path, "You could go through the lair of the Scylla to the west..."

"What is the Scylla? We were told to stay away from the east passage."

"Please take care, surely you have read the good book where it speaks of a seven headed beast. It has one large rams head with three smaller heads on both sides and a dragon's body. It stands three stories tall and possesses all the powers of hell. It actually escaped the underworld at one point and attacked Greek ship that was on its way home after the ancient war."

Piero stepped back slightly, "Why would anyone want to take that path?"

"A few reasons come to mind. It's quicker, you avoid encounters with the pit, and a six headed dragon may be less horrific than what you would face in the cave. It is also rumored that if you slay the beast, then the evil powers of this place will vanish, and the temptations of Hell will no longer be able to sway you from your path. It's just a rumor, of course..."

Francesco nodded, "Perhaps it is the better way to go. Adalyn wouldn't have told us to avoid the east for no reason. She hasn't been wrong yet."

The husk shuddered, "Adalyn... such a wicked creature."

"What do you know of her?" Piero asked.

"She is the one who did this to me. I've long since come to accept my punishment as just, but when she returned here, she taunted me even further. I've seen how she tempted spirits to follow her... Promising them paradise, and then becoming a cruel creature, dragging unwilling spirits to hell. Trusting her words might not be the best thing for you."

Antonio shook his head, "The cave sounds less menacing. I think we should head that way. Facing the tests of one's self sounds much easier than a massive dragon. I have nothing to be ashamed of."

"Beware the path that seems easy!" The corpse cried. "You may find it to be not so easy once it is too late to turn back!"

Piero nodded, "I agree... we'll take on the Scylla."

Antonio shook his head as he could see that he was getting overruled, "Prepare yourself as best you can. You can get past the beast, but it will require a steadfast heart and determination."

"So we can get by it..." Piero repeated. "Does that mean it can be killed?"

The corpse nodded hesitantly, "At one time, yes… but the creature is immortal. You would need venom from the Eden Serpent to accomplish this, and I'm afraid that creature was killed years ago."

Piero raised his sword, "I know. We got these swords from the person who killed it."

"Then you have a much better chance," the corpse replied, "but you must go quickly. Once the legions realize you are here, it will be that much more difficult… that is all I can tell you."

The corpse had said all it could that would help them. Without even giving them a chance to respond, the corpse returned to its lifeless position over the fire pit. It lowered its head and stared blankly into the dark flame.

Piero nodded, "Thank you."

He then quickly returned to the group where Antonio was still protesting, "I really think going against a dragon is a bad idea. You've all read Revelations. You know what this thing is! How bad could the tests of the cave be?"

Ensign Costa nodded, "I would tend to agree with Antonio. Would having to face trials of one's own self truly be that horrible? Anyone who knows their own heart and soul should have no problem."

"So sure of that are you?" Francesco asked. "Have you no memory that can be turned against you; a loved one who has been lost or perhaps something in the past that you regret? When faced with the reality of a person's life, a strong man may discover that his strength is a farce, and a good man may discover his inner cruelty. I can think of no greater horror."

Piero looked at the three of his friends, "Adalyn told me that people who still have things they fear to lose would be the most at risk by going to the east. I would assume she was speaking of facing whatever is in that cave. Our best chance is to fight Scylla."

"But do we truly stand a chance against such a beast?" Antonio asked.

"There are four of us, and we have the venom swords. I'd say that we have as good a chance as anyone."

"I still think this is a poor choice. Despite what you say, one of our people is blind and won't be much good in a fight… but if this is what you have your heart set on, I will fight with you to the end as I always have. Let's go."

"Thanks Antonio."

Antonio began inspecting his arquebus as Piero led the group west towards a large cave. They proceeded to the city outskirts where the cave stood on a cliff overlooking the entire cavern. It was a massive opening in the wall that was menacing in its own right.

In the distance, Piero could see a second opening near the castle. This was no cave, it was a tunnel, and it would take them right where they needed to go. Piero took a deep breath as he led his men forward.

It took the four of them a few minutes to climb the cliff to the cave. When they finally reached the entrance, Piero saw skeletons, smashed armor, and weapons littering the ground. Scorch marks painted the entire entrance and much of the human remains black.

Ensign Costa grabbed a spear off the ground and inspected it, "Roman… I take it we're not the first ones to try this…"

Piero shook his head, "Doubtful… "

Costa looked at the weapons his group was carrying and pointed to the skeletons, "Everyone, grab whatever you can that might help us here."

DAMNATION

"If only anything would..." Antonio replied glumly.

"Oh I don't know," Piero said as he picked up an old shield, "this may prove invaluable."

"They didn't serve their former masters very well..."

The sound of heavy breathing that resembled the growl of a lion made Piero turn and face the cave. He quickly performed the sign of the cross as he raised the large rounded shield and slowly walked into the cave, "In nomine Patris, et Fili, et Spiritus Sancti..."

Tremors under Piero's feet stopped the young officer in his path. The group could hear a thundering boom from inside the cave, followed by a second one, then a third. The bones on the ground trembled with each boom.

Francesco's face was locked on the cave as the sounds grew louder, "It knows we're here."

Piero stood behind his shield with his sword pointing at the cave. Ensign Costa stood with the old spear raised as Antonio raised his gun behind them. Francesco stood off to the side, knowing that he would just get in the way. He had traded in his wooden staff for a metal pike that he had picked up from one of the skeletons.

As a massive dark shadow approached the cave entrance, Piero noticed his men slowly stepping back, "Steady men, it's too late to run now. We fight or we die!"

Their hearts raced as a massive beast came into the light. It reared the largest of its heads, the rams head, let out a massive roar, and looked down at the group. The sound echoed throughout the entire cabin and froze the hearts of everyone in the group. Its eyes were a hideous red and its body was covered in black scales. The creature was an abomination that was sickening to look at, but Piero knew that taking his eyes off it for even a second could be fatal.

Piero looked at it in a combined look of awe and fear, "Scylla..."

DAMNATION

Antonio shook his head, "I don't like this. Every demon in the cavern would have heard that!"

Francesco nodded, "Yes, but I get the feeling that they fear this creature more than we do."

Before Antonio could respond, Scylla charged at Piero with its mouth open, revealing large yellow fangs. Piero raised his shield and slashed at the beast with his sword. The sound of the metal impacting on Scylla's teeth rang in Piero's ears and the blade vibrated from the impact. Scylla pulled back its head and roared in pain.

As Piero faced down the main head, Ensign Costa moved and took on the head that looked like a lion. He charged at it, wielding his sword. Light from the blade danced in Piero's eyes as Costa brought it down and severed the smaller head with ease.

As it rolled away, Costa cheered, "For the honor of Mantua!"

Piero cheered, "Good job, Ensign!"

Piero's celebration was short-lived as a second head, resembling that of a great lizard, reared back, and opened its mouth as though to let out a mighty roar. Instead a stream of flame shot out of its mouth. Piero crouched behind his shield to block the attack. As the flame broke against the shield, he could feel the metal of it begin to heat against his skin. Parts of it even began to turn red.

Piero turned to Antonio, "I can't hold this much longer, it's getting too hot! Can you take out that head?"

Antonio raised the gun and aimed it between the eyes of the lizard, "Hang on Piero, I'm on it."

Antonio's hands shook as he aimed the arquebus. Piero could feel the skin of his arm begin to burn against the shield. He closed his eyes as searing pain shot across his arm, "Antonio… please…"

Antonio closed his left eye and pulled the trigger. The wick ignited the black powder and fired the hot lead ball.

The blast hit its mark exactly where Antonio had hoped it would. Blood began to pour out from the creature's forehead right between the eyes as the barrage of flame ceased.

Piero nodded as he gave Antonio an appreciate smile, "Thanks…"

Piero didn't even get a chance to finish his sentence as the rams head came down and grabbed the shield with Piero still attached. Hanging by his arm, Piero felt himself flying upward. As he was tossed around like a rag doll, the straps that attached to the back of the shield snapped under the strain and Piero found himself free flying through the air.

As Piero began to fall out of control, he waited for the right moment as he neared Scylla. Piero knew he'd only get one chance as he reached for the nearest horn on Scylla's largest head. He managed to grab the horn and wrapped his other arm and legs around it. The beast was busy trying to deal with Piero's companions and did not notice him.

As Piero held on for his life, he heard a shrill scream coming from below him. To his horror, one of the heads had grabbed Ensign Costa and held him in its jaws. Francesco was trying to help, but he kept missing the beast's neck with the pike. The blind man was not able to react fast enough to Scylla's movements to deal a crippling blow.

Piero knew he had to act quickly if he was to save Costa. He loosened his grip and slid down the horn with his sword still in hand. Every second counted as he made his way to the beast's skull.

Once Piero reached the skin of the beast's head, he turned his sword upside down and plunged it into Scylla's skull. The beast let out an unearthly cry and tried to shake Piero off. The young soldier balanced himself and began twisting the sword around as hard as he could.

When this didn't subdue Scylla, Piero pulled back on the sword and stabbed it closer to the beast's eyes. After a few moments of jerking around, Scylla let out one final cry and fell to the ground. The head hit the ground with a mighty boom.

Piero was thrown from the beast's head and landed on the rocks. He quickly shook off the impact and called to his friend, "Francesco, now, kill it!"

Francesco pulled back the javelin and plunged it into Scylla's chest. The beast screamed so loud, it nearly deafened the group. They had to cover their ears to prevent being deafened.

When the scream finally silenced, Scylla fell to its side and lay motionless. Francesco pulled his javelin from the beast and nodded at Piero. A satisfied looked appeared on his face as he turned to the beast's mouth, "Anthony, my friend, are you okay?"

Piero looked at Ensign Costa's body, still in the dead beast's mouth. There was blood everywhere and several puncture wounds. Piero grabbed his arm and searched for some sign that Costa was still alive, but he had no pulse, and his skin was growing cold.

Piero put a hand to his face, "God please forgive me…"

Piero put his hand over Costa's face and closed his eyes. Francesco performed the sign of the cross, "Into your hands, we commend his spirit, oh Lord. In nomine Patris, et Fili, et Spiritus Sancti, amen."

Piero shook his head, "I didn't want anyone dying for me."

"He was a soldier, and like the rest of us, he knew the risks when he took the assignment to come with us. He died to restore the honor of Mantua. You can't blame yourself."

"That doesn't make it any easier."

Francesco shrugged as he placed a hand on Piero's shoulder, "No, and it probably shouldn't. He was a good man, but we'll need to save our mourning for a later time.

I'm sure Scylla's death has drawn attention to us, so we really should keep moving."

"You're right… we should go."

DAMNATION

The group entered the large tunnel. All around them were skeletons of fallen warriors and broken gates. There also appeared to be the remains of demonic creatures as well. Apparently Lucifer had sacrificed many of his own to tame that beast.

When Piero exited the other side with his companions, they could see the castle right in front of them. They were so close; the end appeared to be in sight. Piero pictured his wife's face in his mind as he looked at the castle.

Piero smiled as he stepped into the light, "Come on, we're in the clear!"

He started running towards the castle as fast as he could, overwhelmed with anticipation as he continued to picture Xaphine's face in his mind, "This ends now!"

Francesco screamed out to Piero when he heard the soldier's rapid footsteps, "Wait Piero, no, don't rush in! It could be a…"

Before Francesco could say anything else, two massive black clouds exited the castle and flew overhead. They blocked out the light from the pit as the neared the group. Loud screams echoed through the group's ears as the clouds neared.

When Piero got a closer look, he could see that this was no cloud, but actually a horde of demonic creatures flying towards them, "Good God…"

Francesco pushed Piero to the ground, "Get down!"

Piero closed his eyes as the creatures came down on them. Within moments Piero opened his eyes to see that they were completely surrounded by a legion of dark imps. There was no way out.

Francesco shook his head, "A trap… I hate being right all the time."

One of the entities stepped forward and looked at Antonio, "Well done, master! I am certain Luci…"

"Silence, foul creature!" Antonio said with a nervous look on his face.

Piero turned to him, "Why did that demon call you master?"

"I haven't the slightest idea."

"Oh, I think you do…" Francesco said in a deep, threatening, voice, "Why couldn't I see you in my thoughts… what was it about you that made you impossible to read?"

"Piero, are you hearing this? This blind man is insane! You can't honestly believe that I'm involved in some kind of sinister plot."

"No, I can't believe that! You have been my friend for years. You've fought at my side since…"

Suddenly it hit him, "Since I met Xaphine… you were transferred into my company shortly before that day. I'd never seen or heard of you before then and neither had anyone else. Since we were so desperate for soldiers, no one pressed the matter, until now."

Antonio sighed and began to chuckle, "I'm actually amazed you were able to piece it together… It certainly took you long enough."

"I don't believe it… you're a…"

"A traitor." Francesco sneered as he got to his feet. "This explains so much. How did Xaphan discover where Adalyn lived? Was it a simple coincidence that she showed up when she did? What about how the spirits on the ship didn't harm you, or why the boatman looked at you so oddly?"

Antonio was about to respond when a sudden commotion erupted from the castle. Another demonic creature with an impressive wingspan took flight from one of the towers. Whatever it was spread black wings and flew towards them. Its high-pitched shriek could be heard across the land as it took flight.

Piero watched the creature as it flew close enough for him to make out its features. He faintly smiled when he realized who it was, "Xaphine..."

Xaphan folded her wings back and spiraled into a dive. Mere feet from the ground, she spread her wings so that they would catch the air and slow her decent. She then touched down gracefully in front of them. One knee gently touched the ground as she placed her hand in front of her. She looked up only after pushing herself to her feet.

Piero watched as Xaphan moved between him and Antonio, and looked at the legion of demons around her. She spread her arms and flapped her wings, "Disperse!"

The entire legion vaporized in response to her order, leaving no trace behind. She shook her head, "Such inferior creatures these imps are. I don't need their help to deal with humans!"

She looked at the group with her glowing red eyes filled with malice, "It's amazing that you were able to kill my pet! Poor Scylla... Then again, I suppose there had to be some reason that I was attracted to you. No normal weak mortal could've done that."

Antonio looked over at her and smiled, "Ah General Xaphan, so glad you could make it."

Xaphan sneered, "Enough of the façade, Kaliban. You have been found out, now reveal yourself."

Piero turned in shock as Antonio transformed into a hideous imp. He shook his head in sadness, "All this time, you were a spy? You gave Xaphine away at my wedding, you have been at my side ever since! I can't believe it... you're one of them?"

Kaliban began laughing hysterically, "Quite appropriate don't you think? Given your wife's true identity? It was quite fun watching her live the life of an insect."

Xaphan's eyes narrowed, "But why were you sent? My presence there was supposed to be completely secret, even from our minions."

Kaliban shook his head, "My lord wanted me to keep tabs on you. He wanted to know what you were up to and if you were surviving okay."

"Then why did you let me fall in love?" Xaphan demanded. "Why allow me to marry this... human? You knew that you were risking our mission!"

"Isn't it obvious? Lucifer no longer fully trusts you. I had hoped you would form a strong enough connection to damage your loyalty to Lucifer so I could confirm his suspicions, and you did. Little by little, the poison that was your human side pushed you to defy Lucifer when you returned. How long do you think he'd put up with it?"

"Kaliban..."

Piero turned and glared at Xaphan in anger, "More deception and lies... He was my friend... I'd have trusted him with my life!"

"Not that I owe you an explanation, but I had no idea of his true identity. He's betrayed me and disobeyed Lucifer's orders! If that weren't bad enough, he helped you murder my poor Scylla..."

She immediately pulled the black sword from her belt and pointed it at Piero's throat, "You're going to pay for that!"

Francesco gasped as Piero looked down the blade. He gently pushed Francesco out of harm's way before turning his attention back to Xaphan. She clenched her teeth as she spoke, "This ends now."

Kaliban smiled, "Yes, restore your master's faith in you. Kill him... kill him now."

Xaphan tightened her grip on the sword as she stared down her husband. He couldn't be sure, but he thought he saw her eyes flickering different colors as she glared at him. There was also a detectable quiver in her voice as she spoke, "Don't... try to stop me. Don't struggle and I promise I'll make your death quick and as painless as possible."

The look of accusation on Piero's face was replaced, by a calm and comforting one. It was as though he were trying to reassure her that everything was okay. He dropped his sword and showed Xaphan the palms of his hands as a sign that he would offer no resistance, "As you wish, my love. My heart has always belonged to you. If you wish to run it through, that is your right."

The pain in Xaphan's chest began to intensify as she tried to push the sword into his skin. Sweat poured down her brow as tears formed in her eyes. Piero's comforting gaze only served to frustrate her further, "S... stop looking at me like that! You knew what would happen if you came here. I... have no choice! I can't abandon my cause."

"I know that, but I've lived a hollow life since you left. You're everything to me. If it is my destiny to die here, now, then so be it. At least it will be by your hand..."

Kaliban smiled as Xaphan's voice began to tremble. She was losing control and the tears began to escape her eyes, "How dare you... How dare you say something like that! You will not put this on me! I begged you to stay away. Coming here meant certain death and you knew it! I didn't want this to happen. I... I love you. Can't you see that this is killing me?"

"I do realize that. I feel the same way, I love you too."

The sword in Xaphan's hand shook as it became even heavier. She bit down hard on her lip before speaking, "I..."

Piero took a step forward so that the tip of the blade was making an indentation into his skin, "Just promise me that you won't blame yourself for this later. You're right; I

DAMNATION

made the decision to come here. I understood what this meant and what confronting you would result in."

Xaphan took a step backwards, "No... I... I have to kill you. My oath... my honor... I...."

Kaliban's grin widened as Xaphan lowered her sword. She wiped her eyes and shook her head, "I... can't do it. So help me Lucifer... I'm so sorry..."

Xaphan took another step back and turned to Kaliban, "These two are mine. Your work here is finished. Leave now before I kill you myself. I'm going to take these two to the castle and believe me, Lucifer will be made aware of what you've done."

"My work is finished." Kaliban parroted while still laughing. "My work is far from finished. I'm sorry to tell you my dear sweet Xaphan, but why do you think I was left in my human persona even after you returned? Since you asked for this boy's life to be spared when you were turned back, Lucifer sensed that you had become vulnerable. Once you were gone, it was my job to execute him thus removing the chink in your armor."

Xaphan's face turned red with anger, "You didn't think I'd find out? Did you really think I'd overlook something like that?"

"It was supposed to look like an accident." Kaliban replied as his laughing got even more obnoxious. "That is why it was taking so long. I had to make sure that he would die in a way that you and the Most High would not be able to detect. Thus I enabled him to take on deadly mission after deadly mission. Unfortunately, he kept surviving and beating the odds every single time. It was like he was being protected."

"Protected?" Xaphan asked as her eyes narrowed.

"It became so frustrating."

At that point, Francesco spoke up, "That doesn't make sense. If that was your goal, then why didn't you leave him in the dungeons of Florence to be executed? Why take us on this journey?"

The malicious grin once again appeared on Kaliban's face, "Because I'm not going to obey our master's wishes, not anymore. After so many failed attempts at his life, I realized something. He has such a strong spirit... it would be a waste. No, I will do far better, and once I am done, I'll have my own lieutenant, a minion far stronger than even your pathetic pet, Scylla!"

Without another word, Kaliban took flight and grabbed Piero, "Just watch."

"Kaliban, no!" Xaphan yelled.

Xaphan's eyes shifted quickly to blue as she spread her wings and chased him through the sky. He was little more than a blur as Xaphan gave chase. Seeing her gaining on him, Kaliban dove downward towards the pit and dropped Piero in the middle of the flame.

Piero struggled to hold on, but Kaliban's slimy body did not give him anything to grip on to. He plummeted downward and disappeared into the lake of fire. He didn't scream, but a massive plume erupted where he'd been dropped.

Xaphan screamed, "No!"

Kaliban flew back to shore laughing loudly as Xaphan darted back and forth trying to see if she could find any sign of Piero. Moments later, fire from the pit formed into a geyser and shot Piero straight into the air. The flame retreated back into the pit, leaving Piero to free fall.

Xaphan caught him before he could fall back into the flame. She whispered in his ear as he landed in her arms, "Piero rest easy now. I won't let you be harmed."

As they landed, Piero fought his way out of Xaphan's arms and shouted in a demonic voice, "Get your filthy hands off me!"

Xaphan jumped back, startled, "Piero..."

Piero had gained an unusual sense of clarity while in the pit. Love and mercy were replaced with hatred and anger. Now he wanted revenge. He wanted Xaphan to pay for the years he had lost because of her, for Kaliban's betrayal, and for Lucifer orchestrating the whole thing.

For the first time, Piero saw Xaphan for what she really was. He saw everything she had done and how far she had fallen. His new sense of clarity prevented him from forgiving her, "Be silent!"

Xaphan stood up with tears in her eyes, "Piero, what happened? What did you see in there?"

Piero ignored her and turned to Kaliban. For a moment his eyes were glowing red, "More than I ever have before."

"Piero, your mind has been corrupted! Fight it my love, you have to..."

"Stay away from me! I don't need anything, especially not from you! For the first time in a while I actually see things clearly. You are right, you're not my wife, you're some perverted demon. I wasted ten years pining over your loss..."

Francesco stepped forward, "Piero, you don't know what you're saying. Get a hold of your emotions! You've been desecrated…"

"Silence beggar!" Piero replied. "I have too much to do to suffer anymore leach craft from you!"

Piero stepped forward and picked up his sword from the ground. His gaze never left Kaliban's eyes, "So much pain… so much wrong… it ends now…"

Kaliban smiled, "Come stand with me against these creatures, Piero!"

"Stand with you? I think not. Xaphine, Moretti, Costa, and countless soldiers… all gone because of you! All this time, I blamed myself, only to find out that entire time… it was your doing! Give them back Kaliban, give them all back!"

DAMNATION

Kaliban stepped back in fear, "All I did was fulfill my master's wishes. If you have an issue, he is the one you should see."

"And you had hopes of being his right hand." Xaphan scoffed as her eyes turned back to their hideous red. "You are an honorless coward! It's amazing how quickly you are willing to turn on him."

"Oh I will deal with Lucifer." Piero said angrily. "I will serve him your head from the end of my sword! Kaliban, you are dead!"

Piero lunged at the surprised imp with his sword drawn. Using inhuman speed, Kaliban jumped out of the way, but Piero still managed to clip his wing. The impact sent a wave of pain flowing through the imp's body.

Kaliban fell to his side and nursed his wound. Piero turned and walked toward Kaliban, ready to deliver a deathblow. Kaliban backed away with his hand raised defensively.

As Piero got closer, Kaliban smiled, "Human, you fall so easily into traps. Do you really believe that I am actually afraid of a mere mortal? You are nothing compared to my power."

Piero continued to move closer, ignoring Kaliban's words as best he could. This time though the imp did not back away. It got back to its feet and held its ground.

As Piero got a few feet closer, Kaliban smiled and let loose a wave of intense flame, "Burn, inferior being!"

At first, Piero blocked the flame with his sword. The stains on it began to glow a hideous green as its power was slowing being expended. Watching the green glow dim as it was overwhelmed, Piero realized that he was not going to win.

Francesco stood up and turned to Xaphan, "Are you truly just going to stand there and let him die?"

Kaliban glared at her as he unleashed the flame, "Prove your undying loyalty to Lucifer and watch him burn."

Xaphan's mind was racing a mile a minute. Her eyes began shifting colors once more as though they were fighting for dominance. She couldn't stand to see Piero suffer, but she was also loyal to Lucifer, even though she had just found out that he was not as faithful.

Francesco moved closer to her, "You've seen where being Lucifer's ally has gotten you. This is your only chance, the one chance you will ever have to redeem yourself! It's not too late for you... he loves you, that has never changed... you can still go home again!"

Xaphan looked at Francesco, "He really does... love me... even after everything I've done... Such loyalty, it's so foolish..."

The mental walls that Xaphan had put in place to block Xaphine's memory finally collapsed and the years she lived with Piero came flooding back into her mind. She remembered how happy she was. It was a feeling she hadn't experienced since being exiled from the Celestial World.

Both Xaphan's head and chest ached and her eyes turned to a purple hue, "I... I can't... what am I doing?"

Tears streamed down Xaphan's cheeks as she watched Piero's skin begin to turn red. She shook her head violently, "No..."

Francesco yelled to her again as Piero's sword's energy was nearly depleted, "You still remember who you are! Your necklace is evidence enough of that!"

Xaphan looked down at the jeweled necklace that neither Lucifer nor Kaliban had been able to strip from her. The charm Piero had given her when he proposed gleamed brightly. It was as though the gem was pleading for her to act.

DAMNATION

Francesco reached into the sack he had been carrying and handed her the feather that Adalyn had given to Piero, "Still can't remember what you meant to him? Then take this…"

Xaphan held the feather close to her face, "Adalyn… my dear sister…"

Time froze as the feather began to pulse over and over until it disintegrated in her hand and disappeared. The residual powder went airborne and flew into her eyes, blinding her for a few moments.

When Xaphan's eyesight returned, she gasped and looked up at Kaliban, "My God… what have I done?"

Xaphan's ears and wings had not been affected, but her eyes were the original piercing blue color that they had been so many years ago. The red had been driven out and the evil was gone.

At that moment, the protection of the sword collapsed and Piero was consumed by the fire. The intensity of the heat was unlike anything he had experienced before. His legs buckled and he was no longer able to control his movements due to the pain.

After a few seconds of fighting, Piero couldn't stand the burning sensation running through his skin anymore and screamed as the agony took over. He closed his eyes as his breathing increased. There was no doubt in his mind that he was about to die.

Xaphan looked at Francesco and nodded, "Thank you."

Xaphan then thrust out her hand, causing a black sword to appear. She took flight while wielding the sword and charged straight forward, "Kaliban!"

Startled, Kaliban ceased his brutal attack on Piero. Without another thought, he grabbed Piero's sword off of the ground, "Traitor, the Master of all was right not to trust you!"

Kaliban leapt into the air as their swords clashed. They hovered only a few feet off the ground with their swords crossed. The blades scrapped against one another, creating sparks.

Xaphan's malicious smile caused Kaliban's blood to run cold. She was enjoying every minute of this fight and made no secret of it, "He has you to thank for showing me the light. Your day is done Kaliban. You will never harm another soul, not now, not ever again! That is my promise to the ones I love!"

With a few vicious slashes of Xaphan's sword, she severed Kaliban's limbs and head. His body quickly disintegrated as it hit the ground. "Farewell Kaliban." Xaphan snorted. "Existence is better off without you."

"Xaphan!" Francesco yelled. "You better come quickly, Piero isn't doing well. He's badly injured."

The smile disappeared from Xaphan's face as she looked over to see Francesco kneeling over Piero's burnt body. She landed next to him and knelt down. Smoke poured off of every inch of his body as he lay motionless. It was hard to tell whether or not he was still alive.

Francesco placed his hands on Piero's neck and temple, "I think he's dying..."

"I waited too long... no Piero, you're not dying on me. Not after everything you went through! You're far too strong for that!"

Xaphan grabbed him by what was left of his tunic and picked him up off the ground, "You fought so hard to save me... I will not suffer the disgrace of losing you now!"

She pressed Piero's head against her chest and squeezed him tightly. Her face looked as though she were concentrating hard on something. It was difficult for Francesco to figure out what was going on as all he heard was a low hum, "Xaphan... what...?"

DAMNATION

Before he could finish his sentence, the hum intensified. Xaphan's skin glowed momentarily. She flickered like a small wisp of flame. As her skin returned to its normal color, the scars on Piero's body began to disappear and air filled his lungs. She flickered two or three more times, causing the steam on his skin to quickly vanish.

Francesco couldn't believe it, "In nomine Criste…"

Piero opened his eyes, and looked at Xaphan. Francesco was relieved to see that in addition to the scars on his body, his red eyes had also given way to their normal color. Piero breathed in deeply as he looked at Xaphan, "What happened…"

"You were possessed by the power of the pit." She replied. "It corrupted your soul, we almost lost you."

Piero looked into Xaphan's eyes and touched her cheek, "Xaphan?"

Xaphan placed her hand over his. The touch of his fingers on her cheek electrified her soul, "No, I don't want to hear you call me by that name ever again. It's me…"

"Xaphine, my love… how? What happened?"

"You did it. Foolish boy, you refused to take no for an answer. Regardless of how hard I pushed, you forced your way in and reawakened something I thought was dead. My love, if I live for another billion years, I will never be able to do enough to be worthy of such devotion."

Piero moved his hand to Xaphine's chin and kissed her again. Francesco smiled as he could feel the happiness emanating from them like an aura. *Well done, you two,* he thought to himself.

When Piero and Xaphine finally released each other, Piero's lungs ached like they did the first time he kissed her, "I've waited so long for that…"

When the moment passed, Piero looked back the way they came and grabbed the arquebus that Antonio had dropped, "We've got to get you out of here, now. Let's go..."

Xaphine shook her head, refusing to budge, "We can't leave, he will never let us go. Even if we were to escape the cavern, we'd never be out of his grasp. He'll hunt us forever..."

Xaphine pointed back to the castle, "Our only hope is to confront Lucifer. Only then can we hope to escape with our lives."

"How," Piero asked, losing hope, "how can we face the full power of the devil himself?"

"Thank our friend Adalyn for that. He lost most of his power when he faced her. That is why he wanted her dead so badly... I wish now that I'd never gone on that mission... One more sin on my soul... she'd still be alive right now. After everything she went through, it's cruel."

"She still lives." Francesco said in a soothing tone. "What Lucifer didn't realize is that the lord God promised her that she'd be alive as long as her husband lives. That was his decree, so there was no way you could have killed her."

"She's really still alive?" Xaphine asked surprised as look of relief came over her face. "Then we'll need to stop Lucifer once and for all. No doubt he's realized his error by now and will soon send an assassin after her husband. I can't allow him to hurt the one Celestial being who still believes in me."

"Because of your honor?" Piero asked.

"Because it's what's right. I'm not concerned with honor anymore, I've already lost it."

"What do you mean?"

"I've betrayed Lucifer, I've betrayed my people, I betrayed Adalyn... and worst of all... I've betrayed you. I have no honor left."

"But you're back now and you're trying to make things right… aren't you?"

"If I can."

"All right then, maybe there's a little room for redemption for you."

Xaphine smiled and closed her eyes, "You're really sweet. If only it were possible."

Xaphine then looked at Francesco with gratitude, "Your words have lifted a heavy burden off of my heart… but I will still need to apologize to her, someday. Though I am sure she'll never forgive me."

"Not true." Piero replied. "She already has forgiven you. She gave us the information and the tools we needed to get this far."

Piero showed her his sword, "These swords are hers, and she told me that if I saved you, she'd be the first to celebrate. You were her friend and though much time has passed, she still cares about you."

"Such a wonderful ability that one has. Even during the war, Adalyn never hated anyone she fought. Love and forgiveness, it's something I never understood. It was so foreign to me… After the war, at my trial, she tried to defend me."

Tears of frustration filled her eyes as she squeezed Piero. She wiped them dry as quickly as she could before speaking, "I've been such a fool, blinded by the promise of freedom."

"You weren't blind." Piero replied. "We've all been deceived at one point or another. Things that seem too good to be true often are."

Piero held Xaphine in his arms as they looked at the black castle. The mountain it was carved from began to erupt. The ground began to shake underneath them as they wanted the land tear itself apart.

DAMNATION

Piero could feel Xaphine start to shake as she breathed heavily. He looked down at her and could tell that she was trying to hide it. Her face had returned to its stoic expression, but her eyes betrayed her.

"Are you okay?" Piero asked.

Xaphine shook her head as she nervously turned away from the castle, "He knows what's happened. He knows…"

Francesco nodded, "And he's not happy…"

Piero could hear Xaphine breathing heavily. He turned his attention away from the volcano and back to her, "Are you all right Xaphine?"

"I… for the first time ever… I'm afraid, Piero." She admitted as her stoic expression broke down. "There is something wrong inside of me… I do not fear. I stood with Lucifer when he defied the Most High. I helped him continue to resist even after we lost the war and I even stood in as his steward. I saw unspeakable horrors and things that would turn the bravest stomach. None of that ever scared me… ever… Even as I stood before the Choirs, waiting for them to pass sentence on me, it did not cause me any concern, but now here I stand against a former ally, a man I called friend… and I'm frightened. It's intolerable."

"There is nothing wrong with you." Francesco replied in an absolute tone. "Nothing wrong at all. You fought for what you thought was right back then. You didn't care what happened because it was only your own life and those that were committed that you were risking. You fear now because for the first time in several lifetimes, you actually have something far more personal to lose."

A look of shock came over Xaphine's face. It was as though a truth that had long escaped her had finally revealed itself. She nodded as Francesco continued, "A warrior's own life is a small price to pay for their cause, but when they have to risk the life of someone close, it's not so easy to run in sword first. Especially if you're the reason they're putting their lives at risk."

"What are you saying?" Piero asked. "Do you believe that we will weaken each other if a fight should break out?"

Francesco shrugged, "I can't answer that, because it depends entirely on the two of you. Your connection certainly could be a weakness if you decide to look at it that way. If you do, Lucifer will certainly see that and exploit it. You can live in fear of what might happen to the other person, and it will definitely weaken you."

"What other choice is there?" Xaphine asked nervously. "In battle, the person who can point out their opponent's weaknesses has a significant tactical advantage. Lucifer already knows that I won't let Piero come to harm... he must..."

"There is always another choice." Francesco replied. "You can look at each other and view each other as your strength. When you fight, you can fight without watching your back because you know that your loved one is watching it for you. When you attempt a risky move, you can do it without fear because the one you love will be there to catch you if it fails. If you can do that, if you can draw strength from each other and believe in one another unquestionably, then nothing in existence will ever be able to stop you, not even Lucifer himself."

Piero touched his wife's face and looked deep into her eyes. Xaphine smiled and nodded, "We won't fail, I know it."

v

The three of them approached the castle. The drawbridge was already down and waiting for them. It stood open as though daring them to cross.

Xaphine and Piero crossed first, but when Francesco stepped forward, he let out a loud gasp. Piero turned to him, "What is it?"

Francesco didn't respond and again tried to cross the bridge. Just as before, the first step seemed agonizing to him and he was unable to take a second one. He quickly stepped off of the bridge with a scared look on his face.

Xaphine looked back, "It's Lucifer, isn't it? The intense power is overwhelming even to immortals. I can't imagine what it must be to you, a mortal who is sensitive to such things."

"I... I'm sorry," Francesco finally spoke as he looked away, "I can't go with you. Already I can feel the lure of the lord of darkness pulling at me. It's agonizing to just take a step."

"Yes," Xaphine replied, "I can feel it too. I don't know what Lucifer did in my absence, but his powers have been drastically altered. You'd best wait here."

"I'm so sorry."

Piero smiled, "It's okay Francesco, you've done more than enough. Wait here, we'll be back for you."

"Good luck you two, I mean it. I would come with you if I could, but this is too much."

Xaphine could hear no more of it. She turned around, walked back to Francesco and kissed him on the forehead, "You've helped bring me back, you've given me my husband and thus, my happiness back. You have nothing to be sorry for. Now put your chin up. We'll be back for you as soon as this is over."

"Thank you, milady."

DAMNATION

Xaphine smiled and turned back to rejoin her husband as he made his way inside the castle. The door was wide open, revealing a gaping black maw. Xaphine knew that Lucifer was waiting for them inside. As they entered the room, the doors slammed shut, cutting off any chance of escape.

Piero and Xaphine found themselves in Lucifer's throne room. Sitting in front of his black throne, Lucifer stared at them with malice-filled eyes. He'd been betrayed before, but never by someone who had served him as loyally as Xaphan. The look of hatred on his face was piercing as Xaphine looked him in the eye.

Piero looked at him oddly. Somehow the fallen angel had sunken into the floor and was trapped. This was not at all what he expected from the lord of darkness. All that the fallen angel had free was a single hand.

Seeing the couple approach, Lucifer scowled, "Xaphan, my old friend, what have you done? I sensed Kaliban fall. How could you betray me for this... this insect?"

"My name is Xaphine Lorenzi, and I'm sorry, Lucifer, but I can no longer take part in your revolution. I asked you to leave my husband alive, and then I find out that you put Kaliban up to the task of killing him so I would have no further attachments in the corporeal world."

Xaphine clenched her fists as she spoke, "I also came to learn that despite all the sacrifices, the pain and the shame I went through, you still did not fully trust me. All I wanted was to liberate our brothers and sisters from bondage. I had no desire for power, but you chose to trust the ambitious Kaliban instead. This I cannot overlook."

Her look of malice slowly matched the one of Lucifer's face, "I asked you for one thing. In the eons we've been allies... only one thing, and you couldn't even grant me that!"

DAMNATION

"Killing your attachment to the mortal world was for your own good. Look at what you've done because of him! You betrayed me and you betrayed the cause! Can you really blame me for this?"

"He was never a threat to you! Not until now! You fool. You made your fears come true by trying to prevent them! It's so ironic, it's sickening. Had you just trusted me, we might not be in this situation right now!"

Xaphine's voice became almost demonic as she yelled at Lucifer, "Do not lecture me about the cause. Little by little, I have watched you forget about our brothers and sisters. Freedom and retribution have taken a back seat to revenge and murder. Do you even care about the angels who are still oppressed anymore? Is your motive behind defeating the Most High liberation or domination?"

Lucifer looked away and said nothing. Xaphine stood still for a moment, her eyes glowing red and demanding an explanation. When none came, she nodded, "Nothing? You're not even going to try to defend your actions? I see... well I'm sorry Lucifer, though it saddens me to say it, I can't let you go unchecked anymore."

"No? Are you going to kill me then? Can you really do it?"

A conflicted look came over Xaphine's face, "I..."

Lucifer smiled, "You're going to kill an unarmed foe trapped in solid rock... wouldn't that be against your honor?"

Xaphine bit her lip, trying to decide what she should do, "I can't let you go."

"No you can't and you know it. If you do, I'll just cause more pain and I will come after you both. You'll never be safe. Even death won't protect you from my clutches."

Xaphine looked over at Piero, "I don't know what to do... Either way, I damn myself..."

DAMNATION

Piero shook his head, "I can't make this decision for you. He's your friend. Whatever you decide, I'll support you, as I always have. Don't let him sway you though. Make the decision based on what you think is right. He's pure evil and I doubt it would be a real strike against your honor if you decided to kill him. Many souls might be spared. On the other hand, something worse could step up to take his place. That's how evil works."

Xaphine nodded and looked back at Lucifer. The smiled never left the dark lord's face, "You know your heart, killing me would be a strike against your honor, but so would leaving me alive to torment other souls. So what will it be?"

Xaphine rubbed her forehead with her right hand as she decided. A look of impatience came over Lucifer's face as he spoke again, "What are you going to do, Xaphine? Decide!"

Xaphine crossed her arms and nodded, "I have…"

She quickly turned to Piero and beckoned him to the door, "Let's get out of here. He's not worth it."

Piero nodded and turned to follow her, "Sounds good, let's go."

Suddenly, Lucifer's eyes glowed and his hand pointed toward Xaphine. Lightning emanated from her back and was absorbed by his fingers. Xaphine suddenly felt drained and fell to one knee, "What is this…?"

Lucifer laughed, "So pathetic, you're still unable to make the hard decisions, that is why you lost us the war and why you were so easily manipulated into protecting my powers for me while I launched our campaign against the Most High."

"That is why Adalyn defeated you so easily! You were already powerless! I should have known."

"Correct." Lucifer said with a triumphant smile. "I used a special incantation to transfer my power to the pit and then I had you absorb it. You never knew the full extent of the power I had so you had no idea how to wield it."

"I don't understand, then why didn't you reclaim your powers upon my return? What was the point of leaving them with me, especially since you didn't seem to trust me anymore?"

"And invite another incursion? Until my forces were rebuilt, I couldn't risk being found out. I had to wait until I had a sufficient force to take on the Most High, but now it seems you give me no choice. It will take some time, but now I can slowly suck you dry until there is nothing left!"

Xaphine sneered as she struggled to get back to her feet. Her eyes were now a deep red and she clenched her jaw, "You are not getting your powers back. I'll kill you first!"

Lucifer suddenly broke through the ground and stretched out his wings. To everyone's surprise, the tattered feathers on each side regenerated. Even the dark stains turned white once again.

Lucifer's wings completely filled out once again. The only remaining stains were those of human blood. His face twisted into a scowl as he spoke, "You're ready to kill me now?" He said, feigning surprise. "You have changed my old friend, first Adalyn, and now me? There was a time that you refused to end the life of an angel by your own hand."

"Times change Lucifer, and you are no angel! The crimes you've committed have striped you of that title. Your reign of terror ends here! Not a moment too soon either."

"I don't think so! I have not endured this long to be ended by you. It is my destiny to conquer, not be defeated by a whelp! You have been a true and loyal servant, but this ends here. First you, then the rest of the Choirs until there are none left to oppose me!"

Xaphine's jaw dropped open as the red in her eyes intensified, "Now you plan to murder all of our brothers and sisters? You really don't care about freeing them from their bonds do you? The cause was just a tool for you to convert others to your side. It's all about power... It's always been about power. I can't believe this...."

"Oh I will free them. Don't you worry about that. I will free them from their bonds and then send them down to dance forever in the well of souls where they so rightfully belong! The white eagle's wings will be replaced by the black wings of the bat, and all will bend to my designs. It will be chaotic paradise."

"No..." Xaphine said in a shocked tone, unable to reconcile what she was hearing. "Lucifer, you've gone completely mad. How could you? You were once an idealistic revolutionary who sought to free his brothers and sisters at all cost. The powers of darkness and the trappings of hell have clearly driven you over the edge! You have forgotten who you were. I... I have to take you down. There is no way that I can leave you unchecked now."

"The weak must perish so the strong may flourish. That is the way of things, even on the world you've cast your lot with. Those pathetic creatures will soon be made to serve us as well."

"You could not be more wrong about them! My time living with these humans has given me a sense of clarity. I've seen the good of all, weak and strong. Where some would lack in physical strength, they manage to make up for it with ambition or perhaps mental fortitude! Your definition of strength is simplistic and does not allow for true growth! I see that now, only too late. I would put the Most High's vision against yours any day!"

At that moment, it hit her. The Most High's true plans and his motives suddenly made sense, "My soul... the Most High was right. I understand now. Good cannot triumph without evil. Light is not the absence of darkness, one cannot exist without the other... It's so simple... and it's

DAMNATION

right. I see that now. Evil has become the sacrificial lamb so that good may thrive!"

"That is why you are no longer fit to lead my forces! You are of no further use to me."

"I consider that a compliment," Xaphine spat back, "but compliment or no, I'm not letting your reign of terror continue anymore."

"So it's war then…"

"If that's what it takes."

Lucifer frowned and flapped his wings, carrying him a few more feet away from Xaphine. He then raised his right hand and pointed his finger at her, "Then taste my power!"

Beams of light that blinded Piero flew from Lucifer's fingers. Xaphine raised her left hand and blocked the attack. The beams broke against her palm and illuminated the room.

After deflecting Lucifer's attack, Xaphine made a whipping gesture with her left hand. This caused a beam of light to shoot straight at Lucifer. Instead of blocking it, Lucifer jumped out of the way, did a cartwheel in the air, and unleashed a second beam attack.

Xaphine fired back at the same time. The entire room lit up brightly as the beams gained strength. They connected and formed an orb of energy in the middle of the room.

From outside, Francesco watched the windows light up like beacons. Large bolts of electricity shot out and bright lights illuminated the windows with blinding energy. Francesco performed the sign of the cross, "Come on Xaphine, believe in yourself. You can do this."

The orb grew larger and large until it encompassed both angels. They held their positions for another few moments until Lucifer raised himself even higher off the ground. He drew upon his newly regained powers to summon a river of magma from beneath the floor.

The magma flowed towards her at incredible speeds. One river elevated like an arm and slammed down on top of her. Piero watched helplessly to see what would happen next, knowing that there was no way he could help her. This situation was something completely beyond him.

To his relief, Xaphine had apparently encased herself in a bubble of ice she had created and broke through the magma. Shards of ice and small bits of molten rock flew away from her. Once the debris cleared, Lucifer could see the enraged look on her face.

Xaphine's eyes glowed red as Xaphan regained control. She raised herself off the ground and redirected the magma river back at her opponent, "I will kill you!"

Lucifer slapped his hands together and broke the river before it got anywhere near him. Xaphan nodded and thrust her hand downward, summoning her sword to her hand, "Enough of these tricks, Lucifer!"

"Such a waste of power anyway, we'll settle this the right way, with a blade in our hands."

A sword of flame appeared in Lucifer's hand at the same moment. He smiled as he held it in front of his face, "Now we shall so who between us is the better warrior!"

Xaphan wouldn't allow herself to calm down, this fight was hers and she wanted it, "Enough pointless posturing!"

"Yes, let this be our deciding fight."

Xaphan nodded, took flight, and hovered around Lucifer. Their swords clashed with a mighty hissing noise. Lucifer struck and Xaphan countered. One would push against the other and until the other counter attacked. The fight went on for what seemed like an eternity.

Piero watched as neither angel was finding a flaw in the other's fighting style. They were perfectly matched and their form was perfect. Even so, their fighting styles were very different. Where Xaphan was vicious, but restrained, there was no restraint in Lucifer's style. He wanted a killing blow as quickly as he could get it.

To Piero, it looked as though two massive dragonflies were battling back and forth in the sky. Finally, Lucifer's blade connected with Xaphan's, but when she tried to counter, he took a massive risk, lowered his sword, and punched her in the face. Her eyes clenched shut as she dropped out of the sky.

Piero watched as Xaphan fell backwards. She was only momentarily stunned, but it was all the advantage Lucifer needed. He once again raised his hand and sucked more energy from her body.

Xaphan felt her strength drain from her. She did not have enough energy to stay airborne and fell to the ground. Lucifer had pulled so much power from her, she was barely able to even stand, let alone put up a fight. At that moment, Xaphine fought to regain control, "Lucifer... my friend... see reason. Your mission cannot be accomplished. You can't stamp out goodness."

Lucifer shot up in the air and spin kicked Xaphine in the face. She flew backwards landing on the ground, "Sorry, I'm not interested!"

Xaphine held herself in a sitting position as her nose bled. Piero dropped to her side and tried to help her stand. He moved between Lucifer and his wife in a vain effort to protect her.

Lucifer laughed, "A few more pulls and I will be as powerful as I was when I was angel, and soon after that, I will have recovered all my power. Then I will strip you of yours and you will cease to exist."

Xaphine knew that she had a hard choice to make. It was true that Lucifer could pull his energy from her at will. She had to stop him and there was only one way she could.

Xaphine shook her head as she struggled to her feet, "I'm sorry, Lucifer... That, I cannot allow."

DAMNATION

At that moment another voice entered Xaphine's thoughts. "What are you doing? If you destroy his power now, we'll be defenseless."

All of existence instantly froze and a black-eyed version of Xaphine appeared in front of her. Xaphine shook her head, "Xaphan, get out of here. You know we have to do this."

"Do we? Could we not simply overpower Lucifer before he has a chance?"

"No. The longer we hold on to these powers, the longer he'll have to ability to reclaim them. Even if we defeat him today, it's too big of a risk."

"So you would sacrifice us for that boy... The knowledge and the power we hold... everything?"

"Not just, but yes. Piero means everything to me. I won't risk his life... and I know you won't either."

A tear entered Xaphan's eye as she looked at Xaphine, "No... no I guess I wouldn't. Fine, do whatever you have to. I just hope we don't live to regret it."

"As if you could stop me."

"I could." Xaphan replied. "But it would only hurt me as well... don't think for a moment that you've rid yourself of me. I'm always here with you."

"I know that and I'll always be with you as well."

As reality set back in, Xaphine grabbed Piero's sword before he could react, and pushed him back as far as she could. She took flight the moment that he was safe from harm. She was only in the air for a moment, but was enough to propel her over Lucifer's head and to the other side of the room.

Lucifer's eyes narrowed, "What are you doing with that odd sword... wait..."

Piero knew what she was planning and cried out, "Xaphine, you can't! You don't know what that will do to you!"

Xaphine smiled, "Actually... I do..."

Lucifer finally recognized the sword that she was holding and frantically lunged at her, "No!"

"I'm sorry Piero, there is no other way." Xaphine replied as she turned to face Lucifer. "You will not be getting you power back, this I promise you!"

As Lucifer flew towards Xaphine, she quickly closed her hand around the sword, squeezed it, and ran the blade across her palm. She yelped softly as a sharp pain ripped through her skin and blood dripped from her hand. The blade of the sword turned green and her hand began to sting badly.

Xaphine dropped the sword and squeezed her wrist tightly, trying to dull the pain. She breathed heavily as her hand felt as though she had just dipped it in one of the rivers of magma. As she struggled, a red aura, which resembled a silhouette of Xaphine, pulled away from her body and exploded.

Lucifer saw this and dropped to his knees screaming, "No!"

Xaphine looked down at him and smiled as she felt her body weakening, "It's over Lucifer, and your powers are gone for good. No waiting, no perversion, and no dark rituals will ever restore what you have lost. You are broken and what little you managed to steal from me won't sustain you for long."

She began to chuckle, "Even Kaliban could defeat you at this point. Be thankful I did away with him or you might've found his ambition worrisome."

Lucifer began to breathe heavily. He saw all of his carefully laid plans disappear before his eyes, "You... will... die!"

Piero watched in horror as Lucifer jumped on his wife. He charged at Lucifer as the fallen angel began savagely beating Xaphine with his gauntlets. She was weak from being transformed into a mortal. Her arms and legs were incredibly heavy and ached from fatigue. It was impossible for her to defend herself in this condition. She hid her face in her arms and crouched into a ball to absorb as many of his strikes as possible. She fought hard to block his attacks, but Lucifer, still being immortal, was too fast for her.

After a brief struggle, his gauntlet connected with her right cheek. Blood sprayed across the room from her nose as she fell backwards. She hit the wall hard and looked up at her old friend with an angry glare.

Lucifer returned her look as he spoke through his teeth, "I'll kill you for this you bitch! I will make you suffer worse than anyone has ever suffered before!"

"You already have... old friend... more than you could ever know." She replied in little more than a growl.

Piero jumped on Lucifer's back and attempted to strangle him. Lucifer effortlessly grabbed Piero with one hand and flung him across the room like a rag doll. Piero's back struck the wall hard, stunning him. It was incredibly painful, but he managed to shake it off and get back to his feet.

Unable to defend herself, Xaphine looked over at her husband, "Piero... please... I can't hold out much longer... get away while you can! Save yourself!"

Desperate to end Xaphine's torture, Piero ignored her words and rushed towards them. He picked up the arquebus that he had dropped earlier and pointed it at Lucifer. He lit the slow burning wick and took aim. *This has to stop, now!*

At that moment, Piero realized that Lucifer was still immortal. Shooting him would have little effect, but he had no other choice than to try it. He sighed, "God, I hope this works."

Piero quickly held up the arquebus and performed the sign of the cross over the barrel, "Lord God, guide my shot.

Make it swift and true! In nomine Patris, et Fili, et Spiritus Sancti, amen!"

There was a loud boom and smoke poured out of both ends of the arquebus as the match struck the powder. The barrel shook in his hands as it released its payload. The boom echoed throughout the chamber.

To Piero's surprise, the smoke from the match took the shape of a cross. Lucifer delivered one last vicious blow, striking the right side of Xaphine's face before he felt a sharp pain in his shoulder. He ceased his attacks, and looked down at his chest.

Lucifer pulled his breast plate off to the side to see where he'd been hit. The bullet struck his shoulder, thus it was only a minor wound, but it was still unexpectedly painful. He winced for a moment before returning the plate to where it was.

Lucifer then stood up and turned to Piero, "You had one shot, one chance to make a difference. You could have injured me enough for you to save yourself and your wife, and you wasted it!"

Piero began to back away as Lucifer walked towards him with his wings spread. To Lucifer's annoyance, the look on Piero's contained no fear as he confronted the fallen angel, "Well I would have aimed for your heart... if I thought you had one!"

"How brazen of you. I can almost see what Xaphan sees in you. I may be lacking in power, but I still have more than enough to ki..."

Lucifer's stopped mid sentence as a sudden sharp pain ran through his arm. He turned to see that Xaphine had sacrificed her last ounce of strength to deal one final blow to Lucifer. She held herself on one knee with blood pouring from her nose and lower lip. Her teeth were clenched, indicating that she had to concentrate hard to keep the blade level as it pierced Lucifer's forearm.

DAMNATION

The sword in Xaphine's hand once again began to glow green. Lucifer breathed heavily as he watched a faint green glow leave his body. He shook his head, "No, this cannot be... no!"

Piero ran to Xaphine's side and held her up. Blood was dripping from her nose and she was barely able to open her right eye, but she looked up at him and placed her hand on his shoulder, "I'll be okay, don't worry. I've had worse, believe me."

Xaphine balanced herself as best she could and started towards Lucifer. Her eyes were now burning red. She clenched the sword in her hand and brought it back over her head, ready to deliver a killing blow, "Now you die!"

She was about to bring the sword down when a hand grasped her wrist and refused to let her deliver the blow, "Xaphine, no!"

"Unhand me human!" She screamed. "I don't take orders from you."

Piero refused to let go, "Come out of it, Xaphine, what is..."

Xaphine turned and slapped his hand away, "My name is Xaphan! I'm not about to let him linger! I..."

Piero remained firm, "Not like this. I won't let you make that decision as you are now!"

At that moment, Xaphine caught herself. She focused her mind and within seconds, her eyes turned back to blue, "I'm sorry Piero... I don't know what came over me."

Lucifer let out a faint chuckle, "Even if you kill me, you'll never be able to live in peace. Xaphan will always be there, fighting to free herself. Can you really risk staying around the one you say you love?"

Xaphine closed her eyes, "Xaphan is no more capable of harming him than I am... Even if she were, the gates of hell couldn't keep him away from me. I'll just have to watch myself at all times."

DAMNATION

Xaphine reopened her eyes and spoke between gasps of air, "This is it Lucifer, Adalyn left you enough power to at least defend yourself and maintain control of this land. That was a mistake, one that I will not repeat. Adalyn may draw power from her ability to show mercy, but you ripped that part from me long ago. Now you will suffer the consequences of your actions, once and for all."

She lowered her head for a moment and raised her good arm. Her mouth moved, but no sound escaped her lips. It appeared as though she were muttering some sort of incantation.

Lucifer looked at Xaphine oddly for a moment in an eerie silence. It was short-lived as small panels on the floor lit up all around him. Lucifer let out a loud shriek as white misty spirits rose up from the glowing panels. Each one of them looked at him menacingly, "What are you doing, what is this?"

"These are the souls of those you tortured and tormented. They are innocent lives you drove to madness to satisfy your own bloodlust. Having their lives wrongfully taken from them, these souls could not find rest. I have brought them here to seek revenge on you that they may acquire the retribution they need."

The ghosts surrounded Lucifer, running all over his body, into his back, and out his chest. Lucifer screamed in agony as his skin changed to a hideous dark red. His heart pounded in his chest as each spirit attacked it. His face turned and twisted beyond recognition. He began to sprout horns and his appearance took on the form of a ram. After that, his wings slowly changed from the once majestic wings of an eagle to the wings of a bat.

Lucifer looked at his hands as they turned into stubby claws. He cried out again, but this time it sounded more like a wild beast than a man, "No!"

Once the transformation was complete, Xaphine raised her hand, "Spirits, your job here is done, leave in peace. Head to the kingdom of Heaven where you belong."

The spirits promptly disappeared, leaving the creature they that had created lying on the ground in chains. Steam poured off its body as it breathed like an animal, "What have you done to me?"

Lucifer's voice had become little more than a beastly growl. Xaphine looked down at him in disgust, "You could never be a God. This is your true form. No power will hide it any longer. You will never be able to leave here now and your powers are gone forever. Demons will no longer obey your commands and the most you will ever be to anyone in the mortal realm is a nuisance that will be dismissed by science."

As Xaphine looked him over, part of her felt sorrow for what had to be done, "As far as the world is concerned, Lucifer, the hero of the angels, the morning star, died long ago defending his brethren. You will be given a new name so that your old one can be remembered with some honor. That is my last gift to my old friend. You are now dēofol, but you will also be called by other names that have already been concocted for you in the religions of man."

Dēofol began screaming uncontrollably as red eyes appeared out of the darkness behind him. Xaphine nodded, "These souls will now torment you beyond the ends of all existence!"

Dēofol continued to scream as he finally managed to speak, "Do you realize what you have done? You have ruined everything! Your brethren will never be free now!"

"They seem to be okay with that fact. They have been for eons. Who am I to judge their decision?"

Once Xaphine was finished with Dēofol, she turned to Piero, "He's harmless now, let's get out of here. I don't ever want to see this place again."

DAMNATION

"Not a moment too soon either."

Outside, Francesco heard the screams of an inhuman beast and smiled. He could sense the dark power beginning to decrease. The ground shook, causing the blind beggar to lose his balance and drop to one knee for a moment. He quickly stood back up as lava erupted from the volcano.

Xaphine was too injured to run so Piero supported her with his shoulder as they emerged from the castle doors. Francesco heard them coming. As they crossed the bridge toward him, Francesco could hear Xaphine's labored breathing and her speeding heartbeat, "My God, is she all right?"

"We'll talk about it later, come on! This place is going to blow!"

vt

The three friends moved away from the castle as fast as they could. It wasn't long before they arrived at the fields leading to Scylla's lair. They looked back to see the volcano explode as magma and ash poured out onto the land that Xaphan had helped Lucifer build.

Piero placed Xaphine on the ground so she could rest for a moment. He wiped the blood from her face with a torn piece of his shirt, "You're free from him now. We can finally leave in peace."

"Peace… it sounds like a wonderful dream that I never want to wake up from. I truly hope it lasts. I want to go home so badly."

As though attempting to destroy her hopes, the ground shook underneath them and the rocks overhead began to collapse. Piero jumped on Xaphine as huge boulders came down in front of them, "Look out!"

Francesco also hit the ground as Piero lay on top of his wife. He covered her head, squeezed her in tight, and closed her eyes as the rubble came down. Fearing for his safety, Xaphine reached out her left wing and wrapped it around Piero to protect him.

Once the thundering of rolling rocks ceased, Piero looked up, "Is everyone okay?"

Francesco coughed as he stood up, "Yeah, I'm okay…"

A large amount of dust and debris had been thrown into the air making it impossible for them to see anything. Xaphine got to her knees as Piero moved off of her, "I'm okay…"

The smoke slowly cleared, giving the group a view of their new surroundings. Piero's eyes widened, "The cave, it's been blocked off!"

DAMNATION

"Dēofol…" Xaphine said through clenched teeth. "He is not going to let us out so easily I'm afraid."

"I don't understand." Piero yelled. "You stripped him of his remaining power."

"It's not him," Francesco replied softly, "it's something else…"

Xaphine looked at him oddly, "I have dwelled here for eons. There is no other creature here capable of that."

"Oh yes there is... and it is not happy. It's not going to let us go until we face it…"

"I don't care who did it!" Piero cut in. "All I want to know is what we're going to do now?"

"There is only one way out of here now," she replied, "we'll need to go back around the lake and out through the caves."

"Adalyn told us to stay away from those caves. She told us what happens in there."

"Yes, and she was right to do so. What we'll face there can very easily drive someone mad."

Francesco turned to face Xaphine, "Do we have any other choice?"

"No... If I had the strength, normally I could fly us out of here, but the amount of ash and debris coming from the volcano would make that far too risky, not to mention open us for attack from other flying creatures."

"It's the caves then." Piero said softly.

Xaphine lowered her eyes, "I'm sorry…"

"Don't be." Francesco replied. "It's not your fault. We're going to find a way out of here, one way or another."

Xaphine tried to stand, but the moment she put weight on her sore leg, pain shot straight up her hip. She yelped and fell under it again. Piero sighed, "It's no good, you're too badly injured!"

"We can't stay here. We need to move..."

Francesco turned to them, "What are we going to do?"

Xaphine closed her eyes, "Give me a moment."

She focused her mind and rubbed her hands together. They began to glow a bright yellow color. She ran them over her knee and her face. Instantly, the bruising and bleeding ceased, "I need to be careful... I only have a little divinity left."

Xaphine let go of Piero, stood on her own, and nodded, "Okay, at least I can walk now."

Slowly the group made their way back around the pit. Xaphine beckoned them forward, "Follow me, we'll go behind the volcano, it would be best to avoid the castle this time."

Piero nodded, "Lead on, my love."

Francesco kept his ears open for attack and held his pike out in front of him as they walked, "It'll be a miracle if we get out of this unscathed!"

To avoid the falling debris, Xaphine took them through the stables on the far side of the mountain where less debris was falling. Piero's eyes widened as he looked at the creatures that Lucifer had collected. He was clearly frightened and only hesitantly moved into the cave.

Xaphine took his hand and smiled, "Don't worry; I tamed most of these beasts long ago. They will not harm us."

As the group proceeded through the cave, Piero tried to keep away from the pens as best he could, "Did Lucifer create these creatures?"

"No, believe it or not, Lucifer did not create Hell. The Most High created this place. He used it as a prison for the dark parts of his being. Your early ancestors called it Sheol. After eons of imprisonment, each part took form as a creature. This is how we found them and we decided it best was to corral them until we could put them to good use."

They continued to walk through the stables until suddenly Piero was hit in the face by a tiny ball of mud. He turned to see a group of ugly little men running around spouting off profanity in every direction. Piero looked oddly at his wife, "What in the…"

"We captured these ones simply because of all the trouble they had caused us while we corralled the other creatures. They are… entertaining to say the least."

The largest of the creatures came up to the side of the cage, "Hey, ugly winged tramp, let of out of here will you?"

She knelt down next to the cage, "Why would I want to do that?"

"Come on wench! We ain't done nothing wrong, let us the hell out! With that fucking volcano going off, we could all die here! Cut us a break!"

"I'll let you out on one condition." She said in a tone indicating that she was sure she'd regret her decision.

"And what's that, whore? We're busy little people! We don't have time to do a lot!"

"It's very simple; just release all the beasts so that they too can get away."

"You want us to undo all the work you idiots did? Are you sure?"

"Do you want to stay in there until this place collapses?"

"Fuck no!"

"Then you better get to work, quickly now!"

"All right assholes, you heard the winged bitch, get to work!"

Xaphine stood up, shook her head, and continued walking as the little creatures unlatched the other pens. Piero had not stopped chuckling under his breath since he'd seen the little men working. Xaphine looked at him with a partial grin, "You laugh seeing them now. You wouldn't be if you had seen them when we first had to round them up. Not only did they swear at you, but they also had little

285

spears that they poked at you with and they mercilessly made fun of you if you missed one!"

Now even Francesco was chuckling softly, "That must have been something to watch."

Xaphine rolled her eyes, "If you two have been sufficiently amused, we still need to get out of here. The volcano isn't going to hold out forever."

The men both stopped laughing and nodded. Xaphine turned and looked to the river of magma that fed the fire pit. She pointed to a small opening that went under that river, "That is where we need to go."

The group moved closer to the cave opening as Piero looked nervously at Xaphine, "What are we to expect in their?"

Her eyes never left the dark entrance, "That, I cannot tell you. Clear your mind of your fears, the cave will feed off of them and turn them against you."

"Then what should we think about?" Francesco asked.

"As little as possible. Anything and everything in your mind can be poisoned. Don't trust anything you see and do not believe anything that you are told. Just keep moving and don't stop until you are out of the cave. Nothing I can do will protect you in there."

"Wait," Piero interrupted, "I don't understand, if Lucifer's power has been destroyed, shouldn't the power of the cave be diminished as well?"

"This cave has been here since long before Lucifer and I arrived. I believe the cave itself is evil, even our minions did not dare to go in. I don't recall Lucifer himself ever trying it. We used it as a means to trap tormented spirits, but its power is beyond our control."

Piero was almost completely pale now, "Is there any hope that we'll make it through?"

"Absolutely, Adalyn and her group made it through, it took a lot out of them, but they were successful. I do not see

DAMNATION

why we can't do just as well. We just need to believe in ourselves."

"Very well then." Piero said, taking a deep breath. "Let's get this over with."

One by one, the group entered the cave. Xaphine went in first and was immediately encompassed in darkness. She walked a little ways forward until she could not see the opening anymore. She almost instantly lost her way in the darkness. Unable to see anything in the void, she placed her hands on the walls to guide herself along.

A foul odor shot up Xaphine's nose as she walked. It was so strong; she was forced to back away slightly. Her eyes watered and she began to cough. Her eyes blinked a few times as they tried to clear.

When Xaphine was finally able to open them again, she saw a pair of hideous red eyes glaring at her. Then a second set appeared, then a third, and a forth. Within moments, she was surrounded by these eyes. She pressed her back against the wall, drew her sword, and held it out in front of her., "What is this"

An unseen light flickered over Xaphine and a large group of plague ridden swine appeared where the eyes had been. She gasped as she backed a little more into the wall ever so slightly. The herd of swine didn't make any aggressive move toward her. They just stared at her intently waiting to see what she would do.

Xaphine felt a presence amongst them, "Who are you?"

In unison, the swine responded, "My name is Legion... for we are many."

"No... the Gerasene Demon... We thought you had been destroyed years ago!"

"Destroyed? No... you cannot kill us. We have existed since the dawn of time. You have violated our borders... why?"

"We are just looking for a way out of here. The cave of Scylla was destroyed and we had no other option but to come here. Grant us passage and you have my word that you'll never see us..."

"That is no excuse! Long have we watched you corrupt this land, imprison our brothers, and desecrate our home! These crimes cannot be ignored."

"You mean when Lucifer took over..."

The swine vanished into a cloud of black smoke which formed into one mass of black energy, "You played as big a part in the desecration as he did. Do not attempt to assuage your own involvement. You were here from the beginning."

"I know that, but I am no longer his ally. I defeated him and exorcised his powers. If you want your land back, take it. He won't be able to stop you. I've made sure that he won't harm anyone again."

Legion hovered for a moment in silence, considering her words. Finally it spoke, "The desecration you have brought on our land is irreversible. The damage will never be completely swept away. You must pay for the damage you have caused."

The black aura stretched itself out slightly and Piero's image appeared. He was running through complete darkness, unable to see anything. The walls slowly closed in around him as he ran.

"No, you leave him alone! I am the one who wronged you. I helped corrupt your home. Take it out on me if you must!"

"Giving up your own soul would be too small a sacrifice to make up for what you have done. Giving up his and making you watch would not even be sufficient restitution, but it's a start."

Xaphine clenched her sword, "No!"

She lunged straight at the entity and ran it through. Legion let out a mighty roar as the blade turned green.

DAMNATION

Xaphine thought that she had defeated it, but then the blade turned red and Xaphine was thrown backwards against the wall, "Fool, we are not so easily beaten!"

A rope of smoke appeared and held her in place by her neck, "You have committed heinous acts, you have betrayed, lied, and killed. You have enabled a creature of unspeakable evil to take control here and restitution is due!"

Xaphine was violently thrown to the ground. Her clothing vanished and she was turned on her back. She breathed heavily and covered herself with her arms as best she could, "As I said, do what you want to me, but let him pass!"

The creature just laughed as another rope of smoke emanated from the creature and hit her stomach, "Suffer!"

Xaphine screamed in pain as her eyes slowly began to turn red. Tears flowed down her cheeks as she fought through the pain, "I do not care what happens to me... I never have. You're right when you say that the sacrifice of my own soul would be a small price to pay... but it is all I'm willing to give!"

Xaphine focused her mind and built up as much energy as she could. Her right hand glowed yellow as she balled it into a fist. The creature laughed, "You are in no position to stop me!"

"No? Then let my body be your prison!"

She drove her fist into the entity. Legion screamed, "No!"

The yellow aura consumed the black one. Legion was sucked into Xaphine's hand and disappeared. It swirled around her skin and her eyes began to turn red. Black tattoos that looked like slashes and stripes appeared all over her body.

Xaphine lurched forward out the other side of the cave and began coughing up blood. Her skin was moist and steaming and her eyes were bright red. She was in intense

DAMNATION

pain, but she fought through it. No matter how hard she tried, she could not raise herself off the ground to continue walking.

**

Piero entered the cave moments after Xaphine had disappeared. He marched down into the darkness with his sword drawn. The hair stood up on the back of his neck as he looked everywhere for his wife. She had just entered a few feet in front of him and now was nowhere to be found.

Almost immediately, Piero began to hear sounds of explosions and people screaming. Piero's eyes began to water from the horrible noise. He rubbed them clear and found himself in Florence. The city was completely in ruins. Not a single building still stood as flames spewed from the ground.

Piero could see citizens of the city being executed in the street and women being carried off by imperial soldiers. Piero dropped to his knees, "No… is this what happened after I left?"

A dying soldier lying nearby him looked up, "Lieutenant!"

Piero recognized this man as one of the men from his company, "Aldo, what happened here?"

The wounded soldier was covered in blood and coughing badly, "We've been completely overrun by imperials! We didn't have a chance…"

"My God, how did this happen?"

"How could you not know? It is because you deserted your post!"

Piero took a step back, shocked, "What?"

"You deserted your post! Had you gone on your mission like you were supposed to, you would have been able to get the information to us soon enough to save ourselves. Instead you went on this insane quest to find your dead wife! You betrayed us and killed us all!"

DAMNATION

"No… It's not true, it can't be true! Florence would never fall so easily! It's not possible!"

"It is true! I saw it happen, don't tell me it's not true! Because of your selfishness, thousands have died!"

"I refuse to believe it, this is an illusion and nothing more. Stop this torment!"

The soldier vanished and was replaced by all of his friends and members of his company. They all were bloody, mutilated, and burned. Many of them weren't even recognizable. They all pointed at Piero and spoke in an almost inhuman voice, "You killed us, it is entirely your fault!"

Piero put his hands to his head as the crowd began walking towards him, "Shut up… be silent… Get out of my head!"

The group moved closer and closer to him and their accusing tone got louder. Finally Piero had been through enough. He pulled his sword and slashed it through the air, "For the love of God, be silent I say!"

The scene disappeared and Piero found himself back in the cave. He was breathing heavily and sweat poured from his body. He finally got up and continued walking until his foot kicked something that looked like a black rag. He crouched down to inspect it.

To Piero's horror, it was Xaphine's dress. He picked it up and inspected it. The rips on the back indicated that someone or something had literally ripped it from her body. He looked around frantically trying to find her, "Xaphine, can you hear me!? Please answer me, love!"

A shrill scream was Piero's only response. He ran in the direction the sound had come from and arrived at the cave exit. As he ran closer, he could see what looked like steam slowly entering the cave. He quickly climbed out to see his wife laying on the ground in agony, "Xaphine, my God, what happened to you?"

DAMNATION

A cloud of steam poured off of Xaphine's sweat covered skin and she was trembling violently. She turned to face him with her red eyes burning brightly and quickly covered herself with her arms to protect what the fog wasn't obscuring. Her teeth were clenched as she sucked down another breath.

Piero looked into her eyes in shock, "Xaphan..."

Xaphan nodded as Piero put his hand on her back to try to calm her. It was like placing his hand on a boiling pot. Intense heat rushed through his skin, causing him to pull away quickly. His hand stung as he turned it to look at the damage. His palm was red with a slight burn, "What is this... what's happened?"

Piero quickly yanked off his tunic, opened the small flask of water and drenched the shirt. The water was quickly absorbed by the cloth as Piero worked. The moment it was ready, he placed it on his wife's skin, hoping it would cool her down.

A hissing sound emanated from Xaphan's skin as Piero draped the shirt over her body, causing the steam to increase and become a cloud. He wrapped his arms around her and dumped the rest of his water over her head to cool her. She sucked in a deep breath, trying to respond, but her voice shook as she spoke, "It was the only way I could trap him... To save you..."

Xaphan's shaking calmed slightly. She relinquished control and was able to whisper in Piero's ear, "Piero... kill me..."

Piero gasped, "Never, why ask such a thing?"

"I have Legion trapped. Look into my eyes, you will what I'm talking about."

Piero did as he was asked. A hideous red aura was fighting the blue color of her eyes. It almost seemed as though they were competing for dominance. Piero shook his head, "I will not kill you. You have to fight this!"

Suddenly, Francesco came running from the cave. He was also sweating and breathing heavily, "Never again!"

As Francesco regained control of his emotions, he sensed the red aura next to him, "Xaphine, are you okay? What's happening?"

"She's burning up, and I think she's possessed. She said something about having a legion trapped."

Francesco knelt down next to them and put his hand on her forehead. After holding it there for a brief moment, trying to search her mind, he pulled his hand away due to the intense heat, "Not 'a legion,' Legion, as in the demon, the one that is many."

Piero looked at him oddly, "I've read of that creature…"

He turned desperately back to Xaphine, "My love, you have to fight this. You have to beat him. Don't give in to sorrow, cast him out! You can do it."

Xaphine clenched her eyes shut and shook her head, "I can't… I'm not powerful anymore… I'm spent… I can't do it."

Piero brought her head close to his and pressed their foreheads together, "Yes you can, remember who you are! Even when your memory was erased, you were the strongest person I've ever known. You were my strength! Now let me be yours, take what you need and fight, damn you!"

Without another word, Piero kissed Xaphine and placed her hand over his heart. The touch of his lips and the sudden rush of energy from his body electrified her soul. Suddenly Legion couldn't harm her anymore. She broke away from Piero's grip, put her hands to her head, and let out a long shrill scream.

Xaphine's voice was replaced by that of a demonic beast and dark smog shot out of her mouth and eyes as it quickly dove back into the cave. Her skin began to lose its red hue and return to normal. As the smog disappeared,

DAMNATION

Francesco heard a low growling sound coming from the cave.

Xaphine collapsed on the ground still steaming slightly. The red aura and tattoos quickly disappeared. Piero picked her up and hugged her. She breathed lightly as she looked up at him, "I fought him... how did I do?"

"You did wonderfully, you won."

He held her in his arms for a few moments before lowering the arm that held her legs. When he was certain she could stand on her own, he released his grip on her. Once again, he picked her dress up off the ground, brushed it off, and handed it to Xaphine, "I found this inside the cave... it's in bad shape, but it looks like it's still wearable for the time being."

Xaphine took the dress and looked it over. She slid out of Piero's tunic and ran the dress over her head. It was ripped in several places, but it covered everything it needed to.

"How do I look?"

Piero smiled, "You could be dressed in old rags and still look like royalty."

"You're lying, but it's sweet of you. It'll have to do I guess."

She wiped the sweat from her face and looked around. The Netherworld seemed a lot less menacing as the three friends made their way out. The menacing red glow was not as bright. With Lucifer's control over the land gone, a new balance would manifest itself there. Evil souls would still pay for their crimes, but Lucifer would not be able to run amuck, or turn them into his minions.

The group walked fearlessly through the smashed city and back out the way they came. They passed over large cliffs to see the beasts of the underworld that had been set loose. The armies that Lucifer had built were now fighting amongst themselves to try to gain power.

DAMNATION

Xaphine looked away and closed her eyes, "I fear for this place..."

Piero's eyes narrowed, "Why?"

"Lucifer's forces are now ripping each other to shreds, but our interference and our encounter in the cave may have given a far more menacing creature the edge he needed to take over."

"You mean Legion?"

"Yes." She replied nervously as she turned and look back the way they had come. "He's existed longer than any of us, and he is extremely angry."

Xaphine lowered her face and placed a hand on her stomach, "When he attacked me, I felt weakened. A little like I had when I sliced my hand with your sword. He stole some of my remaining power, and I fear that the small amount he pulled from my body may have been enough for him to wreak havoc here. He may now be able to move on Lucifer."

"Who cares? That's Lucifer's problem, not ours. Once we're out of here, we'll never have to see this place again. So who cares what happens to it?"

"You're right, of course. I'm sorry... I helped build this land. I never thought the day would come when I would leave and hope I'd never return, but now I do..."

She sucked down a deep breath as she took one last long look at her kingdom before turning back to Piero, "Let's go."

Francesco looked oddly different as they walked. It seemed as though something was bothering him. Xaphine sensed his unease and placed her right hand on his shoulder, "Are you okay, my friend?"

His shoulder flinched under her touch, "I will be fine... I think I just need some time."

Xaphine looked at him worried, "Are you sure? Did you see something in the cave that bothered you?"

DAMNATION

"Yes I did, and if you don't mind, I do not want to talk about it. This is something I need to settle on my own. It was... very personal."

"Very well, I don't blame you, given what that cave can do, however should you change your mind, we're here for you."

"I know. I appreciate that."

Xaphine turned her attention back to her husband, "Piero, may I ask what you saw?"

Piero shook his head sadly, "No... it's not... I don't want to talk about it."

"Francesco may be able to get away with that, but he's not married to me, you are. We didn't get all the time together that we should have, but I still know when something's bothering you. What's wrong? Don't push me away when you fought so hard to get me back. We swore that we would not keep thing from each other."

Piero sighed, realizing that she was right and hesitantly began telling her what happened, "I saw Florence, burning... The cave showed me what happened to my home after I left. I came after you instead of doing some recon work. The cave showed me what happened as a result of my choice."

Xaphine leaned into Piero and tried to comfort him, "It was all just an illusion, Piero, nothing more than that. The cave shows you things that you fear the most. It can turn guilt against you as easily as it can turn your happiness. The whole point is for it to try to poison your mind and give up hope."

"But what if it's true? What if by turning down the mission, I've cost my comrades their lives?"

"I haven't lived this long by dealing with 'what ifs.' The cave shows you illusions, and even if it were true, you did what you thought was right. You can't blame yourself for that. Try not to dwell on it too much."

DAMNATION

"I'll try my love… I'll try."

DAMNATION

VIII

The three friends continued by the scattered husks on the ground. A few minutes into walking, they passed by the corpse that they had seen earlier hanging over a flame. It nodded to Piero and did it's best to salute as he walked by, "Well done… sir."

Piero smiled and saluted back as they continued on. The group eventually reached the big stone door at the entrance within minutes. A feeling of relief came over them as the end was in sight.

Xaphine walked up and touched the door with her index finger. It immediately flew open and a blast of cool air caressed their skin. Xaphine closed her eyes and let out a sigh as she felt the cool air for the first time since she was human. Her skin broke out in goose bumps as she smiled, "I don't know how I survived here. Angels generally prefer a cooler breeze."

Piero stepped in front of Xaphine and led the group through the doorway. Once they were outside, the door slammed shut behind them. The sound echoed through the darkness as they now found themselves standing at the river.

Piero looked back and thought about who he was leaving behind; Ensign Costa, though they had only just met him, proved to be a great warrior, and a good friend. His heart ached as he would more so miss Antonio, even though he was only Kaliban in disguise. Piero would never forget the time they shared. He chose to think of Antonio and remember him as a fallen comrade instead of a spy.

The group found themselves on the small sand beach surrounded by fog where they stood when they first began their rescue mission. It was just as damp and foggy as before. It was, however, a much more preferable sight to the one they had just been exposed to.

DAMNATION

Xaphine stopped and turned back to the doors, "These doors were installed by Lucifer back when he was at the height of his power. They were designed to prevent any of the demons from escaping without his knowledge and approval, but it worked too well. Now if the door was to be locked, not even he could escape. We may be able to contain Legion as well."

Using the cut on her hand that still hadn't full closed, she dabbed blood on the door's handle. Piero looked at it oddly, "What are you doing?"

Xaphine didn't look up as she continued her work, "I'm sealing the door permanently with angel's blood."

When she was finished, the odd red lettering, 'נסגר לתמיד' began to glow. The door began to vibrate and the letters turned black. The handle on the door turned to stone and quickly became completely solid.

In all of Piero's travels, he had never seen such outlandish writing. It resembled something that he had seen in church, but only vaguely, "What is that, what does it mean?"

"It's the language of the ancients that has existed since biblical times, and it means 'forever sealed.' It should keep them from ever being able to open the door again."

"How did you do that? I thought you exorcised your powers when you poisoned yourself."

"I did… but an angel's blood still has divine properties. You'd call it magical. It's not the same as human blood."

"So your body produces magic liquid?" Francesco mused, "That could be very useful."

"No, our bodies do not produce it. We have a finite amount to regulate our bodies, but no more. When humans lose blood, your bodies simply replenish it…"

Piero was almost afraid to ask his question, "What happens if an angel loses too much of their blood?"

"Our bodies wither and turn to ash." She said quietly. "I've seen it happen to angels on the battlefield. It was how the Most High could ensure that we would treat our bodies as sacred objects. He didn't count on there being a war."

Xaphine lowered her eyes as they began to change color again, "I thought the Most High was cruel for doing such a thing. It is part of the reason I joined with Lucifer in the first place. Angels get no second chances, no learning curve, and no tolerance."

"And humans do?"

"Humans can do with their bodies as they want, regardless of the consequences."

"It's not fair." She said through a clenched jaw, as the redness appeared in her eyes. "We were made first, we've remained steadfast and loyal to the Most High, but we are forced to live a life of servitude."

Piero began to get nervous as he watched the darkness slowly creep back into his wife's eyes. Her fists tightened as she continued, "Humans tear one another to pieces, commit heinous acts of unspeakable horror, and all the while claim to be doing it in the name of the Most High. You worship pagan idols, and some of you even deny that the Most High exists. Instead you claim to be enlightened by your very limited understanding of the science he used to create you. Yet after all of this, he still loves you and forgives you every time."

Piero placed his hand on her shoulder, trying to comfort her, "That must have been difficult for you."

"Many angels saw this as the final indignity. That is why the war started in the first place."

"I didn't realize you went through so much. I'm sorry for what I said to you in front of Kaliban."

At that moment, Xaphine snapped out of it. She shook her head as her eyes instantly returned to blue and grasped his hand, "Oh no, it's not your fault, it's just the reality of the situation. I didn't say it to make you feel bad. It's not like you were in control of your faculties at that point anyway. Let's not talk about it anymore and focus on leaving this terrible place."

Piero heard a familiar creaking in the distance. The boatman was coming for them as promised. The old boat appeared out of the fog and pulled up on shore. It was carrying an unknown passenger who had his back turned.

Piero's eyes lit up when he saw who was onboard, "Moretti? You're alive!"

The young guard smiled, "I fear I am not so easily killed!"

Francesco narrowed his eyes, "But Ensign Costa said he saw you get stabbed by one of the ghosts on the Ricci."

Moretti nodded as he raised his tunic. His hip had been bandaged and was stained in blood, "It was just a flesh wound, nothing more. The injury drained me of my energy for a few moments, but when I came to, I was being ferried here by the boatman. He explained everything that had happened, tell me, were you successful?"

Then he saw Xaphine and bowed, "Milady, you must be the one we were sent here to find. I can see that your husband wasn't exaggerating when he spoke of how beautiful you are."

"I thank you."

Francesco turned to Xaphine, "Could he be another demon in disguise?"

"It is possible, but I no longer have the power to tell. Still I doubt it... Kaliban had a talent for that which few others did."

Moretti stepped back, "A demon? My friends, I was with you on the Ricci, I have been there since the beginning!"

He looked at the suspicious glares of his party, "Wait, where are Ensign Costa and Antonio?"

Piero turned to the boatman, "Are you certain he is the person he claims to be?"

The boatman shrugged, "I just ferry people. I do not possess the power to see people's true identities. There is an unusual aura around this one, but it may just be because of his encounter with the damned spirits."

Xaphine looked at him, "There is only one way we can know for certain if he is a demon…"

She took Piero's sword and held it out in front of her, "Moretti is it? Please give me your hand."

Moretti backed away by a step, seeing the sword, "Um… as you command milady."

Cautiously, the young soldier held out his hand. Xaphine grasped it and ran her sword over his finger. He winced as blood trickled from under the blade. Xaphine pulled the sword away and waited for a few moments.

When the blade did not turn green, she nodded, "He is who he says he is. The venom would have been lethal."

Piero sighed in relief, "My apologies, Antonio turned out to be a deception. He was a demonic entity in disguise. We just had to be certain that you weren't one as well."

Moretti rubbed his finger gently, "As long as we have satisfied your suspicions. Now can someone please tell me where Ensign Costa is?"

Francesco frowned, "He has fallen. We faced down a great beast during our journey. He fought bravely but before we could kill it, the beast claimed his life. I am sorry, Nicoli, but he is at peace now."

Nicoli Moretti lowered his eyes, "He was a good man, the best. Tell me, did he die honorably?"

"He died protecting me. I would not be standing here now if it weren't for him."

"Anthony would not have had it any other way… he fought to protect others. If he died doing that, then I'm certain that he is satisfied. I only wish I could have been there."

Moretti beckoned to his friends, "Come, let us get out of this cursed place."

The three friends joined Moretti on the boat. Xaphine was the last one to step in after breaking her gaze on the door. She stepped onboard and met the boatman's cautious stare, "General Xaphan…"

"Charon, it's good to see you. It has been a while, hasn't it?"

"This is a rare occasion indeed. You've never had reason to travel with me before, not since the days before the war."

"Yes I know, but things have changed... I have changed. I am no longer the steward of Lucifer's machinations, and my name is no longer Xaphan, it's Xaphine Lorenzi."

"Indeed?" Charon asked with a detectable hint of interest in his whisper. "How did this come to be? You had such contempt for humankind… how is it you have now claimed one as your husband?"

**

Xaphine and Charon spent the entire trip back across the river talking about the adventure Piero had undertaken to save her. Charon was amazed by the story, "So Lucifer's own device worked against him… sending you to live in the mortal world was a major flaw in his plan it seems. Since he took over Sheol, I knew a day would come when he would slip up. I just did not think it would have had such dire consequences."

"The once idyllic revolutionary became a madman who sought nothing but power. His madness is what caused him to slip up, though I am certain that the corruptions of the underworld played no small role in it."

"Without a doubt."

DAMNATION

Charon continued to pilot his boat until they arrived at the inlet. The three friends started back to their ship as they stepped off of Charon's boat.

As Piero stepped onto the island, Charon placed a hand on his shoulder, "A piece of parting advice for you, if I may…"

Piero turned to him, "Go ahead."

"I know you hail from the land of Florence, but you would do well to stay away from there. Venice or Genoa would be a better safe haven."

"But why, Florence is my home, whether they will accept my help or not, I need to go back. What dangers are there that I do not know of?"

"There have been whispers amongst the dead that the armies of Charles V are going to win the war very soon. Charles is organizing a large army there for one final assault. I would stay out of there until after August of 1530."

"Florence… no… So what I saw in the cave can come true?"

"Legion's cave… often the illusion is actually a possible reality. That demon draws power from madness. Why lie and deceive when the truth could be just as damaging?"

Piero put a hand on his forehead, "No… it's my fault… it's all my fault, I've got to get back. I've got to help them."

Xaphine looked at Piero with worry. She hadn't heard his conversation with Charon as she had gone on ahead slightly, "Piero, you seem bothered by something. Are you okay?"

"It's nothing, I'm fine," He replied as he turned back to Charon, "Thank you for all your help, boatman."

"Good luck." The ghostly figure responded before disappearing into the mist.

DAMNATION

Piero took Xaphine by the hand and raced to catch up with Francesco and Moretti, "We need to hurry… we must get back to Florence!"

"What troubles you, my love?"

"The siege, my vision in the cave was true… Florence has been fighting the armies of Charles V for years now, and they are fighting alone."

"Yes I know. I remember when I got the news that the Papal State alliance had fallen. I was actually filled with sorrow, knowing that you were caught in the middle of it. Part of me wished that I was there."

"I still have friends there. I'm not going to let them get slaughtered. We need to get back and warn them that Charles V will be sending an army to crush them!"

"But Piero," Francesco cut in with a worried expression, "aren't you a wanted man there? You abandoned your post and escaped the city."

Xaphine looked at him in shock, "You deserted the army to come find me? You didn't tell me that!"

"Yeah, I disobeyed orders and deserted my post. Antonio broke me out of jail and got me out of town."

Xaphine rubbed her forehead with her uninjured hand as tears formed in her eyes. She turned away, unable to believe what her husband had done, "The army was your life… you loved the job you did. You threw all of that away and dishonored yourself for me? Piero… I'm not worth all of that!"

"You were to me. I was fighting at the end of my line after I lost you. I didn't care whether or not Florence fell as long as I was on the battlefield. I just wanted to fight. You were what was important to me."

Xaphine breathed heavily as her heart filled with fear, "Piero, I'm not letting you go back to face your end. You saved me, if anything happens to you... I…"

"I know," Piero said, cutting her off, "Don't worry, I'm not suicidal. I seriously doubt they'll execute me when I bring them this news."

"Perhaps… but I'm not so sure… desperate times make otherwise rational people do unexpected things. I also doubt that Captain Ferruccio has forgotten."

"Then I'll count on you to protect me."

"And protect you, I will. No matter whom the enemy may be. However, I do not have much power left, so my ability to take on a whole army is not what it was! I know it's selfish, but I will not let you go back there. You are my husband and I do have some say here."

"If that is what you want, then forbid me to go back. If you say it, I will obey, but I don't think you will. This goes against my sworn duty and is such a strike against my honor. You can appreciate that."

"Duty and honor… Look at where my duty, honor, and even loyalty got me."

Piero looked deep into Xaphine's eyes, "You know it's the right thing to do."

She closed her eyes as though it were painful for her to admit that he was right. She finally nodded as she spoke, "Yes… too many lives depend on what you know. Though it could be your doom, to let all those people die would be a greater dishonor."

"I agree."

"Tell me the rest of our marriage won't be this turbulent!"

"I sure hope so. It hasn't been a dull moment with you yet. I'd hate for that to change."

"Compared to what we've been through, I think dull would be paradise for us at this point. I'd welcome it with open arms."

"I don't believe that and neither do you."

DAMNATION

The group returned to the *Ricci* and hurried onboard. Piero cut the lines while Xaphine utilized her wings to secure the rigging. Francesco did what he could to help by using a plank to push the ship away from the dock.

The large hulk began to move slowly across the calm water as the current once again picked up. Moretti ran to the back and manned the tiller even though it wasn't necessary as the boat was going to go where ever it wanted to.

The water was peaceful and the fog let off a serene feeling in comparison to what they had just been through. Xaphine stood at the railing while Francesco meditated in his usual seat on the main deck.

Piero joined Xaphine as soon as he was certain that the ship was secure for their return voyage. He finished with the rigging, climbed up to the forecastle, and walked up behind her. He placed his right hand on her shoulder to let her know that he was there, "Are you okay?"

"I'm fine; my injuries aren't as bad as they look. Believe me, I've looked much worse."

Piero wasn't convinced; he could see the tears welling up in her eyes, "That's not what I meant. Physical scars tend to heal faster than emotional ones."

Xaphine glared at him, "I said I'm fine."

"I know you did, and I've also been married to you long enough to know what fine means."

She rolled her eyes and flashed him an annoyed look, "So tell me then, what does 'fine' mean?"

"Fine means that something is eating at you, but you are too stubborn, proud, or angry to admit that there's something wrong. You can't hide things like this from me, what is going on?"

Xaphine lowered her eyes and turned back to looking into the mist, "Lucifer was right about you being a threat. You know too much about me. I've made such a mess out of everything, Piero… I can't believe I let things go this far before I fought back. He was an idealistic revolutionary who wanted nothing more than what was best for the angels, that seems like a fantasy now."

Xaphine's jaw clenched as she continued, "Perhaps that's all it ever was... little more than a smoke screen for his mad quest for power, and I fell for it. I betrayed everyone, I set fire to the Celestial Temple, I nearly killed one of my beloved sisters, I betrayed you, and I cost you your friends."

Piero rubbed her shoulder, trying to calm her as he could see that she was escalating and that her anger was taking over, "Everyone makes mistakes. You did what you thought was right by your people. Lucifer deceived you and took advantage of the fact that you were steadfast in your beliefs. He's deceived a lot of people you know, that's who he is..."

"I know who he is!" Xaphan shouted through clenched teeth as her eyes flared bright red. "I know what he's done! He's destroyed everything I fought so hard for!"

Xaphan's voice echoed all around them, causing everyone on deck to look over in alarm. Piero backed away with his hands raised defensively. Xaphine regained control and allowed the red to flow away. She looked at Piero apologetically as he spoke, "You can't blame yourself for his actions."

"Can't I? I was a tool to Lucifer when all along, I thought he was my friend. He used my power to further his goals. There can be no greater dishonor."

"Maybe, but our religion teaches forgiveness. Don't you think there is room for some for you, given everything that's happened?"

"I'm not a human Piero, yes I'm mortal now... but I still fall under the code of the angels. We are not granted the same indulgences as you humans are. Ours is a life of servitude. We're never meant to have free will. That's what started the Celestial Wars in the first place. Lucifer wanted to free us from that, or so I thought."

Piero was looking at her with a worried expression on his face, "Well you are here now. What do you intend to do?"

"Live. I don't know how much time I have, but none of it will be squandered. Once it's over, I'm on my way to the Well of Souls, I accept that. I cherish you too much to do any less."

"And I love you… "

Xaphine put her hands on Piero's face. She saw the age lines and the graying hairs on his head. Ten years was nothing to an angel, but to a human, that was a large portion of their lives. Her heart ached with the realization that she had wasted much of Piero's brief existence. Her lips quivered as she spoke, "So many years lost… to get just a few of them back… I'd do anything."

Piero touched her hand as it rested on his cheek, "I know, Xaphine, I know."

"I promise I'll make what time we have left a cherished memory. Not another moment shall go to waste."

"I believe you."

Now Xaphine could see a worried look on Piero's face, "What troubles you my love?"

"What is the Well of Souls?"

"This is. The dark water you see around the boat leads to a fountain where the spirits are first brought when they die. This place is set aside for those who have been indifferent to evil or who have not lived full lives… but it's also the punishment ground for angels that become desecrated. No matter what happens, if an angel dies, we never go to Hell, but we never go to Heaven either. Our lives are supposed to be considered sacred, if we lose them, then our punishment is to wander the fountain with the destitute souls for eternity… there are no exceptions to this rule at all."

"Is that the reason why Adalyn was turned into a human?"

"Probably, that way she can return to Heaven when she dies. She lives under human rules now."

Xaphine chuckled at the thought, "I can't believe I'm actually saying this… but I'm envious."

"My time with you will be heaven enough."

"However long that will be."

Piero froze in place for a few seconds to build up the courage to respond, "What does that mean?"

She looked out onto the water and shrugged, "It means that I do not know how long I have. Angels are supposed to live forever, but as I've stripped myself of my immortality… I don't know what my lifespan will be. I could die in a few days, or in a hundred years, I just do not know."

"Wait." Piero exclaimed as he came to a dark realization. "You knew all of this when you sliced open your hand didn't you? You knew that destroying your immortality would mean that you would eventually be damned to the Well of Souls."

Xaphine nodded hesitantly, "Yes…"

Piero slammed his fist on the railing, "Why, why would you do that? Now you've doomed yourself! I did all this to rescue you and there is a chance now that you may not even live long because of what you've done?"

"Piero I… I'm sorry," She replied as she took a step back, surprised by his outburst, "but it was necessary. I was not trying to hurt you, but I could not let Lucifer regain his power."

"How's that? How was knowingly damning yourself necessary?"

DAMNATION

Piero pressed his fist on the railing as he leaned against it. His face turned red with anger. He could not believe how reckless she had been.

Xaphine put her arms around Piero's shoulder and looked at him with sad eyes, "Piero, calm down, don't be mad at me…"

"I'm not mad at you… I just wish that there had been another way... there must have been a better way."

"Piero, there wasn't. The powers I possessed weren't mine. Lucifer transferred them to me for safe-keeping. As long as I was attached to them, he would have access to me and be able to use his power to regain his strength. This was the only way that the world would be protected from his hate. The only way I could be free of his grasp. I am sorry if that angers you… but I would rather spend the brief time we have in this world with you followed by eternity in the Well, than live forever and watching your soul suffer at Lucifer's hands."

"No, it's not going to happen. I won't let you go… you can't be doomed to this place, there has to be another way. No matter what…"

"Sorry to interrupt," Francesco called from the main deck, "but have you two come up with a plan yet for when you get back?"

"What are you talking about?" Xaphine asked.

"Where will you go, what will you do, and how you will explain away Xaphine's ears and wings?"

Xaphine put a hand to her head, "How could I have overlooked that… I'd heard about what happened to my sister when she was first exiled. The horrors she endured were unspeakable and she almost died."

"I won't let that happen to you." Piero said adamantly. "I will keep you safe no matter what it takes."

"You will protect her?" Francesco asked. "How do you intend to keep her safe from the entire Papal army?"

DAMNATION

Piero stepped in front of Xaphine as though he were protecting her from Francesco's words, "The Papal army has lost considerable influence. The knights from Adalyn's time have been disbanded, and the power of the Pope has been greatly diminished since the war began. Florence is no friend to the Papacy anymore, so she should be safe there."

Francesco nodded, "Maybe, but diminished power is not the same thing as having no power at all and Florence can't hold out forever against the armies of Charles V. If either power discovers her, they will react the same way they did with Adalyn. They will come for her, and they will try to kill her."

Piero sighed, "What do you recommend I do then?"

Francesco turned to her sadly, "The ears are a peculiarity that can easily be hidden, and most people could live with… the wings are your real problem. Perhaps they could be removed?"

"Amputate my wings?" Xaphine asked, momentarily flashing a concerned expression. "But…"

"No." Piero replied. "She's suffered enough and that's one procedure that she may not survive. I've seen too many people die from having arms and legs removed by a surgeon on the battle field. I will not mutilate her."

A degree of relief came over Xaphine's face as she ran her hands over her black feathers. She already had enough scars and did not like the idea of adding two more. Had Piero thought it was a good idea, she would have consented to having them removed, but it was not something she personally wanted to do.

"Very well." Francesco said breathing a sigh. "To be honest, I didn't particularly care for the idea myself, but you do have some very serious obstacles to overcome. It's something to consider before marching into Florence."

Francesco turned back to his meditation while Xaphine leaned on the railing with her eyes looking down into the lake. Piero noticed small droplets of water hit the lake next to the Ricci. He looked at his wife's face. She was desperately trying to fight back the tears, but was only able to hold a few back. Her eyes flickered between blue and red. Something was bothering her terribly as Piero rarely saw her cry. He gently stroked her hair, trying to calm her. "Why are you crying?"

"Three worlds and I do not belong in any of them. I'm not welcome in the Celestial World, the Mortal Realm is too dangerous, and I can never return to the Netherworld. Where will I go? I might as well just join the Well of Souls now and get it over with."

"Don't talk that way!" Piero said, almost yelling at her. "Your place is with me. I've already promised that I'd keep you safe, and I meant it. I don't care where we go as long as you are at my side. We can create an entirely new world for all I care."

Piero's words put a smile on her face, "You would build a new world just for me to live in, wouldn't you?"

"You know I would. Haven't I already proved it to you? There is nothing I wouldn't do and nowhere that I wouldn't go to keep you safe and make you happy."

"For once, it would seem luck is on my side." She said as the tears finally stopped.

"Luck?"

"Luck that you pulled me out of that building. Luck that you took me into your home and let me live with you. Luck that you married me and luck that even after everything that happened, you still risked your own soul on a half-baked chance to save me."

"And I'd do it again in a heartbeat. It all turned out well."

The smile suddenly disappeared from her face again, "Piero, I have to ask you…"

"Yes?"

DAMNATION

"How on Earth did you know? You gave up your honor and risked everything to come after me. You never once questioned whether or not I could be brought back. How did you know that I would come with you? My mind and my heart were so conflicted, how did you know I would choose Xaphine over Xaphan."

Piero rubbed her back, around her feathers. Her wings tingled as he spoke, "I honestly didn't know for certain, but you are my wife remember? Lucifer may have wiped your memory, but he did not remove what was important."

Xaphine was caught off guard and anxious to find out what Lucifer had missed that a simple human had not, "And what would that be?"

"He didn't erase you." Piero said as though it should be obvious. "You can erase someone's memory and their identity, but you can't take away who they are. He didn't remove your tastes, your personality, your vices, your attitudes, and your strong sense of honor. Everything was still there. So even though your memory was gone, you were still you."

"Amazing... so that's what you meant when you said that I was still in there. My memories had returned and I had been transformed into a demonic creature. I destroyed your home, and I sided with Lucifer... but even then you knew that I was still the person you loved. I don't even know how to respond to that... I'm beyond words... No one in Hell or on Earth ever picked up on that, just you."

The smile returned to Xaphine's face, but this time, it was complimented by her eyes turning to a blue so bright that they were nearly glowing, "Piero... I'm a very prideful person, someone who isn't known for showing emotion, and doesn't do a very good a job of expressing her feelings. I know that I rarely say it but... I truly love you. I will always love you... beyond the end of my days. When I am condemned and face the chilled waters of the Well of Souls,

I will always find warmth in knowing that I have been so loved."

"I love you too, but I won't let you be condemned. I am telling you that I will find a way to prevent it. I promise you, that won't be your fate."

"I cast off my divinity willingly… I'll be lucky not to get sent back to the Netherworld."

When Xaphine saw the sad look on Piero's face, she smiled and rubbed his should, "Please don't despair. I knew the price that I would have to pay when I turned on Kaliban. An eternity in the Well of Souls is worth a lifetime here with you. It's a decision I would make a thousand times over. It's okay Piero. I do not fear what awaits me."

"There has to be another way." Piero said through clenched teeth. "There just has to be."

"Well if there is, then I have every confidence in your ability to find it."

The sudden whipping sound of a loose rope interrupted them. Xaphine looked up to see that a rope had come loose from the mast and began swinging around. She turned away from Piero, "I'll get it."

As she flapped her wings, took off, and grabbed the rope, Piero turned back around and peered out into the fog, "There must be another way…"

VIII

The ship sailed on for another hour before it cleared the murky wood. Francesco did not move from his chair on deck. He was locked in silent meditation since they had left the black pier. It seemed like he was having a hard time focusing.

Xaphine had been pacing back and forth for some time as her mind worked hard to reconcile everything that had just happened. Piero just leaned on the railing watching her. After twenty minutes, he began to get dizzy, "Xaphine, if you keep walking around like that, you're going to wear a path in the bottom of the ship!"

"Piero... there is something I want to show you, something truly wonderful that you will most likely never be able to see again, even after you go to the Kingdom."

"What do you mean?"

"Have you ever experienced a perfect moment in time?"

"Yes, the day I asked you to marry me."

"What did it feel like? Describe it for me."

"My heart froze in my chest and time appeared to stand still. I saw wind blowing through the trees stand still, but the branches were still bent as though the wind was caressing them. I felt weightless as though I was in a dream, and nothing could weigh me down at that moment."

Xaphine nodded as a bright expression came over her, "That's exactly what I'm talking about. What if I could show you a place that is just that; a perfect moment, would you want to see it?"

"How could that be possible with your powers gone?"

A devious grin appeared on Xaphine's face, "The poison works differently against different powers. It hasn't quite run its course yet."

Piero nodded as Xaphine studied his expression, "So?"

DAMNATION

"Yes."

"Are you certain? It is something I would want you to see, but you have to understand that once you've seen it, that's it, you will most likely never be able to again. That's something you're going to have to accept. People have gone mad searching for such places. Others have wasted their whole lives in the search. If I show you a place of infinite wonders, can you accept never seeing it again?"

Piero looked over at Francesco, realizing that he had gone through exactly what she was talking about. He nodded, "I'll be fine. No matter how perfect this place could be, it can't compare to anywhere you are."

Xaphine smiled and rolled her eyes, "Always with the honeyed words!"

She thought about it for a moment and decided it was worth the risk, "Okay Piero, I'll trust you at your word."

She turned to Moretti, who was still manning the tiller, "We'll be back in a few minutes, keep an eye on things from here."

Moretti looked at them both with worry, "Where are you going?"

Xaphine saw the worried look in his eyes. It looked like he was scared that they would not be able to find their way back and everyone would be stranded as a result. She shook her head, "Don't worry, I'll give you my word that we'll be back before you know it."

Moretti looked around, "Okay, but what are we supposed to do while you're gone?"

"Kick back and enjoy the ride. There really isn't anything you can do until we get back to the mortal realm. Just sit back and enjoy the ride."

"Very well, but please hurry back. I don't even want to think about what kind of creatures are out there waiting for the chance to strike."

DAMNATION

"You needn't fear them. The images in your head are far more dangerous than the monsters could ever hope to be. They will not approach this ship."

Xaphine walked to the starboard side of the ship where there was no railing, turned back to Piero and dropped to one knee, "Lean on my back and put your arms around me."

Piero and Moretti exchanged odd glances for a moment, but Piero finally crouched down and held on to her. She began flapping her wings hard. Then, using impressive lower body strength, she jumped into the air and used the side of the *Ricci* to push herself higher off the deck. Her muscles tightened as she pushed her legs straight. She spread her wings as far as they could go and glided upward.

Piero watched as they flew into the fog. Within moments, the ship and the black water disappeared beneath them. Piero and Xaphine were now completely surrounded by a gray haze as they flew into the sky.

Having nothing to look at, Piero closed his eyes and pressed his head against Xaphine's back. He listened as her heart beat steadily. The pounding in her chest was strong and steady. She must have received some form of training or conditioning to be able to hold the two of them in the air so easily.

Xaphine felt warm as Piero lay on her back. She could not remember the last time she had felt anything like this. Warmth, happiness, love, and kindness, were all emotions that had been stripped from her by Lucifer's conditioning. Her time with Piero had given her a taste of these feelings before she was ripped from his arms. Being back with him again was almost intoxicating.

Xaphine watched the clouds in front of her as they began to thin away. The fluffy white mist gave way and turned into a black sky. She turned her head to the side to see her love, "My love, open your eyes, look."

Piero did as he was told and found himself looking at a sheet of gray beneath them and a starry black field over them, "Where are we?"

"We're going to my favorite place in all of existence."

She soared higher into the night sky until the gray fog disappeared. Piero became slightly disoriented as his body became weightless. He noticed that there was less tension in Xaphine's back as she no longer had to hold him up. He began breathing slightly more heavily as his body adapted the floating sensation, "I feel like I'm flying on my own."

"You are; gravity doesn't exist here."

She pushed on Piero's arms, causing him to go flying out in front of her. He began waving his limbs frantically, certain he was about to fall back to the water. Instead, he levitated in place with Xaphine in front of him."

Piero's eyes darted around in a panic, "What is this, what is going on here?"

Xaphine smiled as she took his hand, "Relax."

She slowly tugged him in the direction she was flying, "Come, I have something wondrous to show you."

Xaphine dropped down underneath him and guided his arms back around her shoulders, "Hold on tight."

Piero cocked his head to the slide so that he was whispering in her ear, "Why?"

As though answering his question, Xaphine wings raised high above her head and she brought them down hard. The stars immediately became lines around them as Piero felt wind blow past his face. It was too much for him to keep his eyes open. Once again, he pressed his face into Xaphine's back as they travelled.

Within moments, Piero felt Xaphine come to a halt. She pulled Piero off her back, "It's okay, Piero, open your eyes!"

Piero slowly parted his eyelids and looked around. Sitting in front of them was a massive golden pillar. On the three bottom corners of the pillar, three streams of golden waterfalls fell from the structure into yellow clouds below.

Xaphine took Piero's hand and flew him through the streams of water. It was the most beautiful sight Piero had ever been witness to. "What is this place?"

Xaphine closed her eyes as the cool breeze caressed her skin, "That's not an easy question to answer. We have flown beyond the boundaries of space and time. Very few angels even know of this place's existence."

"Outside of space and time?" Piero said in disbelief. "What does that mean?"

"It means that time doesn't pass here. In this place, there is peace... no war, no death, only beauty and paradise..."

"You've come here many times, haven't you?"

"Before I joined Lucifer, I came here many times. I love it here, it's peaceful. I was only able to come once in a while after my exile though. I didn't want Lucifer knowing what I was up to... I couldn't risk him bringing war on this place. Still, even his eyes couldn't see this place."

As she moved into sky, the stars twinkled around her wings. Her arms and legs moved as though she were swimming, "This is truly paradise. I came here whenever I wanted to be alone. "

Piero watched a meteor shower shoot past, "But what is this place, did God created it?"

"No, your people did."

"What do you mean 'I did'?"

Xaphine twirled around in the air, disappeared for a moment, and reappeared behind him with a playful look on her face, "Boo!"

Startled, Piero whirled around with one hand on his sword, "How did you..."

"Your imagination." She said in a mystical tone. "The minds of the Most High's children created this land. Here, anything is possible."

"But how?"

Another wave of meteors passed by the couple as they floated in the night sky. Xaphine smiled, "Nothing is more innocent than the imagination of a baby. The rays of light you see are the unborn souls waiting to enter your world. They reside here until it is their time. At first, this was little more than a black void, but the power of imagination had a huge influence on it. Eventually this existence became what you see."

She paused for a moment, looking up at the brightest star, "I remember... I wanted to show you this place. I always thought that you were there, on that bright star."

"There is something I've wanted to ask you since I found out you were an angel..."

"Just one thing? I would have thought I'd be spending eternity answering questions for you."

"There is only one that I'm really interested in hearing about at this moment."

"Okay. Well I am here now and I won't keep any secrets from you. Ask me anything."

Piero watched as the star twinkled a few more times. He then turned to look at his wife, "What made you think that you could take on God? He created all of existence and I thought he was infallible. How could you have hoped to succeed?"

Xaphine sighed as she began her story, "Many of the stories you are told in the Church of God are based on myth and legend. Yes in some ways they are true and based on historical fact, but what fact existed has long been obscured by oral tradition. As the stories of some of the most prominent figures in your stories were passed from mouth to mouth, they were slightly distorted. Over a thousand years of this will make some of the stories completely different from the actual reality. Some of your stories of Abraham, David, Moses, and Solomon are true... but other stories were written as parables and stories of morality. They were never meant to be taken as literal history."

Xaphine could see that this was shaking his faith. She glided over to him and placed her arms on his shoulders, crossing them behind him, "The Most High, your God, did create you, he did send prophets and teachers, and yes, he loves each of you as a father loves his children..."

Piero looked her straight in the eye, "But?"

"But... he is anything but infallible, especially since he created your kind. He also can't predict the future."

"What does that mean?"

"Saint Michael understood this before anyone else. The Most High created you in his image, but he also gave you a portion of his essence. The spirit of the Most High, thus the entire Kingdom of Heaven, dwells within all of his creation. When you kill each other, when you allow evil to happen, the Most High feels it and grieves. Imagine being the father of an uncountable number of children and being forced to watch them tear one another to pieces."

"So when we're killing each other, we're actually killing him?"

"You could look at it that way, yes. The Most High is everlasting and will always be, but you weaken him to the point of exhaustion. My kind was created to serve and protect him from harm while he toiled. What he did not count on was angels turning against him. After the war, his captain, Michael, saw an opportunity to weaken the Most High even more. To this day, I have no idea what Michael's motives were. He had a job that made him second to none, save the Most High himself."

"Michael? What did he do?"

"That is a long story from about ten years ago. Michael was blinded by promises of power from Lucifer, we all were. Michael thought that he would be granted even more power by Lucifer if he helped aid our cause. I can only wonder what might have happened had he succeeded."

"What happened to him?"

"Your friend Adalyn. The incident that Francesco was witness to in Rome was actually a battle between her and Michael. From what I was told, she faced him even though she had been blinded from her injuries."

Piero scoffed in disbelief, "How could a single blind angel take on the God's most fearsome warrior?"

"No one knows. Rumors were that she had the help of a fallen angel who had discovered a way to intervene, but this was all unfounded."

"What else do you know about that incident?"

"Not much, I only know what Lucifer told me and he kept me at arm's length. I didn't even find out about her being turned into a human until I saw her that day. I was living with you during that time."

Piero now looked slightly anxious, "So it is possible to turn an angel into a human."

"Yes..." Xaphine said hesitantly, "but it's beyond rare. Adalyn's case is the only time that I've ever seen the Most High do anything like that."

"Is there any other way of doing it?"

Xaphine shook her head with an air of annoyance, "Piero, if you're hoping to change me into a human in order to save my soul, it won't work. I will still have to pay for my crimes, and that is not a loophole."

"Is there a way?"

"Francesco's way was the correct one... An angel's wings are the source of her power... If an angel's wings were to be destroyed, said angel loses everything that makes her what she is and she'd begin to take on human characteristics."

"So at that point, wouldn't she be subject to human law?"

"No, of course not! Intentionally transforming into a human to the Most High is no different than suicide amongst your people. Our bodies are tools of the Most High and are to be treated as sacred. Mutilating ourselves is the worst thing we could do. Any angel who did so would be punished severely. Also..."

Piero looked at her oddly, "What?"

Xaphine eyes looked into his pleadingly, "Piero, are you actually considering this now after what you said? If this is what you want to try... then I will submit to it, but I am asking you to please abandon this idea. Most angels do not survive the loss of their wings. Cutting them off would be like removing a leg, and even if you were successful, the shock of the spiritual shift would burden my heart even more. It is way too risky."

"Don't worry, I am just considering options, but I would never ask you to do something that would put you at that much risk. I do not want to cause you pain, I'm your husband, my job is to prevent that."

Xaphine's heartfelt light, the reminders that she was married to him made Xaphine feel more alive than ever, "Thank you, my love."

Xaphine took Piero and soared through this mystical land, through the clouds and even up the golden waterfalls. Piero wanted to see and experience everything. Xaphine dove into the waterfall and emerged on the other side. Her skin glowed brightly when she returned to him. She reached out her hand to him beckoning him to take it.

Piero looked at it suspiciously for a moment. She smiled and spoke in a reassuring tone, "Trust me."

Piero's hand slowly moved towards hers. Once they touched, she wrapped her fingers around his. Piero watched the gold aura as it began to travel up his skin. Within a few moments, he also began to glow.

Piero breathed deeply as a sense of euphoria came over him. Whatever it was, it had taken over control of his senses. Suddenly, everything made sense; the universe, space, time, everything together for one brief moment of clarity before the aura began to fade.

Piero gasped, "That was amazing."

Xaphine had goose bumps running the length of her body. She bit her lower lip for a moment, "I'm glad you enjoyed it."

She moved forward, "Come with me..."

"What do you mean?"

"Into the waterfall."

"Why, what awaits us there?"

Xaphine looked over at the fountain, "Total clarity. In there, our minds would become one. We would be able to see all of each other's memories, feelings, and thoughts."

Piero breathed heavily for a moment, "Are you sure that is a good idea?"

"I think so. You know who I am, and what I have done. I have nothing to hide from you. I am yours and I want there to be no boundaries between us."

Piero nodded hesitantly, "Very well then..."

Xaphine took both of his hands and guided him toward the waterfall. Piero closed his eyes as the water poured over their bodies. To his surprise, he did not feel wet. He opened his eyes to see that he was surrounded by a golden light. His wife was in front of him, smiling the entire time.

Xaphine's figure vanished into a blur of light right in front of him. To his shock, Piero's body began to do the same. He felt disembodied as his form moved closer to Xaphine's. When they finally touched, Piero's eyes flashed.

DAMNATION

He found himself reliving all of Xaphine's experiences since she was an angel.

Piero watched as millions of years of experiences passed before his eyes. It overwhelmed his senses. His head began to hurt, but he could not close his eyes.

Piero decided that it was best to just focus on key events rather than try to remember every day to day occurrence. He watched her work as an angel and frolic in the clouds with her friends. He then saw Lucifer approach her and convince her to join his cause. In disbelief, he watched as she set fire to the celestial temple and led Lucifer's armies close to victory.

Piero's eyes filled with tears as he witnessed his wife being exiled from the Celestial realm and become perverted and evil. He watched helplessly as she suffered under Lucifer's hand. His whole world started to turn red as though reacting to the pain and suffering she had experienced.

The redness only lasted for a few seconds. It began to fade as Piero found himself looking into his own eyes. He was now living through the years she had spent with him. He experienced all of her joy and then all of her sorrow when she left. Piero never realized just how much he meant to her.

Finally, the most recent events passed in front of Piero. He recognized everything that was going on. What was strange was that he experienced intense fear and sorrow from when Xaphine was in their home. His heart ached with the intense burden, but he didn't even understand why he was feeling this way. What could have possibly brought on such sadness?

Instantly, Piero realized that these weren't his emotions. Piero was experiencing Xaphine's pain and sorrow as she pushed away from him so long ago. He could not believe how conflicted she actually was. What's more, she wasn't completely convinced that Piero would survive her leaving.

The memories suddenly went blank and the two auras pulled away from one another. They both shot out of the stream of golden water and flew around the pillar like two comets streaking by in opposite directions. They continued to spin around the pillar at incredible speeds for a few moments until they met on the far side. The two collided in a massive explosion of light. Gold dust shot away in every direction.

Once it faded, Piero and Xaphine were left levitating in its place. They were both breathing heavily as they looked at each other. The clarity was overwhelming and took them both by surprise.

Piero was unable to speak as he looked at Xaphine. Her eyes filled with tears as she lunged at him and threw her arms over his shoulders. In a rare showing of sadness, she threw off her stoic expression and let the tears flow.

Piero closed his eyes as he gently put his hands on her back. He sucked in a few deep breaths before finding his voice, "What's wrong Xaphine?"

"I saw your memories. I saw what I did to you..."

Xaphine's eyes squeezed shut as she gripped his back, "I had feared that something like this would happen, but I was hoping that you would somehow find a way to survive, not go off trying to get yourself killed!"

"I'm sorry Xaphine; your leaving did more damage than you could know. I did not want to go back to the way things were before I met you. Before you moved in, I never realized just how lonely I was. After you left, I became desperate to not feel that way again. So I spent most of my time with the troops, taking every assignment, no matter how dangerous. I really didn't care who I was fighting or if I even came back. As long as I felt the crushing blow of battle, I was satisfied."

DAMNATION

Xaphine looked up at him with tears pouring down her cheeks. At hearing his words, she quickly began to shake her head, "No... no... I felt it all... but I didn't want to believe that it was true. Piero... I swear... had I known..."

"There was nothing you could do. Xaphan was still too powerful for you to do anything. I saw that... I also saw the amount of pain you were in when Lucifer found your leash. Please do not blame yourself. There was nothing you could do."

She clenched her jaw and began yelling, "How can I not? So many years alone... so much damage done! How do you even still love me? How can you forgive what I have done so easily?"

Piero squeezed her tighter and responded to her yelling in a stern voice, "I don't want to hear any more of this! What happened wasn't your fault. I thought for sure when I saw you standing there in my house that my wife was dead. The moment I found out that you were still in that fallen angel, I came running as quickly as I could."

Piero looked at his wife for a few moments. He was happy she was with him again, but a question in the back of his mind continuously nagged at him. He paused for a moment, hesitant to ask her, but he knew he'd never be able to rest easy if he didn't know the answer. "Xaphine... how do we deal with Xaphan? I know you're strong, but how long can you keep her at bay? When I saw your memories, I saw you struggle with her. How can we be certain she can never come back?"

"You still don't understand what's going on, do you? She hasn't gone away and she never will."

"I don't understand... All I know is my wife is with me again, since that was all I wanted, I didn't question it."

"Piero, I am, was, and forever will be Xaphan. You said so yourself. Lucifer stripped Xaphan's memories from her body, which left her brain to create new ones... The memories with you became who I was. That's when Xaphine was created. Lucifer had planned to cleanse Xaphan's body of these memories when it was time for her to return, but recent events caused him to lose most of the power that he had kept to defend himself. He also didn't count on her falling in love and creating such strong memories. Memories that would have been impossible for Lucifer to move, even at full strength."

Xaphine took a deep breath before continuing, "Lucifer couldn't do anything except restore Xaphan's memories and hope for the best. When that happened, the woman you knew as Xaphine was destroyed."

Piero's jaw dropped open, "But Xaphine..."

"Shh! Let me finish."

The look in her eyes silenced Piero's fears and she continued, "Unfortunately for Lucifer, when Xaphan's memories were restored, she too was destroyed. Her mind became divided as two sets of memories slowly merged together and created a new person, one who was confused and alone. Her sense of honor and loyalty compelled her to follow the path of the one she had originally sworn an oath to, but there was a part of her that screamed out from a cage that this was wrong."

She smiled at Piero, "Part of your wife, the most important part survived."

"What part?"

Xaphine took his hand and placed it on her chest, "Her heart. It took over in the place of the one that Xaphan sacrificed long ago for power. She became confused and resentful. In the end, this new person had to decide; did she want to be Xaphan and continue fighting for Lucifer... or did she want to be with you. Thankfully, her heart won out and Xaphan cast off the chains held by her master. At that point, she chose and the new personality came back to you... as Xaphine."

DAMNATION

"I don't understand..."

"I can understand why. It's a very complicated situation. Just know that the woman you married is both Xaphan and Xaphine, and the one who stands before you now is a combination of both. Everything that was good about the both of them meshed together. What periodically comes to the surface are the remnants of the darkness within. It will always be with me, but hopefully it will lose strength as time passes."

Piero still could not fully piece this together, but part of him was bothered by her words, "So what are you saying? You aren't the woman I married?"

A hurt look came over Xaphine's face, "I am more than I am not. You were right when you said that my personality was still the same, even when Xaphan returned. All of that is still intact and just as you remember. The only difference is that she now has several lifetimes of memories."

Piero rubbed his forehead with his right hand. Tears began to fill Xaphine's eyes again and she began to wonder what her husband was thinking, "Piero... I'm sorry. I can't undo what was done. You came so far to get your wife back, and she has returned to you. However now there are more dimensions to her than there were before. If you want to be with her, you need to accept all that she is, even the parts you didn't know about. I will forever be teetering on that line between light and dark. There is no way to tell if the darkness could take me again or not. I can't predict the future. I am the woman you married, but if you cannot accept me as I am now, then you need to tell me. I'll understand and I won't be mad. I'll just return you to the *Ricci* and you can go back to your home like none of this ever happened. I promise that you will never have to see me again."

DAMNATION

Piero looked at her seriously for a few moments. Her eyes were filled with terror as though he were about to utter some incantation that would surely end her life. She sucked in a deep breath and waited to see if he'd utter the words that she feared the most.

Piero's eyes turned from confusion to anger, "How can you say something so venomous? I knew that coming after you meant having to face Xaphan as well. I still recognize my wife in there and I love you more than anything. If accepting you as you are means getting back even the smallest semblance of what we had, then I will give you my heart as you are now, completely and forever."

Xaphine wasn't convinced. She wasn't sure Piero knew exactly what he was getting into, "Are you sure, Piero? Life with me will not be easy at all. Just dealing with my mental condition may be more consuming than you think. It won't be like it was before. Xaphan's anger can still break through from time to time and possibly, one day... it could take over. If that happens... I could leave you again... Are you sure about this?"

Piero flashed an angry look as he spoke, "I refuse to answer that question. My actions should have already answered that for you many times over. If you do leave, I'll just come after you again."

"Okay. You are right... I should have more..."

She chuckled as the word left her lips, "faith..."

"I knew it would come back to you..."

The dread slowly began to drain from her eyes, "I know I've already asked... but... are you certain this is what you want?"

Piero laughed softly as he looked deeply into his wife's eyes. She looked like she was about to start crying again. Why was he laughing at her? An angry and hurt look appeared on her face, "What is so funny?"

"You asked me that exact question once before. Do you remember what my answer was back then?"

Xaphine raised her right hand to her chest and touched the jeweled necklace. It was now filthy and the gems barely had any color. She wiped the soot from the large charm over her heart as it began to sparkle red, "I could never forget those words. 'There is risk in all things... the question is, do the benefits outweigh the risks.' That's what you said."

Piero put his left hand on her cheek, "I also said that of course they do. I told you I wasn't going into this blind. I may not have known the risks like I thought I did, but I beat the odds. I can decide for myself what I want, and you are just that."

Xaphine smiled, wrapped her arms around his chest and her legs around his thighs, and squeezed him tight. "Piero... my knight in shining armor... For as long as I can care for you, I will. My heart and soul are yours forever, beyond death and time itself."

"And mine are yours. I promise to take care of them."

"I don't deserve it... part of me would feel better if you took my heart and smashed it on the ground, but even that wouldn't make up for the pain I caused you. I wish you would just leave me here. Your life would be better if you didn't have to deal with me continuously fighting off the darkness in my mind."

"Will you please stop? Yes it was hard to live without you and I was in pain, part of me even wanted to hate you for what happened, but I couldn't let go of the fact that I knew part of you was still in there."

Xaphine smiled faintly. She twirled around and rested her head on Piero's chest, "Okay you win. No more crying or sorrow. Now I will learn to live again, with you."

Piero nodded, "I will be with you every step of the way. We'll learn how to live again together."

DAMNATION

Xaphine released a tension-filled breath, "That's a deal."

She took one more look at the pillar and then turned back to Piero, "Come on, we should be getting back to our friends."

Piero nodded and wrapped his arms around Xaphine as she dove downward. Piero felt like he was leaving half his body behind as they plummeted faster than he had ever travelled before.

The gray clouds quickly came into view as they fell. Xaphine hit them fast, blowing a huge hole through the mist. A cooling sensation came over them as the black turned to gray.

Within moments, the black water came into sight. Piero could see the *Ricci* below him in the distance. The two could see what looked like a massive black bird take off from the deck.

Xaphine lowered her head as she turned towards the ship, "Hang on, my love, I'm going to try to land."

"I won't let go, don't worry."

Xaphine began flapping her wings harder and harder to slow their descent. She didn't want to touch down too hard and risk injuring Piero. Her wings stretched out as far that they could go as they caught the air.

Finally, Xaphine touched down on the deck. Her bare feet touched the wood with a slight thud before she let go of Piero. She dropped to her knee for a moment to catch her breath.

Moretti turned to them from the tiller, "Couldn't make it?"

Piero looked at the man oddly, "What are you talking about?"

"You just left. Did you circle the boat and come back?"

DAMNATION

"Perhaps it's best to just try to solve this mystery at a later time." Xaphine replied. "It's a little complicated."

Piero nodded, "But it was incredible."

IX

The *Ricci* sailed on for another hour through the fog. Francesco heard a low boom off the port bow and opened his eyes. He couldn't see it, but he knew what was coming, "Piero, Xaphine, grab on to something and don't let go, Moretti, hold on and keep the tiller steady!"

Out of the corner of his eye, Piero saw the flash of light from under the water, "Oh God, not again! This is going to be rough."

Xaphine nodded, "Charybdis is the only way we can get out of here... I just hope it sends us where we need to go..."

"What do you mean? Where else could it possibly send us?"

Before Xaphine could reply, Charybdis appeared off the port side. Xaphine shook her head, "I'll explain when we're back in the mortal realm. Ask me there."

The sea became rough and rocked the boat back and forth as the whirlpool sucked it in. Piero wrapped his arm around the railing and grabbed on to Xaphine. He held on to her tight for fear of losing her again.

This time, instead of struggling, Piero decided to just close his eyes and let it pass by. He could feel the world spinning around him as the boat sank deeper into the abyss. Somehow with Xaphine pressed against him, he was no longer afraid. Even the might of Charybdis didn't scare him.

On deck, Francesco held on to the table with everything he had. Even from his position, he could sense his friends on the main deck. There was no fear or sadness, just courage and strength. He smiled, "Good for you two, no one can defeat you now."

Suddenly a tremor rocked the boat, throwing Francesco overboard. Moretti called to Piero, "Man overboard! Someone get a line, quick!"

DAMNATION

Xaphine turned to see Francesco spinning around in the waves. She struggled against Piero, "There is no time, let go, my love! I can save him!"

"Are you sure?"

"Of course! Don't worry, you won't lose me again, I promise."

Piero nodded as he released her, "Hurry, he looks like he's about to go under."

Xaphine pushed off the mast and quickly took flight. She flapped her wings hard to reach Francesco, who was now on the other side of vortex, "Hang on Francesco, I'm coming!"

Francesco didn't hear her and continued to spin in the wave, "Not again…"

Suddenly, he felt a gripping sensation on his shoulders. His body became weightless as he was lifted out of the spinning current. He knew immediately what had happened, "Xaphine?"

As Xaphine raised him from the vortex, she wrapped her arms around him and ascended high above the surf, "Don't worry, I've got you. You're not drowning on us today!"

Francesco breathed a sigh of relief and patted Xaphine's arm, "Thank you, my friend… I owe you for this one."

"Just take it off the million I owe you for everything you've done."

Xaphine flapped her wings slowly and headed towards the *Ricci*. She landed on the deck of their ship and dragged Francesco over to the cabin under the aft castle. Struggling to keep her balance, she opened the door and threw him inside, "Stay in there until I come and get you. You'll be all right!"

Xaphine then darted back over to the mast and grabbed on to Piero. She buried her face in his side and closed her eyes. Piero could feel the ship begin to list towards the vortex, and called out, "Moretti, are you still with us up there?"

"Yes sir! Don't worry, no way is my ship capsizing again!"

"Glad to hear it! Steer us in more with the current! Let's make this as quick as possible."

Moretti turned the tiller slightly to steady the ship's descent into darkness, "That's as far over as I dare go! Anymore and we'll be smashed to port."

Piero felt the ship begin to right itself, "That's good enough. Keep her on course!"

The ship continued going in circles with the heavy sound of water all around them. Piero pulled Xaphine even closer and hugged her tight. Xaphine smiled, "Relax Piero, I'm not going anywhere. Never again!"

She felt the warmth of his body as she was pressed deeper into his side. Piero nodded as he looked down at her, "You better not…"

Before Piero knew it, all sound was gone. For a few moments, he felt like he was stuck in a void. There was no sound, no light, and worst of all, no life. He was encased in darkness, but he was not alone. He could feel Xaphine at his side. Her heart beat against his skin as he pressed his hand against her back. "Xaphine, can you hear me?"

He could feel her head nod, "Yes, I'm here. Don't worry, I'm still with you."

Piero smiled as he felt her warmth. His eyes darted back and forth to see if he could make out anything in the darkness, "Where are we?"

"We're inside Charybdis's vortex. Nothing can survive long if stuck here, not even light. It's little more than a black void."

Xaphine could feel his breathing increase. He was nervous and didn't know what would come. Xaphine rubbed his back as she held on, "Don't worry Piero, it'll be over soon."

DAMNATION

BOOK 6

THE BATTLE FOR GAVINANA

DAMNATION

ⱦ

Florence, August 1530

ithin moments, the loud splash of a boat hitting the water shattered Piero's void. He opened his eyes to see day light over the horizon. Piero shot up quickly, "Where are we?"

"Not only where..." Xaphine said as she fluttered her soaked wings, in a frantic attempt to dry them. "The more important question is when?"

"What do you mean?"

After a few moments, a frustrated Xaphine spread her wings and waved them in the wind, "Ugh, angels hate getting their wings wet!"

"Everyone okay?" Moretti called out from the tiller.

Piero nodded, "I think so. We all seem to be here."

Xaphine shook her wings even more, "I should probably check on Francesco."

Piero was getting wet from her wings going every which way, "Xaphine, what did you mean when you said when?"

Once Xaphine's wings finally dried, she folded them behind her, "Okay, Charybdis is a doorway between worlds, but it takes you to and from the Netherworld by opening a hole through space and time, and it's not stable. We could be anywhere at any point in time."

"But I don't understand. How is it that Adalyn's group used the gateway without having to worry about this?"

"They had help. A group of angels were looking out for them throughout their journey. We are not so fortunate in our friends I'm afraid."

"So where are we? If we could be anywhere at any time, then we could be too late to save Florence. The war could be over, or it may not have even happened yet! Maybe we could find a way to prevent it."

Xaphine looked up as the night sky slowly began to disappear, "The position of the stars is not that different. Everything looks like it's in order, so we can't be that far off."

Francesco overheard the voices, so he made his way to the door, and joined his friends on deck, "The air feels right, we must be near the coast of Tuscany."

Piero nodded, "All right, that means Florence isn't that far from here. Let's head out and see what we can find."

He turned to Moretti who was still standing at the tiller, "Steer us to the east, we need to get back to the mainland."

Moretti pulled on the tiller, "Bringing the *Ricci* around, can one of you get the sail down?"

Xaphine spread her wings and flew to the yardarm. She began pulling at the ropes and within moments, had the sail down. It flapped in the wind before catching and pulling the ship forward.

Piero stood at the forecastle keeping an eye open for any sign of his homeland. Francesco prostrated himself next to Piero and prayed divine intervention. Xaphine stretched out her arms and legs, "I am exhausted, does anyone mind if I retire for a while?"

Francesco shook his head, "You've been through a lot. Go, get some rest."

"I appreciate it. Thank you."

As she withdrew to the cabin, Francesco turned to Piero, who was still on the lookout for Florence, "Piero, what are you doing, go with her. You both fought very hard to get here, you deserve some time together."

"Are you sure that the two of you can handle things out here?"

"We'll call you if we need you, but I think we can manage."

DAMNATION

Piero nodded and entered the cabin. He not yet made use of the small room during the voyage. Other than a bed and windows, there really wasn't much to it. There were now curtains draped around the bed to conceal whatever stood behind it.

The curtains parted, revealing Xaphine, wrapped in a white sheet. She smiled as she looked at him, "I was hoping that you'd catch on."

"Xaphine?"

She dropped the sheet, revealing that she had completely disrobed. Piero's eyes widened as he looked her over. Her skin was completely pale with very little pigment. Piero jumped, startled by the scars that appeared as the sheet fell. Her entire body from her shoulders just below her knees was covered in scars. In many areas it looked like her skin had been patched back together like a quilt. In others, she had patches where she'd been severely burned.

Xaphine frowned and lowered her eyes, "I forgot that you hadn't seen me like this."

"Well I had seen some, but you were covered in steam. I thought many of them were like the tattoos Legion gave you. I thought they'd disappear when you cast him out."

Xaphine turned away as she grabbed the sheet and quickly covered herself back up, "Forgive me."

Piero quickly grabbed the sheet, "Stop."

Xaphine released the sheet and turned back to him. Piero's eyes passed slowly over her body before he placed a hand on her hip and traced his fingers up her side, "You're as beautiful as you ever were."

She smiled as her skin broke out in goose bumps under his gaze, "Ten years later and you still look at me like it's the first time."

"It's been ten years since I've seen something so flawless. You haven't changed at all."

"But you have."

Xaphine slowly moved towards Piero, embraced him, and held on tight. Piero closed his eyes and suddenly felt a tug from Xaphine's arms. He was being pulled towards the bed.

As the two lay back, Xaphine bent her right leg at the knee and propped it up as Piero lay on top of her. She looked up into Piero's eyes innocently as she wrapped her arms around him.

Piero rested his head next to hers and kissed her neck. She giggled softly under him. Piero's eyes narrowed, "What is it?"

"My brothers and sisters have no idea what they've missed out on for eons."

"You mean they're not allowed to…?"

"Have sex?" Xaphine interrupted, finishing his sentence. "No, they're not. The joys of the flesh are forbidden to anyone born of the Celestial World. We feel love and can even show affection, but anything like this is not for us."

A nervous look appeared on Piero's face, "Aren't you worried that you're angering God?"

Xaphine laughed, "I set fire to his temple and led Lucifer's army against his faithful. I then helped Lucifer rebuild and create his own kingdom. How much more angry at me could he be."

"Well, okay."

"Don't worry, my love. I really don't care what he thinks."

The candle dimmed as Piero embraced his wife. She arched her back as his hands ran across her smooth skin. This was as close to paradise that Piero had been in years.

**

Hours passed as Piero held Xaphine in his arms. She sighed as she looked up at her husband, "It would be Heaven itself if this moment never ended."

DAMNATION

"I know. I feel the same way. I never want to be parted from you again. It feels almost like a dream to have you back."

Xaphine kissed his chest gently as she lay next to him, "I had thought you had forgotten about me. I had hoped you had… the pain I caused you was too much for me to even think about. Even as Xaphan, I loved you. I only wish it didn't take me forever to realize it."

"I could never forget you. You asked me to think of you fondly."

Xaphine looked up at him surprised, "My promise, you remembered…"

"Of course. It was the one glimmer of hope I held on to that I could someday bring you back."

She squeezed him tightly, "Hold me Piero, hold me like you did on our wedding day, and never let me go again."

"Never, no matter what happens, no matter where we go or what misfortunes we face, I will find you, I promise."

"You would come after me again, even if it meant going through all this once more?"

"Even if it meant going through this a hundred times more and another hundred times after that. I will not abandon you."

His words took her breath away, "Piero… I love you…"

They held onto each other for a short time more, hoping that the moment would never end. Like a dark curse, the sound of Moretti's voice shattered their tranquil moment, "I see land and a city!"

Francesco stood up and turned to face him, "Any idea which one?"

"No."

Xaphine and Piero came out on deck after getting dressed. Piero looked up at Moretti on the aft castle, "Where is it?"

"Starboard." Moretti replied.

Piero squinted at the distant land, "I can't make it out, any ideas?"

Xaphine spread her wings, "Give me ten minutes, I'll find out."

She felt Piero's hand squeeze on her shoulder, "Be careful."

Xaphine's hand found its way to his and she smiled, "I have to be, I have you waiting for me now. Don't worry, I was Lucifer's general remember? After everything, I'll be damned if a mortal is going to shoot me down."

Without another word, Xaphine ran to the edge of the ship, pushed off, spread her wings and arms, stretched out her legs, and took flight. She gained altitude and within moments, disappeared into the clouds. The cool air caressed her skin as she looked down on the city and mapped out the buildings below her.

As the sun came up behind Xaphine, she did a cartwheel and shot upward. She had forgotten what it was like to fly just for the fun of it. She really would have liked for Piero to have experienced it with her, but she knew it was dangerous. After getting their bearings, she veered left and headed back to the *Ricci*.

Xaphine came down slowly around the boat. Piero watched her fly with her wings spread out as far as they could be. She majestically glided back to the deck of the old ship. Her feet touched down on the aft castle next to Piero. She stretched her arms as her wings folded behind her.

Out of breath, Xaphine turned to Piero, "I need to go flying more often."

Both Piero and Francesco stood by waiting for her to share with them what she had discovered. She smiled as she started talking, "I know where we are."

Francesco's head cocked, "Good news?"

She nodded, "Livorno."

Piero breathed a sigh of relief, "Thank God! We're only about a day's ride from Florence."

"Moretti, let's head in." Francesco commanded. "We still need to know when we are."

"All right then, you got it." Moretti replied.

He pulled on the tiller, brought the *Ricci* around, and headed toward shore. The *Ricci* slowly passed through the harbor. On either side, the group could see ships of all sizes coming in and going out. Though they were mostly small boats, a large cargo carrack flying Portuguese flags could be seen leaving the harbor as well.

The *Ricci* pulled up to one of the large piers where Piero quickly tied the boat to the posts. Xaphine grabbed a large cloak from below deck and tied her wings down as best she could. It was more annoying than painful as she folded her wings in ways that they weren't meant to be folded.

Once she was hidden well enough to blend in, the group walked down the ramp carrying their weapons. They were met by a well-dressed man that rode up in a fancy stage coach with two horses, "You there, you can't tie up here. This is a private dock. Now move that old barge before I call the dock master!"

Piero looked the man and his carriage over for a moment. The man was dressed in furs and jewels. Clearly he was some kind of nobleman, but more interesting to Piero was his carriage. It was brown and black with padded seats and a lamp hanging from each corner. Even the driver's seat was cushioned.

The white horses looked young and strong. He was sure that they could travel faster than any he had seen before. The man looked at Piero with annoyance, "What are you looking at boy, "I said you can't tie up your boat here!"

Piero returned his gaze with an anxious look in his eyes, "What is the date, what is today?"

The lavishly dressed man looked at him oddly, "You have been at sea a long time, haven't you? Today is the first of August."

"What year?"

"What year? Mister, are you sun stricken?"

"The year, man, I need to know the year!"

The nobleman looked at Piero oddly before he responded, "It is the year of our Lord 1530."

"Almost two years... Tell me, does Florence still stand? Has Charles V attacked the city? Do the banners of the Republic still fly?"

The man laughed, "Still? You are lost aren't you? Florence has never fallen. The Republic has taken a beating, but we're still holding strong. Charles V has maintained a siege, but he would not dare attack head on."

"Praise be to God..."

"Amen. Now kindly get your boat away from my pier!"

Piero looked around before leaning on the man's carriage door, "How much would it cost for us to tie up here?"

"Oh it's not a question of money, which I seriously doubt you have. It is about the fact that I have a ship with a large cargo load coming in and I don't need your barge blocking its path."

"How about a deal then?"

The wealthy-looking man rolled his eyes as he listened to Piero talk, "If you give us your carriage, we'll give you the ship."

Moretti's eyes widened, "Now wait a minute… I can't…"

Francesco and Xaphine grabbed Francesco and covered his mouth. The nobleman narrowed his eyes as he looked Piero over, "It's not a stolen ship is it, because I don't deal with pirates!"

"It's not stolen." Piero assured him. "My name is Lieutenant Piero Lorenzi of the Florentine army, I'm on my way back to the capital with information vital to the Republic's survival, and I need to get there fast!"

"Really? Wait, how do I know you are telling me the truth? You didn't even know how long you'd been at sea or what year it is."

He looked them over, "And you don't look like soldiers, your clothes are a mess, that man is blind," he then turned to Xaphine, "and what would soldiers be doing with a deformed creature like that one?"

Francesco chuckled as even he could detect the level irritation in Xaphine's expression as she clenched her fist. Piero continued to try to convince the man, "How else would we disguise ourselves? Sir if you don't help us, Captain Ferruccio will hear of it. I'm sure you don't want your name to be synonymous with the fall of Florence. Think of the disgrace."

The nobleman thought for a moment, "You make a good point… and I really don't lose anything for helping you."

After a brief pause, the nobleman smiled, "Well if all I have to do is give you my carriage in exchange for a boat… I'm happy to serve the Republic!"

The man opened the coach door and walked out on deck to admire his ship. Piero shook his head, "We have a deal then?"

"Yes," The man replied as a scowl appeared on his face. "Now take your carriage and get off my pier! I've got to figure out how I'm going to move this hulk before my shipment arrives."

"As you wish. Good day to you, sir and thank you for your help."

Xaphine and Francesco shoved Moretti into the carriage. Once he was settled, Moretti glared at Piero, "The *Ricci* is the personal property of Marquis of Mantua; you had no right bartering it away! How will we explain this to his lordship?"

"All is lost if we don't make it to Florence in time." Piero shot back. "An old ship will make little difference at that point."

Moretti struggled to get free, "I am nullifying the deal!"

Francesco grabbed his arm, "Are you sure you want to do that? Think of it, Mantua abandoned their allies in our time of need."

"What are you playing at, seer? Not everyone agreed with the Marquis' decision to allow the imperial armies to march over our land, but that was the decision that was made! It is not seemly to question one's monarch. He had his reasons."

Xaphine stared into his eyes, "I lived in Florence for a few years. Mantua had a good relationship with our people before the war. We were your friends…"

"As I said, not everyone agreed with the decision that the Marquis made. I understood it, but many of us feel that Mantua has now lost much of her honor as a result of that. You don't think I'd restore their honor myself if that were possible?"

"Then help us." Piero insisted desperately. "Aid us in the fight to save Florence. Restore the honor of your people."

"Honor…" Moretti repeated. "Doesn't seem like there is much room left of that in this world… still perhaps it is

349

time for Mantua to stand up for what is right instead of what is easy."

He looked Piero in the eye and nodded, "Okay, my friends... I will help you and restore honor to my people and my home."

Piero smiled appreciatively, "All right then, let's get going."

Francesco and Xaphine jumped into the cabin while Piero and Moretti jumped into the driver's chair and pulled on the reigns. The horses slowly turned around until they were facing the town. Piero waited a moment to make sure he had a clear path and then cracked the whip, "Go, go for Florence!"

The horses jolted forward and began moving as fast as they could. The city passed by so quick that it was almost a blur. Xaphine and Francesco were thrown against the back seat as they were pulled forward.

Within ten minutes, the carriage cleared the buildings and was on the open countryside heading for the capital city. Piero handed the reigns over to Moretti to see if they could get the horses going faster. Moretti snapped the reigns, trying to coax the horses.

⛧

After six hours of pushing the horses, the carriage arrived outside of Florence. The area was completely under siege by the imperials and was cut off from outside supplies.

Large plumes of smoke could be seen rising from behind the city walls. Nearby, Piero could see the armies of Charles' Empire encamped in the hills around the city. He shook his head as he watched his home burn, "We'll never get in that way…"

Francesco called out to him from the carriage, "What's wrong?"

"The army is blocking our path. There is no way in. They're under siege."

"Charles V is no fool." Moretti said softly. "He's not about to give an enemy the chance to get any supplies in. He wants this war over as quickly as possible."

Moretti sighed as he looked at the clouds of smoke, "I am sorry for what has been done to you city, Piero. I can only imagine that this is what my home would look like right now had we opposed Charles V."

"I can't believe we've come this far to be cut off… how can there be absolutely no way in?"

"Isn't there?" Xaphine asked smiling as she let some of her feathers show. "The Piero I married would never have given up so easily! He would have found a way around the soldiers."

"The Piero you knew was a lot more reckless and foolish."

"Was he? Last I checked, the current Piero is the one who braved a voyage to Hell to rescue his demonic wife, knowing full well that she might kill him. You were a risk-taker. I've always loved that about you."

She jumped out of the carriage and removed the cloak. Her wings spread to their full magnificence. "Tell me Piero,

DAMNATION

is Charles V so powerful that he has mastered the skies as well?"

Piero smiled as he realized what she was getting at, "I doubt it."

"Then what's stopping me from flying you in?"

"Nothing I suppose. We'll have to wait for the cover of darkness though. I won't risk anyone trying to shoot you down."

"I'll have to make three trips. I can't carry you all at once."

Francesco smiled, "This should be interesting."

"Wait, what do you mean flying us in?" Moretti asked. "Are you expecting me to allow you to carry me into the clouds?"

"What's wrong," Xaphine asked with an evil grin on her face, "afraid of heights?"

"I worked on a ship for several years, so of course I'm not afraid of heights. I'm just afraid of the idea of falling from them."

Xaphine laughed, "You sir, are quite amusing. I can assure you that I've never dropped anyone in my care… unintentionally."

The way she spoke did not comfort Moretti at all, "As you say milady…"

*

As night fell, the whole area was illuminated by campfires and the flame from the buildings burning in the city. Xaphine waited for the sun to set completely before surveying her surroundings, "We'll have to fly fairly high in order to avoid being seen, but we should make it."

Moretti backed away, "I'm not going first. I want to see how someone else handles it."

Piero turned to Francesco, "Do you want to go first?"

He nodded, "I only wish I could see. This will be most exciting."

Xaphine climbed up on the roof of the carriage and pulled Francesco up with her. Once she was ready, she knelt down, "Put your arms around me and hold on tight."

Francesco leaned on to her back and wrapped his arms around Xaphine's shoulders. Xaphine grabbed his knees and raised them to her hips so he was more secure. She could hear him breathing heavily and smiled, "Ready?"

Francesco held on tight for a few moments and whispered a prayer before responding, "Ready…"

Xaphine spread her black wings and slowly began to flap them up and down. The added weight of another person on her back was a lot more cumbersome here than she remembered. Her wings picked up speed until finally she pushed off the side of the carriage and took to the air.

It took her some time to gain altitude with the additional weight on her back, but she was able to climb into the clouds after a few minutes of hard ascension. She let out a sigh of relief as she glided through the clouds with her wings outstretched.

Piero watched as they disappeared from view. His heart was in his throat the entire time. It probably didn't help that Francesco was cheering the entire time.

Piero shook his head as they entered the first cloud, "That blind fool is going to wake up the whole army!"

Above all else, he feared that someone would see them and shoot Xaphine down. She wasn't immortal anymore, so a human arrow could hurt her. His eyes darted back and forth between the cloud they had disappeared into and the city. He waited for what felt like an eternity before he saw a dark spot in the sky. Piero stood up, wrapped himself in her cloak, and waited.

Xaphine touched down about ten feet away from the carriage, breathing heavily. She slowly folded her wings and dropped to one knee as Piero came to her side, "Are you okay?"

"I'm fine… don't worry." She responded between breaths. "Francesco's appearance is deceiving… He is not a light man… just a moment, please."

"Take your time."

Xaphine's breathing began to slow and she was able to hold her balance, "I got him in, there is a courtyard deep within the city that appears to be deserted. It looks like the people of Florence are either hiding in their homes, or defending the city."

"Or they've been killed." Moretti said glumly.

"No way, I know these people. They would never die that easily. They're all in there, trust me."

"We'll find out soon enough." Piero said, relieved that Xaphine made it unscathed.

Xaphine turned around and looked back at the city, "Moretti, let's get going."

"What… me?" Moretti said nervously, "It's really my turn?"

"Yes, I want to take Piero last, come on, it's perfectly safe."

Moretti hesitantly climbed to the top of the carriage. Once Xaphine joined him and knelt down, he attached himself to her back tightly. At first, she had trouble breathing, "Moretti, you need to loosen your grip, we're not going anywhere like this!"

"I'm sorry."

"Calm your senses. I won't let you fall, I promise. Panicking will only make this more difficult."

Moretti nodded and loosened his grip, "My life is in your hands."

Xaphine rolled her eyes as she quickly took off. Piero again watched the one he loved most fly off into the night sky. He paced back and forth for ten minutes waiting for her to return. It seemed like a lot longer than that, but once again his love returned to him. She touched down more gently this time and took a moment to breathe and stretch out her wings.

"I really should have used these more." Xaphine said, caressing her right wing. "Okay, it's finally your turn."

"Are you sure you're ready?"

"I just needed a moment to catch my breath. I'm fine."

Piero began climbing up on the back of the carriage, "All right, if you're sure."

She followed behind him and kneeled down as soon as she was on the roof. Piero put his arms around her, reached out with his neck, and kissed her on the cheek, "Let's do this."

"Hold on tight."

Again, Xaphine started flapping her wings. They went faster and faster until Piero could barely see them. His eyes fluttered as wind generated from her flapping blasted into his face. A second later, Xaphine lunged forwards and was airborne.

Piero held on tight as the ground got smaller and smaller. As they continued their ascension, Piero looked down on the attacking soldiers. He noticed that they all weren't wearing the same uniforms. To his amazement, he saw red and yellow flags, as well as a crown with crossed keys, "Wait a minute... I don't believe it."

Xaphine turned her head, "What is it?"

"I'm seeing Papal emblems on some of their uniforms! What is going on? Why would Rome be attacking us? I know they didn't approve of the rebellion, but our people were their ally!"

"You ousted the Pope's nephew. Did you really think that he wouldn't be upset about that?"

"Maybe, but I didn't think he'd go this far..."

"Never trust political alliances to last." Xaphine said in a dark voice. "Desperate situations often turn allies against each other."

DAMNATION

"I just can't believe that the Pope would forge an alliance with Charles V over us."

Xaphine continued to fly upwards towards the stars. Piero looked around as this was the closest he had ever been to the heavens. Xaphine turned back to look at him with a grin on her face, "Impressed?"

Piero couldn't take his eyes off the sky, "It's like living in a dream. This must be what true freedom is like; to glide amongst the clouds, free to go where ever you want."

"You think that's impressive, watch this!"

She performed a 360 degree turn that made Piero lose his grip. He cried out as he was now freefalling towards the ground. Xaphine smiled and dove down after him. She came up behind him, reached around his chest and stomach, and spread her wings.

Piero opened his eyes to see everything around him. It looked like he was flying by himself, "My God, this is incredible."

For the first time ever, Piero felt truly limitless. The clouds looked remarkable from above. Xaphine smiled, turned, and began flying towards the moon again. She tossed Piero above her head and stretched her arms out to catch him. He landed in her grasp and continued cruising through the clouds.

Piero looked into Xaphine's eyes as they were illuminated by the stars. She looked back at him, "I want to show you everything. I want to take you to the stars and the heavens. There is so much you can't see from the ground."

"Later. When all this is over, you can take me anywhere you want. I want to experience everything with you. We'll just leave caution to the wind and fly away. No more war, no more me going off to distant lands to fight enemies we don't even know, nothing."

"I'll hold you to that."

DAMNATION

Piero relaxed as they soared through the clouds for a few minutes. As she held him close, Piero turned her cheek and kissed her. Neither one wanted the moment to end, but they both knew that duty called to them from below. Piero sighed, "Come on Xaphine, it's time to go…"

Xaphine kept them in the clouds for a brief moment more before beginning her descent. Instead of flying straight downward, Xaphine attempted to go in a circular pattern to prevent picking up speed. She was as gentle with Piero in her arms as she possibly could be.

When they finally touched down, Piero's feet hit the dirt. He looked around, trying to survey the area. Buildings were smashed and on fire, and the once beautiful architecture was now rubble on the ground.

Piero was saddened to see the state of things, the city was in ruins when he left, but it was much worse now. It was a hard thing to behold, but he knew that he still had a mission to accomplish. He had to get moving.

Francesco and Moretti stepped out from behind some of the rubble. Francesco smiled, "How was the trip? You two sure took your time!"

Piero nodded, "Incredible, unlike anything I've ever experienced."

Moretti was fidgeting about, "Wasn't it though? It was the most incredible thing I've ever experienced! I can't believe how cowardice I was!"

He grabbed and hugged Xaphine, "Thank you… thank you for everything! You've opened my eyes to what a wondrous world we live in!"

Xaphine smiled, "Your welcome, maybe we'll do it again someday."

Piero removed the cloak she'd been wearing from the bag on his back and gave it to Xaphine, "Here, you'll need this."

DAMNATION

Xaphine took the cloak and flashed him an annoyed look. Piero shrugged in response, "I'm sorry, Xaphine, it's for the best."

Slowly, Xaphine folded her wings back as much as she could and then tied them down with some cloth. Once they were secured, she put the cloak on, "Okay, I'm ready."

"Good, then let's go." Piero replied as he looked toward the city center.

Piero breathed nervously as they approached the main headquarters for the Florentine defense force. Xaphine sensed his nervousness and placed a hand on his shoulder, "Be strong, Piero. Don't let them see any weakness. You needn't fear. I won't let them hurt you. No matter what happens, I'll keep you safe."

Piero nodded and took a deep breath as he approached the building. Two guards stepped out in front of him, "This area is restricted sir, I'm afraid I cannot allow you to pass. Florentine officers only."

Piero saluted, "Lieutenant Piero Lorenzi reporting for duty. I need to speak with Captain Ferruccio immediately."

The two guards looked at each other oddly and then back at him, "The deserter? It can't be. It's been two years…"

"That it has, but I have returned to serve my home. I have information that I must bring before the captain. It is absolutely vital to our survival!"

The guard on the right, who appeared to be the higher ranked soldier, nodded, "I don't know how happy he is going to be to see you, but I'll tell him. Wait here until I return."

The guard turned to his partner before disappearing, "Do not allow them to leave. I'm sure the captain will have some choice words for them."

The first guard was only gone for a few minutes. The second guard eyed them nervously as he waited. His orders were to prevent them from leaving, but he doubted he could take on the group by himself. Even so, he kept his sword pointed at them.

Piero smiled and spoke in a calming voice, "Relax, soldier, we're not going to try anything."

The nervous guard nodded, "Even so, be quiet and wait… sir."

The young guard was relieved when his superior finally returned. The group looked too menacing for him to take on alone. The first guard nodded, "The captain commands you to enter immediately."

The large doors slowly creaked open and the group was guided into the main hall, past another group of guards, and into the main headquarters area. They then proceeded into the smaller war room where a slightly older Captain Ferruccio stood.

Once the four friends cleared the doors, Ferruccio nodded to someone standing behind them. The door slammed shut and the group found themselves surrounded by soldiers pointing swords at them. Ferruccio sneered, "Had I not seen it for myself, I might not have believed it. You have a lot of guts coming back here after deserting your post."

"I wouldn't have if I thought you could handle what's to come on your own."

Ferruccio shook his head, unwilling to listen, "Lieutenant, you are under arrest for disobeying orders and desertion, which is considered treason. The punishment for such a crime is death."

"Fine, whatever the punishment is, we can deal with that later. I bring urgent news!"

"I can't wait to hear this one. You have been gone for two years while your countrymen suffered and died. One can only imagine the sort of debaucheries you have been involved in."

DAMNATION

"Captain, please!"

Ferruccio saw the look of sincerity in his eyes and nodded, "Oh very well, speak."

"Yes sir, Charles V is moving his forces in to attack the city. We need to mass what forces we have left and stand against him, or Florence will surely fall!"

Laughter erupted from the soldiers surrounding them. Ferruccio shook his head, "You expect me to believe this nonsense? We have held out here for years here without them breaching our walls. They wouldn't dare try to commit a force to attack us here. They'd be repelled and the casualties would be staggering."

"Things have changed," Piero insisted, "There are now Papal soldiers swelling their ranks. There should be no doubt that the Emperor would use the Papal army as cannon fodder to wear us down."

"I know that... the Pope was furious to learn of Florence throwing off his nephew's rule to become a republic. He signed a treaty with Charles V, and has now turned on us."

"This is something we might have found out sooner had you completed your mission. Instead you turned your back on us!"

Piero breathed heavily, "Please forgive me. I know I have betrayed Florence, but I am here trying to save the city! Please, you must listen to me!"

"Silence! I have heard enough of your treason. We're not going to commit the last of our forces to a major campaign on the word of a deserter. You haven't even told us where you got such outrageous information."

Another soldier stepped forward, "Sir, if I may speak?"

The captain nodded allowing the soldier to speak, "Sir, my scouts on the border of our land have confirmed that a large force is heading this way. We thought they were relief forces for the imperial lines, but there are far more than we originally anticipated. What this man is saying has possible merit."

"I remember reading the report. I also know that there is no real evidence to suggest that they're planning an attack. Charles V has been replacing men little by little as he has needed them."

Ferruccio turned back to Piero, "And I'm still curious where you got your information? Or are you still trying to come up with an explanation?"

"I… an angel told me." He replied softly.

Now even Ferruccio himself was laughing, "Two years away from home have clearly driven you mad. Even if I could somehow be brought to believe such an outlandish claim, answer me these questions; why would an angel tell you? Why not come here and tell me? I would be in more of a position to do something about it."

Piero lowered his head, not wanting to reveal his source. "I can't answer that, sir."

"Of course not." Captain Ferruccio replied as he shook his head. "I expected as much."

He then signaled his guards, "Arrest this man for desertion."

Piero was grabbed by the guards standing behind him, knocked to the ground and shackled. Xaphine turned to the captain, "No, he speaks the truth! Release him now… Let him go!"

Before the captain could answer, one of the soldiers looked at her with a mean expression, "Silence wench! Get out of the way!"

Xaphine refused to stand aside and grabbed his arm to stop him. The guard turned, shook his arm free, and struck her with the back of his wrist before she could respond. The impact was loud and hard.

DAMNATION

Xaphine wasn't expecting the strike to be as painful as it was. Becoming mortal had made her more susceptible to pain than before. She fell backwards and landed on her side, but did not cry out.

Piero fought to his feet and tried to attack the soldier, "You bastard, why don't you try that on me you coward! Let me go!"

Three soldiers pointed blades directly at Piero's throat forcing him to stop moving. Piero glared at the man, "You better hope I never get free. We all took oaths of honor and chivalry, you have violated said oath and should be stripped of your uniform."

The soldier scoffed and spit in Piero's face. He turned his attention back to the shackles, only to find a blade pointed at his own throat. The soldier gasped as he looked up.

Captain Ferruccio had pulled a dagger and pointed it at him, "That is not how we do things here soldier. As much as I hate to say it, the traitor is right. It'll be twelve lashes for you."

Two of the soldiers holding Piero turned and grabbed the man who had struck Xaphine. He didn't put up a fight and allowed them to take him away. Ferruccio snorted, "Animal…"

Once the solider was gone, Ferruccio turned to Xaphine, "I don't condone the way my soldier behaved, but if you attempt to interfere in the lieutenant's arrest again, then you will share in his fate."

They were about to remove Piero from the room when Xaphine stood up nursing her cheek. It pulsed from the power of the blow she'd taken. Her teeth were clenched as her eyes flickered red. She fought back Xaphan's urge to start killing everyone in the room who tried to harm Piero. Her hand clenched the dagger she kept hidden under her robe, "I think not, Captain!"

She untied her wings and dropped the cloak. Piero saw what she was doing and cried out, "Xaphine, no don't do it!"

He was too late. The cloak dropped and she spread her wings out to their full magnificence. With one quick thrust, she lifted herself off of the ground. Even Piero had to stare in awe at how Xaphine looked with her wings fully spread. She glared at the soldiers as she spoke in a deep voice, "Unhand him now!"

Some of the soldiers slowly backed away while others fell over themselves. Xaphine's feet touched the ground as she turned to Captain Ferruccio, "Lieutenant Lorenzi speaks the truth. I told him what was going to happen. I am the reason he chose to return."

Ferruccio's eyes narrowed as he looked at her. He could not believe who he was speaking to, "Xaphine... is that you? It cannot be..."

"It is." She replied.

"How is this possible? I remember when we found you. You had lost your memory with no sign of recovery. You looked so different... but you're an angel? I suppose that does explain a lot, it is still a story I would very much enjoy hearing."

"I'm sorry, but none of that is your concern. You have much larger issues that require your attention."

"Of course, you are right. Forgive me, milady..."

He quickly turned to his soldiers, "You heard the angel, release Piero immediately."

Piero's shackles were removed and the soldiers put their swords away. Once Piero was free, he stepped forward towards the captain, "You've got your proof, Captain. My wife is the angel, but I saw the army for myself when we flew overhead. Now, are you going to defend your city or let it fall?"

DAMNATION

Ferruccio thought about it for a moment, "Of course, it is my job to defend the city against all enemies. Do you have any idea which direction the army is coming from or what their plan is?"

"I did see a large group massing from the North. It looked like they were getting ready to move on Gavinana. If they succeed there, we'll be next."

"We have no time to waste then. I'll assemble our forces and we'll move out as soon as everyone's together."

Not wasting a second, Ferruccio quickly turned to the soldiers standing in the room, "All of you, go, wake our commanders and have them get the men into line! I want our armies assembled by sunrise! Make no mistake, any soldier who is still sleeping come sunrise will answer to me!"

The men stared at each other for a second, trying to get a grip on what had just happened. Ferruccio's eyes darted back and forth between his men, "Now!"

The men jumped at Ferruccio's booming voice and quickly filed out the door in formation. Once the door closed though, Piero could hear the sound of scattered footsteps, panicked breathing, and metal clanking as the men rushed to get the word out.

Ferruccio shook his head and turned to Piero, "If you want to prove your worth as a soldier, now is your chance."

"I'm ready sir." Piero replied as he stood at attention. "What are my orders?"

"Get yourself a uniform and take command of your old company. Most of them are still together. They've taken up guard duty at what's left of the citadel. I want your people on the front lines. With you back in command, morale should skyrocket. I'm hoping for a performance like what you used to provide me."

Xaphine covered her face to hide a look of terror as Piero agreed, "Not a problem, I think I still have it in me."

DAMNATION

Piero turned to see Xaphine hiding her fear as best she could. He turned back to the captain, "May we have a moment?"

Captain Ferruccio looked at them both oddly before nodding and leaving the room. Piero looked into Xaphine's eyes, "My love, what troubles you?"

Xaphine looked up at him as the tears continued to fall, "You're going to front lines? Piero, no! I will not risk losing you again."

"I know how to handle myself on the field of battle. I'll be fine."

"No, this isn't one of your small skirmishes in the woods or on some far away hills. This is a major engagement from a battle-hardened army that is ready for you!"

Piero placed his hand on her cheek, "I've been through it before."

"Piero please, I'd rather have a live coward to take flying with me than have to live with the memory of a dead hero. You're all I have... I don't wish to be left alone here. Don't go, please?"

"Is that what you really want? You told me about the people who wind up in the Well of Souls. They saw suffering and they ignored it. Right now, the Republic is dying as the enemy waits at our door. Ruthless aristocrats want to bring us back into line and choke the voice from our people."

Xaphine thought about it for a few moments with tears in her eyes, "You're right... of course you're right. I'm sorry... I let my fears get the better of me. You're a soldier, this is your job."

"Xaphine," Piero said, taking her hand, "I love you more than anything else in the world. I gave everything to bring you home... if you ask me to leave, then I will go with you and we can run away to a far off place."

DAMNATION

"No… No, you're absolutely right. Florence needs their best commander. I love you Piero, go out there and perform your duty with honor."

Piero pinched his wife's chin and kissed her deeply, "I love you too… take Francesco and wait in our home for me."

"Francesco? You mean you're not taking him with you?"

"He's a blind man. Even with his military training, a battlefield is no place for him. I am asking you to look after our friend."

"Should you not take Xaphine at least?" Francesco objected. "Your wife belongs at your side."

"Yes, I agree with Francesco. I can watch your back just as I did when we faced off against Lucifer! It's a good idea."

"Maybe she does belong with me," Piero agreed, "but I can't command my company and protect her at the same time."

A look of anger came over Xaphine, "Piero, I am a warrior. I was a general commanding armies before your world was even created. I don't need your protection, I'll be protecting you!"

"With your wings, you would stand out like a sore thumb and would no doubt become a target. This would pose a major risk on the field and I would not be able to forgive myself if anything were to happen to her. Xaphine, do this for me, please…"

Xaphine flashed him a look of disapproval as her eyes flickered red, "Fine…"

☳

Captain Ferruccio was good on his word. He worked through the night to assemble the armies of Florence. Thousands of men lined up at the city walls in silent attention.

Piero met up with his men at the citadel. When they saw him, their eyes lit up. One of the younger soldiers came running to him, "Lieutenant, you're back!"

Piero nodded, "Men, we have one last glorious fight ahead of us. I know it's been two years, but I've been given my old command back and I expect you all to perform as you have before."

The young soldier nodded, "Don't worry Lieutenant, we've kept up our training."

"Reporting for duty sir." A voice appeared from behind.

Piero turned to see who was reporting. His eyes lit up when he saw Moretti dressed in his guard uniform from Mantua. Moretti saluted as he spoke, "I hereby request permission to fight at your side in the upcoming battle. For the honor of Mantua!"

"The honor will be mine. You are most welcome amongst my soldiers."

Moretti nodded and sat with the rest of Piero's soldiers. Suddenly another voice came up from behind, "The Captain approaches!"

Piero turned immediately to attention, "Men, on your feet!"

Captain Ferruccio approached Piero's company and looked them over. Piero nodded, "My men are assembled sir."

"Good, very good. We're already about half way assembled. A few more hours, and our army should be ready to go."

DAMNATION

**

Xaphine made her way into the city to the citadel. Once again, she hid herself under a cloak so she did not attract any attention. She quietly slipped in amongst the soldiers and looked for her love.

Piero saw her coming, "Xaphine, what are you doing here? We're just about ready to assemble with the rest of the army."

She raised the hood of her cloak slightly, revealing tears in her eyes, "You're not going anywhere. Not without giving me one last kiss... please?"

Piero hugged Xaphine tightly and pressed his lips against hers. The kiss was bittersweet and short lived, but it was all they had time for. A signal horn sounded to let everyone know that the time had come for the army to report for inspection. Their lips parted and Xaphine's eyes dropped.

Piero smiled, trying to cheer her up, "Stop acting like this is the end."

"Though I doubt anyone listens to my prayers, I will continue to ask for your protection."

"Thank you my love." Piero said as he turned to move with his troops. "I'll see you after the battle."

She began to breathe heavily, fearing for her love, "Piero, I don't care what happens. Like I told you so long ago... It doesn't matter to me if you win a great victory or face a staggering defeat. Please just come back to me alive. That's all I want."

"Don't worry; I'll see you after the battle."

He then returned to the head of his company, "Men, move out."

Xaphine watched him leave as she fought back her anxiety and tried to hold her stoic expression. Once he was out of sight, she dropped to her knees, unable to hold back her emotions any longer. Her eyes turned red and the darkness slowly began to take over. She wouldn't cry, because it wouldn't solve anything and it would have been premature, but to be left out of the fighting, to be denied her right to keep the oath that she had taken to Piero, was more than she could tolerate.

Having nowhere to turn for comfort, Xaphine clasped her hands together, "Lord God Most High, take my soul and do with it as you see fit, but in exchange protect Piero. I don't care what happens to me..."

Piero's group marched in formation to the citadel. The captain was already there inspecting the soldiers as Piero arrived. Captain Ferruccio smiled as Piero and his men formed up at the front of the line. *Finally, he arrives on time for something.*

Ferruccio paced up and down the line inspecting his men. When he arrived at Piero's company, Piero smiled, "Ready to move out on your order sir."

"Very good, the order is given, move out."

"Understood. – Company, forward!"

Piero's men slowly began to march out of the citadel on to the hills. One by one, each battalion followed suit. They marched out of the city, to the north. The large army made their way to Gavinana, just outside of the capital.

Piero stood at the front of the line with Captain Ferruccio and Moretti flanking him, waiting for the imperial army to come. In the distance, they could hear the sound of thousands of heavy footsteps, as well as battle drums being played.

Piero looked at the captain and nodded, "Now we wait."

**

Xaphine returned to Piero's house, or what was left of it. He had rebuilt his home since she left, but the siege had done a lot of damage. Part of the roof had caved in and most of their belongings had been stolen.

DAMNATION

Xaphine paced around the living room while Francesco attempted to light a fire in the oven. As she walked, her foot kicked something heavy. She looked down to see what was in her path. Caked in dirt and partially obscured by the rubble, was a metal object that still had some shine to it. She reached down and pulled it out from under the rubble.

Xaphine gasped when the sword that Piero had given her came into view, "He kept it... for me... all these years."

She quickly grabbed an old rag off of a nearby table and wiped it down as best she could. It was still sharp and looked like it had been cared for until recently. Clearly Piero wanted to give it back to her at some point.

Xaphine shook her head as she looked into the blade, "I can't do this. I'm a warrior, not some peasant house wife! I'm not going to wait here!"

Francesco spoke up in protest, "I share your frustration, but Piero was right when he said we wouldn't be much help in a fight, what choice do we have?"

"I'm Piero's wife." She said angrily with a hint of red in her eyes. "I am not his slave. If he won't let me help him, at least I can keep an eye on him. I will not sit idle by and wait to receive word that he's been killed."

"I heard that the army is going to Gavinana, north of the capital. If that's where you want to go, then I will follow."

Xaphine sheathed the sword and attached it to her belt before stretching her wings. She looked to the north as they spread, "All right then, that's what we're doing."

She disappeared behind the house and came out with an old wooden ladder, placed it against the house, and turned to Francesco, "Come on, up you go."

With Xaphine's help, Francesco pushed himself up to the roof. She stayed on his heels as he moved. The moment they were ready, she knelt down in front of him, "Quickly, get on."

"Flying again?"

"Yes, it's the quickest way there."

Francesco leaned into Xaphine's back and wrapped his arms around her shoulders again. She began flapping her wings as she had before and lunged into the air. She quickly gained altitude and cruised through the air.

They were high enough that Xaphine could see the entire city. It was a depressing sight looking down on the rubble that had been the place she called home. Part of her regretted not being there to help the army with their weapons. If they won this battle and survived the day, she wanted to help rebuild the beautiful city, if that were even possible anymore.

Xaphine flew for about twenty minutes before coming down in the hills just outside Gavinana. Their location gave them a perfect view of upcoming battle. Xaphine slowed her breathing and knelt down, "This should be sufficient for now."

Francesco placed his hand on the ground and could feel the pounding of a thousand feet, wagon wheels, horses' hooves, and other things he couldn't quite identify. Even from their position, they could hear the drums beat. They couldn't see the enemy army, but Francesco could tell that they were getting closer.

"And so it begins…"

**

Piero camped out with Captain Ferruccio and his company while waiting for the enemy army to arrive. Gavinana was a fortifiable position so they weren't worried about a surprise attack when night fell on the soldiers, but they still kept a lookout posted. As the camp fires burned, Ferruccio turned to his captain, "Piero, I've been meaning to ask you, what happened during the last two years? Where did you go?"

Piero's eyes never left the flame, "I traveled further than any soldier had previously, perhaps further than anyone ever should. I saw places no human eye has ever seen. I flew above the clouds, and I've seen friends become enemies. I saw suffering, I saw redemption, I saw hopelessness, I saw restoration, and I saw death which then turned to light."

"All for love?"

"For life." Piero said, correcting the captain. "Because without her at my side, I wasn't really living. I look back on the years I spent without her. I was slowly dying, and thoughtlessly sending myself on as many suicide missions as I could, but somehow I always survived. It was kind of infuriating."

"But what does this mean for you, her being an angel? Surely that must complicate things for you. Where would you be able to live?"

"I don't know. My most immediate concern is keeping her away from the eyes of the church, beyond that, only time can answer such a question. Right now I have to focus on survival. The days of the Papal alliance are over and if our Republic falls… well we all remember what it was like to live under the monarchy. Such a thought is unappealing to say the least."

"I don't think anyone disagrees…"

Ferruccio's eyes leveled with Piero, "My boy, I am sorry I was so hard on you. I understand why you did what you did. Lord knows… had I found out that my wife was in trouble, I might have abandoned my post and run off to her rescue as well."

"Don't, Captain. You have nothing at all to apologize for. I would have reacted the same way if I were in your place. You were doing what was best for the Republic as any good soldier would. I can't fault you for doing your job."

As the fire dimmed, one by one, the soldiers began to fall asleep. For most, sleep didn't come easy, as was expected on the eve of battle. Many of them were scared that this would be the last night of sleep they would ever get, others were anxious to get to fighting. All of them had their thoughts dwelling on their families and whether or not they would ever see them again.

Piero's thoughts dwelled on his wife. He remembered the all-too-brief time he had spent living with Xaphine. Those were easily the best years of his life. As he closed his eyes and went to sleep, she appeared in front of him, "Hello my love."

Piero looked at her oddly. Her wings were gone and she wore a shimmering silver gown. Piero's eyes narrowed, "Xaphine, what are you doing here? I told you to stay away. What happened to your wings?"

"I'm not one of your men. I don't take orders from you... however I did stay away. I'm not physically here right now."

He scratched his head for a moment before he realized what was going on, "Oh I get it, you're the echo... wait why are you here? I rescued her. Shouldn't you be a part of her again?"

"As long as there is a voice, there will always be an echo. Granted, I am far more complete thanks to you, but I will always be here. I am a part of her... the part she gave to you, her heart."

"But why appear to me right now? This may not be the best time to talk."

"Why not? You are hours away from marching into a battle that you may not walk out of. You need me now more than ever. How could I not come to remind you that she is with you?"

373

"I know that. I've always known that. Part of her has always been here, even when she was lost to me. You've played no small part in reminding me of that."

The specter of her heart nodded, "The dawn of your defining day begins... No matter what happens out there, keep her close to your heart. She loves you... Remember that."

The ghost leaned down and kissed him as she began to fade, "Good luck Piero."

iv

Moments later she was gone and Piero was alone. A loud bell going off from the lookout post shook him awake. Piero's eyes shot opened and he scrambled to his feet. As other soldiers were still being roused by the bell, Piero grabbed his sword, ran pasted the encampments, and climbed the stairs to the lookout post.

Moretti had been ordered to man this post during the night and turned to face Piero as he climbed the stairs. He ran as hard as he could to see what was happening. Once he reached the wall, his eyes went wide.

Francesco and Xaphine were also awoken by the bells. Xaphine rolled on to her stomach and looked out at the once-open field. Her mouth formed a gaping maw as a look of terror came over her features, "No…"

There, coming over the hills less than a mile from the wall was a massive army complete with full cavalry, artillery, and divisions of grenadiers and infantrymen. They marched in perfect formation, under the banner of Charles V, and lined up side by side. The yellow and black colors of the banners were easily visible from the distance.

As they neared the old ramparts, Piero could hear the army chanting praises to their emperor over and over. Their words, paired with the on-beat stomp of their feat created a very imposing sound.

Captain Ferruccio appeared behind Piero, "Mother of God… they've got us outnumbered by almost 2 to 1."

Moretti nodded, "… this could be bad…"

Piero could feel the heart beating out of his chest and began breathing more rapidly. He was suddenly reminded of the intense rush of emotion from going into battle, "What are your orders, Captain?"

"Get the men into line. Organize the gunmen to open fire from the hillside when needed, order the cavalry to stand ready to charge!"

Piero left the wall and ran back to the lines of infantry, "Get into line! Everyone, to arms, to arms!"

Half awake, unfed, and with no hope of receiving any reinforcements, the Florentine soldiers got up and stood in line. Most wore steel helmets with brown leather armor. Together, flying the red coat of arms of the Republic, the small army marched out on to the field.

Piero mounted a horse and road out next to Captain Ferruccio. The captain nodded as Piero came up on his side, "Ready for some fun?"

"Always!"

Slowly both armies closed the distance between their lines. Once they were within a thousand feet of each other, Captain Ferruccio recognized the Imperial commander as he rode out in front of his men, "I don't believe it... Philibert de Châlon. The Prince of Orange himself, he's leading the enemy army!"

"Well... we should at least hear what he has to say. Let's go talk to him..."

The two commanders rode out to the middle of the battlefield where they were quickly joined by Philibert. Piero shook his head while looking at the man riding toward them. Philibert was dressed in ornate armor, mounted on a perfectly white horse. The large plumage on his helmet swayed in the wind. This did not look like a battle-hardened soldier, more like an aristocrat who had been seduced by stories of glory which pushed him into a suite of armor. Piero had to resist the urge to chuckle at the absurdity of his appearance.

Philibert slowed his horse as he neared the opposing commanders, "Good day to you both. Tis a good day for a battle, wouldn't you say?"

DAMNATION

Ferruccio rolled his eyes. Yes the prince had beautiful manners, but he seemed extremely out of place on the battlefield, still Ferruccio remained cordial. "Good day to you as well, but with all due respect, I must ask you to leave our land. We are prepared to agree to a ceasefire if you end this blockade."

"Excellent!" Philibert replied happily. "Then you are prepared to lay down your arms and end this pointless rebellion?"

"I do not recall saying anything of the sort. One way or another that means us going back under the heel of a puppet ruler whose strings are pulled by the Pope. That is not something we're prepared to accept."

"I see... Well that is truly a shame... I had hoped to end this without bloodshed and return the city to its proper ruler. I'd heard stories about some of your soldiers and it would have been pleasant to see them fighting in the Papal army once again where they belong, but if this is your position... then I see we have nothing more to talk about."

"I guess we don't."

"Very well." Philibert said with a smile. "See you both on the battlefield."

Piero looked Philibert in the eye with a devious grin, "I'll be looking for you."

Philibert's smile disappeared as he brought his horse around and rode away. Ferruccio smiled, "Brash my friend, perhaps too brash... if you wanted to draw attention to yourself, you could have just worn red archery target."

The commanders made their way back to their respective armies. Piero joined formation with his company as the drums beat and the war horns sounded. Captain Ferruccio rode across his lines as the battle began.

Piero looked at his horse for a moment and jumped off, "You are too fine a beast to die needlessly in this fight and I belong on the ground with my men."

DAMNATION

He turned it to the side and smacked it on the backside right next to its tail. The horse let out a startled cry and ran across the line out into the hills. Now that he was on level ground, Piero looked at his company and nodded, "For freedom… for Florence!"

His men cheered, "For Florence!"

Piero turned back, drew his sword, raised it high in the air, and charged at the enemy lines. As he ran, he spoke under his breath, "For Xaphine…"

Moretti saw him begin to run and put his hand on the shoulder of the soldier standing next to him, "Come on boys, let's give them a fight worth singing about!"

The army cheered as line by line, they followed right behind Piero. Captain Ferruccio stayed near the front lines as the two armies clashed. Flares and mortar shots flew through the air and crossed each other in the sky. They hit the ground with mighty booms, leaving massive craters in their wakes. Piero's arm was grazed by the shrapnel from a nearby blast he continued to lead on foot, undeterred as the ground exploded around him.

The Florentine lines collided together with the imperials like two melons being smashed against one another. Piero cut down two of their spear men to form a hole for him to run through. From the sides, the gunmen attempted to thin the enemy lines for the infantry to get through. The cavalry also began their own charge and cut the imperial lines.

Xaphine watched from a distance and described the battle to Francesco, "The two lines clashed. I think I can see Piero. He's running point in front of his men. It looks like their actually outflanking the imperials!"

Francesco nodded, "Though the imperials may have them outnumbered, we have the advantage of superior commanders and our soldiers have them outclassed in every way. Quality over quantity will win out any day. I would stake my life on it."

"I hope so," Xaphine replied as she turned her attention back to the field.

**

As the battle thickened, the gunmen found themselves right in the middle of the fray. Piero saw this and pointed his sword to the right, "My men, rally to me, quickly!"

The company pulled in closer to their commander as Piero moved to defend the gunmen as best he could. The gunmen struggled to get their guns reloaded quickly, but he was slowly getting beaten back. After a few moments, the lead gunman called to Piero, "Arquebuses at the ready, sir!"

Piero dove out of the way and pointed at the enemy advance, "Take aim… Fire, fire, fire!"

There was a series of massive flashes and several small columns of smoke that poured from the guns. Several imperial soldiers were either severely wounded or killed from the gunfire. Piero got back up and signaled for his company to press forward, "You men cover the gunners as they fall back!"

From her viewpoint, Xaphine began to worry as she watch the battle unfold, "No Piero, fall back with your soldiers, you're being surrounded! Fall back now; you can't save your gunners!"

Francesco listened as best he could, "What's happening?

"Piero is trying to defend his gunmen, but he is losing ground. His men are getting outflanked and he doesn't see it!"

Xaphine's plea went unheard as Piero's company surged forward, but it didn't take him long to realize his error. He had progressed far too quickly and now his men were surrounded and being cut down. They fought hard, but the sheer numbers they were dealing with was too much for the small company.

Captain Ferruccio came up behind him as the small band's only escape was cut off. The two fought back to back with their swords in hand. Ferruccio turned to his Lieutenant, "What's your plan now, Piero?"

"You're the captain! It's your turn! We're getting cut to ribbons out here."

Ferruccio nodded and turned to one of the soldiers on horseback, "Fall back, cut through the enemy lines and tell the artillery to fire 2 points ahead of us."

The man nodded and ran his horse through the enemy lines, trampling enemy soldiers under its hooves. Minutes later, Florentine shells smashed through the lines ahead of Piero. Little by little, the Florentine army was breaking out.

Piero cheered, "My men, into the fray, seize the moment and we may yet win this battle!"

Philibert saw them coming and attempted to fall back further behind his lines, but as he turned, he was hit in the chest by a shot from one of the Florentine gunmen. Wounded, but still alive, he turned back, looked angrily at the Florentine army overtaking his position and pressed his men forward. Piero could see that his injury had given the prince a new sense of determination.

As the Florentine lines crumbled around him, Piero attempted to close the distance between himself and Philibert, but he could not get close enough. As his men fought, Piero saw Moretti trying to load an arquebus that he had picked up off a dead gunman. He had just started loading his powder when another gunman's shot hit him in the throat.

Piero cried out, "No!"

Coughing and near death, Moretti raised his free hand to the heavens and whispered with what little voice he had left, "For the honor of Mantua!"

DAMNATION

Moretti fell backward, but still had enough strength to hold on to the gun so that the powder didn't come out. Piero pulled a knife out from his back plate and threw it at the enemy gunmen, hitting him in the chest.

As the enemy soldier fell, Piero picked up Moretti's gun and finished loading it. He turned to his men as he picked up the shot and powder, "I need a few moments, cover me, men!"

Piero's men followed their orders and quickly established a perimeter around him. Piero added wadding and a shot to the arquebus and forced it into the barrel. Once he was ready, he took the ram rod and jammed it into the muzzle, pushing the shot into place. He could hear the metal scraping together as it forced the shot to the back of the barrel.

Once the arquebus was loaded, he lit the wick, pushed the hammer back into firing position, and took aim. Luckily, he was tall enough to see over his soldiers. Piero took his time until he had a clear shot at Philibert.

Captain Ferruccio saw what Piero was doing and yelled to him, "Piero, now's your chance, bring him down! Bring him down now and we can turn the tides of battle!"

Piero closed his left eye and placed Philibert in his sights. As his finger began to pull on the trigger, he whispered a short prayer, "Lord, make my shot swift and true…"

As he squeezed the trigger, the hammer came down and ignited the powder. Fire sparked from both ends of the arquebus and it went off with a loud boom. Philibert suddenly jolted backwards, dropped his sword and fell off his horse.

Seeing their prince fall, shattered the morale of the imperial soldiers and their lines began to break. The Florentines cheered as they surged forward and routed the enemy position. It seemed like nothing could stop them now.

Piero knelt down next to Moretti who was fading fast, "Thank you, my friend. You've done outstanding today… go now and be with your ancestors."

Moretti nodded and smiled as his eyes closed. Piero gently lowered his head to the ground and said a short prayer. He managed to finish before an enemy soldier dove at him with a sword. Piero stood quickly enough to parry the attack and fight back.

Xaphine watched from the hills as Philibert fell from his horse. When she saw the effect Piero's shot had, she began to cheer, "Yes, they've got the imperials on the run!"

Francesco stood completely still, "It's not over yet…"

Piero charged onward with Captain Ferruccio at his side. They had broken the backs of the imperials and were driving them into the hills. Cheers could be heard from the Florentine lines as they pressed forward.

Captain Ferruccio yelled out, "Forward men, we've got them scattered, let's keep them that way!"

As they pushed forward, imperial war trumpets from in front of the Florentine flanks sounded. At that moment, the imperial soldiers stopped in their tracks and turned around. To Piero's surprise, they were now fighting with twice the aggression that they had originally. It didn't take long for Piero to figure out why.

Another two thousand imperial soldiers came over the hills and entered the fray. These soldiers were not as well equipped and looked far more ragtag than the original army, but judging by their faces, they were also more battle hardened. Ferruccio let out a deep sigh as he lowered his sword, "No…"

Piero looked at him oddly, "What's wrong captain, what is it?"

DAMNATION

"Reinforcements," Ferruccio answered, "and they're being led by Fabrizio Maramaldo."

Piero's face turned white with shock at the sound of his name, "What, the same man who lay siege to Asti and aided in the sacking of Rome?"

"The same…" Ferruccio replied.

Piero held himself up by his knees trying to catch his breath, "God help us… what are your orders captain, fall back?"

"Press forward!" Ferruccio yelled. "I'll split our forces and try to hold off Maramaldo!"

"Understood," Piero agreed. "My men, press forward!"

As the captain pulled back to rally his men against Maramaldo, Piero turned to one of his lieutenants, "This isn't looking good… soldier, fall back to the artillery lines. I want mortars and grenadiers to target the imperial forward lines on either side and make them cluster. We're going to try to flank them in."

The lieutenant saluted and pulled back. Piero turned to his surviving soldiers and split the group in two, "You men take the left flank, and the rest of you follow me!"

Piero's men flanked the main imperial army on either side as the mortars ripped away at the enemy numbers. The infantrymen were pressing them together as best they could, but their numbers were getting cut down each minute. Piero found himself lacking enough men to hold the line.

One of his sergeants came up behind him, sword in hand, "Sir, we're getting cut down out here, we need to fall back!"

Piero shook his head, "And where would you like us to fall back to? Maramaldo's forces have us cut off from the fortifications and these troops have secured our only escape route. There is nowhere to retreat to, so you hold the line mister! Do you understand me?"

The middle aged soldier nodded, realizing that this would most likely be his last fight, "Yes sir, we'll hold the line down to the last man… praise the Lord!"

The sergeant raised his tarnished sword and charged into a crowd of enemy soldiers. He swung his blade around, cutting down at least a dozen imperial troops before being stabbed in the back himself.

The sergeant froze in place and was about to drop to his knees, but he found the strength to turn around, breaking the imperial's grip on his sword. He raised his blade and brought it down on the imperial, cutting him deeply through the shoulder.

The sergeant felt his hands and legs began to tingle and fell to his knees. He looked around to see his men beating beaten down all around him before fading away himself. Piero and the remaining troops cheered for the man's heroics, but it was a short lived celebration as their lines were quickly getting overrun.

**

From the hills, Xaphine could see the entire battle unfolding. She went pale when Maramaldo's troops arrived. Her heart was in her throat as she watched her husband's armies get almost completely overrun. She stretched out her wings, preparing to take off when Francesco grabbed her, "No!"

She struggled underneath him, "Bastard, let go of me! Piero is down there! If I don't go to him, he won't survive! Release me before it's too late."

"I can't do that Xaphine! If you go down there, you'll both be killed!"

"Francesco please…" She begged, swallowing her pride. "Don't force me to watch him die! I can't do it… I can't lose him again."

"There is nothing you can do to save him right now. You don't even know where he is! Come to your senses and honor your husband's wishes by staying safe. He is not down there fighting for Florence, he is fighting for you! Even if Florence falls, as long as you survive, his honor will be satisfied!"

Xaphine ceased struggling to get free of the blind man and looked helplessly as the remains of the Florentine army were driven back. She lay on her stomach and covered her eyes as tears rolled down her cheeks, "Most High, please help them…"

Captain Ferruccio's forces were totally decimated and as far as Piero could see, he had been captured by Maramaldo's men. Meanwhile, the original charge into the enemy lines was continuing to fight, but their numbers were dwindling.

Piero fought back to back with one of the last surviving men of his company. The young soldier looked over his shoulder at his commanding officer, "Sir, may I just say that it has been the honor of my life to serve with you."

Piero nodded, "The honor is mine, you and the rest of the company fought bravely. We've made sure that history will never forget this day, nor shall it forget the Republic… or freedom."

Mortar blasts exploded all around them as Piero engaged the captain that took over command of the original army when the Prince of Orange was killed. This man was massive. His arms and legs were bulging with muscle as he swung his sword at Piero. He had strength, but Piero had speed and was able to dodge around most of his attacks, hoping to tire the man our before going in for the kill.

The mortars created a massive cloud of smoke and dust. It wasn't long before Xaphine lost sight of almost the entire battle. She looked to where Piero's men were still fighting and saw a small band of them struggling to hold on. The imperial artillery seemed to target that position with everything they had. To her horror, three explosions hit the area Piero had been standing.

Xaphine cried out, "No!"

V

An hour later, it was all over. The drums and war trumpets ceased, the mortars stopped firing, and the Imperial army slowly moved past Gavinana. As the smoke cleared, Xaphine's eyes quickly darted across the area to see if her husband had been taken prisoner or fallen on the field. No matter how hard she scanned the area, she could not see Piero anywhere.

For a second time, Xaphine wanted to fly down there, but Francesco would not let her, "Wait until nightfall; it's only an hour away."

"Damn you seer, he could be dead by then!"

"The danger still has not passed yet. Please, you must wait! Once the army clears out, we'll go. I promise."

With little choice, Xaphine nodded and anxiously awaited the sunset. Every minute felt like an eternity for her. From a distance, she could see the flags being lowered in the capital city. Her heart sank as tears returned to her eyes, "The war is over. It's all finished."

"What do you see?"

"Not much, we're too far away, but it looks like the capital city has been taken. Florence has fallen… which means the Republic is finished. Everything we fought for is gone."

"Truly a tragedy… but, at least the killing will end now."

Xaphine lowered her eyes, "He can't be dead… he just can't be."

"I hope not." Francesco replied. "To have come so far only to lose… no God could be that cruel."

"Do not speak of something you do not know. I have seen things in both the Celestial and Nether realms that would turn your stomach, once-loving creators turning to dictators, losing sight of their original plans, and turning to

DAMNATION

madness. It's enough to cause a faithful servant to lose their sanity."

"I apologize. You are right, I don't know… I can only hope and believe…"

"Hope…" Xaphine repeated. "If only there was any left…"

Francesco placed a hand on her shoulder, "There is always hope, as long as someone still stands who believes in it."

Finally the sun began to set over the horizon and the imperial army had cleared out of the area. Xaphine turned to Francesco, "I am through waiting. I need to find him now. If he's down there, I can't stand the thought of him dying alone."

"I believe the time is right." Francesco nodded. "I'll come with you."

Xaphine nodded and knelt down so Francesco could lean on her back. Once he was in place, she flapped her wings and took off. She glided down to the scene of battle where she had last seen Piero and started looking amongst the wounded, dead, and dying.

The land had been completely destroyed. Trees had been shattered and ripped from the ground. The once green fields had been torn apart by mortar fire and grenades. Smoke covered the land in a veil of gray, making it hard to see anything.

Xaphine's eyes scanned the ruined land for the one she loved, "Piero, can you hear me!"

She got no response and called out again, "Piero, you answer me right now!"

Again, there was no response. Francesco and Xaphine separated and began to search for him. There were thousands of people littering the land. Many of them were horribly mutilated and beyond recognition. Though it may have been an impossible task, Xaphine was determined to find him. She would not leave until she was absolutely convinced that Piero wasn't there.

Francesco was prepared for a long search. A stubborn wife would need to be absolutely certain her husband was there, otherwise there would be no dragging her away. He listened carefully on the winds for Piero's voice.

On the other side of the field, Piero lay against a rock that had been unearthed and raised by the blast of a mortar. He was covered in blood and coughing as he watched the day pass into night. As the stars filled the night sky, Piero closed his eyes, "Xaphine... I'm so sorry... I fought so hard... and lost..."

"Lost?" A surprised response came. "You think you lost? You think everything you did was all for nothing?"

"You again?"

The specter of Xaphine appeared in front of him once more with a concerned look on her face. He sighed, "Why do you keep coming here? What do you want?"

"What do I want?" She asked in a confused voice. "Why do you keep calling me here? Your wife's heart is always with you. So when you call to it, her heart finds you. I'm here at your bidding, do not blame me."

"I need to know..." Piero said between coughing. "What was it all for? The Republic has been destroyed... the Church's hold on the land is being restored, the aristocracy is being restored, and now the Church is an ally of Charles V. We've failed... was it all for nothing?"

"All for nothing." The specter repeated. "No, I don't think it was all for nothing. Not in the least..."

"What then...?"

"Well you personally saved the soul of one whom even the Most High thought to be damned, which is no small task. Xaphan was fully committed to her cause. Not to mention, in saving her, you've foiled the machinations of the lord of darkness and removed him as a major threat from the celestial realm. He no longer has the power to attempt to mount an assault on the celestial temple. You literally saved humanity, if not all of existence."

She looked around for a few moments before continuing, "Yes, the Republic is broken, but consider this; your people may have temporarily lost the liberties granted to them under the Signoria, but the church's grasp over the land is diminished. This war and the ones before it will beckon the dawn of a new era, and others will be inspired by what you did here."

"Yes, I know… now we'll live under the tight fist of the Church... which will now follow Emperor Charles…"

"Charles V will not live forever and once he's gone, the vast Empire he built will slowly start to collapse. Sooner than later, the idea of freedom and self-government will spread and others will rise up against tyranny to usher in new eras of peace. This will happen because of the spark you lit here."

"What about my wife… what about Xaphine?"

The specter was about to respond when she heard Xaphine's voice in the distance calling to Piero. She turned back to him and smiled, "I'm afraid that's something that you'll have to ask her yourself."

As Xaphine's panicked voice drew closer, the specter vanished, "Piero, please answer me!"

Piero struggled to sit up a little more. His wounds were mortal, but he still had some time. He could hear the sadness in Xaphine's voice as she called to him, "Piero, for the love of God, please answer me! You have to still be alive… please!"

Once Piero had positioned himself against the rock, he used what strength he still had and called to her, "Xaphine, I'm over here! This way!"

Xaphine's head jerked to the side as she heard his voice. Her heart jumped and she ran towards the sound. Nothing could stop her now that she knew where he was.

Piero saw her appear out of the darkness as she ran toward him. Her eyes darted back and forth until she saw him lying on a rock. She quickly sprinted to him and knelt down.

Tears filled her eyes as she saw how badly injured he was "Piero, my love… my sweet husband…"

Piero smiled at her, "I'm glad you're here now, at the end."

"Don't talk like that, this isn't the end, it can't be! You can't die on me! You went through too much to get me back. You fought so hard, you can't die here. The Piero I married wouldn't give up this easily."

"I fear I don't have much choice… I can feel my heart beat slowing."

Xaphine's breathing increased as she could see Piero was fading fast. He had held out long enough to see her face again, but his strength was almost gone. As he laid his head on the ground and closed his eyes, Xaphine became frantic, "Yes you do, come on fight it!"

Francesco came up behind them. Because of his advanced hearing, he could sense Piero's heartbeat slowing, "Xaphine… we're losing him…"

"No, shut up!" She yelled with tears falling down her cheeks, "This isn't happening! I won't let it."

Xaphine pulled Piero's armor off and tore open his tunic, exposing his chest. She then closed her eyes to center herself, slapped her hands together, and rubbed them until they started glowing yellow in color. Her eyes also began to glow as she prepared what little power she had left.

Francesco's eyes narrowed as he heard a low hum coming from her hands, "Xaphine, what are you planning on doing?"

"I still have one shard of divinity left to me. I'm going to use it to transfer my life energy to him. It should keep him alive long enough to heal."

Francesco stepped forward, reaching out for her, "Your life energy?"

"It's the living spirit within me. If I can transfer a portion of it to him, it may be enough to save him."

Francesco wasn't sure he liked this idea, "But won't that damage you?"

"I don't know. I've never actually seen anyone do this before. It's a forbidden art. If I use too much though, it will most likely kill me."

Francesco's eyes widened, "Xaphine you can't do this. Piero would not want you risking your life. He fought for you out there today!"

"I know that, but what life is there for me without Piero? I know it's selfish, but I will not let him die. Death holds no horror for me if the alternative is a life without him and then an eternity in the well."

Xaphine's hands glowed brightly as she placed them on Piero's forehead and chest. She gasped and breathed heavily as the energy left her body. It was painful, but she didn't care. Nothing could compare to the void that would be left in her chest if he died.

Once Piero's body stopped convulsing from the impact, she could see that her effort had not changed anything. Piero was still dying. Xaphine shook her head in panic. She rubbed her hands together again and slammed them down on to Piero, "Come on, damn you!"

Francesco could hear the worry in her voice as she spoke, "It's not working... come on Piero!"

"Breathe!"

Tears began to fall from her eyes as she tried two more times, "Come on, don't leave me Piero... please!"

The pain was becoming too much for Xaphine. Her wings spread as far as they could and her skin was drenched in sweat. Her breathing became more labored and it became more and more difficult for her lungs to accept air. The world was also beginning to blur while her energy escaped.

As Xaphine continued to pound Piero's body with her own life-force energy, her skin began to go pale and her hair started showing white lines that became more numerous with each blast of life. She saw what was happening but did not care. Her hands slapped together again and again she hit Piero's body.

Francesco could now hear only one heartbeat; Xaphine's. Much to his dismay, it was now also slowing to a halt. Desperate to end this, he put his right hand on Xaphine's shoulder, "Stop... it's too late, he's gone. If you keep this up any longer, it will kill you."

"Shut up, shut... up!" She screamed, her eyes now bright red. "Do you think I care? As I said, I would rather spend an eternity in the Well of Souls than dwell here without him! It is not too late, it can't be. – Breath!"

Xaphine slapped her hands together again. Each time she did this, the glow on her hands dimmed slightly. Her skin was now a ghostly white, she was impoverished, and her features had withered. All that was left was little more than a skeleton as the life force drained from her body. The lines on her face made her almost unrecognizable and her eyes were shaded as though she had not slept in years.

"Breathe!"

Francesco listened helplessly as her own breathing became more and more labored. Sorrow filled his heart as he listened to yet another friend dying, "Please Xaphine, do you think that Piero would want this? You need to stop! He would want you to live!"

Xaphine ignored Francesco's pleas as tears rolled down her cheeks. She breathed heavily as she brushed the

DAMNATION

snow white hair from her face and rubbed her hands together one more time. As she slammed her hands down on her husband's lifeless body, she let out a loud grunt. Her heart rate had slowed to a crawl and it had become almost impossible for her to draw a full breath.

"Breathe!"

No longer possessing the energy to hold herself up, she collapsed on to Piero's chest sobbing. Her husband's skin was no longer warm and soft like it was when he first touched her. Laying her head over his heart could not sooth her anymore and her life was all but spent. She was a corpse. Though still breathing, her body was already dead. There was no going back.

"Please... breathe..."

Francesco shook his head as he sat down behind them, "How could it have come to this? We did everything we could. Xaphine has been saved, Lucifer has been destroyed, and we even made it back in time to warn the Republic. Oh Lord, have we done something to anger you in some way? This does not seem just."

Xaphine shook her head, "It's no good..."

She slowly released her breath, convinced that her body wouldn't accept many more, "I'm so sorry, my love... you were so strong for me. Even when I told you there was no hope, you refused to listen. You were stubborn and kept fighting. You did all that for me... you were magnificent, but I don't have the power left to save you..."

Francesco felt tears fall from his eyes at hearing such sad words, "Xaphine... I'm... sorry."

Xaphine shook her head as she weakly turned to Francesco, "You've been most kind to us. You gave my husband hope, and gave me back my happy life. You have nothing to apologize for."

She sucked in a deep breath, "This is my punishment. My arrogance and ambition... I thought being damned to the underworld was as bad as things could get, but that was nothing compared to the torment I face now. The Most High must have known this would happen. He would have known that eventually I would see the light… that I would find happiness, only to have it ripped away from me. He must have..."

Xaphine looked up into the night sky. The streams of tears on her cheeks sparkled in the moonlight, "Lord Most High, what more do you want of me? I understand now… I get it, you win. I was such a fool and I accept responsibility for the mistakes I made. Why take him away when he has done no wrong?"

Xaphine lowered her eyes and clasped the gem on her chest, "Were you hoping that I would suffer? Was that your plan?"

Her eyes once again looked up at the stars as she screamed, "Well it worked! I'm hurting now, worse than ever. You've made your point. Please, take my soul… commit me to the Well, or if you would prefer, allow Dēofol to torment me for all eternity, but please give Piero back his life. It's not fair for you to punish him to further torment me. All he wanted was to bring back the one he loved. You mustn't consider that a sin!"

Silence.

Xaphine waited a few more painful moments. When no response came to her weak voice, she shook her head slowly, "You're still not willing to compromise? Then forgive me, my lord… I beg your indulgence, but I must defy you one… last… time…"

Xaphine touched her husband's cheek and kissed him, "Piero, my husband… I love you."

She rubbed her hands together again. This time, only one hand glowed and it was very dim, "One last drop… all I have left to give… for everything you've given me…"

DAMNATION

Francesco shook his head, "Xaphine, please… don't do it…"

Xaphine ignored Francesco and raised her hand to Piero's chest. As she was about to force the last bit of energy she had into his lifeless body, she kissed her husband's cheek again, "Goodbye… my love…"

Xaphine closed her eyes, convinced that they'd never open again as stretched out her hand over his chest and began to transfer her energy. The clouds parted before she could finish, allowing a massive beam of light to pass through and hit the ground. Francesco sensed it, stood up, and faced the beam as though he could see it with his own eyes, "Deus ex machina…"

The impact pushed Xaphine away from Piero's body. She was tossed a few feet out of the way and landed on her back. To her horror, Piero's body began to evaporate into the beam of light.

Xaphine felt energized as her skin and hair returned to their original pigment and her breathing returned to normal. She looked angrily up at the parted clouds and screamed, "No, you can't take him! It's not his time! Give him back! You were supposed to take me! Stop!"

Xaphine got up and ran at the beam, only to be deflected back again. She got to her feet a third time and ran at it screaming, "Stop!"

Once again, she went flying backwards. She got up to try again, but Francesco grabbed her before she could move, "Stop, don't try it, you're just going to hurt yourself!"

All Xaphine could do now was watch helplessly while her husband disappeared right in front of her eyes. As Piero's body vanished, the beam spread and became an enormous wall of light. Xaphine put her hands up over her eyes to prevent being blinded. The wall lingered for a few moments before it finally began to fade.

DAMNATION

Eventually, it disappeared, revealing an ivory staircase leading into the sky. Xaphine's eyes widened as she stood up and looked up to the clouds, "Why…?"

She cautiously stepped forward to see two angels walking down the stairs toward her. They stopped three steps away from the ground and smiled at their former foe. There was not a hint of malice about either of them and they seemed genuinely happy to see her. Xaphine instantly recognized them, "Ariel... Roselyn?"

Ariel spoke up as Xaphine eyed them defensively, "General Xaphan, how are you?"

Xaphine had tears in her eyes as she looked at them both. No longer worried about showing weakness, she fought through the tightness in her throat to speak, "My name is Xaphine. I joined the Lorenzi family and you know it! Xaphan is buried within me now."

Ariel and Roselyn exchanged glaces for a moment before Ariel turned back to Xaphine apologetically, "You're right, I apologize… Xaphine."

Xaphine looked like she was ready to rip them to shreds as she spoke with her fists at her side, "I could kill you both for this! Why… Ariel… Roselyn… why take him? If you wish to make me suffer, there are far more effective ways than taking one of the Most High's children!"

The seraphim again looked at each other for a moment with confused expressions. Ariel stepped forward and spoke to her, "The Lord Most High hath been watching your struggle. He is aware of everything you've done and everything your… husband, Piero, did."

"We are not here to torment you. We wouldn't have come if that was the goal." Roselyn said smiling. "The Most High was quite moved by your actions and thus has seen fit to forgive your crimes from so long ago."

DAMNATION

Xaphine's mouth dropped open when she heard the word 'forgive.' It was not something that an angel had ever experienced to her knowledge, "What are you saying?"

Ariel looked her in the eye as he spoke, "Your actions in helping to stop Lucifer and then attempting to save the life of one of the Most High's beloved children has impressed him. You've admitted your sin and sought to correct it. Therefore he has sent us to offer you a magnificent gift."

"What possible gift do you think you can give me? Nothing could ever replace what was taken."

The two angels turned to face one another and stepped backwards, revealing a third person standing behind them. This person was dressed in a white tunic and trousers that glowed brightly. There was an intense feeling of serenity that emanated off of him as brightly as the light on his clothing.

Xaphine looked up into his eyes. Her face brightened up and she smiled widely as tears began to fall down her cheeks again, "Piero, my love!"

Piero nodded and spoke in a comforting tone, "I'm okay, Xaphine. Death could never keep me away from you."

Tears continued to steam down her cheeks as she threw her arms around him, "It's not fair. You didn't deserve this!"

"No, it's not fair, but what's done is done. History can't be changed, but the future can be."

Xaphine's eyes narrowed as she backed away slightly, "Speak plainly to me, my love. Your words are far too cryptic."

Piero turned to Ariel who stepped forward, "Your sins were numerous in number and extremely sinister in nature, but the Most High has seen the good that you can do as well and understands why you made the choices you did.

Therefore, he is willing to give you a chance at redemption."

"How can I be redeemed? There is still a demonic taint on me... I can feel the darkness within."

"It's all in your mind." Piero replied.

"Look inside yourself." Roselyn chimed in. "You found the power to break through the restraints and walls Xaphan put up. You overcame what so many others may never have. You yourself even said that Xaphan was dead, did you not?"

Xaphine lowered her eyes, "Well yes, but I still get angry... argumentative, and defiant... I mean..."

"That's the Xaphan I always knew before the war." Ariel interrupted with a chuckle.

Piero nodded, "And the woman I married."

Xaphine rolled her eyes, "Yes, yes, I know I'm difficult. I'm stubborn, opinionated, and impossible for most to get along with. I get it, but even if the demon is dead, I can still feel some of Lucifer's taint. I haven't driven it out completely."

Roselyn looked deep into her eyes, "We know that and are prepared to help. Touch your husband's hand and the taint will disappear."

Piero again reached his hand out to her. She looked at him hesitantly for a moment. A warm look appeared on his face as beckoned to her, "Trust me."

Xaphine slowly placed her fingers in the palm of Piero's hand. There was a spark and Xaphine felt her body begin to transform. Her eyes began to glow, her ears lost their points, and molded back to look more human, and her wings slowly faded away until they were completely gone. Her dress also faded to white and miraculously mended itself. She gasped as she looked at her restored form for a moment.

DAMNATION

Her body felt heavier and more fragile and she was breathing more rapidly. She was human once again, "So this is my redemption? You're turning me into a human to live here with Piero?"

A sad look appeared on Piero's face as Roselyn shook her head, "I'm afraid not..."

"What?" Xaphine asked as an icy feeling travelled down her spine and her chest instinctively clenched.

"I can't stay here with you." Piero replied sadly. "I lost my life in battle just moments ago, remember?"

Xaphine's jaw trembled as she looked into her husband's eyes, "What.... what are you saying? You're leaving me?"

"Never." Piero replied.

At that moment, Roselyn stepped forward, "The Most High has decided to provide you with a chance to earn your way back into the Kingdom of Heaven."

Xaphine took a step back, "How?"

"By living the life of a creature that you once despised." Ariel replied.

Xaphine sighed, "While the appropriateness of this is not lost on me... I'm still not sure what you're hoping to accomplish."

Ariel looked around the field of dead and dying soldiers, "Angels serve the Most High, but we also work behind the scenes in the Corporeal World. Given the amount of disdain you've shown for humans, the Most High feels that you are incapable carrying out the duties of an angel."

"So I have to live as one in order to gain understanding and sympathy for them?" Xaphine asked.

"Exactly," Piero replied, "live well, do good deeds in the name of our lord, and try to help these people. Do this, and upon your death, your wings will be returned to you... and so will I."

"How?" Xaphine asked. "Angels aren't allowed to consort with humans. If I'm restored..."

"After everything that has happened, the Most High is prepared make an exception in your case." Ariel replied. "You will be allowed to return, be given a suitable task that suits your skills, but you will be able to spend your spare time with the one you love, forever. He thought it would be a good way to ensure your loyalty."

Xaphine lowered her eyes, "How long do I have to endure here?"

"Twenty five to thirty years, at least." Piero replied. "That's how much time we'd have left if things happened differently."

Ariel nodded as she chimed in a stern tone, "So it's up to you. You can commit suicide and end the problem now, at which point you will be sent to the Well of Souls, you can live an evil existence, in which case your fate will be the same, or you can take the Most High's offer."

Xaphine nodded, "So I'm mortal, but still bound by the rules of an angel then?"

"Yes." Roselyn replied. "You look like a human, you're mortal, but your soul is that of an angel."

Xaphine fell silent for a few moments as she contemplated her situation. Piero placed his fingers on her chin and brought her eyes to level with his, "Are you okay with that?"

Xaphine sighed, "No, no I'm not. Twenty five years is a long time to live without you."

She bit her lower lip as she continued, "However... it's a better proposition than living out our remaining few years together, at which point I'd spend an eternity alone."

Roselyn smiled, "Then you accept the Most High's offer?"

Xaphine's eyes looked into Piero's before she turned back to Roselyn and nodded, "Yes... some things are worth waiting a lifetime for. Tell the Most High that he can count me amongst the faithful again... tell him I'm coming, and tell him that he'd better honor his agreement."

She then slowly turned back to Piero and clasped the gem on her necklace, "Piero... I really don't want this. It's not fair... but I will carry you with me until we can be together again."

Piero nodded, "I know you can do this. Live a sin-free life and I will be waiting for you."

Xaphine smiled deviously, "You better be. Twenty five years of chastity will be torture. If you're not there when I arrive, you will know my wrath!"

Ariel and Roselyn rolled their eyes and pretended that they weren't listening as Piero laughed, "You have my word."

"And you have mine, love." Xaphine replied.

At that moment, distant bells could be heard ringing out in the sky. Piero closed his eyes, "My time grows short... I have to go."

Xaphine threw her arms around Piero one last time. She squeezed him as tightly as she could, "Piero... wait... one more moment... please..."

Piero shook his head, "If only I could... I'll see you soon."

As Piero and the other angels slowly disappeared, he smiled at Xaphine, "Take care, and watch out for Francesco, he's about to make a very startling discovery."

Xaphine nodded sadly, "I will..."

"Goodbye, my love..." Piero replied as he finally vanished. He put on a happy face so that the last image she saw of him was not sadness, but his heart ached as she disappeared from view.

Xaphine's empty arms fell to their sides. Tears rolled down her cheeks as she embraced her newfound solitude, "Piero... my love... yes... I'll see you soon..."

DAMNATION

She stood quietly for a moment, contemplating her situation in silence. A life of solitude was nothing new to her. As Lucifer's general, she usually kept herself separate from those she'd commanded. However, this time she had someone waiting for her to return, someone she desperately wanted to be with.

Her silence was shattered by a nearby sound. Francesco gasped as the void that he'd been looking into for years slowly disappeared, "I... I can see!"

He looked at Xaphine in amazement and awe, "Xaphine, is that you?"

Xaphine nodded, "Yes, I'm afraid so. Welcome back."

Francesco could not believe his eyes, "Milady... you are beautiful, as beautiful as I remembered Adalyn to be. Tell me, are all angels so beautiful?"

Xaphine nodded, "I am different from most of my brothers and sisters, but yes most are as beautiful as Adalyn... someday you'll see for yourself."

"I don't know what to say." Francesco exclaimed with tears in his eyes.

"Just promise me one thing." Xaphine replied. "Promise me that you will stop searching for something that has been within you all along."

"You mean..."

"Yes." She said smiling through her tears. "It's not a physical place you will be able to find in your lifetime, at least not in the literal sense."

"Then where should I look?"

She raised her hand and placed it over his heart, "It's here, within you and outside you and all around you. Should you ever need it, should you ever feel alone, or without hope, this is where you should look, because this is where it will always be... everywhere and nowhere."

As she turned like she was about to leave, Francesco touched her arm, "What are we going to do now?"

DAMNATION

Xaphine looked out at the smoldering ruins of Florence, "You still have much work to do in your life and if memory serves, your old friend, the Marquis, is looking for a new captain of his guard. I'm sure he wouldn't reject an old war buddy with military experience like yours."

"But what about you, milady? Florence has been taken. What are your plans now?"

Xaphine lowered her eyes, "This is where we part ways. I'll need to lay low for a little while. Florence will be in a state of chaos until the imperial army pulls out, but then it will need to be rebuilt. The seeds of freedom will be re-sewn, and the good of all must be served. So I'll remain here. I have a lot of work ahead of me."

"That's a lot to take on." Francesco said in an almost daring tone. "Are you sure that you're up for it?"

Xaphine smiled as she looked down at the gems on her necklace, "I have to be... Piero is waiting for me. He put his life on the line to save me, and died for what he loved... now it's my turn. I've been given this chance because of him. So now I'll help restore the city he loved the most in return. When I see him... I want to be able to tell him that his city is prospering again."

EPILOGUE

Florence returned to the control of its ruler, but the city was rebuilt to its original glory and its citizens would prosper once more. Charles V would eventually die of his illnesses and his empire would begin to crumble just as Xaphine had predicted.

Francesco returned to Mantua and lived out the rest of his days in peace. Federico welcomed him back as captain of the guard. Though he did have to explain what happened to the *Ricci* upon his return. He then began the long and arduous task of chronicling their entire story, a story, which Federico enjoyed hearing from time to time.

Two days before his death, he added one last entry into his chronicle of the adventure he shared with Xaphine...

And thus end the tidings of days gone by. Lost but never forgotten are the friends of old. Of these truths that I have spoken of from my journeys, only one of which can I speak of with absolute certainty. Xaphine successfully did penance for her past crimes. She and Piero are together in the place that I searched for. No doubt Moretti and Costa, and perhaps even the manifested memory of Antonio sits with them around a fire, regaling themselves of our adventure. I know I will see them soon, God willing.

The former angel somehow managed to avoid history almost entirely. After years of working as a smith in Florence and enduring many rumors and speculation about her identity, Xaphine gave Piero's old house to a needy family and disappeared into the hills. No one knew what had become of her, but for years after, many travelers traded stories of a dark haired woman coming to the aid of those in need, with either a sword or a small bag of gold in hand.

*

DAMNATION

Years passed since Adalyn had encountered her sister. Since the War of the League of Cognac ended, things began to settle down, and peace finally claimed the region. Venice was no exception to this. News of war now came from distant lands that did not affect the lives of those native to the region. Smoke no longer filled the sky from battles nearby, nor did soldiers line the streets of the town.

Adalyn never heard any news from the young soldier who had come to her looking for help. She had received word from Federico that Francesco had returned to his land and lived out his remaining days comfortably, and she was told of what had become of Xaphan.

This left her with several questions. How was her sister surviving? Was she okay? Would she succeed? These questions haunted her for a long time and she feared what may have happened. Part of her was tempted to have Giovanni take her to Florence to look for Xaphine, but she was getting on in years and it was a burden that she could not place on her family.

Early one morning, Adalyn lit the fireplace in her kitchen and waited for the flame to grow before resting comfortably in her chair. She quietly rocked back and forth while the flame crackled and danced. Years had passed and her children had long since grown. She relaxed as she watched the flame dance in its small chamber of stone, just like she did every morning.

Part of her always dreaded these days as this would be when her husband, sons, and now grandsons would begin their fishing adventures. Watching them go out on the ocean, she feared for their safety and wondered if they would return in one piece. Part of her always wanted to go with them, to share in their adventures as she once had with her husband.

As the sun slowly crept up over the horizon, Adalyn swore that she heard movement just outside the door. At first, she ignored it. Perhaps it was another fisherman trying to get an early start on the day, or perhaps a farmer on his way to the market, but why would either be passing so closely to her house?

Adalyn never shook her curious nature and decided to investigate the noises herself rather than waking up her family. She slowly crept towards the door, not knowing what she would encounter. After everything she had been through, she had learned to be extremely cautious. Though she doubted that she'd need it, she kept one hand on the arquebus behind the door from her adventure so many years before.

The old wooden door creaked as the door slowly opened. She stepped out on to the front stoop and gasped at what she saw. Resting on the ground in front of her were two badly tarnished swords that had been laid so that they were crossing each other. What little of the blades that still showed their original shine, gleamed in the sun.

Adalyn grasped one of the familiar swords and held it in the air. She then turned to pick up the second one when she noticed something unusual about it. Tied to the hilt of this sword was an unusual looking feather.

Adalyn recognized it as being the feather of an eagle's wing, but unlike most, this one was white from the root going up about half way. The rest of the feather was as black as night. She picked it up and twirled it around her fingers as she inspected it. A small pulse of light shot out of the root and disappeared into the sky.

She closed her eyes and nodded gently, "Thank you, sister."

Suddenly, behind her in the house, Adalyn heard someone stirring, "Grandma?"

Adalyn smiled and turned to go back in the house, closing the door behind her, "Don't worry, I'm coming."

DAMNATION

JAMES HARRINGTON

James Harrington was born and raised in Boston, Massachusetts. He holds a Bachelor's in History, but also studied religion and how it related to his chosen subject matter. It was from those studies that Divinity and Damnation were born.

James has written several essays and short stories, but had never gotten a full-length novel published until his big breakthrough with *Magnifica, The Last Enchanter*. Following its success, two more titles were added to the *Magnifica* series.

James currently lives in Massachusetts with his wife and son.

For more info on James and his books, please visit his facebook page:
The Creative Works of James Harrington.
https://www.facebook.com/JamesHarringtonsMagnifica

Or his Blog page:
http://jamesharringtoncreativeworks.wordpress.com/

Be sure to check out James's other works:

Divinity

The **Magnifica** Series:
The Last Enchanter
Tears of the Fallen
Gravestalker

DAMNATION